About the Author

Pratibha Ray is an eminent novelist and short story writer of Orissa. In her stories she has tried to unravel the underlying mysteries of society. From romanticism she moved into the realities of life. Her interest and choice of a subject for novel or short story are varied. The innumerable strains of modern life, the alienation of individuals, hedonistic philosophy, corruption in the narrow lanes of politics and moral degradation which comprises the nucleus of her thoughts are reflected in her novels. Pratibha Ray's *Yajnaseni* is the best seller of Orissa and her novels have gone into several editions. The author was presented the Bharatiya Jnanpith's prestigious ninth Moortidevi Award in 1993 for her novel *Yajnaseni*.

About the Translator

Pradip Bhattacharya is the author of 14 published books covering English literature, rural development, homoeopathy, children's stories, ancient Indian history, the Mahabharata. He has also translated Rabindranath Tagore's *Shantiniketan* and Bankim Chandra Chatterjee's *Krishnacharita* into English for the first time.

He is the only Indian to be awarded the International Human Resource Development Fellowship (1989) by Manchester University and the Institute of Training and Development, U.K. He is a member of the Indian Administrative Service and a Secretary to the Government of West Bengal.

YAJNASENI
The Story of Draupadi

Pratibha Ray

Original Oriya novel
YAJNASENI

Translated by
Pradip Bhattacharya

Rupa & Co

© Pratibha Ray 1995

Translation © Pradip Bhattacharya

An Original Rupa Paperback 1995
Second impression 1997

Published by
Rupa & Co

15 Bankim Chatterjee Street, Calcutta 700 073
135 South Malaka, Allahabad 211 001
P. G. Solanki Path, Lamington Road, Bombay 400 007
7/16, Ansari Road, Daryaganj, New Delhi 110 002

Typeset in Palatino by
Megatechnics
19A Ansari Road
New Delhi 110 002

Printed in India by
Gopsons Papers Ltd
A-28 Sector IX
Noida 201 301

Rs 145

ISBN 81-7167-323-6

1

"Finis,"

your dear *sakhi.*

But after writing *finis* it seems as though I have not been able to write anything at all. The long-drawn tale of life brimming with tears and laughter lies fluttering like a blank scroll on the breast of inexorable Time. As if the pilgrim on the road to Death leaves behind everything in this world! Though we may well so imagine, actually he leaves behind nothing. Just this crumbling body is left here and even that is not his own. The soul flies away — when was it his, anyway?

The skies have no beginning and no end. The ocean neither wastes away nor increases. The sun neither rises nor sets. Your heart's desire is neither fulfilled nor left empty. Our relationship too has no name and no end. Therefore, in this insignificant letter what final word will I be able to set down? Even after relating everything of life the last word is invariably left unsaid. After receiving everything, fulfilment is left. After all has ended, the auspicious beginning remains. Beginning of what and whose end? That which is creation is annihilation. Inauguration is itself dissolution — that is mighty Time, eternal and infinite.

As the breeze carries scent from flowers, I wonder: attracted by whose perfume does life leave this body? Where does it go and where does it come from?

Lust, anger and greed are the doors to hell. O Lord! Is hell the end? Till the last moment when death's icy hands freeze a creature's soul, is doubt finally dispelled while struggling to utter the last word on life? The golden dust of Mount Meru is slipping underfoot. There is no feeling left in the feet. They are gone, those people, who knows where, following whom throughout life these tender feet shed blood, bore pain. Not once did any of them

1

exclaim, "Oh!" and look back. What mighty obstacle would that "Oh!" have created to their attaining heaven? Who had wanted heaven? Who had craved a kingdom? And you had wanted war? Despite someone else being the root of all the causes, they emptied the entire cup of blame on my head and went away — leaving me thus at death's door!

Giving the innocent child a toy and snatching it away the next moment to make it cry! Why fabricate this elaborate drama of taking along all this? It is fun to play with one who asks with hands outspread. But one who asks for nothing — with her such toying! If this is not cruelty, what is? He who is far from the perishable, who is beyond the imperishable, is Purushottam to whom all is owed. He is the lord of supreme bliss. Why does He play such a game? To whom does He give and from whom does He take?

Life is slipping away underfoot. Those who were my companions have gone ahead on the road to heaven. In the great blue expanse everything seems empty, meaningless. Yet today on the way to death all of life's congealed pride and hurt begins to flow like melting wax. Query after query dashes against the shores of the heart. Still, the last word cannot be said. *Finis* has been written to the letter. Moment by moment as I slide down the path of Death I begin to read the letter again. Perhaps the secret of this creation is infinite, unplumbed curiosity about life! That is why despite the varied experience of life it remains shrouded perpetually in the mystery of joy and sorrow, prosperity and poverty, love and loss, life and death. This letter, written with my blood, is my only companion on the road to death. While reading my own letter should my soul leave the body, remember that it is you who are its recipient, Priya Sakha! Govind! O best of all men, Krishna! O Madhusudan! Krishnaa's *pranam!*

All the grievances, all the silent hurts and reproaches of life, today, in these last moments, I place here. In life regrets will remain.

What agonies did I not suffer for preserving dharma? I had thought that on the strength of my adherence to dharma and fidelity as a wife I would be able to accompany my husbands to heaven. Yet, I had but touched the golden dust of Himalaya's foothills when my feet slipped and I fell! Five husbands — but not one turned back even to look. Rather, Dharmaraj Yudhishthir, lord of righteousness, said to Bhim, "Do not turn back to look! Come forward!"

Those very words of his shattered my heart. I mused: how false is this bond between husband and wife! Affection, love, sacrifice and surrender! If man suffers the consequences of his own deeds, then offering myself at the feet of five husbands for the sake of preserving Yudhishthir's dharma, why did I have to bear the burden of the whole world's mockery, sneers, innuendos, abuse, scorn and slander?

Dvaparyuga was about to end. The day Abhimanyu's son Parikshit was anointed king on the throne of Hastinapur from that very day the Kaliyuga commenced. It is said that my name will be counted as one of the five *satis*, renowned for chastity. Men and women of Kaliyuga will laugh scornfully saying, "If with five husbands Draupadi could be a *sati*, then what is the need for fidelity to one husband?" With many husbands why can't the women of Kaliyuga be *satis*? Draupadi will be food for mockery and jest amid the perverted sexuality of Kaliyuga's debauched men and women. How will these people appreciate that five-husbanded Draupadi had to burn inch by inch in the cause of chastity? Then the heroine of Hastinapur, Draupadi, will become a condemned soul, the heroine of a tale of calumny. O Krishna! O Vasudev, you are omnipotent! It is by your wish that Draupadi has made this long journey from birth till now. By your wish Draupadi's eyes have opened and shut, her breath has come and gone. Then, have you no share in her praise and blame?

Today with the blood dripping from her heart Draupadi is writing about the start of her life on the stones of the holy Himalayas. Some day, for saving the oppressed world, you will arrive on earth by way of the Himalayas. That day you will read this blood-drenched autobiography written in indelible letters.

3

"Aha!" — the exclamation will be voiced for Draupadi. Enough — that is all I want for myself.

You are the knower of hearts. What is unknown to you? Yet, the tormented cry does not reach you unless it is voiced aloud. Therefore, I am placing everything before you.

Time may transform me into a goddess, but I appeared on this earth with this body in human form. My five husbands are each a creature of this mortal world. Our master, the great sage, Krishna Dvaipayan, has established me as a deity. In his eyes I appear divine. The cause of my having five husbands he has attributed to some boon by Shiva. But I am no goddess and no knower of past births. Therefore, today on the road to death whatever I say I shall speak the truth. The story of my life, is nothing other than the life-story of any human being on this mortal world. Read the indelible words of this letter. Seeing each hair-raising incident of my life the people of Kaliyuga will be able to decide whether the insults Draupadi suffered have ever been borne by any woman of any time. God forbid that in future anyone should ever suffer such abuse.

O *Sakha!* The day I was insulted in the Kuru court, having lost confidence in the five husbands, casting all shame aside, with both hands uplifted, it was you I called, it was before you that I surrendered. And today when once again my five husbands have gone ahead leaving me helpless, I am offering myself to you. All my grief and agony, insults and heartbreaks — I am offering you everything. If I am no longer my own, why should my grief remain mine?

O Krishna, knower of hearts! What is unknown to you? Yet I am setting down my story. Grief is lessened by unburdening the heart. And when I am unburdening the heart then everything — my faults, weaknesses, illusions — all will be exposed. If the world blames me for this, what can I say? I could not rise above mistakes and avoid false steps, perhaps that is why the road to heaven was blocked to me.

Time is passing away. My body is lacerated, my heart is shattered. Blood is dripping from my heart and it is in this blood that

4

my story is drenched. At the time of death, whatever a man says or does is beyond his control. May the accumulated agony of so many years gush out as a libation at your feet. Let the world see. O Govind! do not turn my mind and heart inert till my story is complete. Do not destroy my memory, do not give it into the hands of death. Only let me tell my story — standing at death's door this little I pray.

From where shall I begin? My birth? But my birth was an exception. I was born nubile. The sacrificial altar is my mother. Yajnasena is my father. So I am Yajnaseni.

Yajnaseni! Panchal princess, Panchali! Drupad's daughter, Draupadi!

2

In the Dvaparyuga it was the area under the Kurus and Panchals which was the Aryan heartland. Bharat's descendants — the Kurus — made Hastinapur on the banks of the Ganga the capital of their kingdom. At this time it was the symbol of the country's pride and glory. The descendants of the Panchal king were not inferior to the Kurus. Actually, between them a sort of rivalry prevailed.

My father's childhood friend was Drona. And he was the tutor of the Pandavs. Once he approached King Drupad for help. Father blurted out in jest, "A begging Brahman and friend to a king! Friendship can be only between equals."

Insulted, Drona left. He got employment in the Kuru court. That insult kept smouldering in his heart. After the weapons-training of the Pandavs was over Drona asked for his fees: "Bind king Drupad and throw him at my feet!"

The third Pandav, Arjun, was Drona's favourite disciple and supremely proficient in archery. In all Aryavart no one except Radheya Karna dared to face him.

It was nothing much for the Pandavs. Arjun imprisoned my father and threw him at Drona's feet.

Drona returned the insult saying, "Only a king can be a king's friend. But today you have no kingdom. From now on the northern portion of Panchal is mine. You shall be the ruler of the southern side of the Ganga river. Now we are equals. Is there any bar to our friendship now?"

Losing half his kingdom, Drupad put forward his hand in false amity. It was the northern part of Panchal that was more prosperous. Drona had kept it for himself.

A kshatriya warrior can never forget an insult. The insult could not be avenged without the killing of Drona. On Drona's side were Bhishma, Karna, Shalya, Jayadrath, Duryodhan and his hundred brothers and then the huge army of Hastinapur! Who was there in Panchal who could slay Drona?

To get a son who could kill Drona, king Drupad gratified Upyaj, descendant of sage Kashyap, and had Upyaj and Yaj conduct a sacrificial ritual.

From the sacred flames of the sacrificial fire a radiant son, my brother Dhrishtadyumna, was born and from the sacrificial altar I was born, like a blue lotus-coloured gem — Yajnaseni!

People said of me — exquisitely beautiful! Amazing! Complexion like the petals of the blue lotus! Thick hair like the waves of the ocean, and large, entrancing blue lotus-like eyes radiant with intelligence! Like an image sculpted by the world's greatest sculptor, with unblemished beauty of face and matching loveliness of figure. Tall, well-formed breasts, narrow waist, plantain-stalk-like rounded firm thighs, fingers and toes like champak petals, palms and soles like red lotuses, pearl-like teeth, a smile that shamed even lightning, moon-like nails. The lotus-fragrance of the body deluded even bees. The serpentine loveliness of my hair would imprison even the breeze into stillness. Poets described my beauty as depriving even sages of their senses.

In white garments, wearing a white crown and holding a white lotus, when I appeared like a blooming blue lotus on the sacrificial altar, every part of my body was resplendent with the glow of youth. Seeing me, even the sages seated around the altar who had controlled their senses were stunned. The chanting lips trembled, the voices grew still. Some young ascetics fell senseless. Even tree leaves were stilled for some moments. The fire flared silent, unflickering. Perhaps mighty Time stood still at that moment.

I am not describing the beauty of my own form. People said so. Father's court poets were exclaiming, "Dark beauty, *Shyama!* However much you may describe her beauty, so much is left out. Even after composing poems all through life one will not find a simile for this incomparable loveliness. Krishnaa is herself her own simile"!

7

At my birth there was a prophecy: "This woman has taken birth to avenge your insult. She has appeared to fulfil a vow. By her, dharma will be preserved on this earth, kshatriyas will be destroyed. She will be the destroyer of the Kauravs."

God had given me a body of unprecedented loveliness and a heart full of goodness. Opening these lovely eyes as I was gazing at this entrancing creation, I heard the utterances of the sages and ascetics performing the sacrifice — my birth was not from my father's seed but from the sacrificial altar built for fulfilling a vow. From even before birth, I was destined to avenge my father's insult! I was going to be the weapon for preserving dharma on this earth and destroying the wicked. It was for this that I was born. Should only woman be forced to be the medium for preserving dharma and annihilating evil throughout the ages? Is it woman who is the cause of creation and destruction? Sita had to become the medium for the destruction of Lanka and the establishment of Ram's rule. For this, she had to discard all the joys of her life and become a forest-dweller. Then, Ravan's lust imprisoned her in the Ashok forest, insulted her, tormented her. Finally, dharma was established on earth. The intention behind Lord Ram's birth was fulfilled. But ultimately what did Sita get? The sentence of exile from Ram! Public test of chastity! The earth cracked open at the calumny. To hide her sorrow, shame and insults Sita sank into Earth's lap.

Even to think of all this makes the heart tremble. My life's goal: preservation of dharma and destruction of the Kauravs! Immersing itself in fantasies of happiness, my mind shivered with some unknown apprehension. Joining my palms, with eyes closed I prayed, "O Lord! If my birth is for preserving dharma on earth then give me all the insults and calumny that are to come, but also give me the strength to bear them all."

Noticing me lost in thought Father was much pleased. Blessing me with his hand on my head he said, "Yajnaseni! It is you who will avenge your father's insult. That is why both of you have been born of the sacrificial fire. My sacrificial ritual has been successful."

8

Touching Father's feet I said, "It is my duty to fulfil your desire. May your blessing be ever on my head."

Father said nothing. His eyes were brimming with tears. Even now his heart was burning with the agony of Drona's insult. I vowed, "If need be, I shall quench this fire with the tears of my life."

Our naming ceremony was held. Brother was born with armour, resplendent with nobility. Sage Upyaja said, "This son is born from fire. It is this famous son who will slay Drona. Let him be named Dhrishtadyumna."

Looking at me affectionately he said, "Let Drupad's daughter, this dark complexioned one, be named Krishnaa."

"Krishnaa!... Krishna and Krishnaa! How beautiful!" Father said and gazed at the sky, his face gleaming with satisfaction. Father's happiness rubbed off on me. I began thinking, "Who is this Krishna whose name itself is so nectarous?"

Father was softly saying, "O Krishna! It is to you that I shall offer my Krishnaa. After all, you are the best of all men in Aryavart! A hero! And the establishment of dharma is the goal of your life. You are pride-humbling Govind. On giving Krishnaa into your hands my lost honour will return. It is for this that Krishnaa's birth has taken place."

Some unknown sensation thrilled me. Every pore in my skin throbbed with joy. The finest of Aryavart's heroes! The greatest warrior and dharma-establisher! Who would not desire him? And moreover I had no separate desire of my own. Just now I had made a vow before my father. So I was an offering to Krishna. If that were not so, why would sage Upyaj have christened me "Krishnaa"?

Krishna and Krishnaa! A heavenly, pure, sweet stream of love drenched my heart. My eyes brimmed over. But who was this greatest of all men, Krishna? I did not know.

3

Nitambini was my favourite *sakhi*. That day I was enjoying the evening breeze in the garden. In private I asked her, "Who is Krishna?"

Sakhi glanced at me out of the corner of her eyes and pursing her lips giggled, "What business has Krishnaa with Krishna?"

I burst out laughing, "I have heard from Father that everyone has some need of Krishna — not just Krishnaa."

"Krishnaa might have some special need?" Even now Nitambini was smiling mischievously.

In a calm voice I said, "I have heard that for some special purpose Krishna has incarnated on earth."

Touching my chin Nitambini said, "Sakhi! Forget Krishna!"

"Why?" I asked in bewilderment.

"Yes, listen to me. It is true that he has wisdom and nobility. He is far-seeing, a master of politics, powerful and heroic in action. He is attractive as the lotus in bloom and as pure. He fulfils the prayer of the oppressed, reciprocates affection. If he accepts with one hand, he gifts with a thousand. His heart is vast, noble. He is incomparably heroic, the best of men, yet...."

"Yet?" I asked in surprise.

"...yes. He is a libertine. He is in love with sixteen thousand *gopis*. He is so adept in winning the female heart that on hearing his enchanting flute women would rush to meet him on the banks of Yamuna. Of course, this was when he was in his teens, and now he is the ruler of Dvaraka, wise in dharma."

He was the receptacle of the finest qualities - it was but natural for them to go mad about him, become oblivious of husband, family and the world. Why sixteen thousand, if hundreds of thousands of women went mad about him, how was it his fault? How I wished I could see this finest of men just once! What did

10

he look like? If I asked Nitambini she would mock me. She would gossip about it with the other *sakhis*, grossly exaggerating it. Then they would tease me unmercifully — I went on thinking in this way. And then, giving it a different tack, I asked, "Do you know of Krishna's ancestry?"

Nitambini burst out laughing, "Family and ancestry are looked into by parents. The woman regards the appearance. If you hear about Krishna's appearance, you will lose your senses. You will say, 'Without Krishna life is meaningless; fetch me Krishna at once or I will die!' Tell me, then-what shall I do?"

I was lost in a dream — Krishna's form! That vision was my constant companion. At that age who did not indulge in fantasy? How much joy there was in imagination! Every fancy of everyone does not come true. Yet, who can live fancy-free?

I was lost in visions of Krishna.

Both of us *sakhis* were seated under the creeper-covered dark *tamal* grove. The colour of the setting sun tinted the blue of the sky and dyed my feet with *aaltaa*. Blue lilies bloomed in the crystal waters of the pool. In the evening sky scattered clouds obstructed the moon, playing with blue lilies. Noticing the clouds in the sky, my pet peacock spread its tail, preparing to dance.

Nitambini continued praising Krishna's beauty. My heart was dancing, keeping time with the peacock.

I was musing: "What is Krishna like? Perhaps like the blue *tamal* tree or like the blue-black clouds? His eyes are like blue lilies. Like the resplendent sapphire blue of peacock feathers is his hair. And his lips will be curved, lovely like *agastya* flowers. Hands and feet like lotus buds, chest broad like the blue sky: his voice like the cuckoo's spring call: the fragrance of his body like henna and his form darkly tender yet tall as the champak tree..."

Entranced, I was listening to Nitambini's description.

She too was watching me out of the corner of her eye. After pausing for a while she talked on — about the honeyed embrace of Krishna and the intoxication of loving Krishna....

Like one drunk, I lay down in Nitambini's lap. My whole body was throbbing. My heart was aching with a peculiar surge of

11

emotion. This feeling I had never had before. What was it? Why did it occur?

Nitambini was whispering into my ear, "Love of Krishna! This is its sign. O Lord! What shall I do now?"

She laid me down under the creepers in the grove and stepped towards the pool to bring water to bring me to my senses. I had not lost consciousness, for I could understand everything. But I was moving in some dream world. Wherever I looked I saw Krishna.... blue.... Krishna.... blue ... the whole world full of Krishna ... full of love ... honeyed. Krishna pervading the world!

Before Nitambini could bring some water, a few drops of water fell from the blue clouds. On my throbbing body drops fell from the Krishna-dark *tamal* tree. Thrill over thrill! My peacock was fanning my face with its tail. Slowly I collected myself and tried to sit up. I was lost in shame. *Chheeh!* what would *sakhi* be thinking? By the time *sakhi* arrived with water, I had covered my face in shame. Along with water she had plucked two lilies. "Alas! Why did you pluck the flowers? All night long the blue lilies would have laughed drinking the moonshine. Nitambini, you are heartless!" But she was sprinkling water on my face. I remained as I was, not being able to say anything — on the one hand was shame and on the other regret that *sakhi* had plucked the lilies!

Slowly she began to stroke my face with the lily petals and whispered in my ears, "I know without the reviving touch of Krishna this illness cannot be cured. But where will I find the Dvaraka-dweller? So, taking Krishna's name, I keep these two blue lilies on your heart. Let that revive you and help you sit up. Otherwise your father will send for the royal physician. Nilanjana has gone to him with the news. What shall I tell the king about the ailment?"

Saying this, Nitambini placed the two flowers on my breast. I embraced them fondly, "Aah! Why did you pluck them?" Carefully I sat up, collecting myself.

Nervously Nitambini exclaimed, "The king has arrived. Someone is following him."

I understood that all this was Nilanjana's doing. Hearing about my condition, Father had arrived with the royal physician. Father could not bear to see me ill. Now what could I tell him? That I had fallen unconscious listening to Krishna being described? If Nitambini blurted this out, how would I lift up my head to face Father?

I was paralysed with shame and was getting angry with Nilanjana. Where was the need to report such a trifling matter? As it was, I detested medicine. Moreover, I was afraid of the royal physician.

Father was saying affectionately, "When the cure of all diseases, Krishna himself, is present, why should I bring along the royal physician? Do not be afraid, Daughter!"

The scent of henna flowers filled the whole garden. A gust of breeze came and some *tamal* flowers fell on me. Blown by it, a peacock feather fell by my side. The thrill was limitless, indescribable. How was all this happening! My pet peacock had left the garden long before.

Father's loving voice was saying, "Take Krishna's blessings, Daughter! His presence here is an indication that you are supremely fortunate."

In case I fainted again touching the peacock feather, I did not pick it up. Nitambini had understood my state of mind. Carefully she picked it up and said, "I shall keep it with your poems." — *Chheeh!* Nitambini did not have the slightest idea of propriety. That I wrote poetry — was this something to mention in Krishna's presence? What would he say when he heard of my writing poetry — the very dust of whose feet permeated the whole world with poetry? And Father was also standing there!

Father continued, "Will you not touch Krishna's feet, Daughter? He has just arrived from Dvaraka. Hearing of your illness, he has come along to the garden."

Both the fresh lilies were still in my hands. Just by the side of Father's feet were two feet like blue lotuses. Even the greatest poet of the world would not be able to describe those feet. I did

13

not know what enchantment lay in them. I placed the lilies on those feet. My tears fell on them.

It was only those feet that I saw at our first encounter. He returned to the palace with Father. Till he passed beyond sight I remained frozen just like that. Nitambini shook me and exclaimed, "What have you done! Gave to Krishna in offering those very blue lilies kept on your breast! What will you do now?"

Helplessly I said, "Yes, what shall I do now?"

All night I was lost in those feet. I did not know how many poems I wrote. Still the heart was not satisfied. I thought if I was unable to describe his feet, how would my poetry ever describe his face, eyes, lips? And if I could not do so, what was the use of poetry?

There is poetry in the heart of every human being. Some pour it out in writing, others do not. I wrote down whatever came to mind in the form of poetry. Father had made arrangements for my education. Both my tutor and my father said that I was scholarly, knowledge-hungry. Quickly I mastered many branches of knowledge. I became an expert in mathematics, music, painting, cookery, flower-arrangement, hospitality and other matters. But writing poetry was an obsession which I went on learning by myself. Father did not know anything about this.

Quite often discussions on various scriptures took place at our place. Poetry also had its turn. Many scholars, poets, wise men used to be invited. These discussions were organised for my sake. Father knew that my interest lay more in these rather than in singing and dancing. At these discussions, my queries were resolved. Attempts were made to quench my thirst for knowledge. But this thirst was limitless.

Once I was listening to Vedvyas Krishna Dvaipayan and agitatedly asked him, "If this life is not long enough to acquire the knowledge of all the books and sciences of the world, then what should man do?"

Vedvyas laughed and said, "It would have been better if your name had been *Trishnaa* [thirst] instead of Krishnaa. Daughter, thirst gives pain, but the thirst for knowledge is full of bliss. It is

14

not quenched in a thousand births, let alone one birth. Thirst is quenched by drinking water. But on drinking knowledge, the thirst for knowledge becomes yet stronger. Once this thirst is quenched the road to knowledge is blocked. The life that ends while gathering multicoloured shells of knowledge from the shores of eternal time — that is a meaningful life."

Delighted I asked, "I have finished all the books given by my tutors. Now what book should I read?"

Vedvyas smiled and said, "Is there any paucity of books of knowledge? This vast cosmos is a library. From each atom and molecule to every planet and star, all are books of His creation. Its pages are the experiences of every moment linked to this earth's dust particles. Therefore, every experience of life is a subject for study. Innumerable scholars, poets, sages, seers, wise men have not been able to unveil the mystery of life. Daughter, what is the need for any more books? Study life. Substantiate the nobility of life. God has created each of us for a particular purpose. Many incidents of your life are waiting for you — they will be your life's supreme study. Go, prepare yourself for them and prove your worth.

Prophetic seer Vedvyas! He described my future indisputably. I began to spin many fantasies and found satisfaction in giving them poetic form.

But the experience of that day! How could I give it utterance? It is indelibly imprinted on my heart. What pen will be able to translate it into language? The rhythm of each line is unique — absolutely its very own.

4

The sun had not yet risen. Some sweet sound broke my sleep. Carefully I listened and heard someone repeating at the door of my bedroom "Krishna! Krishna!" Who was calling in such a sweet voice so early in the morning? I continued to listen.

Krishna.... Krishna.... Krishna — someone was murmuring the name at the door of my heart. Was it rising out of my own heart or was someone reciting it on the other side of the shut door? Perhaps both were true. I opened the door. The courtyard of my palace was strewn with red. This dawn was quite distinct from other dawns. There was something special in it. But who was it that was singing Krishna's name?

Krishna.... Krishna.... Krishna — the sweet voice was floating towards me from a gilded cage. My favourite blackbird 'Nilmani' was repeating Krishna's name. The night before, Nitambini had been narrating stories about Krishna's birth, the miraculous feats of his childhood, the adolescent romance with the gopis and Radha's love, then in youth the abduction of Rukmini.... she had gone on recounting many other incidents. The more she criticised Krishna's faults, the more I found my respect for him increasing. I kept thinking: he could become the favourite of all Gokul at the age of twelve, so what if he was beloved of the gopis? Were the gopis distinct from the inhabitants of Gokul? Although besides Rukmini and Satyabhama he had many other wives in Dvaraka, he married them solely to protect dharma, for preserving the honour of women. Krishna who was more radiant than the blue sapphire could never be soiled. If Krishna, who was world-enchanter, turned heart-stealer, then what was the harm?

Nilmani had overheard my talk last night. The bird had started reciting Krishna's name right from early dawn as though its chirping were echoing the feelings of Krishnaa's heart.

Opening the gilded cage I petted Nilmani and said more softly than its own voice, "Nilmani!." And it replied, "Krishna. Krishna!" Again I called, "Nilmani!" It repeated, "Krishna. Krishna!" Again I called, "Nilmani!" It repeated, "Krishna. Krishna!"

As often as I called it would respond with Krishna's name. As if by uttering "Krishna" Nilmani was returning the love I was displaying. I wondered how Nilmani had managed to understand that it was the name of Krishna which was giving me the greatest pleasure.

I showed some mock annoyance, "Nilmani, stop this!"

Teasing me it said, "Krishna! Krishna! Krishna! Krishna!"

"Nilmani, Nilmani!" "Krishna!...Krishna!"

"Oh Nilmani! You'll drive me mad!"

I heard laughter — Nilmani was laughing! Behind me *sakhi* Nitambini had arrived and touching my unbound hair she said, "Reciting Krishna's name from the very morning! The entire day is still left."

Startled, I turned around and said in annoyance, "Not me, it is this bird Nilmani who is reciting his name! I was just rebuking it."

Nitambini swayed her hips exaggeratedly before me and shaking her head said, "Oh yes — yes, your heart's treasured blue sapphire is truly Krishna; Krishna who is like a blue sapphire. It is Krishna who is lovingly called Nilmani. And you, right from the moment of awakening, are going on reciting 'Nilmani! Nilmani'."

Ashamed I bit my tongue and muttered, "*Chheeh!* How would I know! My pet bird is named Nilmani, so what can I do?"

"It is you who have named the bird", retorted Nitambini with her eyes dancing. Defeated, I said, "Yes, it is I who named it. But I do not know why I liked the name Nilmani. The day my bird's christening was celebrated, the court poet had brought a long list of names among which this name sounded best to my ears."

"That is how it happens, my princess! Otherwise with so many

17

names available why would your name be Krishnaa? How sweet does 'Nilmani' sound on your lips!"

Shutting Nitambini up I said, "Really! Is today the first day when you are hearing it? I call 'Nilmani' day in and day out."

Apologetically Nitambini said, "It is not new for me to hear you call 'Nilmani', but it is new for the special guest resting in the guest-chambers. Will it be all right to disturb his sleep?"

Irritated, I asked, "Who are you talking about? Why should I disturb anyone's rest?"

Nitambini's eyes were dancing with naughtiness. She said, "This loving repetition of 'Nilmani' by you and the bird's calling out 'Krishna...Krishna' is resounding through the guest-chambers. The real Nilmani — poor thing — is getting restless like a bee maddened by the fragrance of flowers. He cannot understand who is calling him with such love. Really, Princess, there is no difference between Nilmani's voice and yours. As I was coming, Krishna asked me, 'Whose voice is this?' I replied, 'It is the voice of our princess.' He laughed. Truly, Princess, that laugh! Lucky, you did not see that laugh. It thrilled me all over."

"What would Krishna be thinking!" I wondered in embarrassment and said, "I was only calling my pet bird. You could have told him."

Nitambini smiled and said, "I replied to just what he asked. How could I say more to such a great person?"

Softly I enquired, "Did Krishna ask anything else?"

"Yes. He said, 'Doesn't the princess sleep at night? The sun is not yet up and she has started calling Nilmani-Nilmani! Not the slightest hint of lassitude in the voice. It is extremely sweet."

I wanted to rebuke Nitambini but a dream-like illusion was enveloping me within and a peculiar happiness was filling my being.

Nitambini said, "I have not finished. How will it do if you lose your senses from now itself?"

I roused myself. Nitambini pursed her lips and continued, "'It is a matter of happiness that your princess remembers me. Convey my thanks to her'."

18

I was dying of embarrassment. What a predicament this Nil-mani bird had thrown me into! How would I face Krishna ever again? Angrily I opened the gilded cage and let Nilmani fly away. I said, "Go, go away. You are now free. So am I!" Nilmani went hopping to the balcony. I expected that as in the past it would fly back to the cage after some time. But after a while it flew far away calling out, "Krishna. Krishna" and became a dot merging into the blue sky. It seemed that Nilmani had not under-stood my mock annoyance and left me for the forest. Now how would I pass the day without Nilmani? Who would beguile me by murmuring in my ears my heart's secrets?

Nitambini understood my dilemma. Softly she said, "Princess, do not worry. He who is named Nilmani never betrays your trust. To tease you it has flown away or has found a companion. Once a mate is found there is no attraction left for the gilded cage just as thoughts of the beloved drive away sleep even on a be-gemmed bed. Princess, you did not sleep the whole night. Your eyes are still heavy, lost in dreams. If one does not sleep properly, one dreams while awake." Nitambini was smiling wickedly with her sari-end between her teeth.

With what cunning had Nitambini changed the level of the discussion! But that day her wit did not please me. I was brood-ing over Nilmani.

Right then from somewhere Nilmani flew back and suddenly perched on my shoulder. It had somethng in its beak which it put into my hair and loudly screeched, "Krishnaa!...Krishnaa!...Krish-naa!"

Nitambini was watching amazed. What was surprising about it? This was no new technique of Nilmani's to placate me. Every time it would bring some flower in its beak and put it in my hair. But it had never called me "Krishnaa". It would always say in my ears, "Princess! Angry? Princess!" just as Nitambini used to en-quire. But who had taught it to say "Krishnaa"?

Nitambini blurted out, "Just see what Krishna has done!"

"What has Krishna done?"

"Taught Nilmani to recite the name Krishnaa."

19

"How?"

"You keep saying 'Krishna-Krishna' here. There he says, 'Krishnaa-Krishnaa'. It is there that it has heard 'Krishnaa-Krishnaa'!"

I got annoyed with Nitambini's mischievousness sometimes. That day, too, I got annoyed and said, "Nilmani went to Krishna? What a story!"

"Notice the peacock feather in your hair fragrant with sandalwood!" She took it out of my hair and waved it before my nose, touched it to my chest and said, "Understand now?"

Thrilled, I stood amazed. This feather did not belong to my pet peacocks. Its blue was deep like the clouds in the evening sky, lovely, vast. And then from where would the fragrance of sandal wood come in peacock feathers?

So, Krishna was taking my name? What was I to him? His beloved wives were in Dvaraka — eight chief queens, Satyabhama, Rukmini...Me, dark-complexioned, why should he suddenly think of me? I had surrendered to him, so I remembered him. But why should he remember me? So many people offered flowers at the feet of gods every day. Did the gods keep an account of them? It was the garland round the neck which enhanced a god's glory and whose fragrance he inhaled. The flowers at the feet roll in the dust.

I was musing thus when Father's commands reached me, "Prepare for Krishna's audience. After giving you his blessing Krishna will leave for Dvaraka."

I got ready. Choosing the best flowers from the garden I prepared a garland. Father had issued directions for greeting him with flower garlands. Shyness would not do. Father would get angry. Quickly I got ready. But I was not pleased with my appearance and dress. If his feet were so enchanting how lovely would his eyes be! Would those eyes be able to tolerate my appearance, my dress and ornaments? Again and again I was standing before the mirror changing my saris, changing my ornaments. Nothing would satisfy me. I was thinking: if it was for facing such lovely eyes that I had been born, then why did the creator not give me a more agreeable appearance?

Irritated with myself and my get-up, I took off all my ornaments. I took off the sari made of golden threads and wearing my usual white sari sat down on the bed and cried helplessly, "Nitambini! *sakhi!* In what form should I meet Krishna? Show me some way out!"

Nitambini put her hand on my shoulder and said afectionately, "Princess! Among the world's beautiful women you are the loveliest. Even if Krishna is the world's most handsome man, why should that bother you? If Krishna were the blue sky then you would be the evening clouds enhancing its beauty. If Krishna were the waters of a blue lake then you would be the mountain ranges reflected swimming in it. If Krishna were the peaceful vast blue sea, then you would be the tender moss on it. Who is greater than whom? One enhances the glory of the other. You and Krishna, too, are like that."

I was thinking: was Nitambini flattering me or speaking the truth? Right then the conch sounded. Nilanjana rushed in flustered and said. "Maharaj is waiting in the audience chamber. Krishna's chariot is ready to return to Dvaraka. Please come to meet Krishna."

There was now no time to adorn myself. I was absolutely unadorned. There was not even time for changing my white sari of silver threads. I set out in that condition.

There was no time to plait my wet hair either. The unbound tresses flowing down to my hips would suddenly toss about but I did not bother.

Nitambini said, "Whom the creator has created from beauty itself, what need does she have of ornaments, dresses, finery? Truly, Princess, this dress which makes you look like a priestess is extremely enchanting. Will Krishna, beloved of the gopis, be able to return to Dvaraka composed?"

I said nothing. Father might be getting anxious! I reached the audience chamber with Nitambini. My eyes were glued to my feet. I did not have the courage to raise my eyes to see Krishna.

If I was unable to withstand the impact of his enchanting form, what would be my condition?

Before I could greet Krishna he said in a musical voice, "Devi Krishnaa! Through you, — powerful and endowed with all auspicious qualities, — many wicked persons on this earth will be destroyed, dharma will be established. I too have taken a life-long vow to protect and establish dharma. You too have taken birth for this. Therefore, accept my *pranam*".

Father said, "That is why I have offered Krishnaa only at Krishna's feet. O Krishna! Right from the time of her christening Krishnaa has remained offered at your feet. Please give her shelter in your lotus feet."

With lowered face I had kept my eyes fixed on Krishna's blue-lotus feet. For some moments I was lost in them. Krishna removed his feet. In a calm, sweet voice he began speaking, "King Drupad! Devi Krishnaa is no ordinary woman. For her arrange a *svayamvar*. The finest hero of Aryavart alone will be the most suitable match for Krishnaa. By offering her like a servant at the feet of someone, you are only insulting her. Only he who will prove himself to be the best of all for Krishnaa, will take Krishnaa's hand in marriage."

Father cried out in distress, "O Krishna! Who besides you can be the finest hero of Aryavart? Where Krishna is the heart's choice what is the need for arranging a *svayamvar*? With you present, who else will have the power to win Krishnaa in the *svayamvar*?"

"Yes, there is someone Therefore, without *svayamvar* none has the authority to take Krishnaa's hand." Saying this Krishna smiled gently. That smile seemed to be meant to churn any young woman's heart and snatch all the nectar stored in it. *Sakhi* was indicating that I should place the garland in my hands round Krishna's neck.

I wanted to do that but my hands would not lift up. I was not mad with love of Krishna, but was helpless. Right then Father enquired, "Who is that? Who is there besides Krishna who is suitable for Krishnaa, the darling of my heart?"

In a voice warm with affection Krishna said, "With the powers of Hari, Hara, Brahma and Indra, a mighty person has taken birth on earth. He is the third Pandav, Arjun, son of my father's sister. He is about a year younger than me. Arjun's and my paternal ancestry is the same. Moreover, it is from a part of me that Arjun has taken birth.

"King Yayati of the Lunar race and Shukracharya's daughter, Devyani, had a son named Yadu. From Yayati's second wife, Sharmishtha, daughter of the Haiheya king, Vrishaparva, Puru was born. He was the ancestor of the Kauravs and the Pandavs. O King, Arjun's heroism is not hidden from you. And with him present, I cannot be suitable for Krishnaa. Arjun is not only my younger brother but my intimate friend. Our bodies are separate, but our souls are one. By making a world-famous hero such as Arjun your son-in-law you will assuredly win fame. This will also make for the fulfilment of your vow."

Father was delighted. The hero who had sometime at Drona's command imprisoned my father would now be his son-in-law. By his prowess Drona's arrogance would be ground in the dust. Through his son-in-law Drupad would take revenge for his insult. When that very hero whom Drona had found in the form of a student became king Drupad's son-in-law, he would be able to stand with his head held high before Drona. He would say, "Drona! Till today you laboured to make my son-in-law adept. If you had known that your best student would become my son-in-law, perhaps you would not have taught him all the arts of warfare. Now my son-in-law can defeat you, so you will have to live under my sufferance now."

Father's thoughts were plain on his face. Be it Krishna or Arjun, his son-in-law must be the best of heroes. If the appropriate son-in-law to take revenge on Drona was Arjun, then what was the objection to that?

But what of me? The garland I had been weaving since the morning to put round Krishna's neck would have to be put round Arjun's. That too at Krishna's behest! Did I have no wish of my own, no desire, no craving simply because I was Yajnaseni-born

23 •

of the sacrificial fire? My birth, life and death — all were dictated by someone else. Why had I come and why should I remain alive? Why should I die? What was the intention? I knew nothing. Ignorance was my only stay. Seeing my disappointed and worried face, Krishna said softly, "Devi Draupadi! You were born to destroy your father's enemies. Not only your father's enemies but the world's evil-doers too. For conquering external enemies we need first to conquer the internal, that is, the senses. Give up desires, cravings, mind, heart and intellect for the establishment of dharma. For the sake of nobler causes selfish interests can be sacrificed. That is what establishes life's nobility."

I realised that Krishna was the dharma-promoter. That very moment I offered myself to Krishna. Silently I said, "O Krishna! If my acts are not my own, then the fruits of my acts, too, are not mine. I know nothing. Whatever commands come for serving the nobler cause, those shall I obey. But I am an ordinary earthly woman. Where do I have the power to conquer lust, anger, greed and delusion? If you do not give me that strength, how shall I turn from a mere woman into a goddess?"

Weaving tears into the flower-garland I placed it not round Krishna's neck but on his feet. It seemed to me that my youth had vanished. I had become an infant. I had not experienced my childhood, having been born with a youthful body. How pleasurable was the delicate, simple, pure ignorance of infancy! Feeling that the ultimate fulfilment of life lay in dripping drops of ignorance on to the feet of the ocean of wisdom, Krishna, with a resolute mind I established his dear *sakha* Arjun in my heart. What alternative did I have? As an ignorant infant I should play with whatever toy my master placed in my hand, be happy, and go on living. Who was I to ask who would be my toy and why?

Before leaving, Krishna quietly spoke to my heart, "Krishnaa! Krishna is ever love-mad, hungry for affection. Never put a knot in the bonds of love in which *sakha* Arjun has bound me. I have the right to share in your love for Arjun. I am a partner in all the victories and defeats of Arjun, in all that he gets and loses. Before eating, Arjun offers the food to me. Without offering it to me,

24

Arjun does not even touch water. But I do not eat the food Arjun offers; I only consume his craving. In the same manner despite belonging to Arjun, my relationship with your subtlest essence is eternal and immortal. Never forget this."

That very moment I split into two. My subtlest essence merged into his deep blue radiant essence. My other portion remained as the body of Draupadi-of-the-*svayamvar*, amid earthly pleasures, desires and anxieties in the royal palace of Panchal, waiting for Arjun.

How strange is man's mind! How many things it forgets and how much remains unforgotten, indelibly imprinted on it!

I forgot that Father had first offered me to Krishna. Now I lost myself in fantasies about Arjun, the noblest of heroes. What would he be like? Just like Krishna? Or a second Krishna? What else could he be if he suited Krishna's heart and mind?

5

Spring was in the air. In the month of Phagun the colour of *phaq* had begun to tinge the arjun forest with red. Thunder-wielder Indra was present on the banks of the pure-watered Ganga. Kunti, the dear daughter of the Bhoj king, had summoned Indra by means of the victory garland obtained from Durvasa. Could Indra reject this summons of spring?

The divine infant who arrived in this arjun forest on the banks of the Ganga with the prowess of Indra from the womb of pure-hearted Kunti in the Uttarphalguni asterism was Arjun — Phalguni, Vishnu, Kiriti, Shvetvahan, Vibhatsu, Vijay, Savyasachi, Dhananjay. After saying this much, Nitambini stopped. She asked, "*Sakhi!* You will be able to remember so many names of your beloved, I trust? Truly, how fortunate you are! He who has so many names — how great must be his fame, his achievements, his knowledge and intelligence! Now forget Krishna and think of Phalguni!"

I said, "*Sakhi!* She who has once established Krishna in her heart can only allow Savyasachi a place there. For, he alone has taken birth from a portion of Krishna. In him, after all, I will find Krishna himself. When Krishna feels that Arjun alone is suitable for me, I believe that it is Arjun who is the world's greatest hero."

Nitambini laughed and said, "*Sakhi!* You haven't heard the stories of Arjun's heroism? He showed his prowess from early childhood. He is the finest disciple of guru Drona. In his amazing weapon-test only Arjun succeeded. There is a hill at a distance of eight thousand eight hundred and twenty-eight miles with a fort on top with a pike fixed above it. On this pike was kept a grain of mustard. The tutor's command was to split that mustard seed into two."

Startled, I kept gazing at Nitambini. How peculiar was this

test! Could anyone be successful in it? Laughing at my stunned aspect, Nitambini continued, "He who passed this test is bound to be either Krishna himself or Krishna's *sakha*, Arjun. Who else can accomplish this impossible feat?"

Surprised I mused: one who had displayed such miraculous ability in weapon-craft — who could he be other than Krishna's *sakha*?

Softly Nitambini whispered in my ear, "It was at Drona's command that Arjun had imprisoned King Drupad. It is he who will win Drupad's daughter at Krishna's bidding. Wah! what a coincidence!"

Warmly I responded, "What option do I have? Whatever Krishna desires, Father will do. It is my duty to honour Father's wishes. Leaving dharma aside, what meaning will my life hold?"

Nitambini smiled and said, "Angry because you did not get Krishna? Despite not getting Krishna you will win Krishna's very life-breath."

"How so?" I asked.

Nitambini explained, "After all, Arjun is Krishna's very life. If Arjun is yours, that means Krishna's soul is yours and you have got Krishna. If you can bring Arjun under your control it will bring Krishna within your grasp. She who can command Krishna — what sorrow can touch her?"

I did not know how I blurted out, "Is there life without grief, Nitambini? If there be, then Krishna does not exist there. Where there is sorrow there is Krishna. It is said he is the friend of the sorrowful."

I did not know then that I was talking about my own future.

27

6

I was preparing to be *svayamvaraa*, to choose my husband, for the Panchal kingdom was preparing for Princess Draupadi's *svayamvar*.

Who was not aware of Arjun's prowess and heroism? Father had suffered defeat at his hands long back. Therefore, without displaying the zenith of his own prowess how could he obtain the finest of women, Draupadi?

Behind the arrangement of such a peculiar *svayamvar* and the conditions of the ceremony there was a double purpose. Firstly, no one other than Arjun would be able to prove himself. Consequently, it would be Arjun who would become the son-in-law of the Panchal monarch. Secondly, Father would be able to compensate before the Panchal people for the humiliation suffered at Arjun's hands in the past.

Sakhi Nitambini announced the conditions of the *svayamvar*. Hearing them, I was stunned. Would anyone succeed in this test?

The bow that had been made for the *svayamvar* was so hard that bending it for stringing would be a difficult task. A lovely dais had been made for the *svayamvar* with a long pole on it. On this pole was a revolving disc. Along with the swiftly revolving disc the picture of the target would be reflected in the water of a vessel kept below. For this, near the pavilion a large water receptacle had been made ready. The target fixed on top of the disc would be in the shape of a small fish. Stringing the bow, and looking at the target's reflection below, the archer would have to pierce the target by shooting five arrows through the eye of the fish. Whereupon the target would slip down. This would be the test to be passed in the Draupadi-*svayamvar* for winning Draupadi.

After knowing these novel conditions stipulated by Father, it seemed to me that in his heart of hearts Father wanted that I should remain unwed forever, helping him in his religious duties, and safeguarding dharma. Otherwise, why would he prescribe conditions which even God Himself would not be able to fulfil? However, I had heard about Krishna-*sakha* Arjun's mastery of archery and infallible aim. Perhaps Father wanted that Draupadi should not be won by anyone but Arjun and that was why such a test had been prescribed.

I had not seen Arjun, but coming to know of the conditions of the *svayamvar* I could hazard a guess at his prowess and heroism. In my heart I thanked Krishna and accepted his guidance. I felt that there was no question at all of doubting any decision of his. He was beneficent, auspicious.

The arrangements were complete. In the whole of Panchal, before the *svayamvar*, for a fortnight there were festivities. The gaiety of spring pervaded the entire kingdom. Rich and poor alike were participating in the celebrations. Palaces were painted afresh. All houses were freshly colour-washed, with their boundaries demarcated. It seemed as if the whole kingdom had been constructed anew. At all entrance gates of mango-branches with water pots had been placed as auspicious signs. All citizens had been provided with new clothes at the cost of the royal treasury. The men and women dressed in new clothes and jewellery were enhancing the glory of the kingdom. The entire capital was decorated with lights. The nights were resplendent. At different places dance, music and fireworks had been arranged round the clock.

For decorating the assembly-hall for the *svayamvar* famous painters and artists had arrived. Those who had not seen the palace of Indra were considering themselves blessed on seeing all the rich illumination, elaborate preparations and pageantry. Appropriate arrangements had been made in the assembly-hall for guests so that they could all watch the target-shooting. Carefully thought out plans had been made for this. A silver canopy shot through with golden threads hung overhead. Fragrant pots of flowers had been kept for the guests right from the entrance up to the *svayamvar* hall. The entire hall was fragrant with their scent. Various types of food had been prepared for everyone right from the poor and humble to the noble guests. Some were thinking that if the princess' *svayamvar* celebration were to stretch on for many years then life would be replete with joy. On seeing the pageantry, guests from far away were wondering whether they had reached some nook of heaven! Surely this was the wedding ceremony of a heavenly *apsara!* From different countries kings, princes, warriors, heroes, priests and scholars had arrived as guests. The capital was resounding with joy, for appropriate arrangements had been made for entertaining the guests.

I was ready to be married. I knew who was to be my husband, who would be able to fulfil the unique conditions of the *svayamvar*. There was no anxiety in my heart, nor any agitation. That would have been there if my husband were the prince of my dreams. I had never seen Arjun; only heard descriptions of his appearance and stories of his famed strength, heroism and personality. Therefore, like a still lake my mind was calm and filled with gladness.

That day I was strolling in the garden with Nitambini. Talking of Arjun's qualities, she was teasing me. Such teasing had become a habit with her. She said, *"Sakhi!* Never trust Krishna. He is such a trickster! Having got such a priceless woman as you, will he hand you over to Arjun from the heart? Do not forget that a portion of Krishna is in Arjun. Even after getting Arjun you will still remain Krishna's. Rightfully, his authority over you will persist. I do not know why my mind is filled with doubts watching the arrangements for the ceremony."

I started and asked, "What doubts? Arjun is bound to be victorious in the test set by Father. Shri Krishna himself has approved this test devised by Father."

In a low voice Nitambini said, "I have heard that the five Pandavs are not in Hastinapur. There are bad rumours circulating about them. I hope to God they are not true! If they turn out to be true then you will have to prepare to remain unwed forever."

My left eye twitched. The heart fluttered. In a weak voice I asked, "The five Pandavas are celebrating a festival in Varanavat. Shri Krishna is bound to inform them about the *svayamvar*. How can there be any doubt about their arrival?"

Nitambini wanted to say something but was unable to say it: "I do not know ... whether the news is true or not ..."

"What news?" I asked anxiously. At that moment wailing was heard from the palace. Maidservants and attendants were lamenting loudly. Both of us were stunned. Why this heart-rending outcry in the midst of joyous celebrations?

Brother Dhrishtadyumna was before me in the garden. His face was pale, eyes downcast. Perhaps father had suddenly taken ill. Agitatedly I asked, "Why this weeping?"

"Shri Krishna has arrived," said Dhrishtadyumna with bowed head.

Surprised I asked, "So what is there in this to weep about?"

Brother said in a thick voice, "We were both born from the sacrificial altar for the protection of dharma. Therefore, like ghee on the flaming altar, we will have to be consecrated to destroying the agony and sins of the world. Krishnaa, you know that the Pandavs had gone to Varanavat."

With bowed head I replied, "Yes, they were halting in the lap of peaceful, beautiful nature at Varanavat. But so what?"

Dhrishtadyumna sat down next to me in the creeper-festooned grove. In a voice heavy with grief he began speaking, "The Pandavs had virtually been sought to be driven away by the conspiring Kauravs. Leaving Hastinapur, they stayed in Varanavat. After their education was over, the blind king Dhritarashtra had no option but to declare Yudhishthir the Crown Prince. The people had faith in him and depended on him. Moreover, Yudhishthir was the eldest. Therefore there was no alternative but to make him the Crown Prince. The Pandavs are brave, strong, discriminating, righteous and peace-loving by nature. Drona, Kripacharya, grandfather Bhishma, minister Vidur and others also strongly supported this decision. After Yudhishthir became the Crown Prince, Duryodhan, Duhshasan and the hundred brothers began to burn with jealousy."

Apprehensively I asked, "Then what happened?"

"That which was inevitable..."

"You mean...!"

Dhrishtadyumna explained, A festival was arranged in Varanavat. The Pandavs were sent off there. Peaceable, simple Yudhishthir — why should he imagine deception? First the Kauravs extolled the merits of Varanavat. So, to have a change of climate the brothers took their mother to Varanavat. A new palace had already been constructed for their stay there. The Pandavs were pleased with the lavish arrangements and decoration of the place. But they did not know that this new palace would open up for them the gates of Yama's kingdom.

I shrieked in distress. Brother caught hold of me, "Yes, Krishnaa! That palace was a house of lac. The Kauravs had engaged Dhritarashtra's cunning minister, Purochan, to seal the Pandavs' fate. He set fire to the house of lac at night. And the Pandavs, Kunti, Purochan — all were burnt to death. It is this terrible news that Krishna has brought, hearing which everyone is grievously stricken. That is why the palace attendants are lamenting. If this is the ultimate fate of the Pandavs, then how will the intention behind our birth ever be fulfilled? Establishing dharma in a world bereft of the Pandavs will be like the blooming of a lotus in a waterless pond."

I sat motionless. What would be my fate now? I had already chosen Arjun in my heart of hearts. I knew that besides him none could fulfil the conditions of the *svayamvar*. This was how one was held up to mockery in the world by depending on Krishna! I was not so sorry for myself, but for those five virtuous brothers — what a fate to overcome! If this was true then Krishna could never have been the *sakha* of the Pandavs and he could not have taken birth for the establishment of dharma. But what should I do? Princes from different kingdoms were flocking to the various guest-houses built for the *svayamvar*. For enjoying the festivities, relatives, friends, foreign guests, all had arrived on being invited.

32

New palaces, eating houses, tourist lodges, entertainment arenas, streets and markets, all were teeming with people. Scholars and priests from various parts of the country had arrived for chanting the hymns. Hoping to win me, many princes were constantly practising with their bows and arrows in the courtyards of the guest-houses neglecting their meals and rest. In such a situation the *svayamvar* would have to be held. But its results were obvious. That there was no one in the world suited to be my spouse would only sully my reputation, not enhance it. That no one was fit for me could hardly be said to be an auspicious omen for me, for I was a woman and that too one who was to choose her spouse. If everyone failed, Father would certainly not relax the conditions of the test. And if he did relax them, why should I silently accept that? First I was offered to Krishna. Krishna did not accept me and ordained that I was for his *sakha*, Arjun. I did not feel any hesitation, for Arjun had been born of a portion of Krishna himself. In Arjun's body it was Krishna who was the life and soul. I had not surrendered myself to Arjun's body. It was before his character, his soul that I had offered myself. In other words, it was to Krishna that I had surrendered myself in a different way. I had thought that in getting Arjun I would find Krishna. But if someone other than Arjun succeeded in the test due to Father's relaxations, how could I taint my soul by wedding that person?

Slowly I said, "Brother! Can't the arrangements for *svayamvar* be stopped?"

Brother was startled and said. "How? Duryodhan with many brothers, Karna, Shakuni, Ashvatthama, Jayadrath, Shalya, Kritavarma, Satyaki, Shishupal, Jarasandh...many competitors have reached the guest-houses. Bhishma, Drona, Kripacharya, Balaram and other respected guests are coming. Scholars from Ang, Vang, Kaling, Chol, Pandya, Magadh, Koshal, Hastinapur, Madra, Kamboj, Gandhar and other kingdoms have come. To speak of aborting the arrangements will be a grave insult to them. Panchal will have to acknowledge defeat before their united strength. Panchal will be gravely endangered. Therefore, for the welfare of the kingdom and to honour the guests, the *svayamvar* assembly will be held at the notified date and time. There is no other choice."

I thought to myself, Krishnaa's danger could never be of greater importance than the danger facing the kingdom. Therefore it was Krishnaa who would face the danger. But who but I could appreciate how terrible that danger would be?

Sighing deeply I said, "It is the same thing. I would have remained an unwed virgin as it is! None will be able to fulfil the conditions of the *svayamvar* and, therefore, I shall remain unmarried. Let only the danger facing the kingdom be averted and Panchal be emptied of enemies.

Brother said, "Hopefully, this is what will happen. They will return with their forces. Why should we test their strength?"

I was silent. All the enthusiasm, dreams, fantasies, desires, anxieties aroused in me by the ceremony had died out. Now I would have to accept the stern ascetic life of a perpetual virgin unmoved by joy and sorrow. After all, if I had no role in what had already occurred and what was going to occur, where was the cause for anxiety?

But that dream-prince of my heart! The thought of that sudden untimely bereavement kept bobbing up in my mind again and again. Remaining unmoved — yes, up to a point. But could anyone ever become emotion-free?

I did not know that my blue eyes were filled with tears. Brother saw it and it pained him. To distract my mind, he said, "Krishnaa! Come, let us go in. Father is expecting us. Krishna has to be greeted. He is Aryavart's finest hero and wisest man. He is our companion in joy and sorrow. It will not be proper to allow any lapse in honouring the guest."

Trying to stem my tears I said, "Will not the greeting of an inconsequential woman like me sully Krishna's glory? These inauspicious eyes of mine had rather not be cast on him. The moment my alliance was proposed with his *priya sakha*, he was taken away. Even after such a disaster will Krishna like to look at my face?"

Suddenly a stream of nectar flowed through my ears touching

the inmost depths of my being. Whose sweet laughter was this? Looking around I found Krishna the most desired of all, standing there! His dark body was looking even more attractive — clad in yellow with auspicious marks on his forehead, rings in his ears, beautiful blue lotus-like eyes, the broad chest adorned with a necklace of gems and a garland of wild flowers, the lips curved in a gentle smile. All my sorrow and distress vanished in a trice. Truly, Krishna was an enchanter. Hypnotised, I began to rise to *pranam* him.

With the same smile he said, "I would prefer your grieved face to a devotional salute. Perhaps you do not know how much more attractive sorrow makes a pretty face. Whether the news of the accidental death of the Pandavs be true or false, had I not brought it, your face would never have expressed the inimitable loveliness of this sorrow. After seeing the beauty of your face, I have forgotten even the sorrow of losing the Pandavs."

The long-restrained tears now flowed down my cheeks and I thought, "Krishna is pleased by my sorrow! How cruel he is!"

Looking at me steadily he said, "After seeing you my mind tells me that the Pandavs are still alive. He whose marriage has been decided with you can never remain hidden from public view like a coward. If the Pandavs have so easily been deluded into the maw of death by being burnt alive in the house of lac, then that is the result of their foolishness. If Krishna's *sakha* is such a fool, then Krishna is an even greater fool! Krishnaa! Do you think that I am a fool?"

Looking at Krishna my heart at once said, "Arjun will come. To keep the vow, to rescue Krishnaa from this extreme danger he will come." Shutting my eyes, I prayed to the Supreme.

The sixteenth day of the celebrations. This was the much awaited day.

At the auspicious moment, before dawn, I bathed in the lake in the garden and entered the golden temple of Parvati with my *sakhis* for worship. I was looking like an ascetic with my entire body unadorned, wet hair left open, falling on my back like waves of the sea. My entire attention was focused on the lotus-feet of Parvati where I bowed after placing the lighted lamp. Silently I prayed, "Devi! Preserve my honour! Refusing to countenance criticism of your husband, you immolated yourself in the sacrificial flames. I was born from that very *yajna*-altar. If the person I have accepted in my heart as my husband has been burnt to death, is that not an insult to me? Then what is the point in my remaining alive? If anyone other than Arjun was successful in passing the test, Father would accept him as son-in-law, but how can I take him as husband? If there is truly something called dharma, then preserve my dharma as a chaste wife."

At that moment a flower fell from the Devi's head. The priest picked it up and offered it to me, "What you have desired will be fulfilled! This is the sign. The Devi is smiling. She does not smile unless there is a sincere cry from within. Good fortune is certain when she smiles."

My heart sang, "Arjun will come! Definitely!"

I touched the sacred flower to my head and returned to the garden. It brought an incident of another day to mind. It was the day of Sita's *svayamvar*. She was returning after having worshipped Parvati and the meeting with Ram took place on the way. The four eyes met and became one. It could so happen that in the Devi's courtyard the meeting with Arjun, the union of four eyes, would take place! But who knew whether Arjun was alive at all or....

My heart grew heavy again. No meeting with Arjun occurred. Every moment I thought, "Arjun will come. Four eyes will meet and unite. My life will be blessed." But he did not come.

Chaste Sita was my ideal. After reading her life story I had turned her devotee, had been immersed in her love, had wept in her sorrow. But why compare myself with her? Would I be able to live like her, silently bearing the agony, burning up within? She was a great lady, the beloved of Ram, the glory of the Raghu dynasty; and I was just Panchal princess Yajnaseni — not even knowing this little, whether I had any husband at all. Why should every incident of her life be repeated in mine? Dejectedly, I returned from the temple, looking with hopeful eyes in all directions. Panchal' streets were ringng with joy. The kings, emperors and honoured guests had all arrived. They had no news of the five Pandavs. No more guests to come. The elaborately decorated guest-house prepared for the stay of the Pandavs was still absolutely empty. If the Pandavs were alive, they should have arrived by now. The *svayamvar* assembly would be held in the forenoon and there was no further possibility of their arrival.

The royal highway was a tree-flanked avenue. Resplendent with new leaves, flowers and loaded with fruit the trees looked like decked-up city women. The cuckoos, parakeets, starlings, thrushes had all got wind of the celebrations in the city. With their heart-stealing songs they were fulfilling their duty by joining in the music for the ceremony, as it were.

In front of the guest-houses the onlookers were fascinated by the swans gracefully swimming in the crystal-clear ponds. There was not a cloud in the sky. Yet at places peacocks were dancing, participating in the singing and dancing of the celebrations, as though they were competing with the dancers.

I returned from the garden with my *sakhis* by way of the *Panchvihar*. Ultimately one would get to know whether the Pandavs had come or not. Through the lattice of leaves and creepers the *Panchvihar* looked most attractive. Dancers were dancing in the entertainment halls of the guest-houses. The *Panchvihar*, decorated with multi-coloured lights, was still resplendent. The entrances to the halls were decorated with many-coloured flowers. Holding garlands in golden trays for greeting guests, lovely maidens still stood waiting. The Pandavs might arrive at any moment. Even the plants and trees of Panchal could not believe that the Pandavs had been burnt alive. Looking at the decorated guest rooms it seemed to be that the Pandavs were about to arrive ... they would surely arrive.

Who was that striking figure in the guest house? Who was that youth, with complexion like blue clouds, in the garden of coloured flowers? Arjun? I was unable to see clearly. My heart started beating fast. Some *sakhi* was saying, "Aah! Shri Krishna remained awake all night in the *Panchvihar* waiting for Arjun.

How pale this freshly blooming blue lotus appears in disappointment! Will Arjun and his four brothers really arrive? See how distracted Krishna is, sitting and waiting!"

At this my eyes brimmed over with tears. My fears that the worship of Parvati had been fruitless became firmer. Hearing the tinkling of our anklets, Krishna too joined us on the pathway. Noticing me he said, "Krishnaa! On this earth it is man who suffers the most. Even when he is immersed in happiness he keeps worrying about grief and danger. While sunk in sorrow, some people keep imagining a state of happiness. True, even in grief joy lies hidden and the tears in your eyes are proof of this." Lifting up my tearful eyes I looked at Krishna. With a smile Krishna said, "These tear-drops of yours are reflecting the vermilion rays of the rising sun, enhancing the beauty of your face and thereby the value of these drops. The sun-rays are themselves glorified. How enchanting they are becoming! Therefore, even tears have a value in life — there is a loveliness even in the shedding of tears. Precisely in the same manner, sorrow too has value, for behind grief happiness lies ready. What is to happen is bound to happen anyway. Therefore, in the moment of joy instead of savouring it, what is the point of weeping and imagining sorrows before the moment for tears has arrived?"

I could not say anything. I *pranam*-ed Krishna. It was my very sorrow which was my offering to him today. There was nothing other than grief in my heart. I began feeling that my heart had become somewhat lighter.

The competing kings, richly dressed, had assumed their seats on the gold-embossed dais. A costly pavilion covered the entire assembly-hall. Wall-hangings woven with gold and silver threads were gleaming in the light. Each king was smug with self-satisfaction considering himself worthy of Krishnaa. Scholars and priests were seated in a separate area. For Brahmins there was a separate arrangement. For accommodating the spectators from the city and the women arrangements had been made on one side. The citizens and subjects had decked themselves out with ornaments. Their seating arrangements were such that while they could overlook the hall, they were not visible to the guests.

But I! I would have to appear in front of everyone for it was my *svayamvar*. I would be on display before all. My beauty and radiance would spur the competitors on.

The *sakhis* had decorated me in many ways. Pure white clothing and flowers covered my whole body. Seeing my reflection in the mirror I thought: "Why don't white flowers look so lovely in the garden?" Sandalwood and heady perfume mingling with the lotus scent of my body were capable of perfuming the entire hall. I had always preferred white clothes and white flowers. So they had adorned me only with diamonds. How attractive and enchanting dark complexion could be I realised only that day after seeing myself. Accompanied by my *sakhis*, seated in a decorated palanquin, escorted by brother Dhrishtadyumna, I entered the hall. As they came to a halt, at my brother's command I alighted from the palanquin. The entire hall filled with murmurs the moment I arrived. Young and old, Brahmin and Kshatriya, men and women — everyone gazed stunned at my dark loveliness. With lowered eyes, slowly I advanced towards the prescribed spot. I was profoundly ashamed to be the target of so many lustful eyes. I wanted to hide my face in the veil. Then, as if in tune with my wish, bees left the bouquets arranged in the hall and began humming around me like a dark blue veil creating a curtain between the greedy eyes of the princes and myself. They got agitated and began breathing in deeply the fragrance of my body. Their breathing could be mistaken for a mild gust of wind.

I did not know whether the lotus scent of my body or the flowers in my hair or the perfumed oils on my body and my hair made the bees leave all the flowers kept in the hall to create all around me a veil like a blue cloud. Bees they were, but how sympathetic! I was grateful for their generous consideration. Only they could feel how painful it was for a woman to have her beauty on display in an assembly hall. Strangely enough, scholars and priests were incapable of sensing this.

Somehow or other I managed to reach the dais and took my

seat there. Then Dhrishtadyumna, greeting all present, spoke: "O assembled kings and princes of high birth! This is my sister, Krishnaa, the eminently desirable one. You have all seen her beauty. She is the finest beauty of all Aryavart. She is also endowed with all desirable qualities. Soft-spoken yet knowledgeable, discriminating, well-versed in scriptures, adept in music, intelligent and goddess-like in appearance. The central tenet of her existence is the establishment of truth on earth and the protection of dharma. Today she is present here to select from amongst you the pre-eminent one. You are aware of the conditions of this bridegroom-choice. O assembled heroes! You have all come here eager for Draupadi's hand. Now before you are the bow and arrows and the target. Only he who, piercing the eye of the golden fish rotating on the discus with five arrows one after another, brings the fish down on the ground, will win Krishnaa. But this hero must be of noble descent."

Then Dhrishtadyumna began introducing one competitor after another. But out of shyness I could not lift my eyes towards any. The name of my heart's desire was nowhere in those introductions. I remained sitting depressed and worried about my fate.

The ambitious suitors began advancing to the sound of conch-shells, bells and other instruments and vedic chants. One after another failed, creating laughable situations. Some failed to string the bow. Others could not even lift it up. Hurt, aggrieved and surprised one king after another went back. The spectators began thinking, "Why did King Drupad keep to this condition even after knowing of the death of the best of warriors, Arjun? Does he want to force the princess to perpetual celibacy?" All the *sakhis* were lamenting in the same fashion. But I was thinking, "World-mother Parvati has heard my prayers. Surely in response to my plea she will send Arjun here. Till now she has not permitted anyone victory only to preserve the honour of an unfortunate pre-pledged woman like me. But if somebody had been victorious? What could I have done then? I would have been forced to honour my father's vow and greet that person as my husband. My dharma as a *sati* would have been shattered." I was finding

40

consolation in this fashion. Deep sighs of defeat, shame and despair were increasing in the hall. Some of the frustrated persons were voicing various types of conjectures. A few were making plans for abducting me by force even if someone succeeded in being victorious. Hearing their words my companions were vastly amused but my heart was grievously pained. I hated myself for having sat so long before such lust-driven sinful eyes. I felt soiled.

Brother Dhrishtadyumna, Father and the elders sat despondent, worried about my fate. But I noticed that among the Yadavs, Krishna was seated with Balaram enjoying the entire scene with a smiling face. For Krishnaa, there was not the slightest anxiety, the least concern, in Krishna! Then there was no doubt that Krishnaa's fate was mocking her. I was preparing myself for the end of the *svayamvar* ceremony. Only a few suitors were left.

Amid all the despair, radiant like the newly risen sun, with complexion enchanting like the setting sun, resplendent with golden armour and earrings, a heroic man arrived at this moment near the target. Everyone was struck dumb with the newcomer's perfect beauty and radiance. Some even forgot their lust for me and began wishing that this hero should pierce the target and win Krishnaa. Some were despondent, contemplating the defeat of even so heroic a person. Delighted Nitambini began whispering in my ears, "*Sakhi!* Prepare yourself. This hero, like the god of love Kama himself, will be victorious and will win you!"

Suddenly my heart beat faster. I thought: if this supremely attractive hero came out victorious, then he could be none other than Arjun. Parvati had fulfilled my heart's desire in the dying moments of the contest. This must be Kunti's son. Who but Kunti's son could pierce the target? Perhaps for a moment I too had this desire — that this hero should be victorious!

Easily and in a pleasing manner the hero lifted the bow. He was getting ready to aim the arrow as the hall resounded with shouts of joy and clapping. The young man got more encouraged. Before shooting the arrow he saluted the sun god. Everyone thought: "At last! The next moment this young man will taste victory. Drupad's royal princess is as good as won."

Suddenly someone among the spectators said, "What is the name of this hero? A condition of the *svayamvar* is that if the suitor is not of noble descent he will not have the right to Krishnaa's hand even if he pierces the target."

Abruptly Dhrishtadyumna said in a loud voice, "The rules of the contest were made clear at the very beginning. Unless the suitor is high-born, my sister cannot wed him. However great a hero Karna, the son of charioteer Adhirath and Radha, might be, he cannot have the right to win my sister."

The moment Dhrishtadyumna had finished, Karna quietly replaced the bow and stared at the sky despondently. He was gazing at the westward inclining noonday sun. Suddenly a cloud obscured the sun. The sun was not prepared to face that silent accusation. Karna returned to his seat. Once he looked at me out of the corner of his eye. Even that sad look of Karna was so enchanting that my companions lost their senses. I was feeling guilty. I felt that even I was responsible to some extent for the insult Karna suffered in this huge assembly. If the peculiar conditions of the *svayamvar* were the cause of the defeat suffered by so many kings and of the insult to Karna, was I also not to blame? Because of me so many heroes had suffered. My heart was full of remorse particularly because Karna had been insulted by raising the question of his birth. In truth, what was the necessity for this *svayamvar*?

I was pledged to be wedded. Everyone knew that. Everyone also knew that the conditions of the *svayamvar* could be fulfilled by none other than Krishna or Arjun. Arjun was dead, Krishna was not among the suitors. Therefore, the result was a foregone conclusion. Even if Karna succeeded, he was not of noble birth. Despite knowing all this, what was the need of making a public display of me and entice everyone?

Every human being is drawn towards a thing of beauty. He dreams of making it his own. If he cannot obtain it through honest means, he tries to acquire it through devious means. At that time the greedy human is unable to determine whether he has the ability to acquire that desired object or not. Unsuccessful despite all efforts, he grieves. Therefore, I was the cause of the sorrow of many kings.

Heroic Karna with bowed head was slowly walking back. The sun had pierced through the cloud and was shining forth once again. In the hall, some people were trying to add to the insult Karna had suffered by making sarcastic remarks. Someone said, "This is the ruler of Ang, the friend of the Kauravs, King Karna! The only warrior equal of the hero Arjun. But who is his father? That's why he suffers insults. Even charioteer Adhirath is not his natural father. It is said that charioteer Adhirath is his foster father." "In other words, brave Karna is a bastard," added someone. "What else? He who cannot give his father's name, what else is he?" said another.

Karna kept silent and moved on hearing all the comments without response, without any sign of agitation.

There are some people who enjoy paining others even though they gain nothing thereby. Most of the people present in the assembaly hall gloated over the sight of Karna returning insulted. But if birth and death were preordained why should one suffer insults on that account? This picture of crestfallen Karna filled my heart with compassion and sympathy. Silently I said to myself, "Heroic Karna, if I have the slightest role in the insult and abuse you have suffered, please forgive me. I feel your anguish with all my heart and soul. After this it is my turn to be insulted and shamed. Is it a petty insult that for the bride-to-be Krishnaa there should be no bridegroom in this world?"

After Karna, Shishupal, Shalya, Jarasandh and other heroes, being unsuccessful, began cursing their fate. All suitors started criticising the conditions laid down by Father. No kshatriya suitor was left for Krishnaa. Now the *svayamvar* assembly could be dissolved. Father and brother were irritated and disappointed. But Krishna was smiling and his face was glowing like a freshly blooming flower. I realised that if there was cruelty incarnate on this earth then that was this Krishna. At this critical juncture of the *svayamvar* ceremony, when an innocent princess' future was at stake, Krishna was not in the least moved. Did Krishna not know all this? If Arjun had been born with a short life-span, why had he chosen him for me?

The assembly was about to be over. The dancing and singing had stopped. Suddenly everyone noticed that Krishna was smilingly looking at the ranks of the seated Brahmins. A resplendent Brahmin youth was asking permission of the assembly to contest as a suitor. All the royalty and the spectators saw clear signs of success in the Brahmin's mighty shoulders, long arms, calm face, handsome limbs, and lotus eyes radiant like the sun. Out of envy, a few protested and in mocking tones said, "Where expert warriors and heroes have accepted defeat, this mendicant Brahmin has stood up in the hope of success!" And some shouted in anger, "The kshatriya race will be grossly insulted if this mendicant Brahmin enters the contest. Even though his failure is inevitable as are night and day, we firmly oppose his participation."

In the midst of this controversy the priests and scholars said, "Kshatriyas are used to battle and are no doubt adept in war. Similarly, Brahmins are used to chanting hymns and, as a result, they are adept in the scriptures and acquire perfection in pronunciation. This does not mean that if a kshatriya practises he will be unable to acquire perfection in chanting or that a Brahmin cannot show expertise in archery. If Lord Parashuram could defeat all the kshatriyas of the world, why should this youth not be victorious? It is not birth but deeds and application that determine the worth of man. Therefore, this highly ambitious, wondrously handsome Brahmin youth can beyond any doubt take part in the contest."

After the priests and wise men had given permission, this young man came forward and stood near the target spot. On seeing him a lightning thrill shot through my despairing heart. I felt I knew this calm, dignified person from long before. But I could not place him.

He stood beside the target and saluted the earth and

Dharma. In a grave, deep voice he said, "Salutations to Krishna and Krishnaa."

Amazed, everyone thought, "Krishna is divinely gifted and is the finest of Aryavart's heroes, therefore it is logical for a Brahmin to greet him. But is it proper for him to salute the princess who might become his wife after a few moments?" It was but natural to entertain doubts about the success, in subtle archery, of a Brahmin youth who was ignorant of such a simple matter of propriety. Some impatient person taunted the Brahmin for making himself a laughing stock by saluting his future spouse.

At that very moment Krishna announced loudly, "By saluting Krishnaa this youth has only revealed his superhuman prescience. Until the conditions are fulfilled, Krishnaa is the unwed princess of Panchal. Any woman, irrespective of age, caste, religion, country, is worthy of a man's respect. For, a woman is formed of Shakti and without worshipping Shakti none can become a hero. Thus, by saluting Krishnaa this wise youth has paid obeisance to Mother Shakti."

Everyone was satisfied with Krishna's explanation. My heart filled with respect for such a wise person. Silently I thought, "Why is Krishna so full of sympathy for this youth?"

Suddenly the hall resounded with shouts and clapping. Stunned, amazed, enchanted, everyone stared at the confident unknown Brahmin standing there with easy grace. Saluting everyone once again, in a moment he had loosed five arrows and, piercing the eye of the golden fish fixed on the discus, shot it down on the ground.

Shouts of joy filled the hall. The *sakhis* were ready with the tray of offerings. Earth and sky trembled with the symphony of conch-shells, ululation, vedic chanting and music.

Directions reached me for alighting from the dais with the marriage garland. But I was already affianced, betrothed to Arjun. How could I wed anyone other than Arjun? The truth of my being as a woman would be destroyed. I had never even imagined that any man other than Arjun would emerge victorious and I would be cast into such a terrible dilemma.

45

Softly I said, "Brother! I offered myself to Arjun long back. How do I wed another now?"

Dhrishtadyumna said clearly, "Not for Arjun but for the preservation of dharma has your birth taken place. It is to dharma that you are offered. The father's dharma is the daughter's dharma. Ramchandra had taken to the forests for preserving his father's dharma. King Drupad had desired to make Aryavart's finest warrior his son-in-law. Today that best of heroes has been tested and he stands before you. Without delay honour your father's vow and discharge the duty of a daughter."

Dhrishtadyumna's words were true. To honour Father's vow if my dharma as a woman was harmed, let that be so. First things first. Even if my dharma was destroyed, my father's dharma must be preserved.

Wedding garland in hand I stepped forward slowly. I saw Krishna smiling at Balaram and standing next to the Brahmin youth. Out of shyness my gaze dropped low. I was feeling shy to look up at the Brahmin youth's face. Fixing my eyes on the youth's tender feet I began stretching up my arms with the garland. *Sakhi* Nitambini softly alerted me saying, "Princess, what are you doing? Around whose neck are you placing the garland? This is Krishna."

Full of shame and embarrassment I shifted a little and saw two pairs of feet, virtually identical, before me. What amazing resemblance between them! Which feet were Krishna's and which the Brahmin youth's? Without looking at their faces the difference could not be made out. I was forced to look up. It seemed to me that blue lotus-eyed Krishna was gazing at me enchanted. The face was moulded in a slightly different fashion. But the eyes! They were absolutely the same! Even this must be Krishna's magic. I heard someone say in my heart, "O Krishna! You are present in everyone, so it is you who must be in *sakha* Arjun and this Brahmin youth. Therefore, he who is Arjun is also this brave youth. In them it is you who are all. Therefore, in this Brahmin youth it is Arjun whom I wed with all my heart and soul. From this day this youth is my Arjun. Whosoever has been graced with

Krishna's love is Arjun." In my heart I determined to request my husband to address Krishna as *sakha* from that day.

Noticing my face suffused with blushes of embarrassment and shyness, he smiled gently. Then I understood that there was a similarity in the face of Krishna and that of this brave youth because of which at first sight he had seemed somehow familiar to me and had attracted me. Actually, there was a charisma in Krishna because of which every grief and sorrow of the world disappeared on catching sight of any part of his body. That was why however much I might be annoyed with Krishna, the moment I caught sight of him I forgot it all.

The flow of my thoughts was obstructed. In an amused yet honeyed tone Krishna said, "Krishnaa! It is not right to make such mistakes from the very inception. If you had not looked up, by now the wedding garland would have been lying on my chest. And the very next moment this unknown brave youth would have taken revenge, robbing me of my life. You are far-seeing and it is your duty to walk looking ahead. Now look up straight and wed this brave youth. How long will the poor youth keep waiting patiently?"

Such mockery in public by Krishna! I got annoyed and at that very moment garlanded the brave youth. The whole hall resounded with sounds of vedic chants, music, ululation and shouts of joyous celebration.

All controversy was now at rest. Even if he was a poor Brahmin, it was with this youth respected by Krishna that I would walk harmoniously on the path of life. But was there any life free from conflict? And then my life, the life of one born of the spark created by the friction of wood and fire — how could that be complete without conflict?

Suddenly the frustrated lust-crazed kings began stepping forward in unison to attack this youth and snatch me away by force. But my husband's massive elder brother uprooted large trees and began whirling them about like clubs. They backed off to save their lives. Duryodhan, Karna, Ashvatthama, Jarasandh everyone turned back, defeated, casting furious glances at me and my calm husband, biting their lips, grinding their teeth, "Beware, some day we will take revenge for this insult. Watch out for that day."

In a short while everything settled down. My husband and his brothers took me with them to their mother who was alone in Ekchakra town. After obtaining her blessings the wedding rituals would be completed. Thus, the five Brahmins, Brother and I set out for Ekchakra.

Father had prepared five chariots. In four, four brothers and in one I with my husband were to leave together, But my husband protested — "We are mendicant Brahmins. We live by begging alms. We go on foot. Krishnaa is to espouse my dharma. Therefore, it will be proper for her to accompany us on foot. True, the princess will find the journey tiring but we are five brothers so going through the forest will be no danger." Dhrishtadyumna wanted to protest, pained at the thought of how difficult it would be for me to go on foot through the forest. But I instantly said, "Brother, now permit me to follow my dharma. This is what is proper for every woman. I, too, should do the same. After all, Janak's daughter following her dharma bore the tribulations of fourteen years of forest exile. This is no exile but only passing through the forest for some distance after which I shall arrive at my husband's home. What trouble is there in this? She who has taken birth from the sacrificial flames can, if the need should arise, immolate herself for the sake of preserving dharma. Now bid me farewell with joy."

Everyone was left speechless at my words. I saw Father's eyes brimming over with tears. Perhaps he was sorrowful. For, instead of having Hastinapur's prince, the third Pandav Savyasachi, as his son-in-law, he had here this mendicant Brahmin youth of unknown parentage. It was not that I had no regrets on this account, but I did not wish to increase the grief of Father and Brother by expressing it. Parents desire that their daughter should remain happy, be married to the best of men. But every daughter does not fall into the hands of an eminent man. And even if that happens, there is no guarantee of her being entirely happy. What was the point of expressing before them that sorrow

48

for which there was no solution, which was not within the capacity of my parents to resolve? With a happy face I left for Ekchakra town. *Pranaming* my father I said, "You wanted the greatest hero of Aryavart to become your son-in-law. That is what has happened. All of us rejoice at this, including myself. May your blessings now be ever with me."

Father responded calmly, "Man's greatest dharma is to carry out his duties patiently. Whenever you have to assume any role, do not draw back from the duty facing you. That is how dharma will be preserved. I bless you. May you attain fame!"

I did not know then that my role would keep changing every moment; that I would have to carry out terrible duties amid an everchanging scenario.

They were ahead, the first two elder brothers, followed by the two younger ones. We were behind everyone else. He was walking keeping step with me, taking care in case I fell behind. I was going to meet my mother-in-law, the mother of a mendicant Brahmin's son, my most venerable mother-in-law! I would stand before her in these royal vestments. When my dress did not match that of her son's, she would at the very beginning consider me not as one of the household but as a visiting guest. That was why before setting out I had left behind all my ornaments except a single diamond nose-stud and two bracelets set with pearls as signs of a married woman. The flower-ornaments in my hair, arms, feet and round my neck felt most pleasant. I was wearing a white sari embroidered with cloud-dark spots. The dress was simple and easy for walking. My husband was glancing at me from time to time. Perhaps he was also praising my beauty silently. On having won me, perhaps some feeling of pride had arisen in his mind. Looking that way I, too, could not help being captivated.

Entrancing as Kamadev, the god of love, himself; a figure like Krishna's, firm and well-made; broad chest, clear lotus-eyes, beautiful limbs distinctively attractive. His face was a clear reflection of his mind. The very first time I looked at him I felt that his heart was pure and vast. He was likely to be unique in the world

49

in generosity and patience. I did not know how such an idea came to occupy my mind at that time. I was counting myself blessed in obtaining him as my husband. Every woman desires in a man — heroism, beauty, courage, knowledge and wealth. I had obtained everything. Only wealth was wanting.

Considering the matter materialistically, it seemed that he possessed no wealth. But if you really looked below the surface, however, it would be clear that all wealth was his. The qualities that a man ought to have were all present in him. If he so desired, he could become the lord of the earth. Defeating all kings, he could acquire every treasure in the world. He had fulfilled the peculiarly difficult conditions of the *svayamvar*. Then wealth could not be something so very difficult for him to attain. Yet he was indifferent to wealth like a yogi, like an ascetic without any adornments. He was a mendicant. As though poverty enhanced his nobility. That such a hero should be poor was nothing but an index of the greatness of his mind.

I was going on walking, arguing with myself to establish my husband as the finest man in the world. Perhaps his poverty was causing some discomfort, but I was consoling myself by considering it as evidence of his nobility of mind.

I was feeling tired. I was stumbling along the forest paths. Pierced by thorns, my tender feet started bleeding and the blood got mixed up in the colour of the *aaltaa* on my feet. That was why it did not become apparent to my husband immediately. However much I was in pain, I did not say a word. So he did not get to know anything. When drops of perspiration began moistening my white dress, my husband said, "Are you suffering much? I am truly grieved. It is not proper that a mendicant Brahmin should marry a princess. Actually, if anyone had won you before me, I would not have pierced the target. We had come with the hope of acquiring gifts and food in the princess' *svayamvar*. What is it other than a quirk of fate that the princess herself should have been won!"

I was taciturn by nature. Over and above that I was hesitant to speak like a garrulous teenager with a husband I hardly knew. I only said, "Whatever is ordained by God is true. Therefore, what is the use of worrying over what might have been? It will be more meaningful to be happy about what has taken place."

In an extremely loving tone my husband said, "Drupad's daughter! I am blessed in having won you."

Shyly I said, "It is equally true for me."

Stumbling over a stone on the path I was about to fall. He stretched out both arms and supported me. Ashamed, I gathered myself. Politely he said, "Devi Krishnaa! Till now I have not taken your hand observing the rituals. Our marriage will take place after mother has blessed it. If you have no objection, you can pass through this difficult forest terrain taking the support of my hand." Saying this he stretched out his strong and beautiful hand to me. Without hesitation I placed my hand in his palm. What of mine could I not give to him who had already won me rightfully?

Holding hands we two kept on walking. Now I could realise why Devi Janaki had chosen to leave the royal palace and proceed to the forest with Ramchandra. She was herself the world-mother and must have known how romantic it was to walk on the perilous forest paths hand-in-hand with her husband. How fulfilling it was and blissful!

While walking, my husband said, "I had heard that King Drupad had resolved to make the third Pandav his son-in-law and that the princess had also acquiesced in this. Unfortunately, all five Pandavs fell into death's maw and finally he was forced to make a poor Brahmin his son-in-law! All Panchal countrymen are grief-stricken over princess Krishnaa's fate. I trust you have not suffered on this account?"

I realised that the brave youth was testing me. He had caught some hint of my weakness for Arjun. Was he jealous of Arjun? Well, he might be. What was unnatural in that? If a woman got attracted to a lovely statue, even that was unbearable to her spouse. This little secret of the hero's heart could not remain hidden from me. Without hesitation I said, "There is pain in my heart. Not for myself, but for him. The very soul of righteousness and courage to meet such an unnatural end! I cannot believe it, but it has happened. He was fated to depart in this fashion. What regret should I have for myself? I, too, knew that the finest hero of Aryavart who would be able to fulfil the conditions of *svayamvar* was Arjun alone. I knew only this much that he who was respected by Krishna was Arjun. Therefore, he whom I have obtained as my husband is in my eyes Arjun himself. I have obtained the greatest hero of Aryavart and he has already won Krishnaa's respect. Is this false?"

In a grave voice he said, "I have heard that thanks to Krishna's foresight the five Pandavs have escaped from the house of lac alive. If Arjun is alive and approaches you someday, then what will you do?"

My heart danced with joy. Spontaneously I said, "Need I say what the duty of a housewife is? If I find so noble a person at my door I shall greet him with appropriate hospitality. The guest is Narayan. If I do not do so, my dharma as a housewife will be destroyed. Not only this, I shall request him to befriend my husband."

"Why so?" he asked, in surprise.

"My husband is Arjun in my eyes. So he will be another Arjun. It will be only natural if the two Arjuns become friends."

My husband smiled in amusement. Touching my hand tenderly he said, "I had heard that the princess is adept in the scriptures. Then I believed that for women to know the scriptures meant learning them by rote like parrots. But now it appears that you have not memorised the scriptures but internalised them. You are not only knowledgeable but full of wisdom too. I admit defeat before you."

We went on walking in step. The other brothers had gone on ahead. Looking at them I was thinking, "I am blessed getting two such elder and two younger brothers-in-law. The eldest brother is courteous, calm and patient like a god. His very sight inspires respect and veneration. The one who is behind him is as huge as he is handsome. Beside him any man is dwarfed. Looking at him my mind is filled with fear. Following him is one who, like the others, is blessed with beauty and is full of happy thoughts and playfulness. His nature is such as evokes the desire to make friends at the very first encounter. Last of all is the youngest brother-in-law. His personality has a unique attractiveness. By nature he appears shy and sparing of speech. He does not open his lips unless it is necessary. Showering affection on him will give joy."

The two of us were behind them, walking hand in hand. Not once did they look back, as though they were keen to walk out of sight as fast as possible. They won my respect at the very first meeting. I wanted to express all my affection and tenderness towards them.

They passed out of sight. Because of keeping pace with me, my husband got left far behind. I was by his side. My hand was caught in his firm grip. As though we two were roaming alone in the desolate forest — engaged in a quest for what happiness? Still, why be deprived of the pleasure of walking together?

Suddenly my husband said poetically, "Princess, do you know what I wish at this moment? I wish we two could get lost in this forest. No one would be able to find us. No one should spoil the bliss of this solitude."

Softly I replied, "There is romance in living incognito. But in the world to roam hiding one's face is to lose fame. Destroying the wicked is the duty of a hero."

In a teasing tone he said, "For living in the forest incognito one has to destroy the wicked at every step. Without killing ferocious beasts one cannot stay alive in the jungle."

Calmly I said, "Wicked human beings are more terrible than the ferocious beasts of the jungle. Beasts kill others in order to live. But a man slays his fellow-men merely to feed his ego. That is why heroes are born on this earth for preserving dharma. *Aryaputra!* It is your heroism that is the consolation of mother earth. For the earth glories in giving birth to heroes."

Taking my hand, my husband was guiding me through a stream flowing below a grove. He said, "Even if I ever have to live in the forest, it will not trouble me, for you will be at my side to keep inspiring me to preserve dharma."

7

The other brothers had reached home some time back. They were waiting for us there. After our arrival they would tell their mother the good news. After some time we two reached there. To get to the courtyard of the frail hut we had to stoop low. Suddenly my mind was filled with despondency: "Alas! Such a strange, untidy, frail hut! Even our horse or dog would not be able to stay here! That my husband is brave there is no doubt. But he is eking out his life in such penury as cannot even be imagined!"

Truly, what a difference there was between the dreams of a virgin's mind and the reality! The palace of Hastinapur and this potter's hut of Ekchakra town — What a contrast! I would have to spend my entire life here!

The next instant I collected myself: "You fool! Take hold of yourself! It will be foolish for princess Krishnaa, bride Krishnaa, to be distraught and agonise. The bride Krishnaa will be able to live tranquilly in this potter's hut."

These five sons. But not the five Pandavs. Still, one was with me and there were four others. It was my good fortune, that they lived harmoniously together in joy and sorrow, danger and distress, of no consequence. My brother was by himself. Moreover, he was my twin brother — neither younger nor older. Since childhood whenever I heard of anyone else having more brothers, I would also wish for several elder and younger brothers. The elder brother would give me a father's affection and the younger brother would provide an offspring's love. Dhrishtadyumna being a brother of my own age was full of his own distinct individuality.

Seeing the five brothers together. I thought: "God has heard my prayers. In the midst of so much penury he has given so much wealth — two senior brothers-in-law like two elder brothers and two younger ones like sons! What do I lack any more? It is the prowess of these brothers that is my wealth, my greatness. I, a kshatriya princess — what more could I expect?"

I was trying to remain happy whatever the circumstances. Perhaps, this is the natural inclination with which man is born. Perhaps, that was why, standing before the frail dwelling house of a potter, I was trying to be happy, considering myself rich.

The elder brother cast a calm, sweet glance at me. He knocked on the door, calling out to his mother. That glance of his immersed my heart in such affection that I began musing in my heart, "This pure-souled great man is worthy of worship."

The elder brother called out exultantly, "Mother, today we have brought a priceless thing. Open the door and see! Your sons have not returned empty-handed."

Overwhelmed with shyness I stood with head bowed. The elder brother was describing me in terms of a priceless object. My heart was thrilled with joy. From within, an easy but firm voice, their mother's, spoke: "My sons, whatever you have brought divide it amongst the five of you equally!"

The elder brother stood stunned and plunged into a deep reverie. The others looked at one other and remained silent, waiting. My husband became grave and appeared depressed. As for me, I was even more confused, surprised and full of shyness. I pulled the *anchal* of my *sari* well over my head.

The door of the hut opened. In front stood the loving, compassionate, beautiful mother. Like *Annapoorna*, Mother appeared to me all-plenitude and calm as the veritable embodiment of all-suffering earth, looking at me with eyes full of surprise and remorse, yet entranced.

I touched Mother's feet. She lifted me up with a touch as delicate as when hands cupped falling flowers. In a faint, remorseful voice she said, "What have I said! I had thought my sons were returning after collecting alms. But this is a princess of heavenly beauty!"

With bowed head the elder brother spoke, "Yes, Mother, this

is Drupad's daughter, princess Krishnaa. According to the conditions of the *svayamvar*, piercing the target your third son has won her. She has come to obtain your blessings before getting married."

"Oh Lord! What a dilemma! What shall we do now? If my word is not obeyed then I shall have spoken an untruth and that will be a gross insult to me. By not obeying your mother's command all of you will violate dharma. And if, following the command, all of you marry Draupadi then that is an insult to her, an undying limitless shame. What shall we do now so that while my word is not proved false and dharma is safeguarded, Draupadi's honour is not tarnished?"

The elder brother said, "Ma, obeying you is our lives' first and supreme aim. Let your words be true. We shall all marry Draupadi."

Possibly the other brothers indicated their agreement in silence. My husband was silent but appeared despondent. My mind rebelled. Did I have no say? Then what was the meaning of the *svayamvar*? Why did Father prescribe such significant conditions for it? Which conditions had these brothers fulfilled for marrying me? I had placed the garland of bridegroom-choice around the neck of one already. By law, and according to dharma, it was he alone who was my husband. He had won the prize. Why should I accept the other brothers as husbands? Would that not destroy my dharma? The very idea was ridiculous: one woman to live as the wife of five men! There would be no other such instance in the world. Why should I silently bear such an insult? Was I a lifeless statue? Lust-crazed by my beauty, bereft of reason and judgment, would these brothers impose upon me their whimsical authority and should I accept that?

Disgust was welling up in my heart for the elder brother. In his eyes I could clearly make out the secret flame of lust.

I was furious with my husband. Was this the same heroic warrior? Why did he not rebel hearing that his wife was to be turned into an object of enjoyment for his elder and younger brothers? With a single exclamation why did he not ring down the curtain on this ludicrous drama? Could any man share his wife equally with others? Was that the proof of manhood?

Perhaps no one paid attention to my rising anger. In a sorrowful voice Mother said, "I know that you will obey my command. All of you are devoted to dharma. But princess Krishnaa has been won by the third one. Therefore, rightfully it is he who is Krishnaa's husband. What about his opinion?"

The elder brother spoke warmly, "True, it is he who has won Krishnaa. Therefore it is up to him to take Krishnaa's hand in marriage. We should not be guilty of disobeying Mother and he should marry Krishnaa — this is the world's judgment. Therefore, Brother, it is you who have to resolve the problem."

With bowed head my husband spoke out clearly, "The command that has issued from Mother's lips and which you have accepted, is my dharma. I would have been happy to have Krishnaa to myself. But that will violate dharma for I would have to defy Mother's command as well as yours. You, too, have already said that we shall all marry Krishnaa. I do not wish to disagree with this and incur sin. With you, the elder brother, yet unmarried, how can I marry first? I would rather my happiness be less than my dharma suffer. Destroying dharma, violating the commands of my mother and elder brother, the happiness that will accrue to me will not really be happiness. This will not bring pure contentment to my mind. Therefore, we shall all enjoy the princess equally. She will be the wife, according to dharma, of us all."

Hearing my husband's words, I flared up. I wished I could turn into a searing flame of the sacrificial fire and destroy the world and in it these five brothers too. If my husband were to turn into a fistful of ashes I would not be sorry. He, who with undisturbed heart, could hand over his wife to another man for fear of his own dharma being destroyed, might be the most virtuous soul in the world, but he could never be a proper husband for any woman of discrimination.

I burnt in inner anguish. But not a word came through my lips. Perhaps Mother understood my inner turmoil. After all, she was a woman and therefore it was natural for her to sense a woman's feelings.

In a soft, sympathetic tone she began speaking, "I have heard that princess Krishnaa is wise, intelligent, learned in scriptures. In this situation of perilous distress let her resolve the dilemma herself. We cannot forcibly impose our wishes on her."

Exactly then scripture-learned Lord Vyas arrived. I thought: "What link does Vyasdev have with this Brahmin family? How did he happen to land up here? Anyhow, as he has arrived by God's grace it will be appropriate for him to resolve this dilemma. By leaving the responsibility of the solution to me, Mother is wanting to keep herself free of all blame. The elder brother, right from the beginning, has been speaking of how to keep both sides happy. My husband, too, is anxious to be free from blame. Then what shall I do?"

Hearing everything, Vyasdev became grave and was lost in thought. Softly, Mother said, "Had they announced right from the beginning that having won Krishnaa they had brought her, all this difficulty would not have arisen. Now please find a way so that my words remain true, my sons honour their mother's command, and yet no sin touches princess Krishnaa."

I wondered how these two conflicting statements could be reconciled? It seemed to me that the elder brother had deliberately uttered such equivocating sentences to convey the news of my arrival to Mother. The elder brother knew that every day the food and money obtained as alms was divided equally amongst themselves. Then why did he not say, "Mother, your third son, having won princess Krishnaa in the *svayamvar*, has brought her here and your third daughter-in-law is waiting at the door for your blessings?" Therefore, if he did not state this openly, clearly there was an ulterior motive behind his words. Mother was bound to say before opening the door that the beautiful object should be enjoyed equally by all the five brothers. That was why he had used such words. Perhaps, like others, he too had been infatuated with my beauty and had conspired in this fashion to obtain me! The other brothers would also have been attracted to

58

me. Therefore, why would they let such an opportunity slip from their grasp?

My mind was whirling with such thoughts. Vyasdev was speaking to Mother — "You know that I had sent you word to send all the five brothers to the *svayamvar* of the princess of Panchal. You knew that the conditions of the *svayamvar* could not be fulfilled by anyone other than your third son. Therefore, despite knowing everything if you gave such a directive to your sons then what is there left for thinking? You knew this too that even if the earth should dissolve your sons would not violate your directive. What was to happen has happened. No amount of regret will call back the words that have been uttered. Therefore, let the entire decision be left to princess Krishnaa. Aryan virgins have been vested with the freedom to choose their husbands. How can we intervene in this?"

I was not pained by the words of Gurudev Dvaipayan. I was astonished, taken aback. I thought in this world no one invited blame upon himself. Everyone was busily shifting the responsibility onto others to remain blameless. What the mother wanted, the elder brother wanted, Gurudev wanted, I knew. I wanted to make it abundantly clear that I had only one husband. It was he who had won me. Him alone I had chosen. But then the mother's words would not be honoured. The brothers would be guilty of violating the mother's command. My husband, too. In fact, his sin would be greater. In such circumstances would I be able to found a household of joy with my husband? From the very beginning I would become the target of everyone's aversion for not honouring the mother's and the elder brother's words. Ultimately my husband, too, would blame me for turning him into a rebel against his mother. In such a situation, how could I speak out my mind openly?

If this was not possible, how could I accept the alternative? There was no precedent for one woman marrying five men. This would not add to the fame of woman as a species.

For all future time Draupadi would remain condemned in the history of the world as a woman of despicable and stained character. So much so that in the Kaliyuga people would call fallen women having many men "Draupadis of this era", making me the butt of scorn. What would they understand of the situation in which Panchali became the wife of five men? I was angry with the mother. Animosity against her rose in me. But the moment I looked at her I forgot the sorrow of leaving my mother. Knowing everything, why did she utter such a sentence? She had sent her sons to Panchal. She knew that her third son would surely win me. Then, why did she say that?

Every mother wants that her daughter-in-law should be beautiful and, if not wise, full of discrimination and knowledge, be of blameless character, chaste and virtuous, spending her entire life concentrating lotus-like on one husband. But how contrary was this situation! For the sake of her own word how she was hinting to her daughter-in-law to take five husbands!

It seemed to me that the matter was not that simple. There was surely some deep mystery behind this. There might, perhaps, be some greater design. But, however noble the intention, how could I marry five men? I had already chosen one husband.

In my heart the memory of Krishna arose. I poured out all my heart's anguish before him. I thought, if he had been present he would have rescued me from this perilous distress. All of them wanted to accomplish their own aims by using me, but were chary of acknowledging it. Krishna was not like that. By a mere gesture he would have conveyed to me what ought to be done. Was it the integrity of my womanhood that was of greater moment to me or the mother's word, the protection of my husband's and his brothers' dharma? To sacrifice myself for safeguarding the dharma of others — was that my duty, or was it my duty to choose one husband for the sake of my self-respect and happiness? This I could not make out! In the secrecy of my heart I cried, "O Govind! I have accepted you as *sakha*. I have offered myself before you. In all Aryavart it is you who are the most wise, qualified and discriminating. Did you not know that these Brahmins would enact such a play for sacrificing Krishnaa in their *dharma-yajna?* Then why did you not give me a hint? Now what am I to do?"

Then, suddenly, it happened. I had just thought of him and Krishna and Balaram appeared at the door!

Both *pranam*-ed Mother. Mother affectionately embraced them. Moved by gratitude, she said, "Govind! Thanks to your limitless foresight we could escape that conspiracy of Duryodhan's. Princess Krishnaa, too, has been won. Now we are in an awkward situation regarding Krishnaa. You have to advise us what we should do so that everyone's dharma is preserved."

Aah! It raised gooseflesh on my whole body. I was bewildered with joy, surprise and imagining happiness beyond expectations. So, it was the third Pandav Arjun who had won me! I had really got the man to whom I had offered myself. Then Govind had created this drama knowing everything all along! But then Govind was a past master in creating drama out of others' joys and sorrows. How should I express my gratitude?

On Krishna's face was a wicked smile. He said, "Who will not be attracted to lovely Krishnaa? Whoever is not attracted is either no man or is a eunuch or lifeless. Grave conflict over Krishnaa has already started throughout Bharat. Arjun has won Krishnaa. Therefore, all the other princes have become impatient. Driven by jealousy and the shame of failure, they are seeking excuses for rebelling. They are not to blame. Whoever has seen Krishnaa once — how can he rest without getting her? There is a chance of fratricidal strife breaking out in future among these five Pandavs. Even though they may deny it out of shame, which of them will swear with Dharma as his witness that he is not infatuated with Krishnaa? If Arjun alone gets Krishnaa, will they not be filled with envy? Bhim! In your heart comparing your *rakshas* wife Hidimbaa with Krishnaa are you not cursing your fate? Are you not envious of Arjun? Rather will it be beneficial for everyone that such a sentence happened to escape Mother's lips. Considering all these matters and for preserving the dharma of everyone and to establish dharma on earth Yudhishthir has created such a situation. Actually, if unity does not prevail among the five

61

Pandavs it will not be possible to subjugate the wicked and villainous Kauravs. It is unity that is the basic *mantra* of organisation and success. The unity of a family is destroyed because of women. So for maintaining unity among the five Pandavs Yudhishthir has thought of making Krishnaa the wife of all of them. What more is to be said in this? I will certainly not be able to shoulder the responsibility of all the five brothers. The person who will take that responsibility should examine whether it is possible or not."

My endurance, wisdom, intelligence, discrimination and chastity — a summons to test them to the ultimate limit was before me. What a desperate dilemma it was! I was full of joy that it was Arjun himself that I had obtained as my husband. Yet I was agitated that along with Arjun I would have to take five husbands.

For preserving unity among the five Pandavs I would have to become the wife of them all. The five Pandavs would establish dharma on earth. If they were not one it would be dharma that would be vanquished. Therefore, my role was clear.

Once Lord Ram had taken birth on earth for the establishment of dharma. He had three brothers. Chaste Sita did not have to face such a situation then. For preserving unity among Ram, Lakshman, Bharat and Shatrughna, Sita did not have to marry all the four brothers. Perhaps she was the World-Creatrix, Mother Lakshmi, and here was I, an ordinary mortal! That was why my ordeal — this dilemma of husband-choice.

Despite not getting Sita as their wife, Lakshman, Bharat, Shatrughna had remained loyal brothers of Ram. Why would the five Pandav brothers not remain loyal to one another without me?

What would *sati* Sita have done if she had found herself in such a situation? Perhaps she would have sought refuge in Mother Earth saying, "Mother Earth! Giving me shelter in your lap, remove my shame." But I was not patient, all-suffering like Sita. If necessary, I could rebel, I could even take revenge. Swiftly I reached a decision. Everyone's eyes were turned towards me.

62

From Krishna's hint I had comprehended this much that for a greater cause a lesser interest could be sacrificed. If I did not take five husbands then my renown as a *sati* would increase, but thereby Mother's words would not be honoured, the Pandavs would not be able to safeguard truth. The establishment of dharma on earth would be hindered. Therefore, I should sacrifice myself.

I, Yajnaseni, born of the sacrificial altar for the preservation of dharma! If, impelled by greed for this mortal body, heroes like the Pandavs had bound themselves by a vow to their mother, then in their dharma-*yajna* let this body become an oblation! In reality what was this body? From where did it come and where will it go? What did I know? For I was not that body. My hands, feet, limbs were not Krishnaa. No one part of my body was Krishnaa. So let everyone be happy getting this body. Let them be united. Why should I be an obstacle? This body made up of five elements — fire, water, earth, air, ether — after offering it to five husbands would I be able to remain a *sati*? What was the definition of *sati*? I knew that remaining faithful to one's husband was chastity. So I would have to remain faithful to five husbands. While offering myself to one, I would have to surrender myself wholly. If I did not do so, I would be unchaste. I thought — man's mind is so distrustful and so full of mysteries that it does not itself know whether it is capable of surrendering itself fully to another or not. Therefore, if for this reason I was called unchaste, that was nothing to grieve over. In having five brothers as husbands I would get Arjun too — this was enough to remove all my depression and sorrow.

In a calm voice I said, "I am ready to accept the five Pandavs as my husbands."

Mother's face lit up. She blessed: "May you be renowned!" Wondering how men and women of coming ages would sing the praises of five-husbanded Panchali, I grew absent-minded. I was lost in my own thoughts.

All events of my life were similarly dramatic. From that day till the last instant of my life I would have to appear in five roles.

I would have to prepare my mind and this body made up of five elements according to the characters and inclinations of my five husbands.

8

That was my first night in the potter's hut — with my husbands, with my mother-in-law. Only one room. My five husbands lay down on beds of grass and went to sleep one after another. Mother-in-law went to sleep at the upper portion of the bed, touching her sons' heads. My bed was at my husbands' feet.

Making a cushion of my body of five elements, all ten feet would be placed on it. This would be my appropriate dharma as a woman!

But a woman going to bed at the same time with more than one man — how shameful and painful it was! Who besides myself would realise this: how shameful it was for me to touch the feet of five husbands all together?

With bowed head I was thinking — till now my marriage had not been completed according to the prescribed rites. Therefore my place was at the mother's feet. I spent all night pressing her feet. I did not know in what grief my tears kept flowing, wetting the earthen floor of the hut. Some drops fell on the mother's feet as I was pressing them. She was not startled. She had known for quite some time that I was weeping. She whispered, "I know your grief. At one time I, too, choosing your father-in-law in *svayamvar*, had dreamt of happiness. But there was a curse on him. Even this did not grieve me. I never blamed fate for frustrating my motherhood. Concentrating on serving my husband, I kept him happy. But for preserving the dynasty, for safeguarding the kingdom, to produce suitable dynasts, at my husband's request I gave birth to sons obtained through various gods — Dharma, Vayu, Indra and the Ashvinikumars. Sometimes I had to face ridicule and scorn on this account. I bore it all. I have not committed any sin, I have practised virtue — this is how I have kept consoling myself. For what I did was necessary for the welfare of the world. The situation you are in today is necessary for the preservation of dharma on earth. Therefore, consider yourself as having earned merit. How many are fortunate enough to be fated to sacrifice themselves for the welfare of the world?"

Suddenly it seemed that Mother had knowingly, deliberately placed me in this predicament. Even though she had had sons through different gods at her husband's request, Mother's own conscience must at times have been weighed down with a sense of sin, shame and hesitation. She would have felt guilty. Perhaps even at such times she would have become the target of scorn and ridicule. In case the mother was shamed before her daughter-in-law and looked small, she had deliberately compelled the daughter-in-law to accept five husbands. For getting children she had slept with different men. Was this conspiracy hatched in case the daughter-in-law, coming to know of this, taunted or looked down on her? Or was it that for subjugating the hundred sons of her elder sister-in-law, Gandhari, and giving the throne to her own sons, it was essential for them to remain one in heart and soul and, therefore, she cast her daughter-in-law into this terrible predicament? In any case, this could not have come about suddenly. Thinking thus, my mind gave way.

My brave brother had quietly followed us in secret. Father had deputed him to find out who these five brahmins were. Having gathered all the information, he returned satisfied to the Panchal capital. Next day in the morning Father despatched palanquins, horses etc. The five Pandavs, Kunti and I went to the capital. Father was overjoyed on getting to know their true identities. His desire was about to be fulfilled.

With great pomp Father was making arrangements for the wedding. When Kunti advised that five wedding altars should be made, Father asked in surprise, "Have you selected four other girls for your third son? Or have you selected brides for the other four sons?"

In a calm voice mother Kunti said, "Your daughter, princess Krishnaa, has already accepted all my five sons as her husbands.

Therefore, the marriages of all five with Krishnaa will be completed according to the rites."

Father was stunned. Agitatedly he said, "What are you saying? There is precedence for the marriage of many women with one man. But if one woman marries many men it will destroy the dharma of the woman. If my daughter concludes such a marriage the world will mock her. Her dharma will be destroyed...!"

In a soft voice Yudhishthir said, "Man's greatest dharma is obeying the commands of his elders. Parashuram, obeying his father's command, became his mother's slayer. We are fatherless since childhood. Mother is our all-powerful governor. Obeying her command, if all five of us marry Krishnaa it will only be following dharma for us."

Dhrishtadyumna was filled with annoyance — "If the command of elders seems unjust, then will compliance with it be following dharma?"

Yudhishthir said in a calm and soft voice, "*Ma* Kunti is a learned lady of Aryavart, devoted to dharma. Her command can never be unjust."

Noticing that the argument was warming up, Father intervened — "Eldest Pandav! I am proud that Arjun won Krishnaa in the *svayamvar*. What if Arjun objects to Krishnaa marrying five husbands?... And has such a thing ever happened?"

Yudhishthir provided Father with instances from the Purans and explained to him that Jatila, too, had married seven husbands for preserving dharma and that for preserving dharma there was no sin in accepting several husbands.

At that moment Krishna Dvaipayan arrived there. Learning of the cause of Father's dilemma he said, "King Drupad! Whether it be pearls or flowers, they have to be strung into necklaces and garlands for adorning the neck of the deity. Without the thin thread it is not possible to string the pearls or flowers together. In the same fashion, for the preservation of dharma in Aryavart today, it is necessary for the five Pandavs to be strung together. Only your beautiful daughter Krishnaa is capable of keeping them tied together. The flower-garland is resplendent on the deity's neck but who can discount the significance of the thread hidden in the flowers? Similarly, even if it is the five Pandavs who will establish dharma in Aryavart, Krishnaa's noble role will be recorded in sacred letters in the annals of time. The life of Krishnaa, who was born of the sacrificial altar is exceptional and incomparable. Then where is the dilemma?"

All conflicts were at an end.

I became the subtle thread for keeping the five flowers bound together, whom no one would see; whose pain and anguish no one would know; word of whose torment would reach none.

9

The wedding festivities continued for five days. The royal priest Dhaumya placed my hand by turn in the hands of the five Pandavs. One by one, five times over, with fire as witness, I married all five of them; swore vows five times — "With body, mind and speech I am yours, only yours. I shall not deceive you. Thrice do I say this is the truth."

In my mind the question arose — was this possible? Was this the truth or self-deception?

On the first occasion at the wedding altar the priest placed my hand in that of Yudhishthir. That night I was to meet him. Father had arranged for five guest rooms for my five husbands. For the nights of the marriages five bedrooms were prepared in five palaces with special pomp and show.

The first night I offered Yudhishthir my devotion. What could I give him other than devotion? Yudhishthir was extremely handsome, with a serene and calm face. At the very first sight all my anger dissolved. That he should arrange things in this fashion being attracted to me — what was his fault in this? He who had poured so much of beauty and youth into this female form and had filled man with the thirst for beauty was to blame.

I *pranam*-ed him. In a calm and soft voice he said — "I hope there is no sorrow in your mind, daughter of Drupad? In a fashion you have been forced into this marriage. Do you think ill of me? Are you depressed?"

With bowed head I thought — "Why this question now? Even if I am depressed, what can be done about it?" But I said, "You are the lord of dharma. Whatever you do has awareness of dharma behind it. If anyone is depressed as a result of that, it means that he does not respect dharma. I have taken birth from

69

the sacrificial altar of dharma. Therefore, I am profoundly attached to dharma."

Yudhishthir grew joyful. Like the sweet face of a child his delicate face appeared incomparable in its innocent beauty. Most respectfully he said, "Yajnaseni! Ever since I heard the account of your birth I have been attracted to you. I knew that without you the preservation of dharma was impossible. So I had to make you my own. With fire as witness you have married me — that is enough. I do not want anything more. You have been won by Arjun. It is he who was victorious in the *svayamvar*. Therefore, I have no objection to his setting up home with you. Let this pure relationship persist between us. That way, Mother's words will not be dishonoured. Your womanhood will not be insulted either. The other brothers will agree with me. What is your view regarding this?"

I was torn asunder with fury, feeling grossly insulted. Shooting a piercing glance at him I said, "You will go on being praised as Lord of Dharma while, I, spending the whole of life in an untruth, go on incurring sin? Having kept fire as witness to make you my husband should I discharge the duties of a wife towards only one husband? Let the world call me unchaste but why should I remain untrue and disloyal to my husbands and spend my entire life feeling guilty?"

Perhaps Yudhishthir was prepared for such a reply from me. In a sweet voice he said, "Who does not desire you? But it is not easy to satisfy all five of us. The five of us have different inclinations and desires. What I like, the others do not. They would not like to see you as I would. If I say, 'Go to the temple', then Bhim will ask you to go to the kitchen, Arjun will want to go hunting; Nakul will wish to go roaming in the forests on horseback; Sahadev will want to sit in private in the courtyard and watch the stars in silence and, (computing their positions) dream of the future. Then what will you do? Whose will you be? Whose demand will you satisfy?"

I was perplexed, but I did not reveal this — "What you

70

command shall be done first. For, your orders are obeyed by the other brothers too."

Yudhishthir said intimately, "It is not such a simple thing, Yajnaseni! You will suffer for this. You are not familiar with the nature of men. Man cannot bear the authority of anyone else over his favourite object. You are, as it is, the beloved of all five. None of us would like to have you out of his sight even for an instant. None will tolerate the slightest indifference. Then what will be the state of affairs?"

I had thought over it, not once but many times, but what was the value of my thoughts? To honour mother Kunti's words I had been offered in oblation. More anger flared up in me against Yudhishthir. Everything had been started by him. But why was he now proffering such explanations? He knew that now no change was possible. Then why was he indulging in useless talk?

In a steady voice I said, "On my account perhaps none of you need to suffer. All will get me wholly, this I vow. Krishnaa is not all-bearing like the earth. Yet she detests cunning and disloyalty."

Yudhishthir was waiting for my reply. Putting a hand on my shoulder he said, "Come Yajnaseni! As partner in my life, in the dharma-yajna, become my wife in dharma — You are the first woman in my life."

I made myself firm. How many princesses of Aryavart would have done penance for becoming the wife of Yudhishthir, the lord of dharma! I was getting him without any power of ascesis. But as yet I was half a virgin. Even now my marriage was not complete. I would have to marry four more with fire as witness. Before that it would not be proper for me to sacrifice my virginity. Before me stood my husband, the soul of righteousness, serene, courageous, wise, Crown Prince of Hastinapur! Today was the first night of our union. But I was unable to surrender myself at his feet. Till my marriage was formalised with the others, I would have to preserve my virginity intact. In no one's life had such a dilemma, such a peril, such a terribly dangerous juncture arisen and it was unlikely that it would occur in future either.

I braced myself for the ordeal. In a soft voice I said, "Forgive me, Lord of Dharma! As yet my marriage is not complete. Before dawn, having purified myself by bathing, I shall again have to sit at the marriage altar. Keeping fire as witness, the right to wed a man according to vedic rites resides only in a woman who is a virgin. You will surely understand me."

Yudhishthir burst into laughter. In that laughter there was no deception, no remorse, no compassion, no distress. Calmly he said, "You have easily passed the first test of life. Yajnaseni! Your devotion to truth and self-control are what I treasure. Tell me now how we shall pass the night."

Inwardly I was sorry for my husband. How easily he had mastered his desire and lust! Would he not be hurt? Would he not be cursing me secretly?

In a calm and tender voice I said, "Please take rest. To ensure that you sleep well I will massage your feet and the night will pass."

He protested and said, "I would rather you got some rest. You must be tired out. You must have undergone much strain walking with us through the forest. Do not worry about me. I shall sit down to play."

"You will play?"

"Yes, at dice — "

"With whom?"

"Alone, by myself." — He was smiling.

Full of surprise I exclaimed, "Alone, by yourself!"

"Everyone does. Everyone means you, myself, all men and women of this world and all insects. We do not play on our own. Someone directs us and we play. In this world everyone leads his own life and lives for him self." Yudhishthir was labouring under strong emotion.

Quietly I said, "But no man can play dice alone."

Yudhishthir said in the same manner, "Yajnaseni! Today in the first night of our union it is my duty to expose before you the weakness of my life. Playing dice is my greatest weakness. I can

72

restrain myself in every sphere except dicing. There is a reason for such a weakness."

I kept looking at him enquiringly. I thought dicing was a royal luxury and entertainment. Kings found pleasure in it. But why should any king be weak because of this? Conquering kingdoms, vanquishing enemies, possessing gems and wealth, weakness for wine and women — kings had many such weaknesses. But why should the Lord of Dharma have a weakness for dicing?

Perhaps behind this lay some obstinate perversity of adolescence which had now turned into a weakness. In childhood while being trained under guru Dronacharya the five Pandavs had never known defeat in anything. They had passed all tests during student days quite well. They had remained favourites of their preceptor. Because of this the hundred Kaurav brothers were full of envy and animosity. They could not defeat the Pandavs in anything. So it was to dicing that they took recourse. Of course, dicing had no special place during student days. Therefore, it was but natural for Yudhishthir to lose in this. But at that tender age the Kauravs neglected their studies and became experts in gambling. They lagged behind in studies. They knew that however brave or intelligent the Pandavs might be, they would never be able to win in dicing, although in other games they might defeat the Kauravs. They had no answer to Bhim in any game. In swimming, too, he would grab hold of ten or twelve Kauravs and duck them for a long time. They would madly struggle and gasp for breath — only then would he release them. While playing with an iron ball in the woods he would throw it so hard that others would get hurt. The Kauravs were worshippers of cruelty in entertainment. Climbing up trees they destroyed nests and throttled the chicks, finding pleasure in that. Bereft of their nests and offspring, the bird-couples would lament grievously. Then the coarse laughter of the Kauravs would broadcast their barbarity. Right then Bhim would shake the tree so hard that they would fall down and get injured. Sometimes he would even uproot the tree and throw it into the stream. But in gambling strength was not needed. Watching out for a suitable time they would challenge the Pandavs to a game of dice. Bhim and the other brothers would not show any interest in that.

Yudhishthir, however, was very conscious of self-respect from childhood. He would participate in the dice-game and invariably lose. He would repeatedly accept their invitation in case the Kauravs thought that he had not responded out of fear of defeat. Despite having lost, he would play again and again. He would think, 'By going on playing I shall surely defeat them in gambling'. Caught in this obsession, whenever he found time he would practise gambling by himself, alone. And this became his weakness. He accorded defeat and victory in this game the status of royal honour. Winning and losing as such did not count for much with him. The shame of that defeat in adolescence had become a blind, perverse obsession with him.

Hearing this, it seemed to me that every human being had some stubborn streak, weakness, addiction or bad habit. Compared to any of these, this simple stubbornness of Yudhishthir was pardonable. How many addictions, weaknesses there could have been in the future king of Hastinapur! Compared to those, this was hardly anything. Moreover, to confess this before his wife on the very first night showed his nobility. The future king was hardly bound to expose before his wife such a minor weakness! From this viewpoint, Yudhishthir was an ideal husband.

I again *pranam*-ed him. In a mild voice he began saying — "Take rest, Princess! Before dawn I will wake you up. I will not be able to sleep tonight. The joy of having obtained you has stolen my sleep. I will play by myself — then four days later when I shall meet you again, then I shall not play alone."

Looking at me he broke into laughter. Internally I was gathering strength. The first night of acting was about to end.

The second night. I did not have to change my body. But one had to change one's character. One had to be transformed. Transformation was nothing but acting!

Bhim was different from Yudhishthir. In appearance, qualities, personality, habits, behaviour and conversation he was distinct. Immediately on entering the bed-chamber he placed his headpiece in my hands, handed over the ornaments and dress saying, "Now all this is your job. You see, besides my stomach I do not bother about any work of mine. I am not conscious about my body or dress. Take care of my stomach first, then come all other things. Only remember that I love eating. My second weakness is that I am somewhat overfond of women. Do not mistake this for a tendency to polygamy. Hidimba is not here. She will never come to Hastinapur. That is the condition with her. The moment I saw you I was attracted, for you are very beautiful. By the mere touch of your hand the simplest food becomes *amrita*. What more do I want? Only delicious food. When I want, give me your company. That is all, you understand? Among us, my share is greater. Mother's direction, too, is that. Similarly, in obtaining you too my share is greater. All the hungers that are in man are present in me powerfully. The responsibility for quenching them is yours." Then he laughed. There was a wicked glint in his eyes.

Depressed, I was thinking, "How shall I divide mind from body? How shall I simultaneously satisfy Bhim's excessive hunger while discharging my responsibilities towards my other four husbands properly?" Bhim did not notice any reaction in me. He was engrossed in his self-expression. I had not even opened my mouth till now. I had not expressed any opinion — whether I had taken in his words or not. He continued saying, "Look, Draupadi! I am rather quick-tempered. I do not tolerate sulking or anger on anyone's part. The moment I notice any neglect of duty I immediately take drastic measures. With me there is no question of forgiveness. However, I do not nurse any grudge. Whatever comes to mind, I speak out. The next moment I forget my anger. Therefore, you will have to tolerate my anger. I know that you are extremely cultured, intelligent and patient. Women ought to be like that. If women are not capable of bearing everything, family ties get loosened. If you do not tolerate my anger it is you who will suffer. For, I shall leave you to live with my *rakshasi* wife Hidimba. Hidimba belongs to the *rakshas* race, but as a wife she is devoted to me. She is afraid of my anger. She saw how with one blow I killed her brother, Hidimb. Who is not afraid for his life!" Bhimsen laughed loudly, mightily pleased with himself.

Even then I sat dumb. It was not pleasant to listen to the praise of my co-wife Hidimba from the lips of my husband. Moreover, Bhim's hectoring tone also pained me. I said nothing at all. A woman had to bear everything. If I said something and Bhim went away to Hidimba, would Yudhishthir ever forgive me? My primary duty was to string all five in the thread of unity. If Bhim left Hastinapur then on the basis of whose strength would the Pandavs raise their voice against the tyranny and injustice of the Kauravs?

The next instant I thought, if out of fear of Bhim's anger and annoyance I gave him more time than the others, expressed greater regard, or took more care of him, then the other husbands would take exception. It would bring about alienation from Bhim. Because of this reason unity would be destroyed. Then what would happen to me? No end to the dilemma was anywhere in sight.

Bhim pulled at my *anchal*. Playfully he said, "Oho! Why are you dumb like a clay doll? I do not understand all this. The learned woman is said to be sparing of speech. But there is no need for my wife to be learned. What is the use of women being learned? Let them be lovely — enough! Let them be good cooks, provide service, laugh with me, talk to me, sing to me, do whatever I command instantly. Understand? Otherwise I'm off to Hidimba. She will be waiting for me. The moment she receives my command, she will start dancing to entertain me. Will you be able to be like that? Do not sit like this pulling a long face. Such a glum face infuriates me! Aha! Scared just by that!"

Bhim laughed out aloud. He was bubbling with glee and curiosity. But my eyes brimmed over. What a terrible test! Yudhishthir wanted a learned lady who would discriminate between dharma and adharma; who would be able to sacrifice life's dearest possession for the sake of dharma; who, having comprehended the essence of the scriptures, practised them in her life. Bhim's inclination was in a different direction. There

76

were still three other husbands whose likes and dislikes were yet to be known.

This body of five elements would be the possession of five persons. How would this be possible?

The dilemma lies stretching endlessly,
The night somehow always ends.

10

The fragrance of Krishna, and only Krishna, pervaded the entire house. He was here just now. Before meeting *sakhi* Krishnaa he was giving *sakha* Arjun some advice.

That day was the first night of union with Arjun! My life's first five nights of union! Each night began amid profound self-control and inner conflict.

But that night was special. It was going to be the night my heart supremely craved. If Arjun could be my only husband! Everything in my life was happening like the unreal scenes in some play! Did anything like this ever happen anywhere else?

The third wedding night. I was thinking this would be the most memorable night in my life. Under the compulsion of circumstances a man does many things. For the sake of the country, for the sake of the community, for preserving dharma, a man does many a gooseflesh-raising deed against his will. As a result, he gains in honour, achieves renown, but one does not know whether his soul too gets peace or not. But where the inner sanction exists, that act gratifies the soul too. My situation was such.

It was only after I had offered my soul to Arjun that I was forced to marry the five brothers. Why? Because as a result of that dharma would be preserved. That among the five husbands my soul was pledged to Arjun, had to be acknowledged.

Sakhi Nitambini knew my mind. So she decorated the bridal chamber elaborately that day. The doors and windows were beautified with garlands of blue lilies, champak and other fragrant flowers. If she had her own way, she would have embellished them with diamonds, pearls and gems. But she knew my taste. Despite being a princess, why was my taste thus? Perhaps there was a fateful purpose behind this! For years this queen of a

78

kingdom would have to remain a queen of the forest — this I did not know, but my fate was not unaware of that.

Nitambini had adorned me with jewels ignoring my protests. "From today you are free from the ascetic life. Now you are a queen. The queen of Hastinapur will wear cloth woven of golden thread. She will put on jewels and ornaments, and anklets of diamond and sapphire when she enters the bridal chamber."

Leaving me in the room, shutting the door, the *sakhis* left. Through the glittering pearl-studded veil I saw my beloved, the heroic Phalguni, waiting.

How wonderful did he look! Tall, firm, well-proportioned body, gentle beauty, bright eyes, face decorated with sandalwood paste, a garland of white flowers round his neck, curly black locks picturing rain clouds, in his eyes the stillness of the blue sea. I looked at him only once. My eyes fell in shyness though I wanted to gaze at that enchanting form for ever.

Very gently Arjun left his seat and approached me. I stood still with a trembling heart. If I surrendered my all to this supremely desired man then for my two other husbands how would I regain virginity before marriage?

But — but this my beloved, beautiful as Kandarpa, the god of love — how could I turn him back from the door of my heart? If I did so, his loving heart would break and before that my heart would shatter into a hundred pieces.

My attention was centred on my breast. How would I make this distressed heart understand? Suddenly I was startled. Whose was this lovely face on my breast! He was standing afar. How was I seeing him on my breast? *Chheeh!* How naughty Nitambini was! In the pendant in my necklace she had placed a tiny mirror of glowing pearl. In that mirror Arjun's face was reflected. He was smiling gently. I was even further immersed in shame. I tore my eyes away from the mirror and fixed my eyes on my hands and feet. But even there it was the same predicament. There on the gems adorning each finger and toe Arjun's reflection was shimmering. In the earrings, the ornaments on my forehead, the nose-stud — everywhere Arjun's bejewelled form was reflected.

In every limb of mine Arjun's picture was being etched. Every pore of mine was thrilled, the body was covered with droplets of sweat. In them, too, Arjun was reflected. Now how would I control myself? How would dharma be protected? Yet two more marriages would have to be gone through with fire as witness. I felt I would faint at the mere touch of Arjun. Thereafter what would take place — what control would I have over that?

When a man loses faith in himself he seeks some different path. He cheats himself till his sorrow has passed to be free from torment.

He had intuited my secret dilemma. Softly he said, "Krishnaa!"

This voice — whose was it? Was it Krishna's? Such a gentle, sweet voice was only his! How did his *sakha* Arjun know that it was one of my names and that it was this name which was dear to me?

My concentration was broken. Arjun was saying, "Why are you anxious? I know your vow. It is the husband's duty, too, to fulfil his wife's vow. Before the marriages are complete not one of your husbands will attempt to put even the hint of a mark on your unsullied virginity. This is the speciality of the Pandavs. But Krishnaa...!" He stopped midway in his speech. Dark clouds of sorrow and depression were obscuring his pleasant face. How could he have a sorrow? Was I the cause of his grief? If this was so, what was the sense in my remaining alive?

In a choked voice he went on, "My supreme moments of happiness with you have gone by. The time that I have been able to have you solely to myself, that remains the most precious period in my life. The rest of life that remains in our hands is solely for the sake of preserving dharma, preserving civilization, for the welfare of the world. Therefore, how can you lose faith in yourself? Now you are no longer your own; you belong to the world! Why should I blame you for having offered yourself for the preservation of dharma in the world?"

Startled, I glanced at my husband. Shyness, hesitation, everything, disappeared. The eager, expectant bride within me had been pushed far away. What was all this that Arjun was saying?

My life with him had just begun that day with this tender moment of union. His days of happiness with me had ended — what was the sense of these words? Moreover, how could he blame me?

Arjun was following everything. Taking my hand he seated me on the be-gemmed bed and said, "When we were returning from the *svayamvar*-assembly by the forest path who knew that you would not be able to remain mine, only mine? It was during those moments that I felt myself to be the world's greatest hero. I thought if sun-rays and moonlight fell on you, I would remove even the sun and the moon! If our pet deer and birds embraced you lovingly, I would behead them! So much so that I was even jealous of your necklace. Only this is my request: Krishnaa! As long as I am before you, remove this necklace and these ear-rings. The necklace touches your breast, the earrings touch your cheeks. How can I, as your husband, tolerate this? But who could imagine that I would have to meet you on the third night and then wait for some more days, till the third night after the marriages with Nakul-Sahadev?"

I complained, "You have won me. You could have said, 'No one else has a right to Krishnaa! Why did you leave everything to me?"

In a voice heavy with sorrow Arjun said, "Brother had spoken thus and Mother had replied! Whatever I said thereafter was as son, as a younger brother. That was what dharma dictated. I could not have spoken otherwise. What my reply would be had been determined by Elder Brother and Mother. But what reply you would give was wholly within your grasp. Unhesitatingly, without any bar, you could give your decision..."

Anger, hurt, self-esteem, mortification were choking me. I sobbed out, "The five Pandavs, their mother, guru Krishna Dvaipayan and your *sakha* Shri Krishna are capable of doing anything on this earth for preserving dharma. Should Draupadi alone, considering her happiness, honour and pride more important, disregarding the views of them all, invite the scorn and curses of the whole world? Is it this that you wanted? If that had happened, your desire would have been fulfilled, Krishnaa would have been exposed — " I checked myself midway trying to suppress my anger.

Arjun placed his hand on my shoulder. Calmly he began speaking, "It is no use crying over spilt milk, Krishnaa. Is it not a matter of good fortune that even for some time we had got each other wholly? There are many instances of sacrificing personal interest in the cause of a greater interest pertaining to the world. The world is now in peril. Just understand this that we have come on this earth not for our own sake, but with a greater aim. I am no different from my brothers. If for any reason I wish to be different, then that will be the beast within me. Even though I am proud of winning you, that is the egotism of my manhood. In truth, who are you? Who am I? Who are these four brothers of mine? Where have we come from? Where are we going? Even this we do not know. By living on this earth for some days if you are able to add to the happiness and prosperity of everyone, why should I be sorry for that? Will that not be gross selfishness on my part?"

I kept listening to his virtuous counsel. Rather than giving me solace, he was actually consoling himself. He was more mortified than I was, more helpless. My heart brimmed over in empathy. I was furious with *sakha* Govind. Arjun was the beloved friend of the finest man in Aryavart, one as learned and discriminating as Govind. For what crime of his could other men lay claim to his wife? Even though they were his own brothers, they were other men! Why had such punishment been meted out to him?

Forgetting my pride, anger and hurt, I got so immersed in Arjun's grief that slipping out of control two tear-drops spilled out of my eyes and fell on his feet like two pearls.

In a pained voice Arjun said, "Krishnaa, you are no mere beautiful princess. You are distinguished in learning and knowledge. You are a poet. There is great need for tears in life. There are times when you faint if you do not cry. Therefore, it is not proper to insult tears whimsically. It is the companions in adversity who are the finest friends, and those are tears. Do not waste them."

82

Wiping my tears, I looked at him. Despite being covered with clouds, the vast expanse of the sky was not affected. Despite being touched with depression, his beauty was not lessened a jot. Rather, the darkness of sorrow had made his manhood all the more impressive. Forgetting my grief, I kept gazing, fascinated, at the beauty of his face. I thought, though life might have to be spent amid slander, calumny, sorrow and conflict, I was blessed as I had got Phalguni. In an instant all the darkness vanished. Arjun, too, was trying to be agreeable. Why cry over what was not under our control?

Arjun sat near me. Like an intimate friend he began saying, "The desire to marry you sprang from two causes. The first was your name itself, 'Krishnaa!' Your name resembled that of my beloved *sakha*, Krishna. So I fell in love with your name. Secondly, you are learned and a poet. I have heard that you have written much about my *sakha*. Can I hear some?"

I cringed in embarrassment. I murmured, "Who told you all this?"

Arjun laughed and said, "My *sakha* is clairvoyant. He has that power. As a child he did many miraculous deeds. He is superhuman. He keeps humming some of your lines."...

83

11

I blushed crimson with embarrassment. Truly my poems had been composed with Krishna in mind. How had he got to read them? Must be Nitambini's work! My poems had been in her custody for some days. She had taken some for reading and had left them behind in the garden. The next day Krishna had gone there for a walk and these fell into his hands. He had returned them. Perhaps at that time Nitambini did not know this. Whatever it might be, how sweet my poems sounded in Arjun's voice! He was such an expert singer!

I was listening with bowed head. Arjun went on speaking — "Krishney! Poetry is fine in itself, but if the poems had been addressed to anyone other than Krishna, I would not have pardoned you today! But even before my telling you, you have wanted my *sakha* heart and soul. I do not know what is that quality in him that makes any woman lose her head and heart the very first time she sees him. Had you not desired him, then sometime or other some unpleasantness was bound to have arisen between ourselves over him. Sometimes he gives such counsel that it may seem he is thrusting you into a chasm. But if we wait with patience, then we realise that behind it lies concern only for our welfare. Had he not given us this information, how would we have come to know of the *svayamvar*? Therefore, will it not be proper for us to be eternally grateful to him?

In jest I said, "So it seems that to you Krishna is dearer than Krishnaa."

Arjun laughed and said, "Krishna is dear to me, and Krishna is dear to Krishnaa; therefore, Krishnaa is exceedingly dear to me."

The night passed in singing the praises of Krishna.

Nakul and Sahadev were the twin sons of the Ashvinikumars.

84

Both were beautiful as Kamadev himself. Faces resplendent as the full moon, eyes calm and compassionate. Obedient to the eldest brother Yudhishthir, exceedingly devoted to their mother, courteous, refined, mild, modest. Both were delighted at getting me as their bride because this happened on account of mother Kunti's command and the elder brother's wish.

Of the two, Nakul was the more handsome. He had more delicacy and grace. Like petals of flowers blooming in the morning sunlight, the touch of grace on the soft, handsome face attracted the heart. Nakul was simple like a child, his heart was open like a blooming, joyous flower. At the first meeting he said, "Devi Panchali, the desire to wed you had awoken from the very day I got to know you. Do you know the reason?" I kept smiling softly at the simple confession. Like a playmate, he caught my hand and drew me to the window.

"Panchali! Do you see my horse? That is my only fascination. I personally tend it. This is what I have heard: you love animals and birds very much; your residence is a beautiful sanctuary; you are able to understand the language of birds and beasts, can follow their gestures; angry elephants calm down on seeing you; poisonous snakes stepped on by you forget to bite back. I am delighted that from now on my horses will be looked after by you too. Getting your loving care they will become the finest horses in the world. If you wish you can bring your pets here. If we ever return to Hastinapur, you will be the queen and your pets will live in royal luxury. I have heard that if they do not eat, you too starve and that you cannot do without them."

"How did you get to know all this?" I asked in amusement.

Nakul replied, "Govind has told us all the events from your birth till now. It is sweet to hear of your qualities from his lips. Actually, having heard of your beauty and qualities from him, we all secretly desired you. Having obtained you, we have become eternally indebted to Govind."

I wondered what Govind's intention was behind this carefully laid out strategy.

Nakul was repeatedly gazing at his reflection in the mirror and admiring himself. His own appearance captivated him more than the new bride dressed for the first tryst. Again and again he was adjusting his ornaments and dress. Looking at himself in the mirror, he felt satisfied. I was vastly amused at his being so child-like, caught up in himself. I wished I could cup that inimitable delicate beauty in my hands and pet and love it. With this husband there would not be much conflict, I felt.

"The horse is, of course, very beautiful and you, too, are beautiful" he would be exceedingly glad to hear this, I thought. But Nakul himself said, "I hope you like me. Is my appearance up to your expectations? I know that a beautiful woman would want that her husband should be beautiful too. It is you who have to judge whether I fill the bill."

I understood the implications of these words. Nakul wanted to say that he would be the best of the five husbands from the viewpoint of beauty. This was what he wanted to hear from me. On the wedding night it was praise of the bride's beauty that suited the husband's lips. But I had to say, "I fade away before your beauty. You should tell me whether you like me. This marriage has, after all, been forced upon you by Yudhishthir, compelled by Mother. You had no chance at all of selecting or rejecting."

Nakul went on looking at me fascinated. In a voice heavy with emotion he began speaking, "Krishnaa! I thought God had poured the entire beauty of creation into me alone. I was worried that my lifemate might be wanting in this. But the Creator is wise. In case I become insignificant beside your world-enchanting beauty, my friend beautified me with very great care."

I laughed out. I liked Nakul's simple and pure self-expression. I thought: now Nakul would be the companion of my joys and sorrows. I would be able to express my mind and heart freely before him.

12

Like Nakul, Sahadev was modest and gentle, but sparing of speech. He did not speak unless it was necessary. Was talking indispensable? Lines of poetry were written in his very limbs. Dreams gathering thick in his eyes conjured up the love-tryst. Though he was ever immersed in profound thought, on looking at him it would seem as if you were hearing the rhythm of poetry.

The moment he saw me poetry bloomed in his dreamy eyes. For some moments he kept staring at me unblinking. Drowned in embarrassment, I sat stiff. He kept gazing, enamoured, lost. Then, somewhat sadly, sighed deeply. I got worried. What was his grief? And why?

He said nothing. Should I speak first on the wedding night?

He spoke first: "Krishnaa! On earth man alone is aware of death and conscious of the future. Therefore, he is afraid, is anxious, has dreams, gets lost in thoughts of the future. He suffers too. The beast has no worry about the future; the present is its supreme moment. This is the difference between man and beast. Man planning for the future commits sins as well as virtuous deeds. Since the ancient times man's mind has been filled with irrepressible curiosity and anxiety regarding the future. Your future flashed before my eyes the moment I saw you in the *svayamvar* hall. Your future is so romantic that on that very day I wished to make myself a partner in it. We are princes of Hastinapur but are facing a severe trial. What his purpose is in uniting you with our lives, only Govind knows. I know only this that you can become a fitting companion on our life-paths. On knowing this, the irrepressible desire to get you that had arisen in my heart has been fulfilled. But remember one thing: when I speak I cannot be wholly frank because since childhood I have been over-sensitive. We are twin sons of mother Madri. Nakul is more handsome than me, lively and strong. Therefore, he leaves me behind in everything. So much so that even in getting the love of our parents I used to be left behind.

"Father left us in childhood. *Ma* Kunti filled that vacancy. As a child, being quiet by nature, I was not able to think about myself. Bhim used to keep *Ma* Kunti so preoccupied that I did not feel like bothering her much. Therefore, I remained content with whatever I got. You are my wife, but the other four brothers have equal rights over you. Because of their power and strength if all leave me behind in the race for your affection, respect, intimacy, I will not blame you. I will not assert my rights by force either. My principle is to remain content with whatever comes my way. But it is the duty of the wife to understand her husband's mind. If you keep performing your duties properly, I will never have to speak my mind about anything."

I sat quiet. Why did God give me so many qualities that all five brothers had found their various inclinations and likes in me? What if I failed to satisfy everyone fully?

Can anyone please everyone? Even God cannot satisfy everyone. If you try to satisfy everyone no one gets satisfied. Your own mind gets weighed down. Merely on thinking of this, you lose confidence in your self. I felt helpless and distressed. I asked myself, "Who will help me? On whom shall I depend? Govind, who has turned my life into a joke? Does he find happiness in this? All right, Govind, I, too, will find happiness in this. Because you are my husband's dear *sakha*. If you are happy, then my husband will be happy. It is just in this that my life will become meaningful."

For five days the marriage festivities went on. Music, lights, dance and song, gifts, feasting — with all this the Panchal capital echoed with joy like Indra's palace.

The weddings were over. Now the bridegrooms and the bride were to be sent off. It was my misfortune that my husbands had been driven out of their kingdom. To save themselves, they were roaming in the forests. Where, in which forest, would they keep the gifts given by Father? He had given each son-in-law a thousand begemmed, gold-plated chariots with pennants, a thousand white elephants decked with gold ornaments, loaded with jewels, many types of luxurious items and beautiful slaves and maids. For each son-in-law expensive garments had been given as presents. For me, specially, pots of my favourite flowers on a thousand chariots, my pets, my library, my musical instruments, various types of clothes and jewellery. Much had come as gifts from Father's allies. Krishna, ruler of Dvaraka, had sent many presents. Among them was a ring set with a blue sapphire and also a maid named Maya.

Then Krishna had said, "These two are my favourite things. I give you this blue-sapphire ring as my blessing. It is my most precious ring. I have been wearing it personally. There is a special quality in it. On gazing at its centre concentratedly for some time many dilemmas are resolved."

Indicating the extremely lovely maid Maya, Govind said, "Since childhood she has been with me. She has always taken full note of my needs. She loves me so much that she cannot tolerate anyone else serving me. In case anyone bothers me, she is ever alert by my side. But, whoever stations her in his heart, she envelops him with her love to such an extent that nothing else is visible to him. This maid of mine, Maya, is as much the cause of grief as the remover of grief. Several tasks of mine are achieved through her. If she did not exist, it would have been difficult to resolve the many problems of Dvaraka, Hastinapur and these Pandavs. Arjun, despite being a younger brother, is also my *priya sakha*. As his wife, from today you are my *priya sakhi*. Hence my first gift to you is dear Maya."

I was grateful and said, "She has been with you for such a long time and is your helper in solving all your problems. How will you carry on your work if you give her away to me? Who will look after your needs and take care of you?"

In a grave voice Govind said, "We shall see. Your predicament is of greater significance at present than my problems. Now you have to live with five husbands. You will have to face new problems all the time. In solving them, Maya will surely be of help to you. That is why I am leaving her with you. Otherwise, you will be in difficulty. Troubled with the difficult responsibility of having five husbands, sometime or other you will want to become an ascetic and take to the forest. At that time who will stand as a barrier in your path?" Govind's soft smile left much unsaid. I forgot everything in that smile. Standing beside Maya, I kept gazing at him. I was grateful to Govind. My helplessness was truly known only to him. However much arrogance I might display outwardly, *sakha* Krishna could comprehend that I was cast into terrible danger because of five husbands. Though Nitambini was dearest to me among the sakhis, she was not as intelligent as Maya. That was why along with other gifts he had given Maya, to me.

But where would I go with so many gifts?

Sizing up the entire situation Father said, "As long as they wish, the five Pandavs and mother Kunti can live as guests in the Panchal kingdom. Glory will redound to Panchal by playing host to them." Father would feel even happier if that happened.

But how could I be pleased with this proposal? Where was my pride in this? In fact, my self-respect would suffer if that happened. I would feel that I was seeking sanctuary in my father's kingdom. For how long would it be tolerable to live as a dependent of my father and my brother? The kingdom which was mine till the day before, I would be a guest there now! Truly, how strange were the ways of society!

How long could one stay as a guest? The reputation of my husbands, too, would suffer. After some time people would start looking down on them. This was the way of the world. It was now my task to see to it that not even the hint of a slur was cast on my husbands in my father's kingdom. How could I tolerate it if it was otherwise? While living in my father's house, I had followed the daughter's dharma. Now the time had come for following the wife's dharma. My five husbands, having lost their kingdom, were poor and without a home. But there had not been any doubt regarding their valour, their heroism and character. Why should I not be proud of them?

Being wealthy may be a cause for prowess and fame, but acquiring wealth by unfair means cannot be termed manhood. The Kauravs, having deprived the Pandavs of their kingdom by unfair means, were now ruling over vast Hastinapur. But that did not mean that their prowess was greater than that of the Pandavs. Now the Kauravs were being condemned all over Aryavart. Bereft of wealth, the five Pandav brothers were the very souls of virtue. That was why throughout Aryavart their praises were being sung. Therefore, despite my not becoming a queen, there was no slur on my reputation. Truly, I was proud of my five husbands.

But it is one thing to be proud of one's husband's prowess and quite another to be happy with one's husband. Keeping the husband happy is an even more complicated task.

This was the problem before me. After the marriage ceremonies were over my actual married life was about to begin. It was easy to get married one by one to five husbands. But how complicated it was to live a married life successfully with them! I did not know how in the past someone had accepted seven husbands or eleven husbands for the sake of dharma. But at that time, in all of Aryavart, except me there was not a single woman married to more than one husband, let alone five husbands! Therefore, Aryavart waited with curiosity and amazement to watch the farce of my married life. I wondered if my life would ultimately turn into such a farce. At one time it was proper for me to accept the wish of everyone. I had never imagined that I would be shouldering such a huge responsibility in life. Then I had not thought that the desires, inclinations, hopes and personalities of five men would be so different from one another. Now, considering the entire matter, I felt utterly helpless.

Even if I devoted three hours of a night to one husband, that would mean one husband's night going fruitless. Then how was I to divide the night or divide myself?

The first day of my married life began. In the morning, having bathed and dressed as a new bride, I *pranam*-ed mother Kunti. Mother's blessing was, "Krishnaa, may God keep you happy!

You have been able to fill my daughter's place. Make your husbands happy with all your heart and soul. Concentrating on their lotus feet, serve guests and visitors as if they were the Divine. I am blessed in having so learned a person as you as my daughter-in-law."

Having taken Mother's blessings, I proceeded towards Yudhishthir's bedroom. Krishna was there. Mother had directed that I should *pranam* him. Some unknown visitor was in Yudhishthir's bedroom. Their conversation could be heard. He was saying, "But Govind! what is the purpose behind your putting Devi Krishnaa into such a terrible predicament? In the abode of the gods everyone is waiting with eager and curious eyes to observe the love, estrangement and conflict of Draupadi, the heroine of five men. Why did you thrust her into such shame? For the gods there is a custom of having many wives. This has enhanced the fame of their prowess. But have you given a thought to the shame and guilt suffered by a woman marrying many husbands? By this, womanhood is insulted. Does the lord of Dvaraka not know this?"

My feet turned to stone. I was listening to the tale of my shame and insult. Whoever the visitor might be I could not make up my mind to face him. I turned back towards the rest-room. Benumbed, I sat down on the bed. My reflection gleamed on the smooth marble of the walls. I felt that I was breaking down under the onslaught of grief, shame and anxiety. The very next moment within the new bride Krishnaa, Yajnaseni, born of the sacrificial flames, rose in revolt. She stood up in revolt against the laws of the abode of the gods, according to which one man might accept as many women as he wished, but if one woman married more than one husband she would be branded a sinner. Who had laid down this law? It must be some male god! Otherwise how could there be such a distinction of virtue and sin between male and female?

All the rituals and rules that had been created in society built around the distinction between rich-poor, high-low, brahmin-chandal, male-female, and such others, the profound inequities that had been set up based upon considerations of virtue and sin — against all of these a lifelong war would have to be waged.

Actually, the acceptance of five husbands was a challenge to the entire race of women. As though it were a golden opportunity for proving that even after marrying many men together, the pristine purity of a woman's character could remain unsullied.

If a woman confined to the inner chambers, having no opportunity to see the face of a man other than her husband, was faithful, some possibility of her chastity being in doubt remained. But even after having married many men if she could remain faithful to them then she could be called *sati*. Perhaps that was why, despite having more than one husband, Tara and Mandodari were still *satis* who were saluted at every dawn. Lakshman's wife Urmila led the life of a prisoner for fourteen years in the inner apartments waiting for her husband. Yet, Ayodhya city did not resound with shouts of praise hailing *sati* Urmila. Devi Sita was abducted by Ravan and imprisoned in the Ashok forest. She lived there in the midst of the demon king Ravan and many demons, facing many lewd advances from them. Yet she spent her time single-mindedly waiting for her husband. Therefore, she could become famous as a *sati*. On the other hand, Urmila remained absent from public view.

What heroism is there in a man clinging on to values in circumstances where he has no alternative but to cling to them? True heroism lies in remaining steadfast in one's values in adverse circumstances. In this world of good and evil it is not possible to appreciate the goodness of virtue without sin. Without sin how can the fame of virtue be established?' If there is no adharma then how can dharma be established? Without darkness how shall we comprehend light? It was, after all, because of the wicked that God incarnated on this earth again and again. I thought it was sin that had made virtue so noble. It was because of the wicked that saints were considered great men. This was the difference between my thoughts and those of an ordinary princess.

When I saw or heard that in every king's royal apartments

many queens, bedecking themselves, kept waiting for him, while, according to his whim, the king might or might not visit one queen's apartments, then I wondered how it would be if it were the other way about? One queen and a thousand kings! They would spend night after night waiting for her! He whom the queen loved best would be made the "Chief King" by her. Hearing my views the *sakhis* used to laugh, "Princess! Keep these thoughts to yourself. Do not open your mouth to anyone. People will cry shame! Everyone will say, the princess is surely unchaste if not physically, at least in thought. One woman accepting many men...what an impossible situation you are imagining!"

I would get angry, "Chaste woman! Unchaste woman! In the same way why don't the scriptures speak of chaste men and unchaste men? Are men's hearts made of gold that sin cannot tarnish them? Have the scriptures prescribed lists of sins only for women?"

Several scenes flashed before my eyes. The Yamuna in spate; while being ferried across the river the great sage Parashar, infatuated with the beauty and loveliness of the fisher-girl Matsyagandha, begged sexual favours of her. Despite repeated protests of adolescent Matsyagandha, the great sage Parashar forced himself upon her in that very boat.

Yamuna in spate! Passengers milling about on both shores. To keep his sexual exploit hidden from the travellers, Parashar, the possessor of miraculous powers created in a trice a mist shrouding the boat all around. In that darkness the sage's lust was satisfied. Krishna Dvaipayan, gifted with supernatural prescience, was born. Taking the son with him, the great sage left after transforming by his blessing fish-odorous Matsyagandha into Yojangandha. The smell of fish disappeared from the body of Yojangandha Satyavati. She was filled with a fragrance that emanated from her for *yojans*.

This Yojangandha in the course of time went on to become the wife of King Shantanu of the Kuru dynasty. Satyavati had two children by Shantanu: Chitrangad and Vichitravirya.

The supremely wise mother, Satyavati, had to suffer the scorn and mockery of society sometimes because of her past. But Parashar? He was respected by all. Rebellion would swell within me as I listened to Lord Vyasdev's narrations of the story of his birth. My face would be red with anger. Vyasdev remained unmoved. He would laughingly say, "Woman is the all-suffering earth. How can her endurance be found in man? That is why it is easy to abuse women. If men were abused like this, then the earth would be filled with violence and only violence. Perhaps that is why none dares to abuse a man. Maintaining the firmness of her character in the midst of slander, censure and infamy, mother Satyavati is the living embodiment of a revered noble lady."

The *svayamvar* of the three daughters of the king of Kashi — Amba, Ambika and Ambalika was taking place. The news reached Devavrat, the son of Shantanu and Ganga. Bhishma's was an inviolable oath! Chitrangad had died unmarried, and Vichitravirya had become old enough to marry. Taking Vichitravirya with him, Bhishma went to the *svayamvar* of the Kashi princesses. Many kings of Aryavart were present there. Bhishma considered that the daughters of the king of Kashi were unlikely to garland Vichitravirya as their choice. Taking the excuse of kshatriya dharma, with the intention of marrying all the three princesses to Vichitravirya, he brought them away by force from the assembly hall. Afraid of the prowess of Bhishma, no one dared protest.

After arriving in Hastinapur, Amba bluntly told Bhishma that she was betrothed to Shalva, the king of Madra country, who had vowed to marry her long back. Seeing him in the *svayamvar* hall, she had lost her heart to him. According to dharma, her marriage ought to be with Shalva. Nobly, Bhishma sent princess Amba with the royal priest and trusted maids to her affianced husband with all honour. But faultless Amba was rejected by the narrow-minded king Shalva. What was her offence?

King Shalva mocked her — "Before everyone Bhishma defeated the kings and abducted you. From that very moment you became Bhishma's leavings. How, then, do you remain fit to become my wife? And now I no longer desire you."

What callous, cruel words! Amba was devastated. She explained to Shalva that Bhishmadev had vowed eternal chastity. Before his father he had vowed, "I shall never marry." No woman had ever been the cause of his deviating from his principles. What Bhishma did was not for himself but for the sake of his younger brother. For Amba, his mind was full of only the purest respect and good wishes untainted with any trace of lust or weakness.

But a woman becomes helpless before a man's egotism. Shalva had no concern for the future of Amba. He turned her down bluntly.

Princess Amba was without refuge. Entering the deep forest she sought advice from the hermits and sages. She did not feel it proper to return to her father's house. It was Bhishma whom she held responsible for her sad plight. For taking revenge she did the harshest penance. No hero of Aryavart stepped forward to ensure justice for her. Only the lord of the gods, Maheshvar, responded. But Bholanath did not give her the boon of vengeance on Bhishma in this birth. He granted her the boon in her next birth. That was when Amba would be able to defeat Bhishma. When would that time come? Before shelterless, slighted, scorned, Amba stretched a life of dilemma like the everflowing current of a river. How long could the adolescent princess live a lonely life only with Shiva's boon for sustenance? Losing patience, Amba immolated herself in fire.

In the next life, too, Amba's dilemma was equally great. As a woman how could she worst Bhishma? Though born of my father as a son, she was a hermaphrodite. Immediately after his birth king Drupad ordered that the new born infant be beheaded. Festivities for the birth of a son were not celebrated.

On seeing my brother, Shikhandi, the mind filled with anguish instead of pity. Through the delicate, refined loveliness of Shikhandi peered the slighted, scorned princess Amba. Without any offence on her part two of her births as a human became cursed. And only because she was a woman! Amba accepted all the injustices piled upon her by society. She immolated herself in fire. And I was born from fire to eradicate adharma and injustice from society. How could my heart not revolt against the self-sacrifice of Amba?

Giving up her life, Amba escaped from one female-birth. The two other sisters were left, Ambika and Ambalika. Their situation was even more grievous.

Vichitravirya died childless. The only dynast of Kuru lineage, Bhishma, was pledged not to marry. How would this lineage be preserved? Would the dynasty sink into oblivion? On the advice of mother Satyavati, for the preservation of the dynasty, Ambika and Ambalika were virtually forced to beget sons by other men. Narrating puranic precedents, Satyavati explained to them, "However much one may perform ascesis, without children the after-life is fruitless." Then, giving many examples she said, "If a woman cannot have a son by her husband, there are eight other methods by which she can beget a son. And this is accepted by society. Among these, one way is begetting a son by another man. Hence, although Vyasdev is your elder brother-in-law, you have to accept him for preserving the royal lineage of Hastinapur." And so it was. By Vyasdev, Ambika and Ambalika had two sons: Dhritarashtra and Pandu. Dhritarashtra was blind and Pandu was sickly. Hence Satyavati requested Vyasdev to impregnate Ambika once more. From the very inception Ambika had opposed the begetting of sons in this fashion. Therefore, for again obtaining a son by Vyasdev she sent her royally adorned maid to him. By Vyasdev this maid gave birth to the exceptionally intelligent and righteous son Vidur. Ambika, afraid and anguished and ashamed of her impregnation, drowned herself in the Yamuna. Yet, Ambika and Ambalika had to bear the brunt of mockery on several occasions. For having becoming pregnant by another man they had to suffer social odium. When Kunti, bowing to her husband's commands, gave birth to sons by various gods, she, too, was insulted several times because of this. Thinking over all these incidents it seemed that if the standards of virtue and sin had been identical for women and men, the female race would not have been oppressed by social tyranny. In the

97

course of discussions with my companions I would often blurt out, "If the need should arise, I too, accepting more than one husband can show that despite having more than one husband a woman can be trustworthy, obedient and chaste." Although I had not thought over the matter that deeply, I would blurt it out under the stress of emotion and then it became a habit to speak thus in anger.

Hearing my arguments, Vyasdev would smile in amusement. I did not know that my fate was playing hide-and-seek with me!

When that predicament appeared in my life, I accepted it as a test of womanhood. It was a challenge for the entire female race. Without protest, I accepted the commands of Yudhishthir and mother Kunti.

But now! I was about to begin conjugal life in right earnest. Now I was feeling that calling man and woman equal for the sake of argument did not settle the issue completely. Like her body, a woman's mind, too, is different from that of a man. Therefore, from age to age society has made different rules for it. If a man takes several wives, then the wives keep trying to win his heart. He may, according to his desire, choose his favourite and be attracted more to her. But what if a woman takes many husbands? Then, taking note of the likes and dislikes of all the husbands, she has to win the hearts of all. Otherwise, life becomes difficult. Now that very situation was before me and I was thinking of everything and nothing! *Sakhi* Nitambini came and informed me, "Maharshi Narad has arrived. He is conversing with Yudhishthir and Govind. Arrangements for a dice game have been made. Yudhishthir has possibly called you." As I was about to leave, another summons came: Bhim was waiting in the bedroom. He had overeaten in the morning and was feeling uneasy. While he was relaxing, my company was necessary.

What was I to do? With whose commands should I comply? In the midst of this a *sakhi* arrived with Arjun's message. He was expecting me in the library. Some scholar had arrived to discuss the scriptures. Considering that at such a time my presence would be appropriate, he had called me.

98

I was thinking over all this when a *sakhi* brought Nakul's directive — he was in the stables, testing the horses received in dowry. Therefore, he had asked for my presence. Immediately after this I received Sahadev's message. He wished to discuss with me whether it was right to stay on in Panchal any longer, for Vyasdev had informed him that I possessed supernatural prescience.

It was from here that a life filled with dilemma began. Now the commands of five husbands had to be obeyed for displaying appropriate respect to all. The neglect of anyone would not be permissible. And I did not wish to ignore anyone either.

So, first the words of Yudhishthir. He was the eldest. He was the head of the family. I was proceeding towards his room when my new sakhi, Maya, blocked my way and said, "Sakhi! Bhim has been waiting for a long time. Will you be able to tackle his anger? And then, Arjun is touchy. How will his hurt be assuaged? He will not, of course, say anything. You can go to Yudhishthir later. It will be right to satisfy Bhimsen first." I was thrown into a dilemma. I knew everything. It was Yudhishthir's command which ought to be complied with first. Then Bhim and then Nakul —

"Intimacy, separation, love and hate in married life are not guided by laws and rules. Justice-injustice, dharma-adharma can be debated in temples, schools, assembly-halls. That has to be acknowledged. But in the intercourse of love all this is invalid. Sometimes, stepping aside from the straight path one has to move at a tangent. Married life is not a matter of partition among brothers that dividing one's own affection, solicitude, love and pride in proportion among the elder and younger brothers one can hand over to the five brothers their several shares." As she spoke, Maya suppressed a smile. I was getting restless. Filled with anxiety, I reached Yudhishthir's room.

I *pranam*-ed Maharshi Narad and Govind. Narad blessed me. Govind, looking at me affectionately, expressed his best wishes.

Having made all arrangements for the dice game, Yudhishthir was waiting. Smiling softly he said, "Sit, Panchali! Today in front

99

of you, Govind and I will compete at dice. Govind says that this world seems like a game to him. Compared to that, dicing is nothing. So he thinks that he will win in this. Let the test be held today!"

Respectfully I said, "Grant me time. Your younger brothers have asked for me. I shall come after meeting them and then watch your dice game."

"What are the other brothers calling you for?" Govind wanted to know. I explained. Hearing it, he laughed out. Mockingly he said, "Yudhishthir! For binding the brothers in the string of unity Panchali was compelled to accept five husbands. Now it seems that over Draupadi competition, jealousy, hatred, enmity, dispute and finally division is going to take place among the five. Now by the time Draupadi arrives after meeting everyone, it will be evening. Then how will your dice game be held? This is but the beginning. Everyday Draupadi's service, company, intimacy and intercourse will be sought by all five brothers. What is unnatural in this after all? But it is by this that the unity of the five will be destroyed."

Firmly Yudhishthir said, "My brothers regard me like God. Therefore, no such dispute can arise among us. At my command the brothers will not hesitate even to go into exile renouncing kingdom, wealth, possessions — everything."

Laughing, Narad said, "Renouncing kingdom, wealth, possessions is easy. But renouncing the infatuation for the finest of women, Draupadi, will not be so easy. You are aware of the story of Sunda and Upsunda. Both brothers were enjoying the kingdom seated on the same throne. They ate from the same dish. Their bedroom was the same and their bed, one. Yet happiness, peace and unity did not persist. Ultimately over a woman, Tilottama, they killed each other."

Fear and anxiety brought me out in goose pimples. In a calm voice Govind said, "Narad's words are true."

Thoughtfully, Narad continued, "At the time of Krishnaa's birth it was prophesied that she would be the cause of the destruction of kshatriyas. Are the Pandavs those kshatriyas? I am

100

now apprehensive. Leave aside the others, will not Bhim alone — were Draupadi not to obey him — smash Draupadi and the other Pandavs with his mace? Anger is no respecter of persons. And then, if it is Bhim's fury! It is better not to say anything about him!"

Distressed with fear I asked, "Devarshi! Your words are making me anxious. I, too, am feeling that many husbands will not be able to receive appropriate service all together. It is exceedingly difficult. As a supremely wise person like Govind is present here, some appropriate arrangement must be settled about this, so that in future no dispute may arise among the Pandavs because of me. Otherwise, splitting myself every instant among them I shall make our married life miserable and distressful."

Narad laughed and said, "Daughter, all this is your personal affair. It is best that between husband and wife no third person plays any role. Moreover, I am absolutely ignorant of domestic quarrels and women's problems. It is Govind who is experienced in these. One may even call him an expert in women's matters. It is he who may be able to find some solution for this."

I looked at Govind. Even the helplessness in my eyes amused Govind. He was laughing. I said, "Govind! I have described my problems before you. I have heard from Mother that whenever you do anything, it is only for our welfare. Please provide the solution. What shall I do?"

Govind joined his palms, "Forgive me, Krishnaa! All these are matters between husband and wife. What advice can I give? You yourself are learned. Do what you feel is proper. Moreover, I have attached Maya to you. What is the need for my advice now?"

Maya! Standing right by my side. She stayed constantly by my side like my shadow. At every step she was my helper. I noticed that Govind was saying something to Maya through gestures. I could not understand anything.

Maya looked at me and said, — "Sakhi, playing the role of the wife of many husbands at one time is extremely painful and shameful. Therefore, adopt the role of being the wife of each

101

Pandav by turn for a year at a time. A woman is mother, wife and sister. Discharge the duties of a mother and a sister all the time with all the Pandavs. But as a wife, stay with each Pandav a year at a time. The five Pandav brothers are each of a different nature. In the course of a year you will get the opportunity for preparing yourself mentally and emotionally for moving in harmony with the nature of one."

Everyone supported what Maya said. Yudhishthir, too, agreed with it. Narad made one more stipulation. While I was living with one brother as his wife, if another brother should disturb our privacy, then for twelve years he shall have to live a celibate life in exile. Such a condition would make the married life of each brother disciplined and enjoyable.

The decision was unanimously accepted. In a way, I was saved. At least for a definite period I would remain the wife of one man and will be able to be faithful to him. I expressed my gratitude to Maya. Taking Yudhishthir's permission I went to the other brothers. Now I was their mother or their sister. I would be able to provide easily responses to the obstinacy, love, anger, problems, complaints, sulking, indifference, petting and whims of one after another.

But only after two years would the union with Arjun be possible. In the morning, completing the purifying bath, when I stood before the mirror decked in bridal finery, my reflection was in the mirror but it was Arjun's calm beauty that was reflected in my heart. I was infatuated. I lost myself not in my beauty, but in thoughts of Arjun. I wished that day itself were the occasion for the honeyed union with Arjun!

In the morning Arjun had softly said, "I shall wait for the third part of the night. The desire to get you in the very first hour is strong. But so long as my fate desires to torment me, what alternative is there?"

I blushed furiously in embarrassment. Looking at me Bhim was trying to understand what words of Arjun were changing the colours of my face. So he promptly demanded some sweets.

Getting up, I offered them to him. Perhaps Bhim was unable to tolerate my private conversation with Arjun.

Now Bhim, too, would have to wait for a year. Would Bhim observe the terms of our married life? But from where would he acquire patience? Still, he was not the one about whom I was worried. If he wished he could go away to his first wife, Hidimba. Nakul, Sahadev were meek and calm and revered Yudhishthir very much as their elder brother. They accepted everything as it came naturally. But Arjun! How would he accept the conditions? Anyway, nothing could be done about it any more. The conditions had been accepted in front of everyone. Yudhishthir had accepted them. Govind's mute sanction, too, was behind it. Therefore, it was useless to keep turning it over in my mind.

I was relieved.

Now I would be able to strike a balance among the five husbands.

13

That the sun of good fortune would rise in this fashion neither I nor even the Pandavs had imagined. A month had not passed since the wedding. From Hastinapur grandfather Bhisma and the elder brother of my father-in-law, Dhritarashtra, sent an honourable invitation. With chariots and horses, servants and maids Vidur, the prime minister of Hastinapur, arrived.

The Pandavs were alive and were married to me. For this, Dhritarashtra and mother Gandhari expressed great joy. Mother Satyavati had also sent her blessings. The citizens of Hastinapur, the hundred Kaurav brothers, gurudev Drona, Kripacharya, Karna, the friend of the Kauravs, were all waiting eagerly. Elaborate arrangements for welcoming us were being made. After the house of lac incident all the sympathy, support and love of the people were with the Pandavs. Now after their return, father Dhritarashtra would give half the kingdom to the Pandavs. However, the subjects desired that Dharmaraj Yudhishthir should sit on the throne of Hastinapur. That way the welfare of the kingdom would be secure. Leaving behind all the heroes of Aryavart by dint of their prowess and manhood, the Pandavs had won me. Therefore, the glory of the Pandavs had multiplied a hundred times in the hearts of the people of Hastinapur. In such circumstances, they decided to return to Hastinapur.

Overwhelmed by the good fortune of her sons, mother Kunti began congratulating me. My good fortune! And I was auspiciously marked, that was why the unfortunate Pandavs' luck had returned to them. All Panchal was buzzing only with this talk.

They, whose wicked plots had pushed the Pandavs to the doors of death, had voluntarily despatched chariots to return them half the kingdom! It was amazing. The miraculous power that lay behind this event — what could it be other than my good fortune? Maya, too, said this very thing to everyone. The husbands were getting a kingdom, yet so much praise for me! I was overwhelmed. I forgot myself. Because of me the Pandavs were getting back their kingdom. Their wealth, honour everything was coming back to them — thinking of this I was perhaps secretly feeling proud too. How did I know that as the flag of my good luck was flying triumphantly, unseen fate was silently laughing. Had I known, would I ever have let Yudhishthir get trapped in the delusion of Hastinapur? Had I not returned to Hastinapur, so grievous and shameful a drama would never have been enacted with my life. But would Yudhishthir have listened to me? Has Yudhishthir ever listened to any advice of mine? That day, too, he would not have listened to me. Alas, man is so naive! For the sake of present happiness, ignoring the ominous hints of the future, he himself invites utter calamity!

That day I, too, was eager to leave my father's place and proceed to my in-laws'. I had never even had a hope of seeing my in-laws' place. Therefore, the thought of taking refuge with my father was paining me. Govind and Balaram were about to return to Dvaraka. After participating in the marriage ceremonies they had stayed back in Panchal for a few days at Father's request.

Along with Govind and Balaram, Arjun too proposed to leave for Dvaraka. I could not understand what attraction lay for Arjun in Dvaraka that leaving his newly married wife behind he should accompany his *sakha* there!

In Govind's presence I asked Arjun about this, although in jest. But it seemed as if Arjun were himself hunting for a reply for some such query. Making a face he said, "In Dvaraka there is no attraction save *sakha*. But now I am thinking that somewhere there ought to be something attractive so that a man can go there — whether it is Dvaraka or hell. At least these two years would get by without suffering!"

After this, what could I say? The hurt in Arjun's mind was but natural. But I was helpless. I thought it best to remain silent. Govind kept smiling — "Friend Bhim, too, was talking of going to Hidimba. But his views have changed after receiving the invitation from Hastinapur. For, the Kauravs will be only too happy not to have to welcome all five Pandavs together. They will think that disputes have arisen among the Pandavs. Seizing upon this opportunity they will mislead the subjects too — 'See, they cannot even maintain unity among brothers. How will they, as rulers of the kingdom, ensure unity among the subjects? Without unity the kingdom cannot be protected from external enemies'. For the sake of general welfare Bhim changed his resolve, forgetting all his hurt and anger. Leaving the Pandavs, how will you go to Dvaraka to enjoy the hospitality of your friends' wives? People will say, 'What sort of effeminate character is Arjun that because he was deprived of his wife's company he went off to live in another's home leaving his own?' Moreover, what will Krishnaa think?"

Arjun, full of hurt, said, "While making such a tremendous promise did Krishnaa even consider how we would feel about this decision? Were our views asked for in this? The implication of this is that whatever decision she takes, whether we like it or not, we should silently accept it."

In a calm voice I said, "This decision is not mine. It is Govind's. Mother says that what Govind does is only for our welfare. Is anyone else's opinion necessary regarding Govind's decision? Therefore, I accepted his decision. If it was an offence, I beg forgiveness."

Feigning ignorance, Govind spoke in amazement, "Krishnaa! Arjun is my *priya sakha*. Having married him, it is through him that you have become my *priya sakhi*. Yet, not finding the means of relieving *sakha's* hurt, you are blaming my innocent friend? When did I stipulate this one-year condition regarding your marital life? Your favourite maid Maya put this forward on your behalf and along with others I also nodded assent. Now let *sakha* himself judge what was my role in this?"

In the same grave tone Arjun said, "Whoever's might be the role, for me the situation is like poison. Whatever people might think, what should I do in Hastinapur? Dvaraka will be suitable. Even if I do not go along, Krishnaa will receive the honours of a queen in Hastinapur. Had Krishnaa married me alone, she would not have ever received this tremendous homage and welcome as the future queen of Hastinapur. By honouring Mother's words, Krishnaa has proved her intelligence."

I understood. Full of hurt, Arjun was saying all this in order to hit back at me. Still my eyes were misting over with anguish. How would Arjun understand my helplessness!

So, Arjun would have to be persuaded in favour of Hastinapur? Otherwise on arrival rumours would spread that the Pandavs had split apart over Krishnaa! Moreover, what happiness would I get in Arjun-less Hastina's royal palace?

It was Krishna whose help would have to be taken for tackling this hurt of Arjun's. It seemed that without Krishna it would be difficult to take even one step forward in my life.

Maya clarified — "If Krishna accompanies us, then how will Arjun go to Dvaraka? He will surely follow Krishna to Hastina. He will never want to leave his *sakha's* company."

Govind agreed to my request. Laughing, he said, "Before the request of a friend's wife the influence of one's own wife has been admitted in age after age to be of no account. The attraction of Dvaraka is today left far behind by the attraction of Hastina. Hastina will have to be the destination." Secretly I was delighted. Yes, *sakha* was no mean wit! Now Arjun was helpless. Without Krishna, what would he do in Dvaraka?

In my mind I began praising Maya's intelligence. I was thinking — "Without Maya how can anyone run this domestic life? She has got totally integrated with our life."

I had not seen heaven — but I had seen the world of dreams. It was in that world that I had imagined the splendour of Hastina. But after getting Phalguni, Hastina had remained a thing of the dream-world. I had forgotten that someday I might even become the royal bride of Hastina. And suddenly, that dream was effortlessly sliding into my grasp.

Filled with grain and wealth, like Indra's abode was this Hastina! It seemed as though I were entering heaven itself. What could this kingdom, which was filled with such splendour and beauty, lack? If anything was lacking it would be sorrow and poverty. I felt proud. Such elaborate paraphernalia to greet and welcome me with the honour and respect due to a royal bride and future queen! It seemed to me that there could be no limit to the happiness of this kingdom. Would it not become impossible at times to bear the burden of so much happiness and honour? I did not know that happiness was born only of the mist of enigma. And the instant the veil of this mist vanished, my sorrows and insults were waiting to scorch me — as plants and herbs shrivel up in the blazing sun.

Clad in white, garlands of white flowers in my hair, decked in eight types of ornaments, I was sitting with the pride and gravity of a royal queen. Slowly my chariot went ahead. With me were my dear *sakhis*, Maya and Nitambini. Before my chariot were the chariots of Govind and Balaram. Following me were my five husbands. Behind everyone mother Kunti's well decorated chariot was coming along the royal highway in the midst of innumerable cheering men and women and various bands of musicians. I was thinking: going ahead was Aryavart's finest man, *sakha* Krishna, and Balaram. Behind me were my great-souled, valorous five husbands and mother-in-law Kunti, full of discrimination, knowledge, merit and sympathy. What else was there for her to worry about? How fortunate was that woman Krishnaa! For a moment, absent-mindedly, I became jealous of myself! The next moment I thought, your own happiness and another person's envy were inextricably linked together. Your own good fortune scorched someone else.

Bedecked women of the town offered their ritual obeisance and greetings. Then we alighted from the chariots. Flowers were being showered from all sides. As though on the entire road a carpet of flowers had been spread so that when setting foot for the first time in Hastina I did not suffer in any way. In actual fact when so much pain and insults were stored in the treasury of Hastina for me, how much proof of their wisdom did the Kauravs display by being thrifty regarding it from the very beginning! I was waiting for the chance to congratulate the hundred Kauravs for these arrangements.

On alighting from the chariot, suddenly, as I looked in front, the Kaurav brothers were in sight. Perhaps the Kauravs were being hypocritical, for they appeared very cheerful though a shadow of gloom would flit across their faces. One among them was gazing at me unblinking. Who was it? In this hour resounding with gaiety who was it that appeared sad?

Maya whispered in my ear — *Sakhi!* It is Vasusen, Radheya Karna, son of charioteer Adhirath. He would have been victorious in the *svayamvar*. Dhrishtadyumna insulted him for not being of kshatriya lineage and royal descent. Poor fellow! Is a man responsible for his own birth? And it is his birth that cursed all his heroism, prowess, manhood."

Maya's words enchanted my mind. My heart melted with sympathy for this cursed hero. A shadow of sadness darkened his face.

Without knowing why somebody is laughing, another person cannot laugh. But seeing someone's tears and grief even without understanding the main cause of his pain, a man can feel pained, his eyes can brim over with tears and his heart can melt in compassion. In this way sadness affects others. When it rains the earth is drenched by the rain. If clouds cover the sun, dark shadows spread over the earth. In exactly the same manner, without knowing the cause of his sorrow, my mind was drenched with pain. The gloom on his lovely face cast a black shadow on my face. I thought — "Oh! Why was he not a kshatriya! Why was he not son of Kunti? If he was, then, whether he had won me or not, in any such *svayamvar*-hall he would surely not have been insulted." Insult is more painful for any man than failure. I determined — if I ever got the chance I would beg forgiveness from this noble youth for that day's insult. What was the sense of my being learned or scholarly if I did not honour the valiant appropriately?

Krishna-Balaram were ahead. Everyone's eyes were on them. The hundred Kaurav brothers and other people were bending at

Krishna-Balaram's feet with offerings of flowers. Karna, too, was standing with a bouquet of flowers, but for greeting whom?

Karna was holding a bunch of roses, freshly blooming roses with leaves and delicate stems. My eyes greedily fixed on them. Maya whispered near my ear, "*Sakhi!* How did Karna get to know that blue roses are dear to you! Look! For giving them as a present, with what care he has selected them. Such rare roses!"

Softly I said, "*Ari!* Not for me but for greeting Krishna everyone is standing with offerings of flowers. Gallant Karna perhaps knows that it is blue roses that will suit dark-complexioned Krishna. Perhaps he will insert these flowers in Krishna's diadem. Wait and see."

I said so to Maya but my heart did not believe this. Surely this bunch of flowers were not for me? I was trying hard to suppress my rapidly throbbing heartbeats. If Maya got to know, she would mock and tease me so much!

White garments and white flowers, both were very dear to me. But blue roses! My very life was in them! How did Karna get to know it? Had he, then, inspected me in the *svayamvar* hall? I was then in white garments, decked in white flowers. But in my hair a garland of white mallika flowers was entwined in a spiral in which Nitambini had stuck blue rose buds. In the garland round my neck too she had strung a rose. And in my hands she had given a bouquet of blue roses. In the assembly, sitting with bowed head, I kept gazing only at the blue roses. Conversing with them secretly I was trying to hide my anguish. At times, touching the blue roses to my cheeks, thrilled, I saw blue-tinged dreams. Did Karna see all this? He understood that though I was dressed in pure white, it was blue roses which were most dear to me.

A woman desires a man full of heroism, prowess, wealth, beauty and other qualities. But among men, he who can apprehend the secret thoughts of a woman is not only desirable but worth meditating upon. How many men understand a woman's mind?

None of the five husbands knew that blue roses were so dear

to me. So many days had passed with Yudhishthir and I as husband and wife. Yet he was unaware of many secrets of my mind. So many days had I passed among them; not once had anyone brought a blue rose to give me. Then was it for me that Karna had brought these roses?

Offering flowers at the feet of Krishna-Balaram, the Kauravs were *pranam*ing them. But Karna was standing like a motinless statue with the bunch of flowers. With an unblinking stare he was gazing at my progress. Out of hesitation and shyness, my steps slowed down. Then were these blue roses for me? Flowers were raining from all sides. I tried to go forward. At that moment the bouquet of blue roses came and fell near my feet. For an instant I was bewildered. I was thinking — "let me gather them up." Just then I stepped right on the bunch of flowers. "Oh!" I exclaimed softly. Not from the pain of any rose-thorn piercing, but because all the tender petals of the blue roses got crushed! The next instant my foot quivered with pain! Exclaiming, "What happened?" Maya bent down at once. My foot was in her hands. Even now a rose-thorn was stuck in my foot. Karna stood anxious and ashamed, thinking, "What is this mishap that has happened? What should be done now?" Gently Maya pulled the rose-thorn out of my foot. A drop of blood had congealed on my sole. My eyes were tearful with pain. Drawing a little near to Maya, Karna said, "Beg forgiveness from the royal bride. I did not pain her deliberately. I know what the pain of being deliberately tormented in public is like. My very token of regard has wounded the royal bride! However, physical pain is much lighter than the agony of the mind — considering this, may she pardon me."

In all the uproar of the cheering crowds no one got to know when all this happened. There was only one witness: Maya. No second person got to know. Karna, too, by a gesture indicated that the way in which he had been insulted in the *svayamvar* assembly had taken place only at my behest. Had I so desired, he could have been saved from such an insulting situation. Truly, was this not correct to some extent? In the *svayamvar* assembly

111

valour and prowess were being tested. There why did I lend mute assent to that narrow condition of my father's?

Maya was saying, "Karna is a handsome man, but is very arrogant. He has not been able to forget the agony of such a grave insult! In the first stage of revenge your feet have been bloodied. Who knows what the state of your heart will be in the last stage? *Sakhi,* that day had you, with a generous heart, honoured Karna's valour then the impossible situation of accepting five husbands would never have arisen. Now, remain entangled all your life and pine away in this situation."

Though Maya's words were true, I was irritated in my heart of hearts. Why was Maya repeatedly making my mind weak, unstable and aimless? Why was she sullying my mind by discussing again and again what had not taken place at all? Removing my gaze from Karna, I turned it towards Krishna's feet. And moving a little ahead I began walking, following Krishna.

Hastinapur's royal bride! Krishnaa! It would not be proper to listen to everyone's chatter and think of this and that.

If Karna was an egotist was I any less? If he was Vasusen, then I was Yajnaseni. Would she who was born of fire be afraid of flames?

112

14

Half of the Hastinapur kingdom, Khandavprasth, was given by Dhritarashtra to the Pandavs. There was not even a livable hut in Khandav. I had never desired Hastina's luxury, splendour and palaces. I had desired acceptance as the royal bride of Hastina, and her rights. Contentment could be found even in the hut of Khandavprasth. I would find fulfilment.

But when Krishna was their friend, how long would it take to transform Khandavprasth to Indraprasth? In a few days the splendour and beauty of the newly constructed city of Indra-prasth surpassed Hastina. The assembly-hall of Indraprasth was the most attractive of all.

During the burning of the Khandav forest the *danav* Maya had been saved because of Arjun's compassion. To express his grati-tude, Maya, after consulting Shri Krishna and taking the permis-sion of Yudhishthir, had built the assembly-hall. Nowhere in the world had such a hall been built. This hall, seventy cubits square, had been constructed on land measuring four thousand cubits in length and breadth. In the walls and ceiling precious stones, and in the floor crystals and pearls had been set. The gems had been so embedded in the ceiling that they seemed like stars and plan-ets in the sky. The ceiling, too, had been coloured so cunningly that like the morning and evening sky its colour would keep changing in tune with the sunlight outside from moment to mo-ment. Even though you were seated inside the hall, you would feel you were seated under the open sky. The floor of the hall, being made of crystal, appeared transparent like water. The stars and planets of the ceiling reflected in it created the illusion of water. Mirrors were so set in the walls that while the assembly was in session king Yudhishthir's reflection could be seen by the audience all around them. The king himself was before them. But

113

the audience would see in the mirrors Yudhishthir's reflection even behind them. A person seated in the hall could not but be aware of the presence of Yudhishthir.

There were flowering shrubs in the garden in front of the hall. At intervals, on plants made of gold, flowers of gems were arranged. On seeing them from a distance it would seem as if in a garden of dreams, flowers of happiness and good fortune were being showered as gems. In the centre of the garden a lake had been dug, with a golden platform all around. Its steps were made of crystal. Golden lotuses had been placed in the lake. Artificial fish made of diamonds and sapphires floated in it. The golden walls had marble ledges set with gleaming pearls. The water of the lake was so clear that everything could be seen down to the bottom. For boating, boats studded with diamonds were tied at one end.

The cunning artistry and beauty of the throne that had been built in the centre of the assembly-hall for Yudhishthir to sit defied description. Even Indra would be allured by this throne to come down from *svarg*.

To keep the entire assembly hall cool many types of flower and fruit bearing trees had been planted. The fragrance of flowers filled the hall. Seeing this assembly-hall like Indra's palace in Khandavprasth, people began calling it Indraprasth. Yudhishthir was anointed king on the throne of Indraprasth. And I became the queen of Indraprasth.

All the five brothers had poured out their energies in constructing Indraprasth. After it was completed in a short while, the Pandavs exulted in joy. The Kauravs raged in jealousy. Many learned men and subjects of Hastina were drawn towards Indraprasth and left Hastina to take shelter in Yudhishthir's kingdom of righteousness. In Indraprasth, comfort, justice, celebrations and festivals turned them away from Hastina. The Kauravs were burning with envy and hatred. The day for inaugurating the new assembly-hall was announced.

Elaborate preparations were made for the inauguration. Seeing all this, for some reason, I do not know why, my mind became anxious. I had no objection to the feeding of ten thousand brahmins, giving new clothes and cows and making other gifts on this occasion. But on that pretext I was not in favour of inviting the Kauravs and their friend Karna, son-in-law Jayadrath and other relatives. The wise never display their wealth to the wicked and the jealousy-prone. This only encourages enmity. Festivities are organised for happiness, not for arousing jealousy or sorrow. There was no doubt that the inaugural celebrations of Indraprasth's assembly-hall would deeply grieve the Kauravs. Then what was the use of such an elaborate celebration, I asked Yudhishthir. But his reply was: "For the inaugural ceremony of the palace it is not possible to invite guests and leave out relatives. Besides, what will people say if the Kauravs are not invited? He who does not maintain relationship with his friends and relations what contact will he keep with his subjects? Just because someone is acutely envious, will joy and festivities disappear from the world? Those who are envious are ever sorrowful. Even if the Kauravs are not invited, they will get all the news sitting in Hastina and will be immersed in greater envy and be all the more pained. Therefore, maintaining friendship by inviting them will be proper."

Yudhishthir's argument was irrefutable. Then what of my opinion? What Yudhishthir once decided, whether it was right or wrong, he never changed it on female advice. I knew this, and remained silent But along with the Kauravs why would their intimate friend, Karna, ruler of Ang, come? And even if he came, why should I serve him food cooked with my own hands?

Of course, all the Kauravs were my brothers-in-law. They were related by blood to my husbands. They belonged to our family. I would welcome them accordingly. But Karna was an outsider. If he did arrive, let him stay in the guest house. Maidservants were there to attend to him. I did not know why, but my mind shied away from facing that man. Those lovely eyes seemed to be filled with all the world's scorn and revenge for me. My guilty mind was unable to face him.

I did not like the ostentation in Yudhishthir's hospitality to

Karna. I had told Maya too about it. But Maya reminded me that Karna was no outsider. He was also one of the Pandav family. Yudhishthir had made this arrangement to please mother Kunti. Hearing Maya's words, I recalled an incident that had happened some days before.

Construction work was in progress in Khandavprasth. One day mother Kunti ordered me to visit her childhood friend, aunt Radha. I got ready immediately. But I could not consider it normal for Hastina's queen-mother to go to the house of Radha, wife of charioteer Adhirath. Had Kunti wanted, she could have summoned Adhirath's wife to the palace. But mother Kunti's going in person to *sakhi* Radha's house, forgetting her royal pride, with sweets and many gifts, and also taking me with her ... this was not just Kunti's magnanimity. Was there something more to it?

Aunt Radha was full of joy and blessed me. She talked to me a great deal. She sent for Karna to *pranam* Kunti.

When Radha went into another room after speaking to us, then Kunti whispered to me, "Do you know, I have one more son! He is older than Yudhishthir. He is as handsome as he is valiant. He is a fine man. But the sad thing is that having been brought up by Radha he is deprived of many of his lawful rights. That is why he could not get you too. Otherwise, he too could have pierced the target easily. I have no doubt on that score."

I stared at her, astonished. Who was this brave son of mother Kunti? Was it Karna? But how could Karna be Kunti's son?

To remove my doubts mother said, "Yes, Karna is my son according to dharma, my *dharma-putra*. I have accepted him as such. Morally, you should consider Karna in the same light as the five Pandav brothers. But it is his misfortune that he is the adopted son of a charioteer." Mother Kunti's voice got choked. I sat stunned and amazed.

Mother Kunti went on, "You may wonder how Karna became my son. He is my *dharma-putra*. The status of a *dharma-putra* is higher than the sons to whom one gives birth. Therefore, my love, affection and good wishes for him are no less than for the Pandavs."

Still I sat bewildered. Not a word would come to my lips. Having five sons, why did mother take a sixth son? Moreover, Karna was the intimate friend of the Kauravs! Mother Kunti understood my confusion. In a voice full of sympathy she said, "Poor Karna is perhaps the son of some unmarried girl. Out of fear of scandal and social stigma, that unfortunate girl, instead of bringing him up, placed him in a river. That infant was saved by Radha's husband, Adhirath, and named Vasusen. Radha was childless. She brought up Karna with a mother's love, but because of the distressful, cursed mystery of birth at every step Karna is insulted and scorned, and is deprived of his lawful rights. His manhood, heroism, ego are crushed at every step. The advantages, honour and respect that the five Pandavs have got on account of being Kunti's sons — Karna has remained deprived of them all till now despite being the equal of the Pandavs. Hearing from Radha of Karna's insults and calumny repeatedly, my mind fills with compassion and maternal love. At the very first sight of Karna, I do not know why, a fountain of maternal love gushed forth from my heart. My heart says that Karna is surely a royal prince. Or he is a cursed son of some god. He has come on this earth carrying the blessings of some god in his human body. It is this human body that is his curse. For, his godly father will never come on this earth to announce his paternity. Therefore, throughout his life Karna will be unable to give his father's name, and will go on suffering infamy. Thinking all this I feel like taking him into my lap. I have five sons. If Karna comes, there wil be six. What is "too many"? A mother's heart is an ocean. However numerous may be the offspring who come into her arms, there is no diminution in the maternal love showered on any. but Karna is arrogant, proud, emotional. Why should he come into my arms? He wants to prove that man may have no control over his birth, but he has control over his action. He is firmly resolved to prove the glory of his manhood by means of action and duty. Even without some such introduction as son of Kunti, he wishes to establish himself."

As mother Kunti was going on narrating, she was growing

117

emotional. Her calm eyes became tearful. Her generous heart was visible in those eyes. Truly, when a woman becomes a mother, how generous and soft she becomes! I, too, was a woman. The distressing story of Karna's life touched my heart. But, it could not mingle and become part of my heartbeats altogether as with mother Kunti. I had not become a mother, so a flood of pure maternal love for another's child did not flow in my heart as in mother Kunti's. That was why mother Kunti's maternal love and compassion for Karna had struck me as unnatural.

Suddenly I recalled the story of Karna's life heard from Maya. It was after that incident that mother Kunti had accepted Karna as *dharma-putra*. She had revealed publicly her irrepressible maternal love and compassion for Karna. That day I had not believed Maya's words. Today tallying all these I wondered how much Maya knew and how much she imagined.

The education of the princes was over. Famous scholars of the entire kingdom were present for the test of knowledge. Many kings, being invited, had also arrived to watch the expertise of the princes. The judges were seated on a large decorated dais. Grandfather Bhishma, mother Satyavati, Gandhari, Kunti, Vidur, counsellor Sanjay, Dhritarashtra, Kripacharya were gracing another dais.

Not just princes, but the disciples had also come to participate. Among them were Karna and Drona's only son, Ashvatthama.

Drona was the master of ceremonies. It was the success of his students that was his achievement. Whoever might win the test, it would be his success and it would be guru Drona's fame that would spread in the world.

After prayers, Drona arrived wearing new clothes. The princes also arrived in the assembly dressed in new clothes and ornaments, smiling. Everyone's forehead was marked with his mother's victory-blessing and the goddess' vermilion mark. Everyone's face was gleaming with the firm assurance of success. All around shouts were raised cheering the princes. Brahmins were feeding the sacred flame. The weapons were worshipped and then one by one each prince displayed his mastery of weapons.

Fighting with the sword, mace and other weapons; wrestling, horse-racing, archery, piercing targets blindfolded and many types of skills were displayed. Then began Bhim-Duryodhan's mace duel and wrestling. The ground shuddered. It seemed as if there was an earthquake. Still, neither of the two was winning or losing. The very dais was in danger of being upset. Drona stepped in between them and stopped the competition. Then came Aryavart's finest warrior, Arjun. The assembly echoed with claps and cheering. Truly, rulers from afar had gathered to watch Arjun's war-skills. First of all, Arjun *pranam*-ed his gurudev devotedly. Then he turned round and saluted everyone. After that the display of weapon-craft began.

Arjun's weapon-craft was so miraculous, so astonishing that spectators could not believe their eyes. It was as though Arjun had magically enchanted everyone. Some wondered whether they were not being deceived. How could the impossible be happening? So difficult was it to comprehend Arjun's skill!

When Arjun loosed the fire-missile, tongues of flame leapt up all around Hastina. The outbreak of fire sent a wave of fear rippling through the spectators — had the princes of Hastinapur plotted to free themselves of all obstacles? Startled, many warriors began to shout and scream like children, and, afraid of dying, fell down unconscious. That was when Arjun loosed the water-missile. Terrific rain and floods appeared. One more doom swept down licking its lips. Terrified, people prayed to their gods. Meanwhile, he loosed the wind-missile. None knew where the waters of the flood were driven away by the wind. Spectators were not only amazed but also grateful and were clapping all around. Commotion broke out among the spactators. Some collapsed clutching pillars and seats. Most lay down clutching the ground itself. Everyone was upset by the force of the wind. Noticing their condition, Arjun used the cloud-weapon. The skies became overcast with clouds. The spectators got some relief. Fear was removed. Everyone was getting acquainted with Arjun's skill. But what was this? The breeze stopped blowing. People were getting stifled. Everyone was restless. In a short while there would be no one left alive to see Arjun's expertise. But Arjun is never the cause of any innocent person's death. Immediately he used the fragrance-missile. A gentle, scented breeze began to waft under Hastinapur's skies. In which kingdom's garden did such fragrant flowers bloom? From where was this breeze blowing? No one knew. Thrilled and gratified spectators stood up to congratulate Arjun. Right then Arjun loosed the earth-weapon. He hid in the earth. The next instant using the mountain-weapon he stunned everyone. The entire Hastina city stood atop a mountain. Sitting in their individual seats the spectators saw Arjun saluting them from the highest peak. They had but raised their hands in response when, using the vanishing-weapon he disappeared. Then, would the spectators remain seated on the mountain? Suddenly he loosed the underground-missile. Hastina was taken netherwards. The spectators were terrified and chaos reigned among them. That was when he used the space-weapon. Everyone was suspended in mid-air. It became an impossible situation. Who would have come to see the display if they had known that such would be the predicament! They began to regret it. But by then the steadiness-weapon had been used. Everyone reverted to the original state and was relieved. All were overwhelmed.

Arjun's skill filled mother Kunti with tears of joy. But the very next instant seeing in front the furious face of Karna, she was stunned. She was aware that Karna was a mighty hero. Since birth he had borne the immortal armour and ear-rings with the blessings of some god. He was roaring out his challenge to Arjun. Karna was Drona's disciple too. He was Arjun's equal as a warrior. But Karna was a charioteer's son and Arjun, a prince of Hastinapur. Knowingly or unknowingly, Dronacharya discriminated against Karna while teaching. Yet neither Karna nor Arjun gave way to the other. Karna himself knew that because of not being a prince, guru Drona's grace was somewhat less in his respect. Daily Drona taught his son, Ashvatthama, and his dear

120

disciple, Arjun, some additional techniques. Karna had always been plain-spoken and upright. He did not fear anyone. He even protested against the preceptor's injustice. Many times he said that he too should be taught for a longer period. In reply, the guru said, "In future the protector of Hastina shall be Arjun. Ashvatthama shall become the weapons-preceptor of the future kings of Hastinapur. Hence, there is need for special education for both of them. What is the need for such special training for you? You will never be king." Karna remained silent. But day by day he grew intolerant of Arjun. Secretly he began to resolve to prove himself in future a greater warrior than even Arjun. He engaged in single-minded ascesis.

And today the day had arrived for establishing himself. He would prove before all that deeds were more significant than birth.

Karna began to display his prowess in arms. In no way was he less skilful than Arjun. But since the miraculous display of Arjun had kept the spectators spellbound still, they were not amazed with Karna's skill. After this Karna directly challenged Arjun to a duel in public: Let his status become crystal clear vis-a-vis Arjun.

Arjun prepared himself. In a loud voice he announced that the result of this duel would be the death of Karna.

On the dais, Kunti lost consciousness. In the duel either Karna would die or Arjun. In her anxiety over whose death did mother Kunti fall unconscious? Arjun was her own son, but Karna, too, was dear like a son. Therefore, she could not face the tragic posibility that either might die. The spectators were applauding this nobility of heart on the part of Kunti.

Here, too, Karna's self-respect and manhood were slighted. Guru Dronacharya knew that the result of a duel between Karna and Arjun would be horrifying. Therefore, he hit at Karna's weak spot — "Duel! That befits between one prince and another. Arjun is a prince of Hastina, and you? Who is your father, who is your mother? You might be a warrior, but how are you an equal to Arjun in status?"

121

Karna was silent! Because of the humiliation and grief, he wished he could vanish into the dust. What was the point of living in a world where manhood was not valued? But Duryodhan was watching all this. Suddenly he announced — "I am installing friend Karna as ruler of Ang country."

Instantly a jewelled throne arrived and the next moment the fate of the charioteer's son changed. But, what did not change was the history of Karna's birth. Bhim commented, "Out of pity anyone might be made a king, but in his body the blood of a royal dynasty cannot be made to flow. Now, instead of holding the reins of a horse, Karna will grasp the reins of government and for this shall ever remain indebted to Duryodhan."

For preventing the battle of Arjun with Karna, right at that time the sun set. Karna felt that even the lord of dharma, Surya, was turning away from him. In such a world pervaded with darkness the establishment of the glory of manhood was but a daydream. Yet he would not admit defeat. For, it was battling throughout life for the glory of manhood and sacrificing his life in that cause, that was preferable to the hero.

On the occasion of the anointing of the king of Ang, celebrations were held throughout the night in Hastinapur. Duryodhan had everyone fed. Having drunk their fill, the citizens of Hastina began praising Duryodhan. It was Karna who should have been the happiest person during this festival. That day, at dawn he was the son of an ordinary charioteer. Now he was the ruler of the rich state of Ang. But where was Karna? In the festive hall all the princes were immersed in gaiety. Other guests, who had come to watch the exhibition of weapon-craft, were also there. But Karna was not there. After eating and drinking he had lost control of himself. No one had the slightest inkling that he, for whom the festivities have been arranged, was not present there at all. Even without Karna the night of Karna's anointing was glittering.

Seated alone in a room, King Karna was seeking to plumb the mystery of his life-story: "who is your father? Who is your mother?" And Bhim's sarcasm — out of pity someone could be seated on a throne, but royal blood could not be made to flow in his body — was ringing in his ears. In anger and fury, his whole body was hot, his mind was going to pieces. By making him a ruler, Duryodhan had displayed his graciousness, had proved his charity. He had become worthy of being thanked. In this Karna did not have the slightest interest. Rather, this singing and dancing, the festivities, were mocking Karna's manhood. At every beat the dance and song were telling him: "Despite there being no royal blood in your body, because of Duryodhan's pity and kindness you are today a king; you ought to be grateful to him. You are favoured, you are dependent!"

Refuse this governance of Ang state, this royal crown, this royal throne? But if he did that people would say, 'Karna is not fit for kingship; the royal throne has filled him with fear; the royal crown does not befit him. Duryodhan has given gifts to one unsuited for them.' No, he would show this world that merely being a prince was not eligibility for becoming king; it was the suitable man who was eligible for it. That it was not the status of parents, but the proof of manhood that was the true proof of manhood.

Karna began musing again: "Who are my parents? As long as I knew that I was the son of charioteer Adhirath, that Radha was my mother, I was happy like all the restless children of the world. I had never even wondered why I had not been born a prince. In the world everyone does not, after all, take birth as a prince. Yet, everyone's parents seem like kings and queens to their children." Karna, too, was happy with his adoptive parents. But in his youth, that day, in those strange moments when, for the first time, he had attempted to overhear from outside the private conversation of mother Radha with Kunti, then he had felt a shock. Mother Kunti was saying, "This son of yours is full of royal signs. Who can say that he is a charioteer and your son? Look at his appearance! If he stands with the princes of Hastinapur, he will surpass all. Oh! How lovely do those ear-rings and armour appear on him? I do not know why on seeing him I long to embrace him. Would it he were my son! Truly, he should have taken birth as a royal prince."

123

Radha had said, "As he is growing up, people are saying that he is not our son, noticing his qualities and appearance. What is the point of hiding the truth from you? Actually, he is not our son. Some unfortunate woman had, after giving him birth, placed him in a box and floated it down the Yamuna. Finding it while bathing, we considered it a divine blessing. He has had these invulnerable armour and ear-rings since his birth."

Then Kunti said, "Alas! Why didn't lightning strike that cruel mother?" Soft-hearted Kunti, bride of the Soma dynasty, cursing that stone-hearted mother that day, began weeping.

Karna returned to his room. In the life of twelve-year-old Karna a new chapter began from that very day. Since then he had been searching for his father's identity. However, he had never spoken of his secret sorrow to his parents. He had no right to destroy their happiness. Rescuing him from the waters of the Yamuna they had given him refuge, otherwise death was inevitable. He would not have had the experience of this precious human life. Therefore, at every step he had been doing his duties towards his parents. Sometimes he would think, "Why did I not become a prince? Mother Kunti had said so the moment she saw me!" Even today he was seeking that stone-hearted mother of his. Bhim's words had cut him to the quick.

Outside Radha called, "Son! Karna! To greet you, mother Kunti herself has arrived. Open the door."

Karna was astonished. On the assembly dais Kunti had lost consciousness at the thought of her son's danger. She had not regained consciousness till the evening. The moment she recovered and heard that Karna had become a king, despite being unwell she had come to congratulate him. He who was the sworn enemy of her dear son, Arjun — on his acquiring kingship Kunti was delighted! was this the generosity of Kunti's heart or some stratagem on her part?

Karna opened the door. He *pranam*ed Kunti. With trembling limbs Kunti embraced him. She was crying. In a faint voice she said, "Karna, my son, may you be immortal and famous. I heard that despite becoming king you are not happy. Bhim has mocked you and this has deeply hurt you. Therefore, I have come myself to beg your forgiveness. Do not take it to heart."

In an agitated voice Karna said, "*Ma*! Your body is hot. Your limbs are trembling in weakness. For such a small matter you have come so far! Bhim's mockery is nothing new. Right from the time of our training Bhim has been reminding me that I am not a prince, that the blood of charioteers flows in my veins. Bhim always speaks the truth. What is there to be agitated about in this?"

Kunti could not remain standing any longer. Karna supported her and took her inside and seated her. In a distressed tone she spoke out, "Right from his birth Bhim has been irritating me. Time and again I have told him not to hurt you. But his arrogance in being the son of Kunti is without any limits. Therefore, at every step he keeps hurting you. I have determined to break his arrogance. I shall accept you as my adopted son. From today you are my eldest son, and the Pandavs are the younger sons." Suddenly Kunti placed Shiva's *prasad* in Karna's mouth. Drawing Karna to her breast she began speaking with tearful eyes, "If your mother had not fallen into such a predicament she would never have consigned a son like you to the waters of the river. Being a woman, I can understand the agony of that helpless mother. If she is alive anywhere, then remembering you she will be bearing mortal pains at every moment. And that is her atonement. What greater punishment than this can there be, Karna, my son? Take it that the unfortunate one is dead. From today I am your mother. From today you are the son of Kunti. I vow I shall announce it to the Pandavs. Then Bhim's arrogance will be destroyed."

Still Karna did not appear satisfied. His mind felt that this was a burden on him of Kunti's infinite kindness and compassion. Till that day he had detested pity. All would bestow favours on him but would deny his manhood. Then, should he be indifferent to this compassion of mother Kunti?

Raising his eyes Karna looked at Kunti. Pale, mournful face; body worn out; in fever; distressed, helpless look and tears brimming over in deeply sad eyes. Bewildered and helpless, Karna kept staring. Karna, too, could not help weeping. Should royally favoured Karna, deprived of maternal love, neglect and reject the veritable embodiment of motherhood?

As if to himself, Karna said, "Mother Kunti, I am not in the least hesitant in sacrificing my manhood for the glory of becoming Kunti's son." Speaking out he said, "Mother, had I been your son, I would have been blessed. But I detest pity and compassion, and in accepting your kindness I feel glorified. I have always regarded you as my mother. From today I will think you are my mother who held me in her womb. Perhaps, there will be some consolation in my distressed life."

Kunti felt hurt. She wept. She said, "This is no pity or compassion, Karna. It is the spontaneous overflow of my heart. This is no ploy, or something put-on. The mother's heart can never be plumbed by the son. For, he is a man. This, too, is the mother's grief." In a choked voice Karna said, "Forgive me, Mother. The hurt of my heart and its wounded honour have been exposed before you." With a wan smile Kunti said, "It is before the mother that the son's entire hurt pride is expressed."

Before leaving, Kunti said, "My son, fighting with Arjun is not good. I feel deeply distressed. May such an event never occur. That will be my greatest good fortune."

Karna was silent. Then was it out of concern for her own son's security that Kunti had poured out all this maternal love before Karna?

The thread of my thoughts was snapped. Maya whispered into my ears, "Karna is coming." Mother Kunti, too, said, "*Bahu*, Karna is coming. *Pranam* him. He is your elder brother-in-law. As it is, Yudhishthir is younger than Karna in age. And Karna is my adopted son."

I drew the *anchal* over my head, keeping eyes lowered, though I wished that I could see that cursed hero from near.

Karna *pranam*-ed Mother. In a soft voice he said, "Why did you take the trouble of coming? You could have sent me a message and I myself would have gone to Khandavprasth." Mother kissed Karna's forehead and blessed him. In a hurt voice she said, "What

126

trouble? Does the mother feel any difficulty in coming to see the son? I came to know that to meet your parents you had come to the Ang kingdom. I could not control myself and came."

Smiling wanly Karna said, "This is my great good fortune."

"Keep quiet. One does not talk to mothers as with kings and emperors. What will *bahu* think? For *pranam*-ing you she has come from so far away. You never came to Khandavprasth to bless her. So I brought her here — reckoning you are the eldest."

Laughing, Karna said, "She who has obtained heroes like the five Pandavs, with whom a *sakha* like Krishna stays — she needs the blessings of an insignificant man like me?"

Mother warned him, "Leave this useless talk. The moment you see me your heart fills with wounded pride. You have not forgotten the childhood quarrels and disputes with the Pandavs."

Mother signalled me to *pranam* Karna. Before *pranam*-ing Karna it would be proper to touch Mother's feet. On *pranam*-ing one person it is necessary to *pranam* all the elders present. My head was bowed. I saw Mother's feet. Bowing I bent forward. Immediately both feet shifted backwards. I was bewildered. Was Mother unwilling to accept my *pranam*? Was she annoyed with me?

The next instant Karna's resonant voice was heard: "Hastinapur's queen Krishnaa will *pranam* the charioteer's son, Karna, by touching his feet? This will be insulting Hastinapur. The five husbands too might be annoyed. Even without the *pranam* my blessings are with them."

I shrank back in shame. Mistaking it to be Mother's feet, I had gone to touch Karna's feet. Mother's and Karna's feet were so similar! Now I noticed that the four feet were truly absolutely identical. That day, noticing the similarity between Krishna and Arjun I had been misled. Here the difference was only that Mother's feet were a little smaller. But how did this happen?

I stretched my hands towards Mother and then *pranam*-ed Karna. *Chheeh!* Karna would have thought that using the excuse of *pranam* I had deliberately gone forward to touch his feet. How ashamed I felt!

127

Maya understood my feelings. "Your feet resemble mother's so much that misled by this the royal bride was going to touch them. It is a good thing that you moved back, otherwise touching the elder brother-in-law the royal bride would have incurred sin."

Karna burst out laughing. "Royal bride Krishnaa and sin! She is the ideal of womanhood in Aryavart. Further, it is in Satyayuga and Tretayuga that sin occurred on touching elder brothers-in-law. In Dvapar even marriage is taking place with the elder brother-in-law."

Karna's sarcasm pierced like an arrow. My heart began bleeding. I controlled the tears. To give importance to the sarcastic comments of such an arrogant and intolerant man would be shameful for the royal bride Krishnaa.

Turning away my face, I returned to my room and from within spoke to Mother so that she could hear, "It will be necessary to return by evening." Mother realised the time. Maya said, "Truly, such similarity between Mother's feet and Karna's is amazing."

Mother said, "Perhaps in some birth Karna was my own son. Otherwise, how can this be!"

15

The inauguration of the assembly-hall was conducted with great pomp. Yudhishthir had greeted the guests seated on the throne in the assembly-hall. Everyone was amazed by its beauty and skilful architecture. In such a situation it was only natural for them to be envious. Having despatched the five Pandavs cunningly to undeveloped Khandavprasth, the Kauravs were rejoicing. But here, seeing the newly constructed Indraprasth and particularly the assembly-hall, they were burning with jealousy. Somehow if the Pandavs could be exiled, then they could enjoy Indraprasth.

Yes, I had myself cooked food for those hundred brothers and served them. I myself. For it was Mother's order. The Kauravs were my brothers-in-law. Therefore, it was my duty to honour them as members of my family. What objection could there be in this? Cooking and serving was a pleasurable activity. I enjoyed it. Therefore, with great care I prepared delectable sweet dishes. Maya and Nitambini too helped a lot.

The hundred Kauravs and five Pandavs sat down together. Balaram and Krishna, too, were with them. Mother had wished that Karna too would eat with them. But Karna was staying in the guest house as ruler of Ang. Mother had invited him for dinner at night. Karna had sent word that he would not like to interfere in anyone's family matters. The Kauravs and the Pandavs were staying together, eating together. This was good. It would increase their friendly relations. His coming might prove an obstacle to this.

Mother understood Karna's hurt pride. Karna had been accepted as her adopted son, but still he wanted this to be clear that he was not of the Kaurav-Pandav clan.

Mother had found out from aunt Radha what type of dishes Karna preferred and had got me to prepare them. I too, because of her love for Karna, had prepared food with great care. But Karna had politely declined even from attending. Mother was disappointed. Amid all the flow of festivities suddenly she became absent-minded. The woman's mind in me was filled with curiosity at Mother's love for Karna which appeared to be without reason. But how to satisfy this curiosity? Silently I went on obeying her.

A hundred and five brothers and Jayadrath, the husband of my only sister-in-law, Duhshala, were eating together. Maya, Nitambini and I were serving. All were praising my cooking and repeatedly asking for more. We became exhausted serving the dishes. They went on eating. Duhshasan caught hold of my hand with his soiled hands a couple of times. Considering the fact that he was my younger brother-in-law, I did not say anything.

When I went to serve *kheer* to Jayadrath, he smiled and said, "Bhabhi, if the food prepared by your hands is so tasty, how would you yourself be?" Duhshasan immediately added, "After returning from here, only burnt things will be available. The beauty we saw in the *svayamvar* is burning us up even now. Today we have witnessed the entire gamut of her qualities and the perfect housewife. It is as though in those flames oil has been poured!"

My body felt as if it were aflame. My face and looks changed. But, while serving food to guests it was not proper to give way to anger. I suppressed my anger and disgust. Yet my face became red. Jayadrath understood and began saying, "*Bhabhi!* Such jokes keep being cracked by husbands' brothers and husbands of sisters-in-law. You ought to have learned that in your father's home. If brothers-in-law do not joke with so lovely a sister-in-law as you, how will they live?"

I, too, pretended as if I was accepting all this as a jest. But the indecent hints lurking behind their words were in no way on the level of jest. I became grave. Duryodhan was repeatedly looking at me while eating. My breathing became deeper. As I served, he

130

would look at me with regret and unsatiated lust and hiss and mutter, "tsk! tsk! tsk!".

I thought that like greeting a defeated enemy by garlanding him with flowers, inviting the Kauravs, who had returned disappointed from the *svayamvar*, to display my beauty before them would appear to them an insult. As it was, the Kauravs were ever intolerant and envious. To irritate them further had not been wise.

I did not know why my joy and good fortune were filling me with fear. My mind was getting hemmed in by anxiety. The body was tired and the mind full of fear. I needed rest. I was proceeding towards the bedroom when I saw Mother standing at the door of the kitchen. I turned that way. I had myself served her food. Mother said, "Now nothing more is needed." She forced me to go and rest. But had she finished eating so quickly?

I saw her food lying untouched. She was standing dejected, absent-minded. I asked, "*Ma*, what is the matter? You did not eat?" In a sad voice she said, "You too did not eat. How could I?" I was perplexed. "After resting for some time I would have eaten. After the cooks, servants and even the pets had been fed, I would have eaten. You know this." "But today you have worked so hard and are looking unwell. So, why not finish eating first? It is one's duty to look after the body's welfare." Embarrassed, I said, "Will you fast because of me today? Then come, I too will eat with you. Perhaps by this time everyone has eaten."

I served for both of us. Mother said softly, "Keeping guests unfed, the housewife does not even take a drink of water." I kept staring in amazement, "Which guest is still unfed? Everyone has been served." Mother said, "The ruler of Ang, Karna, is in the guest house still unfed. He was invited here today. There has been no arrangement for food for the night in the guest house. Should we finish eating and go to bed?"

I grew annoyed at Mother's words. She would fast because Karna had not eaten? I asked, "So?" In a steady voice Mother said, "It will be necessary to go to the guest house with food for Karna." "You will go?" I asked with a simple heart. Mother said,

"After Yudhishthir's becoming the king of Indraprasth, you are in charge of the household. Karna is your guest, not mine. Looking after guests is your duty." "I shall go to the guest house?" I asked in surprise. In a grave voice mother said, "What is so surprising in this? Karna is not just a guest but is also your elder brother-in-law. Take along Maya and Nitambini too. Moreover, Karna is after all staying in the private guest house in the palace."

Hiding my unwillingness and irritation I said, "Just as you wish. I have no objection."

Eagerly Mother arranged everything. It was more than was necessary for one person. She began to explain to me, "The guest is God. If the guest is satisfied, God Himself is satisfied. If you do not go yourself, Karna will not accept food. You are in truth the ruler of the household. I know Karna. In every matter he seeks out dharma, duty, rule and law. If you go with the food, he will be pleased."

I thought, whether Karna was pleased or not, Mother would surely be glad and that was what I ought to do. The three of us arrived at the door of the guest house. In Maya's hands was the dish of food and in Nitambini's the vessel of water.

I kept waiting outside. Both of them went inside and sent word by the attendant that a message had come from Mother Kunti. Karna was getting ready to go to bed. He came out into the sitting room and asked, "What message so late at night?" "Food for the night has been sent for you," said Maya. Karna was taken aback and said, "The lunch was so heavy that there is no need for dinner. However, as Mother has sent it, I shall have to take a little."

"No, No, not a little. You must eat your fill. That is why Mother has sent us. Your favourite dishes have been made by queen Krishnaa on Mother's orders. Queen Krishnaa has herself come with the food. Mother's orders are that the guest must be served by the queen herself."

Karna became grave. He appeared somewhat sad. Hesitantly he said, "It is not proper for the queen to come to the guest house

132

so late at night. Mother Kunti has been blinded by maternal love and has forgotten what is proper and what is not."

Quietly Maya said, "You are the Queen Mother's adopted son and the guest of honour of the palace, staying in the rooms where only the members of the royal family stay. Therefore, as she is in charge of the household, it is proper for Queen Krishnaa to take care of the guest."

Thoughtfully Karna said, "When the queen has herself brought the dish, it will be a crime to return it. But, I will have only fruits. Put the fruits down and take back the cooked dishes."

"Why only fruits? Is today any particular day of worship?" enquired Maya, surprised. Karna kept quiet. After a few moments he said, "Whatever anyone might think I want to say clearly that first I beg Queen Krishnaa's forgiveness. I am speaking only of the usual customs. It is the dharma of a woman to have only one husband. If the first husband dies, then in some circumstances there is sanction for a second husband. But at one time to share the beds of five husbands is not sanctioned anywhere. There is no instance of this in the past and will perhaps not occur in the future. Such a woman, despite being married, is considered a public woman. Even to touch water from her hands is to lose one's dharma. Look, in these matters I am very rigid and traditional. your queen, being Yajnaseni, despite marrying five husbands can be famed as chaste. But the ordinary woman in such circumstances is termed unchaste. How can I accept food cooked by her? In these matters I am extremely particular."

On the veranda of the guest house both my feet were frozen. So much insult, calumny, slander! I would not be able to answer back, for Karna was our guest and the guest was God. In anger and sorrow my entire being was shuddering, but the unperturbed body kept standing. Maya was saying, "Sir, you are insulting our queen. Because you could not win her, is this your reaction?" Karna grew pale. Laughing he said, "I am saying what is sanctioned by scriptures. I have heard the queen is learned and wise. Ask her whether my words are according to the scriptures or not.

133

Actually, I do not wish to hurt anyone. But even if the truth is unpleasant, I have the habit of uttering it."

Sending the tray of fruits within, I returned. It seemed to me that this was the beginning of the insults I would have to suffer. I felt angry with Phalguni, with Mother, and most of all with Yudhishthir. My appetite was gone. Anguish and sadness brought tears to my eyes. I did not like weeping at the slightest excuse. Tears represented weakness. But sometimes even tears become companions of human beings when they are helpless. They reduce the burden of sorrow pressing on the heart. They wash away anguish and depression and help gather new strength.

I detested tears. But were tears under anyone's control? That was my state that day. Yet, Mother would have to be informed. I was standing in the veranda of her bedroom. *Ma!* Karna only accepted fruits and returned all the food." "Why?" enquired Mother in pain. I said, "It was late at night and the afternoon repast had been heavy. So now he was not hungry. You had sent it, therefore he ate the fruits."

"Then for tomorrow morning you will have to prepare his favourite dishes. Now rest. Get up a little early in the morning."

Mother became so anxious for Karna that she even forgot to ask whether I had had my dinner or not. And she did not notice the tears in my eyes.

I was returning to the bedroom. I thought, in the morning, pretending to be unwell I would not get up. Otherwise, Karna would not take breakfast either. It would be a grave sin if the guest remained unfed. If I did not cook, Mother herself would and then Karna, after breakfast, would depart for his kingdom.

On reaching the bedroom I saw Phalguni coming. I was wanting to pour out on his broad, generous chest the burden of my helpless tears and ask, "Phalguni, why give me this punishment? For epochs this calumny will remain inscribed in the history of the world. Is Krishnaa responsible for this? Did Krishnaa want this? Then why should she bear the burden and pain of this insult?"

134

On seeing a sympathetic friend, the dams of the river of sorrow break. I sobbed. I stood like a stone statue at the door of the bedroom. Tears were glistening on my checks. Phalguni was about to pass me by with bowed head. Without even looking at me he said, "What do you want?"

The tear-drops fell. Suppressing my agony I said, "Phalguni, I am not well. My heart is heavy with sorrow." I thought that hearing this Phalguni would become anxious. But in a calm voice he said, "It is natural because of the day-long weary labour. I am informing Elder Brother. Rest." Glancing at me sideways, he returned towards the sitting room. It seemed as though he were reminding me of Karna's mockery, "Krishnaa! I am helpless. At this point of time late at night this first husband of yours can provide no help, for at this time you are in the role of Yudhishthir's wife and I am but a mere spectator."

I entered the bedroom. I ought to rest only after my husband had gone to bed. I kept sitting and waiting for Yudhishthir, but he would not understand my pain. He was a detached, unperturbed man. Worldly hurt, anger, hatred never touched his inner being. He was a god and therefore, in one sense, like stone.

My body wanted rest; my mind wanted consolation and patience. I had five husbands, but nothing was forthcoming from anyone.

Outside, Phalguni's feet were visible. They were looking as attractive as blue lotuses on the marble floor. They halted on the other side of the door. Phalguni might not enter the bedroom of Yudhishthir's wife, Krishnaa.

From outside Phalguni said, "Elder Brother is now seated with Duryodhan playing dice. This night he is winning every time. He will play all night. For, occasions to win come only rarely and when they do it is not wise to let go of them. Do not wait for him. Rest. Brother has sent this message."

Phalguni would not come inside, but I could go out. Removing the curtain, I came out, and stood in front of Phalguni. In a steady voice I said, "Phalguni, even after hearing of my not being well he will pass the night in the hall absorbed in the intoxication of

135

victory? Will this not produce any reaction in my mind? I do not know why, this dice business scares me. Whatever be the addiction, it is dangerous. It is because of the obsession to give things away Bali was consigned to the nether regions. Duryodhan may not perhaps forget all his life the shame and insult of defeat at Yudhishthir's hands. I do not know what means of revenge he may seek secretly."

Carelessy Phalguni said, "Dicing is for pleasure, entertainment. What is the link between life and defeat and victory in a game? Women are suspicious by nature and habitually look at everything in a devious manner. That is why they suffer more."

I know the Pandavs. While they might blame a brother for something, they would not tolerate from the wife's mouth any complaint against a brother. Calmly I said, "Phalguni, till your brother arrives I shall not lie down. Come let us talk for some time. Let us talk of your *sakha's* philosophy of life. Why does your *sakha* devote so much of his energies to matters which concern others?"

Phalguni looked at me gravely. His blue-lake eyes were lookng bloodshot. Perhaps it was late at night or perhaps he had had a drop too much. In a grave voice he said: "Krishnaa! For two years I have to keep a vow. It is you who have laid this down. Then why this attempt to break the vow? Do you want that I should undergo a twelve-year exile in the forest?"

I was taken aback. How would Phalguni know what I wanted? He was not a woman. How would he understand that every instant I sought his company.

The silent voice of my hurt pride was perhaps sensed by Phalguni. Softly he said, "From the point of view of honouring the vow, not to desire you for two years does not mean that I am an impassive ascetic or eunuch. On such a quiet night, if I indulge in intimate conversation with you, it will be breaking my vow. Who will know this better than me! Forgive me, Krishnaa, we will discuss this tomorrow. There will be time in the afternoon. Then, in the very presence of *sakha*, we shall discuss this. If *sakha* is beside us, there will be no anxiety about breaking the vow either."

Like an unperturbed man, he left spurning my plea. Not even once did he turn back to know my reaction.

Once I thought of sending a message through Maya that I was extremely unwell. But would that be proper? The Kauravs would take it otherwise. And even if Yudhishthir did arrive would it cool the burning of this insult? Rather, immediately on seeing him my anger would flare up. This night of festivities would be filled with thorns. Yudhishthir in the joy of victory had neglected his wife. He was winning. In the self-satisfaction of winning, the sorrow of anyone's else's defeat could not touch him.

I was restless and the message arrived for joining him in the hall in the joy of his first victory. I was helpless. In such matters the husband's request had to be complied with otherwise Yudhishthir would be demeaned before the Kauravs. With great difficulty, I got ready. Taking Maya along I arrived in the hall. Yudhishthir noticed neither my illness nor my depression. Full of joy he said, "Yajnaseni, without you there is no joy in being victorious. Come, sit down! For the first time in my life I am winning at dice. Without you, how will I be able to enjoy this pleasure?"

Enthusiastically Bhim said, "After winning Draupadi, the Pandavs will win in everything. This is clearly proved in the dice-game. Therefore, this victory is Draupadi's."

Duryodhan was burning with anger having been defeated. At that very moment Bhim reminded him of his ultimate defeat in life. Duryodhan threw a burning glance at me. It seemed as though in that gaze were flames of desire, embers of revenge, and the fire of horrible lust.

Duhshasan was aflame with intolerance. Laughing out loud, he said, "Because of the supremacy of the chastity of Devi Draupadi, wife of five husbands, the flood of victory will sweep the Pandavs into the womb of the ocean."

I felt more distressed. It is not wise to sing to the defeated enemy songs of one's own victory. This increases enmity, not decreases it. Immediately on seeing me, the Kauravs had spontaneously erupted in lust and were burning in the ignominy of defeat. Then what was the benefit in irritating them further?

I thought my presence here was not desirable. It would be proper for me to return. Somehow Krishna understood my secret thoughts and said, "Yudhishthir, Krishnaa has worked hard and looks tired. Give her permission to rest." Yudhishthir concentrated all his attention on throwing the dice. Without raising his head he said, "Then Yajnaseni may leave."

Like an automaton I returned. Tears, though suppressed, would flow. These tears were not the molten form of agony, not born of the pain of insult, nor emerging from physical weariness. They had sprung from helplessness, and loneliness. The woman who was mocked at every step for being loved by five husbands — how lonely she was, how friendless! Who would understand that?

It was not possible to sleep. It was stifling in the room. Taking Maya along I went to the terrace. In the open air and in the moonlight, the sky full of stars might perhaps share my pain. Standing in a corner, I was seeking some solace from the vast sky. I saw on the roof of the guest house a tall, well-formed, strong shadowy form appearing restless, anxious, at times looking towards the sky and stopping as though asking questions. Who was it? Guest Karna? Why was he restless, impatient? Did he have any problem?

The sounds of joy were floating up from the hall. Yudhishthir was winning again. The shadowy form was seeking from the sky answers to the questions of life. On the roof of Mother's palace yet another sad shadowy form was fixedly staring at the roof of the guest house. Repeatedly, the dim outline of the shadow was shuddering with deep sighs. Who was it? Mother Kunti? The eldest son Yudhishthir was winning, but in what secret agony had she lost her sleep?

Forgetting my own pain and sorrow, I lost myself in Mother's pain and secret sorrow. Kunti, mother of five heroes — her secret pain would be deeper than my pain. This was what I thought to myself.

I thought, removing the mother-in-law's sorrow was the duty of the *bahu* of the family. But from whom would I ask the cause of Mother's sorrow? Who would tell me? I decided that if an opportunity arose, I would, with folded hands, ask her. Mingling my tears with Mother's, I would reduce her sorrow.

16

Despite the body being unwell, the mind can stil remain well, but if the mind is sick the body cannot remain healthy. I lay sick for several days in bed. Yudhishthir remained content handing over the responsibility of my treatment to the royal physician. He had considerable faith in the royal physician. But I had lost faith in myself. I was sceptical — with five husbands and insulted by the Kauravs all through life, would I be able to lead a healthy life?

I was constantly thinking about my five husbands. Now I realised that no one can ever satisfy everyone. For maintaining order in our joint life the rules that I had made had perhaps given me some advantages but they had pained others. Every night, before going to Yudhishthir's bed-chamber after dinner and after completing all the work, when I would go to wish them good night, Sahadev would be fast asleep like an innocent child. Nakul would be in the pleasure-chamber, lost in music and dance. He was rather too engrossed these days in the dance of dancing girls. And Arjun would be seen engrossed in studying scriptures in the library. During his study of the scriptures and practising weapon-craft none would go before him so that his concentration would not be dibturbed. These were his clear directives. He would deliberately keep himself engaged in some task of this sort till late at night. Perhaps, by not giving me the chance to bid good night he was assuaging his heart's resentment.

But Bhim would be waiting for my arrival. The moment he heard my footsteps outside the door he would say as if issuing a command, "Panchali, enter within! I am extremely unwell. I cannot get up from bed and go to the door."

Without entering from the other side of the door I would reply, "Why do you usually fall ill late at night, as I notice?"

"Because of you."

140

"Because of me?"

"Certainly. You serve such food that every day after dinner I become inert. You know that I am rather fond of food. Now it is for you to tackle the situation." Bhim would be restless. He would groan as if in pain. He would ask for water to drink and some digestive. I would be compelled to enter and try to remove the discomfort. Bhim would say, "Panchali, for a full year you will not be my wife. But there is no bar to your being sister and mother. I am unwell. You ought to adopt the role of mother and sister. You cannot leave till I fall asleep."

Bhim was hinting at massaging his feet. This might alleviate his pain. Sleep too might come quickly. Thinking thus, I would sit down to take care of him. Sometimes it would be day-break and yet Bhim's pain would not subside, sleep would not come properly. The whole night I would be devoted to serving him. I would think "Yudhishthir will be waiting. He will be getting annoyed." But I could not openly tell Bhim anything. Silently I would massage Bhim's feet. To irritate me he would keep narrating accounts of his love and dalliance with Hidimba. At times showing pity he would say, "Yes, now you may go, Panchali. Yudhishthir will be waiting. It was not my intention to trouble you. Therefore, tomorrow I shall go away to Hidimba who will know of my heart's condition better than you. At her slightest touch, sleep closes the eyes. At your touch, instead of sleep coming, if it is anywhere near, it goes far away. Hidimba is a *rakshasi* but as a wife she is superior to you."

Bhim wanted to hurt me, but I would not protest. I had got used to his barbs. Quietly I would return to Yudhishthir's chamber. Perhaps now, asserting the authority of a normal husband, he might be somewhat angry. It might be that he would even be agitated and furious. Anyone would react thus. But there would be no sign of Yudhishthir waiting for me. Like a sense-controlled hermit he would adopt a detached attitude and in an unperturbed voice say, "So Bhim finally went to sleep? I have heard that every night after dinner he feels unwell. Keep watch over his eating and drinking, Yajnaseni. On seeing good food, he completely forgets what is healthy and what is not. Exercise control over him. It is Bhim's strength that is the treasure of the Pandavs. If he remains continually unwell then it is on me that the danger will fall. As the eldest brother, it is I who have to take care of everyone."

I looked at Yudhishthir with a deep, penetrating gaze. That he was anxiously waiting for me all night — even this he would not acknowledge! For, if he did so, would he not be diminished in the eyes of his wife? Therefore, in a roundabout way he wished to convey that he was not pleased with Bhim's ill health. He felt anxious, insecure and dissatisfied. In every matter displaying such generosity, Yudhishthir would never be able to express his inner thoughts before me. In case my faith in him was shaken, he felt hesitant even to say, "Give me food", even if he was hungry. My heart would soften with pity to see such hesitation in a husband greedy for fame. In a mild, sweet tone I would say, "Because of Bhim's ill health, I have neglected my duty towards you. I am sorry. But if Bhim keeps feeling unwell at a particular time every day, what am I to do?"

Immediately Yudhishthir would respond, "That does not trouble me in the least. But if you remain without sleep every night, engaged in his service, then you will fall ill. Therefore, do not bother too much about this childish behaviour of Bhim. He will become all right by himself soon. That a responsible warrior like him should become ill because of over-eating is not good."

I laughed to myself. That Yudhishthir did not like this deliberate illness on Bhim's part, I understood. And that Bhim detained me without cause, making a pretence, was not hidden from me either. Neither was Yudhishthir's annoyance. Yet, leaving one husband in a state of ill health, in pain, how could I enjoy with another husband?

I would think of means to escape from this danger — if Bhim should go for some days to Hidimba, I would bear that. Besides this, I could see no other resolution of this dilemma.

Even if the irritation of Bhim's tantrums could be borne, the cold indifference of Phalguni was beyond tolerance. I felt as if

every nerve in my body were snapping. Secretly I would wish —
like Bhim, why doesn't Phalguni make me suffer? Put me in
difficulty? I would feel as though I were being swept far away
from Phalguni on the swift current of hurt pride.

I fell ill after the following event.

Those days on the excuse of practising weapon-craft, Phalguni
would go far into the jungle. At times he would return long after
sunset. After returning, he would engage himself in the evening
worship. He would eat lightly at night and then again get engrossed in studying in the library. Or, discussions would begin
with *sakha* Krishna on the scriptures.

At times Phalguni would come so late from the jungle that I
would grow anxious. *Sakha* Krishna would understand the state
of my mind. Reassuring me he would say, "*Sakhi*, you are insulting my dear *sakha!*" I would keep gazing at him with questioning
eyes. Laughing, *sakha* would say, "What can my *sakha* not do
alone in the forest? Tigers, bears, serpents and other savage creatures he can render powerless. If you knew this, you would not
be so anxious. It seems you have no confidence in my *sakha's*
prowess and skill in arms. Is this not insulting Phalguni? You are
his wife, yet you entertain such thoughts about him! If he gets to
know of this, he will curse his deeds. So, do not worry about
Phalguni."

Listening to *sakha's* reassurance, I would try to console myself.
That day when Phalguni returned, he was covered with blood
and wounded. No one knew how this had happened. The attendants who had accompanied him related that on that day somehow Phalguni was unmindful and in that state was riding a
spirited horse from Panchal. The horse sped away with him into
the forest. After a long time the horse was seen racing back by
itself. The attendants wore out themselves searching for the master. Finally they found him lying unconscious below a hill and
brought him back in a wounded condition. From his very birth
Phalguni had been obsessed with the desire to be the hero of
romantic adventures. Perhaps to get rid of idleness and depression, he had become careless while gazing at the beauty of that

forested area from the back of that fiery spirited horse. Taking advantage of that, the horse had slipped out of his control and so he was thrown off and got hurt.

There was no time to think of how this had happened. I got busy in treating and nursing him. The royal physician inspected him immediately and said, "Considerable blood has been lost but there is no danger. He will regain consciousness soon. But he needs complete rest for two full weeks. Nursing will be more effective than medicines."

Laughing, *sakha* Krishna said, "Now I understand why, despite there being so many horses in the stables of Indraprasth, he invited danger by choosing the unruly Panchal steed. Otherwise how will the company of lovely young Krishnaa be available! Gentlemanly, polite and restrained, Phalguni is unable like undisciplined Bhim to exact forcibly service, company and sympathy from Krishnaa."

Despite every word of *sakha's* being full of gentle mockery, there was no end to my sorrow and depression. I was thinking, "What is the real reason for Phalguni doing such a reckless thing? To get my company or take revenge on me?"

I was seated near Phalguni's feet. Mother was seated by his head. Phalguni was regaining consciousness. The moment he opened his eyes, they fell on me. My eyes filled with tears. Mother was present, so I controlled myself. After opening his eyes once, Phalguni closed them again. The next moment, looking up at Mother he smiled and said, "Over such a slight matter you get so worried! The loss of blood is nothing new for me."

Kunti did not reply. She only kept running her fingers through his hair. Her eyes were tearful. Mother left to prepare food for Phalguni telling me, "Keep rubbing the soles of his feet gently." I, too, wanted precisely this. Gently, with all the tenderness of my heart, I began rubbing those blue-lotus like feet. That is when *sakha* Krishna mockingly said, "*Sakha*, I hope my presence is not creating any hindrance to your rest?"

Phalguni opened his eyes, "*Sakha*, where you are absent there is no rest. Therefore, without you, is there any joy in relaxing?"

Laughing, *sakha* said, "Even if I am not present, Krishnaa is there after all. For getting Krishnaa's nursing and company the most worldly-wise of men will not think twice before falling ill. Are you sure that you have not fallen off the horse to achieve this state out of that greed?"

I was overwhelmed with shame and grief. Phalguni became grave. In a stern voice he said, "*Sakha*, blood has ever been shed for every dispute in the world. It is necessary to shed some blood to destroy the demonic."

Like an innocent child *sakha* looked at Phalguni and said, "What are you saying? Which demon? What dispute?"

Looking at him steadily, Phalguni continued, "It is man's desire and lust that are the wicked demon. And the dispute is between the mind and the conscience. When the desire demon grows strong, then one loses control of oneself. Lust swallows up conscience. That is precisely when, on blood being shed from the head, the demon admits defeat."

Sakha Krishna asked, "About whom are you talking?"

"About myself, about man, about the lust of man. *Sakha*, do you think that I am not a man? That I am a stone?..." Phalguni appeared very excited and stopped in mid-speech.

Sakha laughed just as before. I kept quiet. But my mind rebelled. I wished to ask, "Phalguni, why this play-acting? Is this what I wanted?" But Phalguni was unwell. It was not right to excite him. I kept smouldering within.

In a calm voice Krishna said, "*Sakha!* You are the finest warrior of Aryavart. You are wise, pure in conduct, and conscientious. Therefore, it is for you that fate has created this test. On passing it, you will be able to become the ruler of all Aryavart. What sort of man is he who cannot conquer his own senses? Desire and lust will remain in man. But they must remain within the boundaries fixed by man.; It is through the union of man and woman that creation is ever new, ever beautiful. Then, should the union of man and woman occur irrespective of place, time, person? Man is a slave of pleasure. But through dedicated vows, worship, meditation, the tongue does not slip out of control despite tasty dishes lying before it. However learned and knowledgeable one might be, if the mind is not controlled by the conscience then that learning and knowledge will destroy the world. Phalguni, you have been born for the welfare of the world. Therefore, you are my dear *sakha* too. Does the battle with lust and desire within befit you?"

An inimitable splendour of scorn bloomed on Phalguni's lips. Pouring sarcasm on Krishna he said, "*Sakha*, right from childhood and teenage till now I can see clearly before my eyes your fame, all your deeds. Besides the eight chief queens in Dvaraka, you have thousands of concubines. Slaying Narakasur, providing them refuge with all honour, you have provided them status in society. And here you are advising me about mind, conscience and self-control. After waiting for four years, a single year of married life will be mine. Have you ever thought how these four years will pass?"

Laughing, *sakha* said, "Krishnaa is your chief queen. Other than her you, too, can have a thousand concubines. But remember, even in this self-control is needed. He who is not enslaved by lust despite living in the midst of lovely young women — it is he who in the midst of so many women with a healthy and calm heart, forgetting his own concerns, can muse on the *sakha's* words. Despite being in the water, the lotus leaf is not wet. That is how I am. Do you not know this? You are speaking to me in this fashion before dear *sakhi* Krishnaa! What will she think? It is her thoughts which are to be feared, for she is a poet, and she is emotional. Considering my philandering as truth if she writes of it in poetry, what will be my state? Will I be able to hold my head high in this world?" Phalguni laughed and said, "Let us ask her! It is you who occupy all the pages in her book. I have read them all. For, every poem of hers gives me pleasure. Will you listen?"

Phalguni went on reciting my poems one after another. Listening to poetry in his voice I forgot all anger and hatred. He had not only memorised my poems, they were in his heart. In the words of the poems I, too, was in his heart! How ineffably profound and heavenly was his love for me! Otherwise, would he

146

have been able to remember the poems? Both friends got engaged in discussing poetry. Quietly taking leave I went towards Yudhishthir's room thinking, "Between husband and wife, the meaning of anger and hurt is not lovelessness. This truth every wife ought to realise."

I had thought he had been deliberately unwell for the sake of my company. Knowing this, Phalguni was secretly happy despite being unwell. "Phalguni wants me" — this was no small thing for me. Even the finest woman of Aryavart would take a life-long vow of virginity on the basis of this feeling.

But when Phalguni rejected my service, my nursing, my company then I felt he was doing so in order to hurt me. What better occasion could there be for telling me that he was indifferent to me?

After completing all my work I came to sit by Phalguni for nursing him. He was appearing drowsy. Gently I began pressing his feet. He was startled. Seeing me he shifted his feet. In a detached tone he said, "You here, so late at night?"

"There is no need to count the hours of the night in nursing you", I said softly. Becoming grave he said, "But Yudhishthir will be waiting in the bed-chamber."

"Permission has been granted for nursing till you have recovered."

"But this is unjust of you."

"Why? Service, company, nursing are, after all, the dharma of a wife, the duties of a housewife."

"Above all it is satisfying the husband that is the wife's duty."

"You too are my husand."

"But for the next two years I cannot look upon you as my wife."

"But you can consider me a nurse. A wife is a nurse too."

"But by this, the condition of married life you have prescribed will be broken. It is prohibited to leave Yudhishthir's bed-chamber and spend the night in someone else's. By this, not only you but I too will be guilty of breaking rules. Therefore, Krishnaa! Kindly return to Yudhishthir. It is in this that your welfare lies

147

and mine too." Phalguni's tone sounded like an order. It was full of hurt pride and sarcasm with traces of mockery. My throat choked with grief, hurt and distress. I thought to myself, "why does Phalguni not notice that today discarding the dress of a lover I have come as a nurse? Does he not understand that I cannot pass the night without nursing him?"

Tearfully I said, "A woman is not merely a wife. She is a mother and a sister too. Now I am not your wife, but your mother, your sister. Therefore, it will not be doing injustice to anyone. Nor will the conditions of marriage be violated. And this will make me happy."

Phalguni laughed out loud in scorn. Full of mockery he said, "Your role as mother and sister is also not very slight. Bhim will fall ill every day. Nakul and Sahadev, too, will ask for some service. What will the poor eldest brother do? Other than cursing us, what is left for him? Moreover, with Kunti present, will you assume the role of mother? Duhshala is born in the Kaurav clan yet she is our only sister. The moment she hears of this tomorrow she will arrive. It will not be proper to take her place either. I am waiting for Mother. She will come any time. She will keep sitting by my head. You should not take a share in that joy. Now go, have pity. In your life there is no season of separation, for you are the heroine of five husbands. Lotus-scented Krishnaa, I fold my palms before you. Go away. Do not make me guilty before my brother. Let him not think that I am pretending illness to keep you by my side. At least, let not any shadow fall on the sweet relationship between the brothers because of you."

In an attitude of prayer Phalguni had folded his palms together. It was impossible for me to bear this insult. I did not wish to have a share in anyone's joy, I did not wish to produce division among any. Only a life of peace and quiet, a world filled with husband and children was what I wanted — which is every woman's desire — not a jot more than that. But why was my life growing so very dramatic?

I suppressed the grief and anguish. I hurried out of Phalguni's bed-chamber.

But the doors of Yudhishthir's room were closed. It was very late in the night. Even the stars in Indraprasth's sky were dozing behind clouds.

I was standing alone. On the corridor running along the closed bed-chambers of five husbands, with all the suppressed agony of her heart, stood Yajnaseni. In the dark sky the constellation of the seven sages was shining in the shape of a question mark.

17

Wealth, prosperity, power, fame, friends and relations, husband, son, daughter, wife — in the midst of all this a man does feel the need of at least one empathetic friend who adding joy to joy will enhance bliss a hundredfold, and sharing his grief will reduce the pain. Truly, Govind was precisely one such empathetic friend. On opening up one's heart to a friend, one's heart becomes free, generously open and radiant as the heavens. But Govind was such a mind-knower that it was not necessary to reveal one's mind to him. Simply on seeing him, as at the touch of the morning sun all the petals of a flower open, the mind revealed itself. Nothing remained secret in the heart. His gaze was like the radiance of the sun and the mind like a flower opening!

Therefore, when mental anguish became unbearable, I made the wish for the appearance of Govind. All this silent agony of the mind could not be poured out before anyone else. All the affairs of conjugal life cannot be expressed before everyone. There are some hurts, many feelings, that remain unexpressed throughout life — even before one's own husband. But before Govind I did not know how all secrecy, all hesitation, all gaps vanished — it left me amazed when I thought of it.

That day too Govind understood the moment he looked at me that in some corner of my mind the tears of an unexpressed pain were being shed. He proposed, "*Sakhi*, come, let us leave for the forest on the banks of the river Shatadru for some entertainment. We shall have a forest picnic. *Sakha* too is recovering and it will divert him as well. Confined at home, Phalguni is appearing somewhat irritable and depressed."

I understood that this entire arrangement was for changing my state of mind. I did not refuse. I did want the open sky, free

150

breeze blowing and greenery, to lose myself for some time in the vibrant beauty of nature.

The chariots were made ready for the five Pandavs, *sakha* Krishna and myself. Some of my attendants came along on this journey to the Shatadru.

Possibly the spring had got to know of our arrival. The season had already completed its toilet, with the Shatadru waters as its mirror. The forest was heavy with the fragrance of Ashok, Champa, honeysuckle and innumerable nameless flowers. On the forest pathways was spread a carpet of Vakul flowers. The restless breeze was ready to welcome us with the scent of perfume. It was broadcasting news of Krishna's coming. In the sunlight, the forest had prepared an offering of fresh blue lotuses in the gleaming tray of silvery waters. The mango groves there were waiting for us, spreading out their cool pandal of mango blossoms. We halted there.

I forgot myself in the ineffable beauty of the forest. I did not remember that I was princess Draupadi, great queen Krishnaa of Indraprasth, Panchali of the five Pandavs. All my grief, anguish, depression and regrets were washed away by pure nature. Enchanted, I lost myself in the love of nature.

Yudhishthir with some attendants left for ascertaining the condition of the forest-dwellers living on the banks of the pure waters of the Shatadru. Bhim went off into the jungle to seek ripe fruits for the afternoon repast. Nakul took the horses to frisk about in the forest. Sahadev sat down in solitude on the river-bank to calculate the auspicious time for *sakha* Krishna's departure for Dvaraka. Now that Yudhishthir had established himself in Indraprasth, Krishna ought to get back to Dvaraka. Kunti had desired that on an auspicious date and time Krishna should leave Indraprasth for Dvaraka. Therefore, Sahadev was calculating.

In the mango grove were both friends, Krishna and Arjun. My attendants, like restless teenagers, left to gather flowers in the forest, flitting about in the midst of bees and butterflies.

Offering betel-leaf to *sakha* I said, "*Sakha!* What was the difficulty in staying on in Indraprasth for a few days longer? Of course, eight queens will be waiting in Dvaraka." Phalguni burst out laughing, "Not just eight queens. The thousands of wives in the inner apartments of Dvaraka will be wasting away in anguish at the separation from *sakha*. The number of days that we could keep *sakha* back in Indraprasth — is that slight? If we keep him here too long, will they not curse us?"

Sakha glanced at me and laughed, "Hearing his remark haven't you decided I am Aryavart's greatest philanderer? Although there is truth underlying *sakha's* words. In the inner apartments of Dvaraka besides eight queens I do have many wives, but there was no way out other than this. Narakasur had raped a thousand virgins and imprisoned them. Narakasur's arrogance and tyranny crossed all limits. Then for establishing peace in his kingdom I killed him. Freeing those unfortunate princesses, I informed their parents. But their fathers, who never tired of complaining of the misfortune of their daughters, would not agree to take them back — not even one. Rather they sent messages, "Suicide is the only path open. After so many days in the custody of Narakasur, no prince — not even the humblest man will take their hand in marriage. If they return to their fathers' kingdoms it will only bring disrepute to their kingdoms. In such circumstances, there is no alternative to suicide."

"Oh! Such injustice!" I exclaimed spontaneously.

Sympathetically *sakha* said, "It is because of that very injustice that Devi Vaidehi had to face trial by fire repeatedly. Ultimately, she took refuge in the womb of Mother Earth."

"Then?" asked Arjun. He used to enjoy very much listening to accounts of Krishna's heroism and nobility.

Sakha continued, "They found that there was no alternative to suicide and approached me for refuge. In distressed tones they said, 'O Krishna, the delight of the gopis, you have thrown us into grave danger by slaying Narakasur. On this earth he was our only refuge. Now, after his death, we have nowhere to go. What shall we do now?" Then I invited all the princes of the world and asked them to marry these princesses. If only even one of them had stepped forward! But none did. Having lived under the control of another man, the women were all soiled. So everyone turned down my request. Distressed, the princesses told me, 'O Krishna, you are our life-giver, our saviour! If you do not save us, you shall be held guilty for our suicide.' I reassured them that they could find shelter in my kingdom. There would be no shortage of food and clothing. All amenities would be made available throughout life.

Abruptly, I protested against *sakha's* words, "Sakha! Can anyone live just on getting food, clothing and a roof? For living, it is necessary to have social status, respect and everyone's sympathy, support. Even in Narakasur's prison food, clothes and accommodation were not lacking. Even then people were sympathetic towards them, respected them. In such circumstances, will food and clothing bring them back their social status? What remedy did you find for the injustice that society does to woman?"

Sakha laughed at my accusation, "The last scene of the drama is the most romantic. A princess like you had asked me this very question. Offering herself at my feet she pleaded, 'O Krishna! By accepting us, save our honour.' Then I realised that it was my duty to accept them as my wives. By this the world's male society would realise that it is not the body of a woman that was the woman; that a woman has a soul too. Though imprisoned in the body, the soul does not become a prisoner. Even if the body is thrown into stinking hell, its sin does not rub off on the soul. Just because the body has been forcibly enjoyed the soul is not fallen. If the soul finds the means of salvation and follows the path of light, then it is without any mark, free, pure. I have respected the immaculate souls of those thousand princesses, married them, accepted them. Where souls unite, bodily relations become a minor matter. Therefore, if I stay back in Indraprasth my wives will not curse you. I have not married them out of lust to enjoy their bodies. I loved their souls and they are all lovers of my soul. Those who cannot understand the nature of my love call me a debauch."

From long back I had been in love with the soul of the perfect lover, Krishna. Now I was regretting in secret why that

Narakasur had not imprisoned me along with those thousand virgins!

Phalguni voiced exactly the opposite of my feelings in jest. Smiling he said, "*Sakha!* The entire news of the world is with you. Will you kindly tell us which are the other demons who have kept lakhs of princesses imprisoned? This very moment I shall slay them and accepting the beautiful souls of those lovely women I shall accommodate them in my inner apartments. Then there will be no need to agonise over separation from Krishnaa."

Sakha laughed at this jest. But there was a hidden barb for me in Arjun's words which, he too, made out. Looking calmly at Arjun he said, "Many lovely women will arrive in a hero's life and in your life, too, this will happen. I have faith that even if a thousand beautiful princesses are in your inner apartments, yet you will ever burn in the anguish of separation from Krishnaa. In your life none can fill the place of Krishnaa."

Arjun asked, "The solution for this pain?"

In a calm voice *sakha* said, "Try to contact the soul of Krishnaa. *Sakha,* there you will see separation has no place. The union of Ramchandra and Vaidehi was a union of souls. That is why, despite remaining separated throughout life from each other, Ram was not consumed by the anguish of separation. Otherwise, he could not have established Ramrajya in Ayodhya. Despite being separated from Janaki, he never discarded work, never neglected any duty towards the kingdom. Therefore, in all Aryavart he is respected as the Man of Honour."

Who knows whether Arjun accepted *sakha's* advice or not, for he joked again, "Then I shall have to go along with you to Dvaraka. Living there I will have to learn the love of soul for soul. You will teach me. Returning, I shall begin a new conjugal life with Krishnaa. To this Krishnaa will have no objection. Krishnaa too..."

Krishna laughed and interrupted, "*Sakha!* The love of soul for soul is not visible to the eyes. Only the soul can see that. It is only by experience and sensitivity that you can learn the technique of that love. Therefore, for this it is not necessary for you to go to

Dvaraka in search of conjugal harmony. Do not imagine that by establishing a capital of the kingdom in Indraprasth your duties have been completed. This is but the beginning..."

Arjun looked annoyed. Since childhood the Pandavs had been battling misfortune and injustice. At every step their life, wealth and honour had been endangered. The fatherless five brothers had grown up under the protection of a mother's sacrifice, dedication and ideals. Now the foundation stone of a peaceful life had been laid in Indraprasth. And Krishna was saying that this was only the beginning of the battle! Krishna was gifted with divine foresight. Was he hearing the footsteps of even more conflict and battle in the lives of the Pandavs?

Like a humble child Arjun asked, "*Sakha!* Yudhishthir should have been the king of all Hastinapur. For avoiding conflict and bloodshed we have remained content with just half the kingdom. We transformed an infertile, undeveloped, jungle like Khandavprasth into a veritable heaven with your help. Yet there is no end to conflict and battle in our lives! Are you worried?"

Krishna became grave. His face changed. It glowed with the splendour of wisdom and superhuman power. I could clearly see a radiant halo around his face. As though enchanted, Phalguni and I lost ourselves in Krishna's halo.

Krishna said, "The day when on the pretext of avoiding conflict the blind king Dhritarashtra split a kingdom into two, made two capitals, Hastinapur and Indraprasth — the seeds of conflict were sown right from then. Dhritarashtra was not able to understand that even on infertile land dedication, application and concentration can create lovely gardens on the strength of righteous thoughts and virtuous acts. Therefore, he was satisfied that by granting infertile Varanavat to his nephews he had displayed magnanimity. But when the prosperity of Indraprasth becomes a matter of envy for the Kauravs, then their minds will be filled with enmity for all Indraprasth. And in this manner, lack of peace and contentment will ever prevail between both capitals. In such a situation, how can the Pandavs pass their days in contented happiness?"

155

Phalguni was astonished and pained by Krishna's explanation. In a voice full of complaint he said, "*Sakha*, you are far-seeing. You know this will happen. Yet, why did you accept the proposal of Dhritarashtra?"

Shri Krishna cast a sidelong glance at Phalguni. On his curved lips a mysterious smile was lending even greater beauty to his radiant face. Softly he said, "Sometimes, despite knowing everything, some decisions have to be taken. For the sake of some nobler cause losses have to be borne on the way, sacrifices have to be accepted. The division of Aryavart was the first oblation in accomplishing this nobler aim. If the kingdom of injustice does not remain, dharma will be established — this no one will understand. For the establishment of justice and dharma, some time is needed for the rule of the Kauravs in Hastinapur. Let the public experience and compare the social life and cultural development of Hastinapur and Indraprasth. It is only then that public opinion will take shape in favour of dharma. Dharma does not need advertisement and publicity. It needs the experience of life and introspection. That is why I accepted the proposal of Dhritarashtra."

Overwhelmed, Phalguni and I went on listening to the amazing strategy of *sakha* Krishna for establishing dharma. In deep thought, Phalguni said, "*Sakha*, Hastinapur is a prosperous and developed area. Indraprasth has been able to equal it. As a consequence of the partition of the kingdom, an undeveloped area has swiftly become a developed and prosperous territory. Therefore, why two, if even four capitals are established what is the harm? Then different areas of the kingdom will be lit up with the light of progress. This, after all, is the aim of your establishment of dharma. That the entire people of the country enjoy happiness and prosperity, is the fundamental intention."

Krishna laughed, "*Sakha*, in your body, if each separate part is healthy, free of illness, powerful and skilled in weapon-craft, yet with the help of one or two limbs you cannot become a master of ~chery. Without the integrated application of the entire body —
~ght, awareness, sight, hearing, hands, fingers, palms — even

an arrow cannot be shot. Without establishing harmony among all the senses and limbs a man cannot even pluck a flower from a tree. Similarly, despite all areas of a kingdom being developed, in the absence of unity and harmony, the future of the country will be shrouded in deep darkness. Every area of a kingdom might be developed, but if it splits into parts, then the sun of its independence sets in the horizon. When civil war breaks out, external enemies get full scope to conquer the country. If the five Pandavs unite they can conquer the whole world. But if they split their defeat is as clear as daylight. Without Arjun and Bhim the heroism of the Pandavs will remain a matter of mockery just as without Yudhishthir or Sahadev the country will be deprived of knowledge of right and wrong and the foresight essential for governance. Of this, there is no doubt. My chief duty is establishment of dharma and national unity in Aryavart. My vow will be accomplished by the efforts of the Pandavs. Therefore, in your life there is no place for inertia and idleness."

Sakha's goal was most noble. But for accomplishing that goal the Pandavs would have to fight injustice, adharma and untruth all through life. Who knows victory would be whose? Suddenly I shivered with the apprehension of something inauspicious. I thought: "Why is all of Hastinapur necessary for us? Happiness, joy, prosperity are not wanting in Indraprasth. Voluntarily citizens of Hastinapur are leaving their ancestral homes to live in Indraprasth, drawn by the justice and good governance of the Pandavs. Let the Kauravs remain in Hastinapur. What is that to us? By fighting others and destroying peace in our own lives what will we gain? Surely *sakha* is not deliberately pushing the Pandavs towards conflict?"

Ma Kunti said *sakha* Krishna was able to plumb the heart's secrets. I had no doubt regarding the truth of Mother's words. Truly, Krishna knew my mind. He looked at me penetratingly, "*Sakhi!* However much you might be educated, sometimes you become self-centred like an ordinary woman. Therefore, the idea of using the Pandavs to accomplish my goal did not please you. But, only think, lakhs of men and women, birds and animals, insects and worms are born and die every moment. The aim of everyone's death is one, but the goal of everyone's birth is not the same. Some are born to live for themselves, some are born for the sake of the oppressed, the poor, the fallen. He who lives for himself invites death. He who lives for the world, despite dying does not fall into the clutches of death. These are the two types of lives in the world. Just understand that the Kauravs and the Pandavs have come into the world with two types of lives. You are the inspiration of the Pandavs. You are Yajnaseni. Why is there any hesitation within you regarding revolution, conflict and sacrifice?"

Out of sheer shame I flushed red. Truly, *sakha* Krishna was a great problem. How he got to know everything in one's mind! Who knew when one might take a false step before him?

Phalguni was lost in thought. With bowed head I was cursing myself — "*Chheeh!* Why such selfishness in me? An ordinary man belongs to his wife, parents, family. But the hero belongs to the country, the people, the society and the world. My five husbands are all heroes. Then how shall I keep them bound for my happiness only?"

Suddenly a smothered hiss escaped *sakha's* lips. Suddenly I saw *sakha's* lotus-petal-like fingers were tinged with blood.

Concerned, I leaned towards *sakha*. Phalguni came up from where he was sitting and asked, "What happened? How did you have this cut?"

With a smile Krishna said, "It is the wound left by the Sudarsan chakra. Sometimes it reminds me that without bloodying my own life I cannot save the world from bloodshed. Look, that innocent tribal boy would have just been dead. At the right moment Sudarshan did its work. Killing the savage tiger, it is coming back. I released it too swiftly and it touched a finger. Blood spurted out. Anyhow, the child is safe."

How petty we are before the nobility of Krishna! I was thinking, "*Sakha's* heart is ever agitated in the cause of the oppressed, the fallen, the injured. He is engaged in sweet conversation with us, yet he is able to see the danger facing that boy so far away! We can see nothing!"

The wound was clearly visible on Krishna's finger. It had not stopped bleeding. Phalguni worriedly said, "Krishnaa! Catch hold of *sakha's* wound tightly so that it stops bleeding. I am getting some medicine", and he disappeared among the vines and leaves. I kept hold of *sakha's* finger tightly. With his eyes shut, Krishna said in a soft voice, "Krishnaa! If I had known that the touch of affection was so sweet and cool, then I would have cut my finger testing the edge of Sudarshan everyday!"

I was not amused with this jest. The bleeding did not stop. Rather, it increased. I did not know what to do. Quickly I tore a strip off my *sari's anchal* and tied a bandage on the wound. On hearing the sound of the tearing, Maya arrived running, I did not know from where, "Maharani! What is this that you have done? Such a costly *sari* torn! Phalguni is coming anyway. The blood would have stopped after applying medicine."

I got annoyed at Maya's words. "*Chheeh*, Maya! You love Krishna so much: in case anyone disturbs him you stand as a barrier in-between. You were his dear attendant. And today, after becoming my companion, such attachment to a petty *sari!* Compared to a single drop of human blood, the valuable things of the world are of no consequence. Moreover, this is not the blood of any ordinary person. It is Shri Krishna's blood, the blood of the noblest human being in the world. I tore the sari — and because of this petty matter you talk like this! What is so great about it?"

With a wicked smile Maya said, "Maharani, just as Shri Krishna's blood is not that of an ordinary man, similarly this *sari* of yours is not an ordinary *sari*. Of course, for Indraprasth's queen a *sari* is nothing of importance. But this *sari* is the symbol of your happiness, safety and honour. On the day the assembly hall of Indraprasth was inaugurated, the five husbands had presented it to you. Wearing this *sari* you had sat with Maharaj Yudhishthir at the fire-altar and had been anointed in the assembly hall on the throne. This *sari* is supposed to be kept in safe custody. *Saris* worn on auspicious occasions are not to be torn up

159

or burnt or even given away as a gift to anyone. Yet, without weighing the matter up you tore it with your own hands and by tying a strip around Krishna's finger even gifted it to him. I hope it is not an inauspicious omen for the future?"

Maya's words awakened in me the foreboding natural to any ordinary woman. But the very next moment I controlled myself. Smiling I said, "Maya, from childhood till now he who has at every step helped in the security, happiness, prosperity and welfare of my husbands — if any valuable thing be sacrificed for him, then it will only be auspicious. I need not have any fear. If anything ill results from this, then I cannot believe that while he is there I shall be in danger. Therefore, if anything ill should occur, it is he who will take care of it. Why do you break your head over this?"

Laughing, Maya said, "I feel that no one other than a friend's wife can make such a sacrifice. Even Rukmini and Satyabhama would not tear the *sari* worn by them on a sacred occasion for a mere drop of blood. Now bound in the affection of a friend's wife, Shri Krishna has forgotten even the city of Dvaraka and his wives."

Maya's wicked joke! I felt like laughing. Carefully tending with affection Krishna's delicate hand I shivered. Oh! How fortunate was I today!

I did not even notice when Phalguni arrived with medicines. I had lost myself. I was blessed having found an occasion to provide the meanest service to Krishna, the best of all men. I remembered nothing when I took Krishna's hand, touched my head with it, expressed my heart's gratitude, thanks and good wishes. Phalguni was laughing and saying, "*Sakha!* is it not your duty to save some affection and good wishes for this unfortunate? Is it not unjust to pour out all good wishes into Krishnaa's *anchal?*"

Laughing, Krishna said, "I am sorry, *sakha!* Unnecessarily you took pains for me. Not only has the bleeding stopped by *sakhi's* affectionate touch, but even the sign of the wound has disappeared. I cannot take off this bandage. The sweet scent of *sakhi's* affection is coming from it. You know so well that pure love, the heart's affection — it is these that are the nectar of immortality. Then what will medicines do?"

The medicines in Phalguni's hand fell to the ground. My torn *anchal* was fluttering in the breeze. Krishna, keeping the bandaged hand on his breast, was looking at Phalguni with loving eyes and smiling. He whispered, *"Sakha!* What is the need of flowers? You know I am mad about perfume. If any flower blooms in any corner of the world and its fragrance is offered to me, I readily accept it. Perfume is pure. The fragrance of memories remains alive in the depths of the mind. And the memory of this day will keep my entire life fragrant. It will keep flooding me with limitless bliss. Some day this debt of Krishnaa's shall have to be repaid. Therefore, do not be jealous of my memories."

18

If *sakha* was not around loneliness became oppressive. Not only I, but Arjun too felt this.

Krishna returned to Dvaraka. Normal life continued in Indraprasth, but the absence of Krishna was making Arjun lonely and was frustrating me.

The celebration of completing a year of life with Yudhishthir would take place a week later. I would lose patience with Bhim's enthusiasm at times which would throw me into difficulties. Arjun was immersed in the pursuit of both weapons and scriptures. I was counting the days. The day of uniting with Arjun was drawing near. A year and a week later I would be able to begin life together with the hero who won me. Then I would make him understand that in household life too there was need of control and rules. It was observing that rule that this year-long agreement had taken place. I was confident that once I got close to him there would no more be any hurt, misunderstanding and anger between us. He would be able to touch my soul and I would be able to lose myself in his soul.

How long drawn-out were the moments of waiting! Till then I had been engrossed in waiting for the day of uniting with Arjun, as though forgetting myself in a dream. Each one of my five husbands except Arjun had more than one wife. Therefore, his entire love was my due. None woud have a share in it. It was this that was the supreme desire of every woman. Therefore, it was natural that my attraction for Arjun was somewhat greater.

It was as I was counting the days for union with Arjun that all my dreams were shattered by Arjun himself.

That day Yudhishthir had called for me. Leaving the task of pressing Mother's feet, I went to Yudhishthir. He was resting. There was but a week left in completing the year-long term with him as husband and wife. Therefore, Yudhishthir would not let me be far off even for a moment. He would say, "Krishnaa, you are the source of my inspiration. If you are with me, I am the lord of dharma and if you are at a distance I fear that perhaps I may slip from the path of dharma. It is not the attraction of your body that is important to me. Important is your practise of dharma, your pure thoughts. I wish you could remain mine, only mine..."

Yudhishthir grew grave hearing his own words, "Now that the time of separating from you is drawing near, see how an improper thought flashed into my mind! Truly, we five brothers have one mind, one life. You are Yajnaseni. Unification and the establishment of dharma are the aims for which you have been born. How can you remain just mine?"

Yudhishthir was lying on the bed in the resting room. Placing his feet in my lap I was gently pressing them. I was profoundly aware of the good fortune of having the opportunity of serving him thus.

Suddenly Phalguni burst into the room like a gust of wind. He was looking extremely frustrated. With lowered head he went ahead, picked up the weapons lying in a corner and dashed out. He did not lift up his eyes either to me or to Yudhishthir.

I was filled with embarrassment. Before I could even arrange my dress, Phalguni had disappeared.

In a detached tone Yudhishthir said, "It seems weapons became necessary all of a sudden. However, with arms in hand Phalguni will be able to manage any situation."

Not only Phalguni, all five Pandavs were altruists. Luxury, dress, happiness, wealth were not at all essential for them. Despite being rulers, they shared the sorrows of the poor and the sorrowful, the oppressed and the fallen. It was for this reason that they had been able to conquer the hearts of the subjects. I wondered what danger had come upon the subjects suddenly! Phalguni would have gone to rid them of that peril. To leap even into fire for that was the quality of Phalguni!

While massaging Yudhishthir's feet I was praising Phalguni and pouring out the respect and honour in which I held him. Just

163

then Maya gave the news, "Phalguni is waiting outside. He wishes to have an audience with Yudhishthir."

Yudhishthir came out. Behind him, I. The curtain was rising before my eyes on yet another gooseflesh-raising scene. Phalguni was standing in the guise of a *brahmachari*. Surrounding him stood the other Pandavs and Mother Kunti.

Surprised, Yudhishthir said, "What is the matter? Why is Arjun in this garb?" With folded palms Arjun said, "Permit me to leave, brother! I have deliberately broken the rule. When Krishnaa is with her husband, should any other Pandav enter that room, he shall have to undergo exile in the forest as a celibate for twelve years. This was the decision arrived at in the presence of Maharshi Narad. It is for the sake of discipline and law that we have made such conditions. Today it is in conformity with those conditions that I am proceeding on twelve years of exile in the forest. With a happy heart, bid me goodbye."

Yudhishthir was pained. I was absolutely stunned. Who had imagined that the conditions that had been laid down for the happiness and peace of conjugal life would ultimately fill my life with so much unhappiness and disturbance? And then it had to be Phalguni who would break the rule and go into exile! I stood there with a broken heart. I could see no way out.

In a voice heavy with sadness Yudhishthir said, "Arjun, you have not committed any mistake. Surely you were forced to enter our rest-room because of some nobler cause. Neither of us took exception to this. Moreover, there is nothing improper if a younger brother enters the room while the elder brother is talking to his wife. Therefore, there is no need for exile."

"Phalguni had gone to get back a Brahmin's cow stolen by some thief and fell into this danger!" Bhim said, mocking Arjun's naivete.

I was thinking: "Why did Arjun really do this? If the Brahman had made this request to him, he could have requested Bhim too. To catch the thief and get the cow back was hardly a difficult job for Bhim! And if he had compelled Phalguni to do it, could he not find weapons anywhere in the entire kingdom except by entering our private chamber without permission? And if those weapons were absolutely indispensable, he could have given advance notice. Maya was waiting outside the room. Through her he could have taken our prior permission. Why did he not do so?"

After these thoughts I became quite sure that Phalguni was deliberately taking revenge on me. A year later the time would have come for uniting with him. And now! He was voluntarily adopting a twelve-year exile. Yudhishthir was trying to stop him, but he would not listen.

Phalguni appeared somewhat angry at Yudhishthir's words. Accusingly he said, "You yourself keep saying that breaking rules is a grave offence. And it is you who are asking me to commit an offence!" Calmly Yudhishthir said, "After all, it is for helping a Brahmin that you entered my room. There is no offence in breaking a rule for doing good to others."

Demolishing Yudhishthir's argument Phalguni said, "To do wrong for right, walking on the path of sin to earn merit, to break rules for doing good to others — all are sins in a way. Therefore, I do not wish to incur sin. Forgive me. I shall have to go into exile."

Phalguni took leave dressed as a celibate brahmin. Everyone was praising him. Because of his dedication to the vow, flowers were being sprinkled on him. Ramchandra had gone to the forest for keeping his father's vow, but his wife and his younger brother were with him. Now Phalguni was going into the forest for having broken a vow. Alone! By going into exile he was acquiring nobility and he would earn fame. I, too, could follow him like Sita and alleviate his sufferings and sorrow. Alone with Phalguni in the midst of nature's beauty I could forget the burden of life. Could I not go into the forest with him? If I went my fame, too, would increase. Happiness would increase. If *sati* Sita could follow the path of her husband, how was it difficult for me?

I too became a *sannyasini;* took off the eight types of jewellery and put on ornaments of flowers, wore white clothing, left my hair open and put bunches of forest flowers in the free tresses. Phalguni would come to take leave of me. Then I would convince him of the logic of taking me with him. How would he be able to leave without me?

Ramchandra had taken Sita with him. I was recalling the arguments Sita had put forward and weighing the consequences.

Maya was astonished to see me in this dress. She said, "Maharani! Living in the palace of Indraprasth in this dress!"

Laughing I replied, "Maya! This is not the dress of the royal palace but of the leaf-hut. I have decided to roam the forests with Phalguni. Will you accompany me?"

Maya said jokingly, "Maharani! How many forest-dwelling ascetics will leave all their penance seeing you in this dress? First of all Phalguni himself will end up breaking the twelve-year long vow of celibacy. Is that what you want?"

In my heart of hearts I wished Maya's words had become true and Phalguni's twelve-year vow was broken. For all the days that he had suffered in separation from me I would, for an equal length of time, give him happiness with heart and soul and make my own life blessed too. Why should a guiltless hero like Phalguni suffer such a stern sentence?

Phalguni arrived. He stood before my door too. But from the outside he said, "Krishnaa, farewell! We will meet again after twelve years. If you are ever in danger, send word to *sakha.* If you keep trust in him, danger will never come near you."

I came out before him. In a firm voice I said, "I too will accompany you to the forest. This is my decision."

Phalguni kept looking at me with dreamy eyes. Then, controlling himself in the next instant he said, "We have obeyed many of your decisions. Krishnaa! By what logic can this decision be accepted?"

I understood Phalguni's hint. The year-long condition of our marriage was my decision. Phalguni reminded me of that. I was hurt by his words, but protested, "To follow the husband is the dharma of the wife. *Sati* Sita had gone into the forest following lord Shri Ram. That I should similarly go into the forest with you is just."

Laughing, Phalguni said, "*Sati* Sita and you! What would she have done if she had not followed her only husband? But you have five husbands!"

Phalguni's statement pierced through me like an arrow. I wished I could weep. But no, weeping was a sign of weakness. Where was there any weakness in accepting five husbands that I should weep? Firmly I said, "I did not accept five husbands on my own. So, why are you bringing up that topic? You are my husband. If you are king, I shall be queen. If you are a forest-dweller then so shall I be. There is no alternative to this."

Phalguni looked grave. In a level tone he said, "Look Krishnaa! In the first place, despite being my wife at this time you are actually Yudhishthir's partner in dharma. It is this that is the condition of our domestic life. This condition all of us have accepted. Today it is this condition that I have violated. Therefore, I am an offender before you. To do penance I have taken a vow of celibacy and also of twelve years in the forest. If she against whom I have committed the crime should accompany me into the forest, then how will the penance be accomplished? In fact, the guilt will be all the greater. Do you want that for all my life I should remain guilty before you and Elder Brother and ultimately go to hell? Is this what you want?"

Where did I have any words left to answer? I was shot by my own arrow. The rules I had made for governing our conjugal life and for happiness had become the cause of my sorrow!

Maya understood my helplessness. Taking my side she said, "Maharani has pardoned your offence. Otherwise why would she have got ready to share your sorrow as forest-dweller? Therefore, in taking her along there will be no violation of the conditions of penance. If the husband becomes a *sannyasin* then for the wife to become a *sannyasini* is sanctioned by the scriptures. What is the bar to this?"

Phalguni laughed and said, "Even if I become a hermit, what is the bar to Krishnaa remaining queen of Indraprasth and glorifying the inner chambers? There is no injustice in this. Yudhishthir is the king and the three other husbands of Krishnaa are the brothers of the king of Indraprasth. Therefore, with four husbands remaining kings, if one becomes a hermit, why should Krishnaa become a *sannyasini*? The welfare of the group is greater than that of the individual. In the history of Bharat so far it is the will of the people that has prevailed. It is Krishnaa's good fortune that even on my becoming a hermit she can remain a queen. If Krishnaa had married me alone then she would not have become Maharani and would also have suffered from time to time because of my bad luck."

Maya said, "Why are you deliberately hurting her?"

Pained, Phalguni said, "If my words have hurt Krishnaa, then pardon me."

Stunned, I looked at Phalguni. From his side Phalguni provided explanation, "With four husbands present Krishnaa cannot follow me. She is not mine alone. She is of us all. Who am I to take her away? That despite this Krishnaa has decided to share my sorrow is no small comfort to me. In this I shall forget the sorrow of forest-exile."

These intimte, soft words of Phalguni, like clouds melting into rain by the touch of monsoon winds, succeeded in drawing out the tears from within me. Seeing them Phalguni said, "With four husbands present, what is your sorrow? In danger, Bhim is there. In a dilemma, Yudhishthir will show the way. With Nakul and Sahadev the time will get by in fun and games. Over and above all, with *sakha* Krishna present, what worry do you have? Whenever you summon him, he will arrive. Remain happy, Krishnaa! Now give me leave!"

I wished I could lay my head on Phalguni's chest and weep my heart out; with all the conviction I could muster, tell him, "Phalguni! Without you how will I live for twelve years in Indraprasth?" But I did not do anything of that sort. For, Phalguni would laugh at my words, would again raise the topic of four husbands. Would he believe that in the midst of all prosperity and comfort it was Phalguni who enveloped me? How would I make him understand that instead of the royal throne of Indraprasth it was the throne of Phalguni's heart that was my heart's desire?

Watching him silently I kept thinking of so many things. I did not know what others would say, but it seemed to me that Phalguni had deliberately violated the conditions in order to go far away. His intention was to punish me. He knew that there was no greater punishment for me in the whole world.

Bidding farewell he said, "Now give me leave, Krishnaa! If I live, we shall meet again after twelve years. After stepping into the jungle who knows what dangers may come?"

With anxiety, worry and foreboding my face paled. I wanted to fall at Phalguni's feet and say, "Reject me and go into exile. Rather than die every moment for twelve years in anxiety and worry it is better to die at your feet." I sensed that noticing my sudden paleness Phalguni was secretly glad. As though he were saying all this in order to distress me. Now I could understand the entire plan he had made. By putting forward arguments, I had prevented his going to Dvaraka with Krishna. Now was this how he would manage that?

I hardened myself — "Aryavart's finest hero Phalguni speaks of unknown dangers in the forest! I am hearing this for the first time. I am sure that Shri Krishna's *sakha* and the finest of warriors, Phalguni, is capable of conquering any danger. There is no power on earth that can defeat him. May Shri Krishna bring you back safely. However much the danger might be in these twelve years, I shall not summon Krishna. For, if you should summon him exactly at the same time then where will he go? Whose cry will he answer? Therefore, only remember that Krishna is with you."

Phalguni softened. In a tender voice he said, "Thanks! Krishnaa, you have completed your duty. I too shall fulfil my duty towards you. Till the year of my turn for living with you comes, I shall send *sakha* a message to give you company. If he is near you, my absence will not distress you. The days will pass comfortably and peacefully. Wherever I might be in the forest, if *sakha* is near you, I will be at peace."

I was silent. What else could I do? I had become dumb. So much was left unsaid.

169

Phalguni caught hold of my hand — "You are learned, wise. What advice can I give you? Still, will you listen to a few words? Walking on the path of dharma Elder Brother becomes very rigid. Do not fall into misapprehension. Do not hurt him. Never anger Bhim. Do not neglect Nakul, Sahadev. And above all is Mother. Let there be no relaxation in performing duties towards her. All through life she has borne, for our sake, grief and pain, hurt and insults. Worship her like your favourite deity. In my absence should *sakha* ever arrive, do not let any flaw occur in extending him hospitality. As for me, never worry at all. Right from birth itself a prince has to battle against exile, danger, starvation, poverty, want and fate. God willing, I shall return. Now give me leave."

Each word of Phalguni's was welcome, inspiring. He mentioned each and every one. But what about me? If a woman was learned or wise did no one think of her? Was there no affection, sympathy, for her in anyone? Was she stone, a lifeless piece of sculpture?

My eyes filled with tears; the throat got choked. Silently I kept nodding to what he said. A moment before he set forth after taking leave I managed to ask him, "Whether anyone else knows or not, at least tell me this much before going that only for punishing me on the pretext of needing weapons you had entered Yudhishthir's room. No weapon was available anywhere in Indraprasth — this I cannot accept. Forest-dwelling hermits are truthful. And if you should speak false before becoming a forest-dweller then it will be a hindrance to your penance, this you also know."

Phalguni looked at me; a happiness filled with compassion, pain and anguish in his eyes. On his lips a slight smile — "I wanted to punish — you have understood that! Because of this, the twelve years of exile will become meaningful."

Even though I should suffer! In punishing me he would find happiness — in this thought, waiting for Phalguni's return, twelve years would go by.

19

Time passes. But, it never ends. The body gets used to bearing grief, however much that might be. The sun rises and sets. Day after day passes. I wondered after how many risings and settings Phalguni would return.

More than a year of the forest exile had passed. In the meantime a year of conjugal life with Bhim had been completed. Now the sweet domestic life with Phalguni would have begun. He was a forest dweller. Therefore, it was Bhim's wish that I should spend another year with him. His argument was: if five persons are responsible by turn to take charge of any valuable thing, and if after a particular time the designated person does not turn up, then that precious gem remains with the earlier holder. From that point of view, in the absence of Arjun I ought to remain another year with Bhim. But my vow was that I would remain celibate, a *brahmacharini*. The type of life that the wife should lead if the husband was far away — precisely that type of unadorned, pure life would I lead.

Bhim was red with fury! As his share of food was the largest, similarly he did not wish to let go the chance of having me too more than the others. But I was firm regarding my resolve. In anger, Bhim went off to my co-wife Hidimba. What control did I have over that?

For a year I remained a dedicated *brahmacharini*. I lived on fruits and maintained celibacy, full of hurt because my husband would remain for twelve years in the forest. Could I not live for a year unadorned?

With Maya and Nitambini I stayed in a hut in the garden. Every morning after bathing in the Yamuna I would perform pooja and complete the other rituals. Then I would prepare food for Mother and the Pandavs. Merit is not earned by neglecting one's duties and performing rituals alone. The whole day I would fast, before sunset bathe again in the Yamuna and take some fruit. At night, I would rest lying on a bed of grass in the leaf-hut. I used to pray to God, "Wherever Phalguni may be, may he be happy! May every difficulty of his be mitigated!"

News of Phalguni would sometimes be available from the divine sage Narad. Along with Phalguni, some brahmins and ascetics were also living in the forest. Building an *ashram* on the banks of the Ganga, Arjun and the other ascetics were passing their time. I was pained all the more by his strict penance, and felt guilty. Loving me, Arjun was deliberately undergoing difficulties. Sometimes I would think, should any heavenly nymph dance before Arjun and enchant him, I would not be jealous of that beauty; I would be grateful. Then I would think, perhaps my wish was useless. For, when I could not break his vow, then what other woman was there in the world who could do so? If Arjun did not undergo hardship during the forest life, and lived in comfort, then longing for him I would not have wasted away thus. But he had acted in this fashion so that I should suffer for his sake. Then how could I be at peace?

The divine sage Narad arrived after many days with news of Phalguni. Noticing my ascetic garb, he smiled to himself and said, "Daughter of Drupad, now you might as well leave the garden hut and return to the apartments! What is the need of all that any more?"

Anxiously I enquired, "Divine sage! Is Phalguni well?"

"What news can there be of Phalguni other than that he is well?" I was reassured. Sitting in the courtyard of the hut, Narad said, "Phalguni is a hero. Despite being dressed as an ascetic, wherever he sets foot he establishes his supremacy. In every kingdom he is receiving rare and varied gifts and honours."

I was thinking, with those gifts our home would be decorated, its beauty would be enhanced. What might those gifts be?

Narad understood. Laughing, he said, "Krishnaa! Man's desires never die. Even after decorating one's home with every good thing in the world, the mind remains empty. The more it

172

gets, the desire to have more increases. Therefore, the greater the number of things Phalguni receives, your desires, attachment, illusion and along with that grief and want, will increase. Therefore, do not think about what Phalguni has received. Perhaps that might bring you grief."

"Bring me grief!" In anxiety I grew pale.

In a gentle voice the divine sage said, "As it is, you are no ordinary princess. You are special. You have noticed many wives in the private apartments of your father and your brother. Save Phalguni, your other husbands have more than one wife. This is a king's glory. Therefore, even while living in the forest should Phalguni, on account of his valour, acquire lovely princesses, you ought to consider that your glory. Though Phalguni should take a hundred wives, you are his first, his dearest. Now you will have the opportunity of establishing your pre-eminence among them and be able to become even dearer to Phalguni."

I was silent, not showing any agitation. I might be Phalguni's first wife, but I will not be the first woman in his life to share with him the bliss of conjugal life, to share the experience of blissful union and separation, love and reproach. Then who is that fortunate princess for whose sake Phalguni has abandoned his stern vow of celibacy and asceticism?

Laughing, the divine sage said, "In Phalguni there is an amazing power to attract. Whichever kingdom he passes through, their princesses voluntarily offer themselves to him. First of all, being thus attracted, Ulupi of the Naga kingdom expressed her desire to take him as her husband. As a man, how could Phalguni refuse?"

"But he had entered the forest in order to observe twelve years of celibacy!", I blurted out.

Laughing Narad said, "Phalguni had put forward this argument at first. But Ulupi, too, is no less intelligent. According to the condition of the vow, Phalguni will not be able to have intercourse only with Draupadi. There is no objection, no prohibition in the condition to taking other wives. Moreover, when Draupadi is leading a conjugal life with the other husbands, it is ridiculous if Arjun as a man should keep roaming celibate. Before this argument Phalguni admitted defeat and accepted Ulupi as his wife."

I, too, was defeated by this logic. There was nothing left to be said. Narad, the divine sage, went on narrating the conquests of Phalguni. Dumb, I went on listening to everything.

In the Naga kingdom some days went by in sweet conjugal happiness with Ulupi, daughter of the Naga king, Kauravya. Then, perhaps, he felt guilty or depressed. For winning back the purity and calm of the past, Phalguni set out to tour all the sacred *teerthas* of Ang and Kaling. In all Bharata, Kaling, being full of sacred spots, was regarded as a holy land. Many yogis, sages, hermits sought to plumb the mystery of life in its generous, calm, enchanting natural surroundings.

Phalguni reached Kaling. He fell in love with its princess Arya. She was returning from the temple after worshipping the sun. He was standing at the doorway with both attractive hands outstretched, joined together, facing the deity. Placing some *prasad* and sacred water in the cupped palms, the princess *pranam*-ed the *sannyasi*. Every day after completing the worship of the sun, the freshly bathed princess distributed *prasad* among all those present.

Even after accepting the *prasad*, the cupped palms of the *sannyasi* remained as they were. The pure, delicate face of the princess was gleaming in his unblinking eyes. In a soft, sweet voice she enquired, "What does the *sannyasi* desire?"

"I am an ascetic from elsewhere. I wish to stay for some time in Kaling." Hearing Phalguni's musical voice, the princess was enchanted.

Like the hum of the *veena*, the princess replied, "There is no lack of hospitality in Kaling, ascetic. You can stay as long as you wish as our guest."

"But one request..."

"Speak, *sannyasi*!"

"Will *prasad* be available from the hands of the princess every day?"

"That will be a matter of great good fortune for me."

174

"What type of husband does the princess desire?"

"Will the *sannyasi* not be knowing a virgin's heart's desire?"

"A befitting husband?"

"*Sannyasis* are omniscient."

"But of what type? Like Kartikeya, Mahadev, the supreme lover Shri Krishna or like Duryodhan? What sort of husband does the princess desire?"

"The finest of husbands, Phalguni, is desired by all princesses of Bharata."

"If someone more suitable than what she imagines became available, would the princess have any objection?"

"How can that be possible?"

"Possible. If gods, yogis, sages are satisfied, everything is possible."

The eyes of the princess were lowered, "But, sir, the only one equal to Phalguni is Phalguni himself. The good fortune of obtaining him as husband has been Yajnaseni's alone."

"Do not worry, princess. You shall obtain Phalguni himself. My words are true thrice over."

Then he entered the royal guest house. Phalguni's vast learning and valour could not remain hidden from the king very long. For ages Kaling had given birth to the brave. How could its king mistake in recognising a hero?

In the meantime Kaling's culture, art, sculpture, vast natural beauty, tradition and heritage, noble humanitarianism and finally Kaling's princess Arya bound Phalguni in bonds of love. After finding out Phalguni's true identity, the king married Arya to him with great pomp. Having spent sweet days of conjugal life with Arya, Phalguni left. Arya wished to follow her husband, but Phalguni told her, "Devi! Stay on in Kaling That is how I shall be able to visit Kaling once a year. My intimacy with Kaling will increase. If I take you with me, it will be as though bidding farewell to Kalinga. The peace that Kalinga has given me — where else can it be found? The day grief, pain, anxiety, anguish become intolerable, I shall return again to your side in the lap of Kaling's earth."

Arya bade farewell to her husband with a smile. Why would she become an obstacle in the path of his fulfilling his vow?

Crossing the borders of Kaling, along the coast-line, drinking deep of the varied loveliness of nature, Phalguni reached the kingdom of Manipur. Infatuated with the youth and beauty of Chitrangada, daughter of Manipur's king Chitravahan, Arjun expressed the desire to marry her. But Chitrangada was Manipur's only heir. Who would be its ruler in future? Phalguni resolved this dilemma. He had no objection to Chitrangada's son becoming the king of Manipur. Peaceful co-existence, friendly relations between kingdoms, were what Phalguni desired. The goal of Shri Krishna's mission of dharma was also this. If the king of Manipur was Phalguni's son, that would contribute to the general welfare.

Phalguni's marriage with Chitrangada was celebrated. In the kingdom of Manipur Arjun lived happily with Chitrangada. He had planned to stay for three years there.

I was relieved on receiving news of Phalguni. But I could not hide my heart's jealousy regarding Ulupi, Arya and Chitrangada. For getting whom all to myself I had practised *sadhana* throughout my life — I did not dare to call him my own. Were they more beautiful than me, more qualified, or more devoted to him?

The divine sage Narad was able to sense my thoughts. In a reassuring tone he said, "Daughter Krishnaa! There is a great design behind these marriages. You know that after the kingdom was partitioned between Hastinapur and Indraprasth, violent feelings and jealousy are smouldering within the Kauravs. One day it will erupt into a great conflagration. A terrible war is feared. These marriages of Phalguni are a preparation for that great war." Amazed, I kept staring at the divine sage. Laughing, Narad continued, "Kaling, Manipur and the Naga kingdom are lands of the brave. For, protecting the motherland, their mighty warriors are ever ready to sacrifice their lives. That is why through marriages Phalguni has established alliances with those kingdoms. In other words, for the coming war he has sent them invitations. Now even if war does break out between the Kauravs and the Pandavs, the Pandavs will receive the full assistance of

176

these kingdoms. From the political viewpoint, these marriages of Phalguni are to be welcomed."

I was reassured. For Political reasons if Phalguni took a hundred wives even then I would not grieve. But if he married someone considering her more beautiful, more learned or more loving than me and was infatuated with her then that would be a gross insult to me. Secretly I prayed to God: "For the welfare of the country, let Phalguni take a hundred wives, but let him not take the hand of anyone in marriage out of love."

The meaning of Maya is magic, affection, attachment, deception. That meaning, which results from mixing all of these, is called life. In other words, life is maya —

It was this that my companion, Maya, was explaining to me. I had become somewhat depressed after the departure of the divine sage Narad. Unawares, I was burning with jealousy and wasting away in reproach. My obstinate heart could not accept Phalguni's taking several wives, even for political reasons.

Maya made innumerable attempts to divert my mind. She was whispering into my ears, "Maharani! For whom is this life of celibacy? This stern asceticism, unadorned life and eager expectation through sleepless nights? For heartless Phalguni? By this time he has already savoured the pleasure of conjugal life with as many as three virgins. He has forgotten you. By the time he returns, will not his anxiety, curiosity and attraction for you become blunted? You are beautiful, learned, desirable. This life is for enjoyment, happiness and joy. It is in the expectation of happiness that man bears even intolerable pain. but Phalguni has extinguished that happiness. Forget him. You have four husbands. Enjoy life with them. You are the chief queen of Indraprasth. There is prosperity all around. In you youth has come to a standstill. But time is a cheat. Ten more years will be needed for Phalguni to return! Every moment of life is valuable. But every instant of youth is priceless! Enjoy life, maharani! Phalguni should see on his return that the plot he made to pain you has failed."

Like a honey-bee Maya goes on murmuring in my ears, unravelling the mystery of life. Sometimes her cunning overwhelms my understanding. I wonder whether I should let myself be swept away in the flow of her words and make every moment of this evanescent life joyful.

That day, on being forced by Maya, I went to enjoy the beauty of the forest on the banks of the Yamuna thinking, perhaps calm nature might lend some peace to my anguished heart.

It was during the rains. The Yamuna was in spate. How peculiar was this flood. Swelling the river, it dragged it on to some unknown path, while at the time of meeting the sea it acted as a pathfinder and made the river steady, calm and full.

Such restless moments arrive in the life of every person. But the goal is steadiness, peace and fullness. But where was steadiness in my life? Where was fulfilment? He whom I wanted near me was far away — like flowers tossed on the river current, like moments slipping through my fingers.

Maya was behind me. Her laughter tinkled. As though she were competing with the waters of the river. She said, "Maharani! If the sky weeps, it does not make any difference in the level of water in the sea. The sea is undisturbed, generous. Is there any lack of space in its heart? As the rivers make their places in its heart, similarly it will be proper for you to find your place in Phalguni's. What will he think if you shed tears reproaching him? Will the sea ever appreciate the river's pain?"

I thought that Maya's words were true. Phalguni was a valorous man. The princesses of the whole world desired him. What was his fault in this?

Maya proposed sporting in the water. This was only to divert my mind. But did one sport in flood waters?

Reassuring me Maya said, "Fear of what? Here the river is not deep. The current too is not fast. Even if it sweeps you away, it will get you to Phalguni. I have heard that by now Phalguni has rescued five apsaras in the five *teerthas* from their existence as crocodiles. From Chitrangada he has had a son named Babhruvahan. Receiving this news, Arjun returned from the five *teerthas* to Manipur. After seeing his son and leaving his wife and child there, Arjun went to Prabhas. Returning from Prabhas he might be resting somewhere on the banks of the Yamuna. You will be carried by the river to that ashram. Taking you out of the water, ascetic Arjun will accommodate you in the ashram. Seeing your ascetic dress he will think to himself, 'It is you who are the true companion of my ascetic life...'"

Maya would have said more but I snapped at her, "Enough! Stop, Maya! Your imagination is wilder than even the river-current. In imagination you have reached Arjun from Ganga to Yamuna! But reality is very far from fantasy." My deep sighs mingled in the roar of the river. Maya could not hear them. Laughing like before she went on, "Test this and see! Sometimes reality and fantasy meet face to face." Catching hold of my hand she dragged me into the river. Nitambini came in behind me.

The cool waters of the Yamuna soothed both body and mind with their sweet, cool touch. I forgot sorrow, frustration, reproach. Laughing, we three *sakhis* sprinkled water on one another, forgetting everything in this sport. To cast away my heart's burden in the flowing water, I became rather too restless. Another companion, Payasvini, threw a flowering twig and said, "Let's see, who reaches this twig first and brings it back."

We three swam to catch hold of it. From the bank Payasvini shouted and clapped like an eager child, filling us even more with enthusiasm.

I did not know how far I had swum in the current. I could not even see where the twig had been swept away. It seemed I was unable to swim and was helplessly being swept along in the current to an unknown destination. My companions were left behind. Not even their voices could be heard. I was just being swept along towards that imaginary ashram where my heart's desire waited in ascetic dress. I did not know whether I was awake or dreaming.

Suddenly it seemed to me that this childishness did not befit the queen of Indraprasth. What had happened to the steady, balanced Krishnaa?

How helpless is man in the grasp of circumstance and yet man

179

does bring about changes in a situation. I was thinking of changing direction and returning to the bank, but I had forgotten that I had lost control over my limbs. The body had become inert, powerless. What a terrible end to a swimming contest with *sakhis!*

Now there was no alternative to leaving my fate in the hands of the current. Death was drawing near. At any moment I might be sucked into a whirlpool. If Phalguni was living in the subterranean Naga kingdom with Ulupi, then there would be no sorrow if I died after I had seen him.

The sunset was tinting the western sky red. The evening of my life was setting in. At that moment I felt intensely attached to life. I wished I could extricate myself from the current, grasping myself tightly with both arms. "How lovely is life, how beautiful! How dear is his life to man," I thought. "Still I will have to feel the cold hand of death. The five husbands are brave and powerful, but none is near to rescue me. Shall I summon *sakha* Krishna? No, no! What if Phalguni is summoning him in distress? Death is better."

My eyes were shut. My inert body was being swept along. My hair was unbound, tossing like some flower on the waves.

Who was that radiant, perfect ascetic? Having bathed in the waters of the Yamuna, *pranam*-ing the setting sun? My entire body, scorning death, was thrilled. It shuderred with a tidal flow of emotion.

Weakly crying out in vague joy, perhaps I was taking Phalguni's name. In the next moment the ascetic's eyes fell on me. In a single leap he seized my arm and pulled me to the shore. Before losing consciousness it seemed to me that someone's reassuring hand was pulling me out of the water. The body was floating somehow, exhausted. It seemed to me as though I were touching Phalguni. That hand in which the royal priest had one day placed mine, how unfamiliar had it become in the meantime!

I was saved from impending death. I was relieved, no doubt, but because of deep hurt and reproach against my dearest, my eyes brimmed over with tears. I was lying flat on the sand, eyes shut. I was thinking: "Forgetting my hurt, shall I say, 'Phalguni,

I cannot bear any more. I have lost the strength and ability to live for ten years more without you. Take me with you.'"

Just then next to my ears I heard a melodious voice, "Indra-prasth's Maharani Krishnaa is committing suicide? What does she lack? During the rains in the evening she jumped into the Yamuna?"

I was startled. Whose voice was this? Not Phalguni's. Then who was that remarkably handsome ascetic?

Slowly I opened my eyes. Before me stood *Ma* Kunti's dharma-son, Karna. I was lost in embarrassment and shame. Slowly I tried to raise myself. The loose wet hair on my back was feeling very heavy. My wet clothes were embarrassing me even more.

Karna understood my predicament. In a friendly tone he said, "You are exhausted. My companion Asmita and Duhshasan's attendants Asuya and Jatila are waiting near the chariot. They will take you up to the chariot and take you in it to Indraprasth."

Surprised, I wondered what it was: this daily indulgence of brave Karna, of coming daily with *sakhis* and attendants from Ang to take his evening bath in the Yamuna!

From above the river bank I heard another voice. It was Duhshasan's —. "Have no fear, Krishnaa! Brave Karna will not take you away to Ang in his chariot. Because Mother is ill he is staying in Hastinapur for a few days. Today we had both come out to hunt. By evening we were in raptures over the beauty of the forest. To bathe and worship at sunrise and sunset is the most important vow of friend Karna's life. After bathing we were to return to Hastinapur. If you do not wish to go back to Indra-prasth, then the doors of Hastinapur and Ang are ever open. The chariot will take you wherever you wish."

I was upset. Looking at Duhshasan I said, "Indraprasth is the place of the gods I worship. My place is there. How did any talk arise of my not returning there?"

Laughing aloud Duhshasan said, "Then why did you leap into the water to commit suicide?"

I protested. In a sharp tone I said, "While sporting in the water I got swept away by the current. To term this as suicide instead of a mishap is improper. Thereby not only am I insulted but the Kuru clan is insulted."

Duhshasan laughed coarsely and said, "I know of your attempted suicide. Among the five husbands it is Phalguni whom you love most. That hypocrite made the pretext of observing twelve years of celibacy. Roaming the kingdoms he sought out the loveliest virgins to marry. And here you are waiting! What sorrow can be greater than this?"

I was not prepared to listen to my husband being insulted, and that too from the lips of wicked, lustful Duhshasan. Gravely I said, "You are mistaken. Phalguni is a hero. Moreover, he is handsome. Beautiful women observe many fasts and vows for getting him as their husband. On finding an opportunity they offer themselves at his feet. By this Phalguni's glory is increased, not lessened."

Duhshasan mocked, "Hail to the hero! And to his heart's dearest whom the charioteer's son Karna saved from the river current! Today not only Phalguni, but none of the other four husbands would even have had news of Panchali's death. Her corpse would not have been found. Each husband better than the other and this is the predicament of Draupadi! Devi! Have your husbands no concern for your welfare? So irresponsibly you set out with female attendants in this deep forest to sport in the water? Not one husband with you for security, not even a single bodyguard! Why are you neglected so much? Perhaps, seeking to satisfy many men you are unable to satisfy even one. So their love is not that profound. Now look at my friend Karna here! Even though he has come to hunt, his beloved wife is with him, the young daughter of Angasen, princess of Kanchan kingdom. He is not prepared to have her far from himself. Therefore, attendants, *sakhis*, all have been brought along. Seeing your miserable condition, Rituvati will express her sympathy for you."

Duhshasan's mockery pierced my heart. On the other hand, I was feeling envious of Karna's wife, Rituvati, too. In my weakened mind many thoughts were rising. Was what Duhshasan saying true? That trying to be everyone's I could not be anyone's?

182

Truly, had I lost my life today in this water-sport, none of the five husbands would have been able to save me. Did anyone have the time to accompany me? I was hardly so fortunate! I was not Karna's wife Rituvati after all!

Noticing my absent-mindedness, Duhshasan continued, "Devi Draupadi, there is nothing to worry about. Even though you had rejected Karna then, he is not averse to you. If you wish, even today he can seat you on the throne of Ang as its queen. What is the dilemma in this? If the five sons of *Ma* Kunti are your husbands, then why should Karna be deprived of that opportunity? Karna is *Ma* Kunti's dharma-son. So, you should make him your husband, there is no adharma in that."

I flared up in anger at Duhshasan's words. Looking at him in disgust, I turned my face away and walked towards the attendants. Glancing out of the corner of my eye at Karna I said, "He who insults another's wife is the worst of men. But he who silently supports such insult, encourages it, is a great sinner. I detest both."

Noticing my face flaming with anger like molten iron, Karna barred my way. Folding his palms together he said, "Devi Draupadi! Karna the great sinner expresses annoyance at the behaviour of his friend, Duhshasan, and begs forgiveness. It is my duty to take you to Mother in the chariot. My wife, Rituvati, will also be with you. Even more than saving a woman's life, it is in the protection of her honour that a brave man finds greater delight. Therefore, I cannot let you depart on foot."

I saw Rituvati before me. She took hold of my hand and led me to the chariot. With due respect she gave her own seat to me. The chariot rolled on. She said, "From long back I have had the desire to call on you. My husband praises you, as though he were speaking of some heroine of his imagination. But after seeing you today I have understood that if my husband had not been so self-controlled, then for winning you he would have engaged in bloody battle in the *svayamvar* hall."

I thought. "Karna praises me! Even after the insult he faced because of me in the *svayamvar* hall, my praise on his lips! Does it not seem like chanting the name of Ram on the the streets of Lanka!"

Looking at me admiringly, Rituvati continued, "Actually, I am Karna's wife but it is you who are the source of his inspiration. The journey that he is beginning today with the inflexible vow to prove his prowess has become possible only because of you. Had his manhood not been wounded that day in the *svayamvar* hall, he would not have taken such a vow. You are the supreme failure of his life. Should Karna's life be crowned with any success, that too will be because of you."

"On failing to win you, every act in Karna's life became controlled. Therefore, you are to be saluted. Karna's wife is not jealous of Yajnaseni, who is the very throb of his heart, but honours her. For a person like my husband, who is the best of all men, you are the befitting woman. Knowing this, I consider myself inferior and feel how unfit I am for my husband."

I became absent-minded. For the first time my heart was accepting that injustice had been done to Karna. That day if my brother Dhrishtadyumna had not raised an objection, then it was Karna who would have been the most fitting son-in-law of king Drupad.

Man has no control over his birth, but over his acts he does have control. What could be more unjust than that on account of the cursed history of his birth, Kunti's dharma-son, Karna, should be deprived of justice at every step of his life?

In spite of myself, my heart softened for Karna, I did not know whether with sympathy or with affection. He who was firmly resolved to be my husbands' enemy — for him my heart was melting! It was an extremely peculiar situation. Truly, who can achieve total control over one's mind?

Yet, the mind has to be reined in. By means of the whiplash of conscience, it has to be brought back on the correct path, even though in that process it bleeds. If that is not done, it keeps advancing on the wrong path and even forgets the very road it was supposed to take. The goal disappears from sight.

Considering the mirage in the desert as true, a man's mind

keeps burning with thirst. I too controlled my mind. Why did I think so much about Karna? Was it necessary that I should think all my life about all those princes who failed in the *svayamvar* hall? He who lost — the sorrow was his. The winner wins applause. Who will sigh in sympathy for the loser?

The chariot stopped before the palace of Indraprasth. I got down. Politely, Karna folded his palms, "Devi! Now give us leave. It is my supreme good fortune that I had the opportunity to save your invaluable life. I was afraid that you might recognise me while being swept along and knowing me as a charioteer's son reject my assistance, considering death to be more welcome. By God's grace you did not recognise me then and were saved."

In Karna's voice was a childlike hurt. Spontaneously I said, "I am sorry for what happened that day. Sometimes out of ignorance a person inflicts hurt on another even though it is not deliberate. Man is the slave of circumstance."

Taking the words out of my mouth Karna said, "I too was a slave of circumstance. But only till the day of that *svayamvar*. Then I vowed to become the master of the situation. Man controls circumstance by the force of his prowess and his effort. He can alter it. I want to show this to the world. It was because of you that I made this vow. Therefore, I salute you."

I sensed that now in Karna's voice mockery for me and arrogance in his own prowess were reflected. So as not to allow the matter to progress further, I said, "I am grateful for your help today. I will tell Mother about your assistance and sympathy."

Karna laughed, "Today I truly performed the duty of a charioteer's son. Who but a charioteer's son would leave hunting aside and bring you to the palace in a chariot?"

Repeating that same refrain again and again Karna mocked me. What a deep wound had the hurt of that day made in his heart! But what alternative did I have?

Ignoring Karna's lovely piercing gaze, full of hurt, sad, then with sharp sarcasm stabbing through the heart, I said, "In another sense I am your enemy. Still, you saved my life. This favour cannot be forgotten. I shall remain indebted for ever."

Karna's companion, Asmita, smiled, "It is said that strategy is strengthened by keeping the enemy alive, not by killing him. Who knows what is the intention behind the act of Karna?"

Suddenly my heart trembled with forehoding. I knew how terrible the desire for revenge in an arrogant man was. But who knew that getting out of water one would have to fall into fire?

20

I heard that Krishna had arrived. Krishna's arrival was like the blooming of a flower in the garden. When a flower blooms its fragrance spreads. Even without seeing the flower it becomes obvious that it has bloomed. The essence of a flower is its fragrance. The desire to have the flower near one does not arise in the mind. For what is the difference even if the flower is far away? After all, the fragrance reaches you, perfumes your mind and heart.

For me the news of the arrival of Krishna was enough. Even without laying my eyes on him I could feel his presence. Even with eyes shut he was visible spontaneously.

That day after returning from the water-sport I had fallen ill. Bathing at an odd hour in the river, the mental shock of being rescued from drowning, Duhshasan's mocking words, and then that day's conversation with Karna — perhaps these had left me somewhat depressed. More than the body, it was the mind that had suffered pain. Who had time to notice that? Who had the strength?

The moment I heard of Krishna's arrival, half my illness disappeared. My mind grew restless. Why had he come? His *sakha* was not here. After knowing that, he had not set foot here even once after that day. What was the cause of this sudden visit? The next moment my heart was oppressed with anxiety. Surely Krishna had not brought some news of Arjun! Was it good news or bad? I could not think much. I busied myself preparing for Krishna's welcome.

Maya had made all the arrangements for Krishna's stay in the guest house. He was resting there. Through Maya he had sent word that he would like to meet me in the evening. He had said that he had particular business with me.

With a smile Maya said, "Hearing the news that you are sad in the absence of Arjun, Krishna has rushed here leaving Dvaraka. Who but Shri Krishna has the power to remove the sorrow of Krishnaa suffering from the pangs of Arjun's absence? The whole world knows of the profound intimacy of Shri Krishna and Arjun. Without offering it to Shri Krishna, Arjun does not even smell the perfume of a flower. Even the air he breathes in is offered much before to Shri Krishna."

I understood Maya's hint, but Krishna had remembered to remove Krishnaa's sadness rather late. A year was left for Arjun to return. The torment of separation no longer existed. I was engrossed in dreams of my husband's return. On his arrival, I would bind him in such bonds of love that he would never again enact the drama of remaining far away from me. So that he would never even recall Ulupi, Chitrangada or Arya. After returning to Indraprasth, Arjun would be only Krishnaa's. I could not bear the thought of any other woman remaining in his mind, at least while living in Indraprasth Palace.

I thought of Krishna more than I thought of Arjun in these eleven years. For I knew that Arjun would not return for twelve years. But on having Krishna near me it would feel like having Arjun with me. Therefore, during the separation from Arjun it was Krishna whom I kept remembering. But I never summoned him, never called for him. I was afraid that during his stay here Arjun might need him and that Maya could create some obstacle to the information reaching Krishna.

But Krishna had arrived on his own! First Arjun's welfare would have to be ascertained.

Maya understood my secret thoughts. She said, "Krishna has come with good news about Arjun. Now Arjun is a guest in Dvaraka. After accepting hospitality there for a year he will then return to Indraprasth."

The news gladdened my heart and mind. If Arjun was in Dvaraka, what worry could there be? The question was, if Arjun was in Dvaraka what was Krishna doing here? Despite weakness and being unwell, I went to the kitchen and prepared food for the noble guest, Krishna. Having lit the evening lamp I was but *pranam*-ing it when I saw Krishna standing before me. Touching his blue-lotus-like feet I saluted him. But my hands would not move from there. Hypnotised I remained for long in the attitude of *pranam*. Through my hands it was as though I poured out my consciousness, thoughts, mind, heart, soul and my entire affection on to those feet. I did not remain mine own any more. Within me no sorrow, happiness, hope, despair, dreams, fantasy remained. I was becoming oblivious of my own entity. Moment by moment I was rising upwards. I did not know how high I was swimming up. In the meanwhile, Maya spoilt it all. She made me get up saying, "Arjun and Krishna's feet are identical. That is why even Rukmini and Satyabhama get misled sometimes."

Ashamed, I got up, secretly annoyed with Maya.

With a slight smile Krishna enquired, "Are you all right?"

Sighing with hurt pride, with tearful eyes I said, "Doesn't *sakha* know?"

In a voice full of sympathy Krishna said, "I notice that thinking of Arjun all the time you have become like a stick."

Eagerly I enquired, "How is he? Is he all right?"

Warmly Krishna responded, "*Sakha*, too, thinking of you, has become like this. But I have made arrangements so that he does not suffer the pains of living in the forest. He is now in Dvaraka. After a Year the vow will be fulfilled. Successful, he will return to you."

Silently I was thanking Krishna. Still I could not understand what necessity had drawn him to Indraprasth leaving his *sakha* in Dvaraka.

Noticing my worried appearance Krishna began to speak, "*Sakhi*, eleven years of *sakha's* forest life are over. Still you never summoned me. So, I have come in person to meet you. Otherwise, what will *sakha* say on returning? That in his absence I did not even come once to look after you. Will you forgive me?"

I was thinking, "Have you come only to look after me?"

Looking at me with deep affection, Krishna went on, "Your responsibilities have increased. Is the responsibility of the five

Pandavs a small matter? Who is there to help you? I feel that you need a trustworthy companion who will assume responsibility of your joys and sorrows, share your chores. What do you think?"

Full of gratitude I said, "You think about me so much. That is enough. Maya is near me. I do not need anyone else."

Laughing, Krishna said, "Maya is your attendant. She is as wicked as she is good. At times she casts one into a great predicament. I am searching for a proper friend for you. You will see that many of your chores she will take upon herself. She will remain with you like a shadow. What do you say?"

Seeing Krishna's concern for me I was overwhelmed. In a choked voice I said, "Who will mind getting a friend? Why shall I object if such a friend can be found? You have seen my miserliness in making friends. During this period I have made friends only with Karna's wife, Rituvati, and Guru Drona's second wife, Harita. Their husbands are in the opposite camp but that has not affected our friendship."

Warmly Krishna responded, "Krishnaa, this is your generosity. You possess the art of making any person your own. I too am bound in the bonds of your friendship. There is no way of getting loose. The wish to do so is not there either. Therefore, leaving *sakha* in Dvaraka I have come here. Tomorrow morning I have to return."

An incomparable gush of bliss wiped out the sense of emptiness in the heart. A stream of pure love flooded the heart. This flood was aching to flow out through the eyes. I lowered my gaze.

Now I was, in a sense, free. This year was for me a year of renunciation. For, this was the year of living with Arjun. I was spending the nights alone. The whole sentient world was asleep, but with me sleep acted like a miser. I came out of the bedroom. I needed fresh air.

But what was this? A faint light in Arjun's bedroom! Had Arjun followed his *sakha* here? This was not impossible for Arjun who lived for Krishna. For the sake of Krishna, Arjun could even break his vow.

Late at night Arjun had come to meet Krishna. Perhaps before sunrise he would return. Would it be proper to go to him at this time? After so many years in the face of the desire to meet my husband once, the considerations of propriety were losing force. He might not see me, for on seeing me his vow of twelve years of celibacy would be broken. But what was the problem if I, remaining hidden, went to see him? What was the necessity to tell anyone that Arjun had come?

Quietly I rose and with soundless steps advanced towards Arjun's bedroom. Before me was the magical moonlight. Everything was lovely, enchanting, dreamy. Someone was coming towards Arjun's bedroom in this magic moonlight. Who was this enchantress? What work did she have in Arjun's bedroom so late at night?

We came face to face. I asked, "Maya! What work do you have with Arjun so late at night?"

Maya broke into laughter and spoke, "As you see Arjun everywhere, similarly I see Krishna everywhere. Where he is, there I am. What is there to be surprised at in this?" Laughing, Maya went away. Perhaps Maya was going to Krishna with the news of Arjun's arrival or in the meantime Krishna had reached Arjun.

I stood silently near the window and saw Arjun lying on the bed, relaxed. Moonlight had covered his entire well-formed body. On his blue body the light looked like an ointment. Gently I went up to the door. From the partly open door the perfume within was wafting out on the veranda. The entire fragrance of the garden gathered by the night breeze was being poured out near Arjun's bed. Would Phalguni ever understand that for eleven long years all the flowers of the garden had been longing for him?

Silently I kept standing by Arjun's door. I was not concerned whether anyone could see me. Had Arjun not gone into exile, this would have been my turn to live with him. So, what was there to be afraid of?

Gradually, from within the room the fragrance of Krishna was emanating. It was overwhelming my consciousness. In all the nerver-centres a wondrous heavenly pulsation was awakening. Krishna was lying on Arjun's bed. For so long, thinking Krishna himself to be Arjun, I had kept standing as a lover at the entrance! If Krishna's sleep broke, what would he think?

I was turning my feet to return, but they would not move. Even if I stood for eternity near Krishna's bed, they would not tire. I repeatedly acknowledged defeat before this amazing power of attraction of Krishna. Spontaneously I became one with him. The soul became free from the cage of the body. The mind wished it could renounce this body and become bodiless and lose itself in love of Krishna. Past, present and future all disappeared.

I kept standing as I was. I did not know for how long. The chirping of the morning birds would wake up Krishna! Now I must go back. I was turning back. Krishna was waking up. In a sweet, soft voice he spoke, "*Sakhi!* You remained standing like this all night! You must have suffered. I too did not ask you to go. Yes, because of your presence I could not sleep; but such tender nearness of yours is far more peaceful than even sleep."

I shrank in shame and said, "I came by mistake. I thought perhaps Arjun had come back."

Laughing, Krishna said, "Can I live in Indraprasth without *sakha?* That is why I had told Maya to arrange for me to sleep in his room. At least by lying in *sakha's* bed I would be able to sleep feeling his presence. However, I shall tell *sakha* that even at his shut doors Krishnaa can keep standing silently throughout the night. Sometimes I feel jealous of *sakha* because of you."

I was not delighted listening to Krishna's flattering words. I knew that while he was clever in making up things, he was even more shrewd in testing the state of one's mind. And, of course, he had the habit of pretending to know nothing despite knowing all. Coming to see Arjun, I stood here the whole night painlessly, enchanted by his magic. Deliberately I kept quiet. While returning, in a voice full of sulk I said, "Kindly do not even take the name of Krishnaa before your *sakha* in case it breaks his vow. He will then incur sin. I have heard that he has earned much merit by staying far from Krishnaa. Now he is again the guest of Krishna-Balaram. Where is any place for Krishnaa there!"

He kept looking at my tearful eyes and said, "These hurt eyes brimming with tears! *Sakha* is not here to see them. Poor man! I feel pity for him! I will paint just such a picture before *sakha*. More beautiful than the beloved's love is her sulking. Only he who is a lover will appreciate this. *Sakha* Arjun will hardly understand."

Glancing at me meaningfully he burst out laughing. I came away, out of his sight, after glancing for an instant at *Sakha*, full of a lover's sulk.

21

Harita is Dronacharya's second wife. To call her wife may not be fully correct. To call her a friend, attendant, servant, nurse, companion will convey Harita's role in Dronacharya's life properly. At the time of the untimely death of his dearly beloved wife, Kripacharya's sister, Kripi, their only child Ashvatthama was only a few months old. It was for his upbringing that Dronacharya married once again young Harita.

Yellow of complexion, from the very beginning Harita was aware that she was to assume the role of a nurse and servant in Dronacharya's household. Lost in the quest for knowledge, Acharya Drona had felt no need for any other woman after Kripi. After Kripi's death he had been regarding every other woman only as mother or as all-suffering earth. He was unable to regard even his second wife, Harita, with a heart moved by emotion. Harita's life was in a way the life of an anchorite. Her husband needed her only because of Ashvatthama. Guru Drona could be said to have been blinded by paternal love. It was for that very son that he had begged his friend Drupad for a cow, and on that account suffered insult of no small dimensions. His son Ashvatthama was his sole weakness. Therefore, guru Drona did not want that Harita should bear children. If Harita should have offspring then she would become Ashvatthama's step-mother. Possibly out of this apprehension guru Drona had kept Harita far from the boundaries of desire and had immersed himself in the sea of knowledge. Harita was like an oyster on the shores of her husband's knowledge-ocean. She took the motherless infant Ashvatthama in her lap like a helpless particle of dust. Drenching him in maternal love, she put in a life-long effort to turn him into a pearl. Ashvatthama was Harita's only possession in life.

I was inspired by the dedicated life of Harita. Spontaneously my head bowed at her feet. But Harita did not want my worship. She desired my friendship and nearness.

Harita was the embodiment of sacrifice and generosity. While admiring her, I began to want her friendship and fell in love with her nobility. Harita welcomed my friendship. After Arjun left for the forest, I stayed a number of times with Harita. I drew strength from Harita's self-control, devotion to her husband, renunciation, and dedication to duty. It was from Harita that I drew inspiration for performing my proper duties towards the five husbands.

Sometimes she would open her heart to me. She would express her regret at Dronacharya supporting the Kaurav cause. But she had never spoken of her unfulfilled desires, as though she had risen far above desires and wants. Except for making Ashvatthama into a proper son of Drona, all other desires were suppressed or dead.

Harita was like the radiant aspect of life. My intimacy with Harita went on increasing and the narrowness of my mind gradually decreased. Needless hurt, pride, arrogance, anger were reduced. Near Harita I always felt small.

But Harita remained full of nobility in her natural generosity. She would say, "Krishnaa, you are the ideal woman of Aryavart. Much is to be learnt from you. Thousands of years later your courage, patience, intelligence, outspokenness, devotion to duty and sense of self-respect will remain the ideal of womanhood. The entire male sex accepts subservience before your chaste beauty. It is for this reason that Karna's wife, Rituvati, secretly envies you."

"Rituvati envies me?" I asked, disturbed.

Calmly Harita replied, "Anyone will. Karna has not forgotten the insult of your rejection. He is restless, distressed because of the pain of that insult. The difference between Karna and Arjun is precisely this that Arjun is humble, free of arrogance. He had surrendered himself to Shri Krishna. But Karna is proud, vindictive. He depends more on his own strength than on God. Man's glory is his strength, manhood, valour. From that viewpoint Karna is not inferior to Arjun in any way. But he absolutely scorns divine power. Just for taking revenge because of your insult he has joined the Kauravs. Otherwise, even without the help of the Kauravs, Karna can become lord of this earth purely on the strength of his own valour and prowess."

At these words of Harita instead of anger or hatred against Karna, my mind filled with sympathy and respect for him. If Karna hated the Pandavs, was there not adequate justification for it? Was it not manly to avenge an insult?

Guru Drona's heart was full of affection for Arjun. Even more than that was Harita's. Because of Arjun's forest-exile, many a time Harita would suffer. With a deep sigh she would say, "Arjun's childhood and adolescence have been spent only in the forest because of the plots of the Kauravs. Arjun again deliberately took to the forest to fulfil his vow! Do not let your love of him lessen, Krishnaa! If your love lessens, he will not create a scene demanding love like Bhim. He will take this pretext to remain at a distance. He will silently practise *sadhana* for your love. During these last twelve years, besides doing *sadhana* in silence for your love, Arjun has not done anything else."

Harita's words would move me deeply. Silently I would vow to myself that this time after Arjun returned leaving aside my learning, intellect, views and opinions — everything, I would offer my life in his service. I would say, "You have won me and brought me. I am yours. Do what you will with me. Now I shall act according to your wishes. In treading the path chosen by you, I will not care about virtue and sin. Win my soul, overcome it. O Phalguni! It is you who are dearest to me..."

Phalguni was returning. After twelve years of silent ascesis he was returning with the hope of getting Draupadi's single-minded love. His wife Ulupi, the Naga princess, remained in the *Patal* kingdom, Chitrangada in Manipur, Arya in Kaling. Leaving them all behind, Phalguni was returning. For whom was he coming back? Leaving his beautiful wives tormented with the pangs of separation, for whom was my husband returning? For me — only for me...

Phalguni was a valiant man. He might have ninety-nine wives.

196

I was not jealous of any. Why should I reproach Phalguni and sulk? To Phalguni I was Krishnaa, queen of Indraprasth. Indra-prasth was not my co-wife. I was Indraprasth's heroine, the wife of the Pandavs — I was Krishnaa.

Waiting, especially waiting for the beloved — how delightful it is! I was decorating Phalguni's room. I was decorating his gar-den, his library, sitting room, prayer room, pleasure room, the entire palace — wherever Phalguni's glance would fall, first that place and then myself. All according to Phalguni's likes and taste. In the kitchen, food had been kept cooked. Whatever Phalguni liked had been arranged. However much I decorated, I was not satisfied. I got annoyed with Maya. One did not know what was the matter with her. She was making arrangements for wel-coming Phalguni in a newly built palace. One room she had decorated like a bridal chamber. Was Phalguni a newcomer that I should meet him in a newly built mansion?

It was true that it seemed as though I was meeting Phalguni all over again for the first time. In my mind was the thrill of an unmarried girl. It is after separation that the joy of union is so great. If there was no separation, how would this be known?

Throughout the kingdom arrangements for celebrations were on. From several kingdoms princes and kings had arrived on invitation. Watching the paraphernalia of the festivities, it seemed to me the celebrations were for my marriage with Phalguni.

I decked myself like a virgin bride. Let not Phalguni feel that twelve years had gone by and that I had grown older by twelve years. The drums were announcing the entrance of Phalguni into the kingdom. My heart too was dancing, throbbing to the beat of the drums.

Maya was coming, laughing, with a tray of offerings in her hand. The husband would have to be greeted and welcomed in. Maya held out the tray towards me. Two wedding garlands in the begemmed tray! For what? Who else was coming with Phalguni? His *sakha* Krishna or Balaram?

Understanding the language of my eyes, Maya began to speak,

"You might as well call her co-wife. None other than Krishna's darling sister, Subhadra! However much anger and hatred there might be in your heart, will you express it the moment they enter home? What will the subjects think? Moreover, what will *sakha* Shri Krishna think? You ought to welcome your co-wife also with flowers. You have to take her into the bridal chamber and leave her with the husband. Will not Yajnaseni be able to do even this little?"

Now I understood why all the pomp and show for Phalguni's welcome. The newly built mansion was not for me, but for Subhadra. The bridal chamber had not been decorated for me. Whereas I had already decked myself, lost to all shame and propriety, as a new bride. I cursed myself. Took off the ornaments and dress. Shaking with anger, I asked, "Maya! How did Phalguni dare to go to this extent? Without the elder brother's permission he married Subhadra in Dvaraka! With what face is he coming to Indraprasth bringing Subhadra along?"

Scattering the dancing radiance of her laughter, Maya said, "*Sakhi!* You have still not understood Phalguni? Is it possible to do all this without the elder brother's permission? Shri Krishna himself had come to take Yudhishthir's permission. It is only after Yudhishthir's permission that Arjun has married Subhadra."

Reproach and hurt against Krishna filled me. So he had come to Yudhishthir for making his own sister my co-wife? He gave a hint that he had found a suitable friend for me. But Phalguni did not wait for my consent or refusal. While getting his brother's permission he did not even inform me once. He said nothing about returning after twelve years of ascesis, bringing along a rare gift.

I heard the account of Phalguni's marriage to Subhadra from Maya. If Subhadra, like other princesses engrossed in love of Phalguni, had desired desperately to become Phalguni's wife, then instead of grieving I would have felt proud. My husband was the finest man of Aryavart. Was that not something for me to be proud of? But the reality was absolutely otherwise. It was

198

shameful. At the very first sight of Subhadra, Phalguni fell in love with her. He was so infatuated that he could not even wait till the bridegroom-choice ceremony. What if in the *svayamvar* Subhadra did not place the garland round his neck? Therefore, he abducted her. Subhadra had gone to perform worship on Raivat hill. Having received the information from Shri Krishna, he was already there with the chariot ready. Phalguni lifted the worshipping princess up on to the chariot. The chariot sped away and disappeared. In this abduction of the sister, it was brother Krishna who helped. He even provided Arjun with his own chariot. Then, appeasing Balaram's anger, he came to Indraprasth for obtaining Yudhishthir's consent. After such a love-marriage, what need had Phalguni of Krishnaa? Krishnaa was dark. What beauty could be hers? Subhadra was said to be fair like the *Kaumudi* flower. Fresh youth had lent her delicate limbs charm. The curves of her body were like the *tamal* creeper; hands and feet like lotus petals; lips like pomegranate; soft, sweet like the blue lily her eyes. No, no, I could not bear any more! She was the sister of the handsomest of all men, Krishna. In the whole world she alone was her simile. I was doubtful whether before her I would even appear an insignificant maidservant or not. In Indraprasth, if Subhadra remained before Phalguni's eyes, then he would not look at me even by mistake. Up till now I was proud of my beauty and personality. I had thought that after winning me no man would fall in love with another woman. No woman of this world could be compared to me. What was my fault in this pride? From my birth, whoever had seen me had invariably been enchanted, would be prepared even to lay down his life to win me. In the *svayamvar* hall, after noticing the pitiable state of all princes, my pride became all the more firm. I had even seen the beautiful eyes of Krishna become lovelier when he was enchanted on seeing me. It was this that had taken my pride to its peak.

But Subhadra had shattered my pride. I had heard that endowed with miraculous powers, Krishna did not tolerate anyone's pride. Perhaps he had sensed my pride and had broken it by means of his own sister.

Alas! How would I know that no one's pride remains for ever? How vast is this earth! In it, how petty and helpless is man! How insubstantial like a speck of dust is man's pride! In an instant it is destroyed. How ridiculous it makes him appear! How much remorse fills the heart — who can say?

Kings and emperors make love to more than one woman. They can marry them or reject them according to their whim. For this no permission of the previous wife is necessary. Therefore, what Arjun had done was fit for a king and a man. But I was suffering on account of my pride. Shame and despair overwhelmed me because of my egotism.

Moreover, Subhadra was more beautiful than me, and loving. Phalguni won me because of his valour. That day it was this that was the matter of my pride. But now I thought: in the *svayamvar* hall after seeing me, why did Phalguni, without waiting for his turn, not bring me away forcibly? Was it that love for me could not blind him? If Karna had not been prevented then perhaps for winning me Phalguni's turn might not have come at all. It was clear from this that Phalguni had been attracted more to Subhadra than to me from the very first meeting. Therefore, was it not natural for me to hate Subhadra?

I did not go to welcome Arjun and Subhadra. Seeing my face next to Subhadra's lovely face, Phalguni would cease to take interest in me.

I sat with doors shut. Tears flowed. Despite all my pride and learning, I was a woman. I felt ashamed to weep before anyone. But how could I deceive myself? My entire pride, tolerance, patience, generosity had to acknowledge defeat before myself. It is not that easy to cheat oneself.

They arrived. Ululation, conch-blowing, shouts of joy wafted from the entrance to the palace. My tears flowed even more copiously.

Someone's sweet voice; "Where is *sakhi?*"

"She is unwell", said Maya.

"In mind or body?"

"That the omniscient knows", said Maya. Waves of soft, sweet laughter beat against the shut doors.

I wiped my tears. *Chheeh, chheeh!* Should I show myself so weak before *sakha*? He was not just *sakha*, he was now also the brother of my co-wife.

Opening the doors I greeted Krishna. With a slight smile Krishna said, "I heard *sakhi* has fallen ill. The responsibilities are not slight after all. Is there no one to help?"

Gravely I said, "One who takes birth from the fire altar does not fall ill. The tongue of flame either burns or is quenched. But the flame of sacrifice dies down only after the oblation is complete, not before that. I was not unwell. I was preparing myself for greeting Phalguni. I was gathering strength for completing the oblation."

Saying that much I stepped forward towards the entrance to the palace. Taking the tray from the attendant, I greeted Arjun-Subhadra. Even after not seeing him for twelve years, I could not look at Arjun's face. For, by then my eyes were drowned in tears of hurt and reproach. With eyes downcast, I kept looking at his blue-lotus feet. Next to them another pair of feet sculptured in gold by an artist! Lovely, enchanting as the feet of Lakshmi in the temple. One whose feet were so beautiful — her face? It was but natural for Arjun to be bound in the coils of love for that glory. It seemed as if those feet were enhancing the beauty of Arjun. Like the feet of Lakshmi next to those of Narayan, the feet of Arjun-Subhadra were setting off each other marvellously. I grew jealous of Subhadra's feet.

After the welcome and greetings I came straight back to my chambers. Shutting the doors, I lay down on the bed. I could not participate in the joyous celebrations of Subhadra's arrival.

Phalguni came to meet me. I showed him due respect. In his habitual calm voice he began saying, "Coming back after twelve years I find no happiness in your mind. The radiance of your face has dimmed. What has happened?" Looking at him angrily I said,

"After seeing Subhadra's face my face cannot but appear pale in your eyes."

Quietly Phalguni said, "Krishnaa! Please do not compare Subhadra with yourself. In knowledge, learning, discrimination, patience, courage, she cannot come anywhere near you. And beauty? The beauty of a woman might be the first thing in a man's eyes, but it is not the most important. It is only when wisdom and character are mingled with beauty that, becoming an ineffable loveliness, it overwhelms a man's soul. With you it is my soul that has established a relationship. Why praise Subhadra here? Ulupi, Chitrangada, Arya or Subhadra, none can ever remove Krishnaa from her seat in Phalguni's heart."

I could not rejoice over Phalguni's flattering words. Rather, even more stridently I said, "Now in Indraprasth Krishnaa is no longer the only heroine. Krishna's sister, Subhadra, has also been established in Indraprasth. Now whether Krishnaa is there or not makes no difference."

Perhaps Phalguni was disgusted with my intolerance. In words dripping with sarcasm he said, "Subhadra will never become queen of Indraprasth, this fact she is well aware of. For, Subhadra is the wife of only the third Pandav Arjun and only Yajnaseni is the queen of Indraprasth."

"And the queen of the kingdom of Phalguni's heart is only Subhadra."

In a hurt voice Phalguni said, "Do not say so, Krishnaa! In future many storm-tossed days will have to be faced. As a result of my marrying Subhadra, the assistance and support of the entire Yadav clan will be with us. *Sakha* is ever ours anyway. But the only means of winning over the elder brother, Balaram, was by marrying Subhadra. Considering all this, it is on *sakha's* advice that I married Subhadra."

Irritated, I flared up, "Phalguni, do not bring politics into domestic life. Your fascination for her is absolutely natural. Why is Phalguni hesitant to acknowledge the truth? Krishnaa cannot prescribe any punishment for Phalguni. Then why these explanations?"

Phalguni was unable to remove the hurt and anger from my mind and heart by any means. He asked for *sakha's* intervention.

Krishna arrived. He was enjoying my anger and hurt. With a smile he said, "I got Phalguni married to Subhadra because of three reasons. The first reason is — the support of the Yadav clan will be available to the Pandavs. The second reason is — *Sakhi* Krishnaa will find a companion who can understand her. Why companion, Subhadra is prepared even to be Krishnaa's slave! The third reason is — because of Phalguni's marrying Subhadra and living with her in Indraprasth, Krishnaa's concentration on him will be reduced to some extent at least. Phalguni will never again become a forest-dweller sulking in reproach against Krishnaa."

Looking at *sakha* I said, "You are the greatest hero of Aryavart. Your sister Subhadra is beautiful, endowed with all qualities. There would have been no lack of valiant suitors for her. What self-interest do you wish to achieve by plotting to bind Phalguni to Subhadra for creating a distance between the two of us?"

Sakha was smiling, pursing his lips. He glanced at Arjun and said, "I have already said that because of Subhadra staying here, your concentration on *sakha* will be somewhat reduced and my self-interest will be served."

"How is that?" I asked, startled.

Smiling, *sakha* said, "On your attention being less concentrated on *sakha*, you will be able to attend to me to some extent. Your entire attention gets tied down to *sakha*, does this not pain me? Once you had said that everything of *sakha's* is offered to me. The flowers *sakha* wears, their fragrance does not remain with him, but is wafted away to me. Therefore, despite your belonging to *sakha*, is it not proper that your attention should be focussed on his friend?"

Even at the time of such a mental crisis I burst out laughing at *sakha's* sweet jest. Precisely at that moment, at Krishna's nod, Subhadra appeared I do not know from where. Touching my feet, with tearful eyes she began saying, "Elder sister-in-law, I am not worthy to become your co-wife. You have won the status of a goddess in my heart. Permit me to remain your slave. I married Arjun, but it is your command and wish that I shall obey. If you permit, then I shall remain in Indraprasth as a slave, otherwise I shall return to Dvaraka with Brother."

Krishna-Balaram's darling sister Subhadra, clasping my feet, was begging my permission for shelter in Indraprasth as a slave! Before her humility and delicate submission I had to acknowledge defeat. How could I remain burning with hatred against such a tender lotus bud! I felt ashamed even thinking of it. Engineering such scenes, why did Krishna throw me into such difficulty repeatedly?

Subhadra was waiting, clasping my feet. Taking her hands, I raised her. Meanwhile her clear eyes had filled with tears. With bowed head, like an offender she went on, "After seeing you I realise how improper, how unjust is Arjun's being attracted to me."

Raising Subhadra's face I said, "If you will obey my desire, then your place..."

Anxiously, eagerly, Subhadra asked, "Where is it?"

"It is here!" Saying this I embraced her. With her breast on my breast, she sobbed like a small child. As it was, tears were flowing uncontrollably from my eyes. Patting her head I said, "Till yesterday you were Krishna's sister. And from today you are Krishnaa's sister. Now what worry do you have? Leave everything to me, and be at peace. Make Phalguni happy."

Phalguni and *sakha* were smiling gently. Looking at *sakha* it seemed that he had known that this would happen. Should Subhadra lean even slightly towards me, I would shower her with affection like a fountain.

If *sakha* knew well ahead every scene of the drama of life, why did he act ignorant?

As the sunlight reflected on the moon cools the earth, so events that bring sorrow, being reflected on the generous coolness of the mind, get transformed into happiness. That in which man finds sorrow — if he but understands it more deeply, it gives him infinite happiness too. '

Seeing Subhadra with Phalguni in the Indraprasth palace, I had broken down in grief. And after making Subhadra my sister, the hour of her union with Phalguni was filling my heart with infinite joy.

Dressing up one's co-wife as a new bride and sending her to the husband's wedding bed was also a peculiar sensation. I had had that experience and with great ease I accepted it. Considering Arjun-Subhadra's first night together in Indraprasth their first wedding-night, it was I who had to make all the arrangements.

While leaving Subhadra on Arjun's bed I felt no jealousy or intolerance. On the other hand, happiness filled me. This happiness was of sacrifice, of generosity, of love. Is there so much happiness if one begins to love another person? But why does so much miserliness remain in a person's love? I found happiness because I began to love Subhadra. Had it been any princess other than Subhadra who had become my co-wife, perhaps I would not have loved her so profoundly. but Subhadra was after all Krishna's sister! Seeing the childlike innocence on Subhadra's delicate features and the chaste intoxication of her deep, large eyes who could refrain from loving her? Like Krishna, Subhadra too had an amazing power of attraction. In this world, who could help loving Krishna? I had loved Krishna. Loving Subhadra was nothing special. Subhadra's speciality was her very own.

I could state with pride, although I had a weakness for Arjun, yet the day on which I was in any husband's apartment, there was in me no weakness regarding the other husbands. Then I convinced myself that I had only one husband. My entire love and dedication I poured out at his feet. Then no other man hid in my subconscious except Krishna. Krishna was within me in sleep, in dreams, while waking. Even in the heartbeats of my husbands it was Krishna whose voice I heard. In every breath that Arjun drew, in every pore of his body I could hear Krishna's name. Therefore, in loving Krishna my chastity or devotion to my husbands was not affected. Love of Krishna was pure, incomparable, far above all hopes and desires. Therefore, I sometimes felt even proud of my own chastity and faithfulness.

Most of the world's women would be called unchaste, if not physically then at least mentally. Even while giving their bodies, secretly they fantasized, enjoying sweet pleasure in bed with some other men. But no such thing happened within me. While being with Yudhishthir I never desired Bhim. While living with Bhim, I never thought of Arjun. The efforts I had to make for a disciplined and controlled life were not very slight. To bring the mind under the control of one's will is the most difficult task in the world.

Ma Kunti said that without suffering Krishna could not be won. In *Ma* Kunti's eyes Krishna was indeed the Divine. It was Krishna who created and destroyed. He was the primal cause and ordained and deereed everything. Listening to the miraculous deeds Krishna did in his childhood, I too had come to believe that Krishna was God. God is the soul-strength of the helpless. Considered from this point of view, Krishna was God for me. It was on the basis of this very faith that in such unnatural circumstances I was leading a normal life. Not only I, my five husbands too believed in this very thing. If Krishna had not been their support, then, despite all their valour and prowess, the Pandavs would have been wiped off the face of the earth long back.

Leaving Subhadra in Arjun's bedroom I came away and was sitting alone in the garden. Sitting there I did not think about Arjun. I was thinking of Krishna. In the moonlit night like the *kaumudi* flower, a tide of nectarous bliss was flooding me within. For, I had made such a great sacrifice for the sake of Krishna's sister! Again my mind was swelling with pride! But at times pride, too, is necessary. Pride motivates a person to do good deeds. However, only if God is behind that pride can man do good things.

Behind my pride was Krishna. I was Krishna's *sakhi*, dear friend. He respected *me*, had regard for me. I could make some sacrifices for him. Such a pride was desired by me, wholly desired.

Krishna was before me. In my unmindfulness it was him that I had been thinking of. He was omniscient. The state of my mind

206

was not hidden from him. Sitting next to me he began speaking in honeyed words, "I am indebted to you for the sacrifice that you have made for my sister, Subhadra. *Sakha* has returned after so many years, yet you are passing the night alone. I am sorry for this."

So, Krishna did understand my grief. I said, "Subhadra has not, after all, snatched Arjun away from me. She has rather provided the opportunity for drawing Arjun even nearer to me. The joy of possessing wealth got without effort gets dissipated. This is also true of the lover in the matter of winning love. Without sacrifice and renunciation the nobility of womanhood gets diminished. In womanhood, too, there is a... She has given me the opportunity of making greater sacrifices and undergoing greater suffering for the sake of Phalguni and has challenged me to enhance the image of my womanhood in Phalguni's eyes. I know that it is for enhancing my value that Subhadra has come here. Therefore, I am grateful to you. *Sakha, sadhana* too is an acquired taste. He who has not tasted this thinks that *sadhana* is painful. It will have to be kept in mind that for becoming a mother it is necessary to suffer labour pains. For coming close to Phalguni, the co-wife will have to be regarded as my sister."

With the same sweet smile Krishna continued, "I know another excellent means of drawing near to Arjun. Will you be able to do it?"

"Definitely! Instead of giving me an easy way, I shall be even happier if you tell me of a difficult one."

Radiating an ineffable radiance Vasudev Krishna burst out laughing. Biting his curved lips slightly he said, "The nearer one is to Krishna, the closer one is to Arjun. Arjun is, after all, my alter ego. How can it be that becoming close to Arjun will mean turning Krishna into a stranger?"

Laughing gently I said, "I was christened Krishnaa after I was born. Father used to say that Krishna and Krishnaa were identical. Therefore, it is you who are truly within me. Whether anyone can see it or not, I can clearly perceive that within me all is pervaded by Krishna."

"The inner being that is pervaded by Krishna is bereft of pride. Where pride rules, there only the shadow of Krishna resides, not Krishna. And to consider just the shadow as Krishna is idiocy," Krishna said with a smile. His words hit me hard. Even a trace of pride within me could not be tolerated by Krishna? But I had never indulged in false pride.

Krishna's mysterious smile was sapping my self-control. As though it were saying, "Whether true or false, pride will have to be got rid of. And for getting rid of pride the ego has to be eliminated. One has to surrender. It is necessary to offer oneself before others like the offerings made to a deity."

This silent voice, it was in this that Krishna's life-story was embodied. Truly, the ruler of Dvaraka was roaming like a nomad for establishing dharma. What was his self-interest behind this? It was for the welfare of the world that he was a nomad!

23

I was finished. I had offered myself for the happiness of the five Pandavs. I had surrendered to my husbands my entire perso-nality and self. I did not have any likes or dislikes of my own. I surrendered myself in the form that any of them wished.

From that day was the start of conjugal life with Phalguni. In the meantime, so many years had gone by. So many changes had occured in our lives. Subhadra had arrived. So much hurt and reproach had come. But, for me, Phalguni still was what he had been. As though for the very first time after the *svayamvar* I was waiting to enter the bridal chamber.

Maya always overdid things. What was the need for so much of decoration and paraphernalia? Wealth, power, panoply — it is these that really blind a person. I did not wish to be blinded. If I could see Phalguni with hundreds of eyes even then I would not be satiated. Phalguni was a second Krishna. When I saw him it was Krishna who stood before me. That day for whom was I waiting? For Phalguni or for Krishna?

He came. Making blue lotuses bloom on the carpet-covered floor, he took a seat. I greeted him. For how many days I had been dreaming of such a night! Such a moonlit night, cool breeze, Phalguni and I — so much of reproach and hurt, so many dreams and whims, so many discussions on poetry, arguments on scrip-tures, could take place only with Phalguni. Yudhishthir was ever solemn and thoughtful. Bhim had nothing to do with poetry or reproach and hurt, dream or fantasy. Nakul was restless like a simple, innocent child. What would he understand about the language of my heart? And Sahadev was lost in himself like a dumb yogi. He never began any conversation on his own. What-ever he said was extremely cryptic, and even if it was unpleasant he would always speak the truth. Therefore, all the poetry within me was reserved only for Phalguni, with whom throughout the night one could discuss poetry. Like Krishna he was poetic, a lover of art and music.

Taking my hand he seated me on the bed. In a soft, gentle voice he said, "Krishnaa, I have to come to beg forgiveness of you."

"What forgiveness?"

"I will have to return to Subhadra's apartments. She fell ill this evening." Phalguni kept looking at me hoping for an answer. I had given Subhadra a place in my heart as a sister. I had never stood in the way of her happiness. Why couldn't she tolerate my happiness?

At this point of time, regarding Subhadra as my co-wife I was jealous of her. I was meeting Phalguni after so many years. But Subhadra could not bear that. Noticing my silence Phalguni said, "You are sitting here waiting for me. But I will spend the night in Subhadra's palace. However painful this might be, I will have to bear it. For you, too, I used to wait every night and you would go to the bedroom of Yudhishthir or Bhim or Nakul or Sahadev according to the yearly condition. This caused me no little agony, though I knew that you were not mine only. Today the extent to which you have authority over me, Subhadra has the same. She is unwell. After knowing this, how can I leave her and come away?"

"But this year is for you to live a united life with me, together. Even if you go to Subhadra I shall wait for you — " With great difficulty I said this.

Immediately Phalguni replied, "But why should Subhadra accept any such condition? With her no such condition has been set that I will live one year with her and one with you. Like any woman she will want to have her husband every day of every year. And that is but natural. Rather than with you, it is with Subhadra that more of my days will be spent. I will be able to have you but once in four years. I will get her every day, every moment. Therefore, how can I annoy her with whom most of my life will be spent?"

210

Now I understood that Phalguni had used my own weapon against me. He was paying me back for the pain he suffered because of me. He would keep waiting for me and I would go to the chambers of others. He wished to convey how much he suffered because of this. But what was my fault in this?

Between Subhadra and me conflict had arisen over Phalguni. In whose apartments would Phalguni spend the night? Realising that I was arguing with him over this, my face turned pale with shame. If Phalguni should desire to remain with Subhadra, then even if I compelled him to stay back, would he be happy? And when he himself was unhappy, how could I be glad? A royal throne could be snatched away by force, but the throne of the heart was not won by force. If Subhadra was established on the throne of Phalguni's heart then even if I kept envying her all through life, by means of envy I could not usurp her. If Subhadra was truly unwell and wanted Phalguni's nearness then to make him stay back would be absolutely unjust.

For twelve years I had borne the pangs of separation from Phalguni patiently. And now would I not be able to bear it for a couple of days more? The difference was only that then he was a celibate in the forest and now he would be staying in the rooms of my co-wife, Subhadra. In a steady voice I said, "If Subhadra is feeling unwell then even your coming here has been improper. It would have been enough if you had sent word through Maya. Go quickly! That poor thing is of a tender age. Finding you delayed she will get upset."

Phalguni caught hold of both my hands, "You will not grieve? What can I do? This is what happens to a person if he runs with the hare and hunts with the hounds."

Hearing Phalguni's warm, sympathetic words my sorrow melted through my eyes. I wanted to compel it to remain hidden within. Was I tender of age like Subhadra that on not getting Phalguni near me I would let flow a stream of tears or fall ill? I was Yajnaseni after all — learned, Queen of Indraprasth, moreover, fire-born. I tried to laugh and said, "I am feeling sorry for

211

Subhadra. Unnecessarily she fell ill. Why? I hope it will not be necessary to summon the royal physician at night?"

In a solemn tone Phalguni said, "Do not worry about Subhadra. Her illness is not so serious. It will be enough if I am with her. But how will you spend the night?"

"Tossing and turning all night!" I said tearfully.

"For whom?" asked Phalguni.

"For Subhadra. Although I have accepted her as my sister even then perhaps she is afraid of me, considering me her co-wife. Otherwise, when you were coming to my rooms today how is it that suddenly she fell ill? Anyway, now you should not delay any more..." Taking Phalguni's hand I raised him and took him up to the door. With head bowed Phalguni silently went towards Subhadra's rooms. The moment I lost sight of him, I shut the doors and collapsed on the bed. I did not know why I was feeling terribly overburdened today. As though Phalguni had stolen away all my strength.

I had just shut my eyes when I sensed Maya's voice approaching me. The moment Maya entered my room I shut the doors. Massaging my feet, Maya said with deep sighs, "Only you could bear this injustice on Arjun's part after twelve long years of waiting. Actually, Subhadra is not unwell. I saw her at her toilet after the evening bath. Arjun cannot stay without seeing Subhadra even for a moment. That is why, spinning a false tale, he has gone off to Subhadra's rooms. And you have been suffering so much in his absence, living like an ascetic."

Maya's words were ringing true and increasing the torment within me. But I did not wish to expose my weakness before Maya. Laughing I said, "Maya! This is but natural. Arjun's relationship with Subhadra is only a few days old. That is why he cannot let her alone."

"But so many years have passed since you married Arjun; your relationship with Arjun is so old."

In a voice choked with dreams I said, "The relationship with Arjun is of this birth and the next. You will not be able to understand, Maya..."

212

24

The moment one looked at Subhadra all the anger, reproach and hurt was left behind like a passing cloud. The heart became clear like the pure heavens. I saw Subhadra and forgot all the conflict of the previous night. I enquired after her welfare. "After arriving in Indraprasth my health has improved. There is no question of any decline," she said.

I was amazed. Then Maya's words were true? Phalguni had spun a false tale about Subhadra's illness and stayed back to spend the night in her chamber. I did not say anything about my suspicion. I asked, "Did you sleep well at night?" She burst out laughing, "Sleep! That is ever my companion. Phalguni was not there, therefore I went to sleep very early. Like other days I did not have to listen to discussions on scriptures and poetry from Phalguni. Regrding these, he praises you a lot. Last night what scriptural discourses went on? On getting an understanding companion his nights are spent in discussing poetry. As long as he was in Dvaraka, the nights would pass by in scriptural discussions with Brother." Subhadra's laughter tinkled. I was flabbergasted. Phalguni was not with me. He was not in Subhadra's room either. Then where did he spend the night? Stating that Subhadra was ill he came away from me. What was the intention behind this? Did Phalguni not crave my nearness? What was his hesitation in being with me? What offence had I committed against him?

To whom would I relate this sorrow, this shame, this insult? Phalguni did not love me — once this became known what would be the sense of my living on? The whole day passed in thought.

Should I say before someone that Phalguni did not love me. Then would I not look small in the eyes of everyone? With what scorn, with pity, would people look at me? Would I be able to bear that?

Evening, alone I sat in the corner of the garden, absent-minded, sad. Perhaps that night, too, Phalguni might not come. Making some pretext he might spend the night somewhere else. Instead of waiting for him in the bedroom, it would be better to pass the night hiding my face in some corner of the garden.

Suddenly, from behind me I heard the voice of Krishna. Startled I looked about. *Sakha* was smiling gently, "Yesterday you cruelly turned my *sakha* back. And today you are seated here in hiding. It seems that today too the poor man will return frustrated from your room and the whole night speak about it sitting next to me. Yesterday he did not sleep the whole night and I too could not rest. *Sakhi*, why are you so cruel to *sakha*?"

Amazed, I kept staring at *sakha*. I was musing on Phalguni's peculiar conduct. To tell such a huge white lie in my name! Why? There Subhadra, here I, both alone, and Phalguni was spending the night with *sakha*. Unnecessarily he was tarnishing my reputation. What was the meaning of this?

I kept looking at *sakha* in amazement. He went on smiling in amusement. Pretending to be angry I said, "In twelve years of celibacy he married four wives only and fathered three sons. And immediately on returning your *sakha* became busy in tarnishing my name. Why? Telling me of Subhadra's illness he went away and the whole night he spent with you. It was not I who pushed him away."

"But you could have forced him to remain."

"Even after hearing of Subhadra's illness would it have been proper to compel him?"

"If not compel, you could surely request him. You could have held him back for a little while."

"Even when Subhadra was unwell?"

"Subhadra was not very unwell, this too Phalguni had stated."

"Even then Phalguni wished to go to Subhadra. How could I hold him back by a request? Do requests win love?"

"But you did not feel sad without Phalguni! After so many

days — and your waiting became fruitless. Even about this you did not feel reproachful? The meaning of this is that within you there is no intense craving for Phalguni's love."

"Does reproach have any language? Eyes, mouth, deep sighs, the choking voice — if from all of these Phalguni could not sense my sorrow, helplessness, reproach, then should I have put all this into words?"

Hearing my words Krishna said, "Krishnaa, last night my *sakha* did not undergo very little suffering. To test whether within you there was any anxious eagerness for him or not he told you of Subhadra's illness. But promptly displaying generosity, you packed him off to Subhadra. Despite Subhadra being unwell had you, by any means, compelled him to stay back in your chambers then he would have been pleased with the intensity of your love. However much learned or wise one might be, with the beloved no discrimination and intellect work. For winning love what is there in this world that the beloved cannot do? And because of your cold generosity my *sakha* was punished not a little throughout the night."

Thrilled with amazement I was searching the reason for this dramatic exit for his. To test my heart's eagerness Phalguni sat with *sakha* all of last night. Hearing this, it seemed to me that Phalguni was mine. Ulupi, Chitrangada, Arya, Subhadra could be Phalguni's wives but I was his beloved, his dearest. Even after several marriages, to me Phalguni was still what he had been before. Now even if Phalguni kept ninety-nine wives in the inner apartments of Indraprasth, still I would not grieve. Phalguni's manhood was vast like the ocean and as generous. Should all the rivers and streams of the world seek shelter there, still there would be place for me.

25

The joint arrival of the great sage Krishna Dvaipayan and the noble soul Krishna Vasudev in Indraprasth was as significant as it was fortunate.

What was the intention of their joint arrival? The public of Indraprasth wondered, startled.

Only a few days before the celebrations to mark the beginning of Subhadra's son Abhimanyu had been held in Indraprasth with great pomp and show. Then both Krishnas had come and after blessing Abhimanyu had gone back. While returning, Krishna Vasudev had said in jest, "Krishnaa! Subhadra's son has arrived as this family's eldest son. Do not grieve over this. This is the tradition of the Puru dynasty. Though Gandhari was pregnant first, still, because the sons of the younger sister-in-law, Kunti, were born first, they are shouldering the grave responsibilities of the first-born. You should be glad that your sons will not have to bear the heavy burden of the royal crown."

Laughing I said, "*Sakha!* Despite being born of Subhadra's womb Abhimanyu is my hushand's son. Therefore, Abhimanyu is my eldest son. Abhimanyu calls me *ma* while he calls Subhadra *chhoti ma*, 'junior mother'. Subhadra has only given him birth but he is growing up in my lap. It is with me that he studies, learns singing, draws pictures. Listening to tales of his ancestors he drops off to sleep in my lap. Subhadra's childishness has not yet gone. Should Abhimanyu insist on anything with her, she teases him all the more. When Abhimanyu weeps, instead of consoling him Subhadra is on the verge of tears. When Abhimanyu chatters away, Subhadra packs him off to me. Now tell me, is he my son or Subhadra's?"

Laughing, Krishna said, "What should I say! Abhimanyu is himself going around saying this. The first day his teacher asked

216

him 'What is your introduction?' Abhimanyu said, 'My father is Arjun, maternal uncle is Krishan and mother is Krishnaa — just this is my introduction.' There is no trace of my darling sister, Subhadra there."

So Krishna was jesting! Still I said, "*Sakha*, since birth Abhimanyu has been listening to the history of his clan from my lips. In his dynasty it is the eldest who has the highest status. Not just because of the respect due to age, but it is because of intellect, discrimination and nobility of heart that the eldest was given the highest status. The sons of Madri, Nakul and Sahadev, too, feel proud to call themselves Kunti's sons. Despite enmity between the Kauravs and the Pandavs, in the eyes of mothers Gandhari and Kunti the hundred Kauravs and the five Pandavs are brothers. So how is it unnatural in any way if Abhimanyu introduces himself as 'son of Krishnaa'?"

Sakha laughed aloud and left. While leaving, he said, "*Sakhi*, my heart is not in Dvaraka. I constantly wait for an opportunity to visit Indraprasth. Do not begin the education of your five sons Prativindhya, Shrutasom, Shrutakarma, Shatanik and Shrutakirti together. I will get the chance of coming each time for the ceremony of each one. Then I will not have to make up false excuses before brother Balaram for coming here."

Hearing *sakha's* words who would not laugh? I said, "Is it a great deal of labour for you to create an excuse for visiting Indraprasth? The Pandavs will seek your help all their lives. Have they been able to do anything without you till today?"

He left that day, promising to return. But that he would return so soon no one had imagined. However, I knew that they were coming, summoned by Yudhishthir. He was in some dilemma which would be resolved after he had had the advice of both Krishnas.

Yudhishthir had dreamt of his father, Pandu. In the dream his father had directed his eldest son to fulfil his unfulfilled desire. It was the supreme duty of the son to fulfil the desires of his ancestors. But Pandu's desire was no ordinary one. He wanted Yudhishthir to perform the *rajasuya yajna* and become emperor.

Pandu too had wanted to perform it. By conquering many kingdoms, he had proved his valour and prowess. He was planning to perform the *rajasuya* sacrifice when because of a hermit's curse he died. The desire to perform the *rajasuya* sacrifice remained unfulfilled. His dissatisfied spirit had been restless ever since.

After the dream broke, Yudhishthir was worried. The divine sage Narad too had seen Pandu at the gates of heaven. He appeared sorrowful. If Yudhishthir performed the *rajasuya yajna* his spirit would be satisfied. Such was the news sent through Narad.

Yudhishthir's dream and Narad's message had produced the desire for the *rajasuya yajna* in the minds of the Pandavs. But what was Yudhishthir's dilemma?

Whoever else might or might not know, I was aware that keen as Yudhishthir was in obeying his father's command, he was equally distressed at the mention of the *rajasuya*. Yudhishthir was ever peace-loving and turned away from battle. His peaceable nature could not tolerate war, bloodshed, cruelty, loss of life and property, grief, sorrow, lamentation etc. He was not afraid of war, though he certainly detested it. But hesitation at the mention of the *rajasuya* was against *kshatriya* dharma. The meaning of *rajasuya* was not conquering kingdoms or establishing a despotism. Rather, as a result of the *rajasuya*, fraternity, dharma and unity were established in the country. Despite this, before taking a decision about it, he wished to have the benefit of the considered views of both noble souls, the two Krishnas. Therefore he had requested them to come.

Krishna Dvaipayan and Krishna Vasudev were seated at the centre. The five Pandavs sat around them. Whether the *rajasuya* would be held or not — grave discussions were on. *Ma* Kunti and I were also present. While taking any decision, in the Pandav family it was customary to take the opinion of the head of the household. My father-in-law, Pandu, too used to respect *ma* Kunti's views on all matters. The elder brother of my father-in-law, Dhritarashtra, also regarded with respect *ma* Gandhari's views. Grandmother Satyavati's opinions were respected by the Puru dynasty. In every sphere the views of the grandmother were honoured. *Ma* Kunti too was in her seat. Even Krishna did not dare to do without her wisdom. But the Kauravs failed to give proper respect to women. They were merely playthings in their inner apartments. They regarded women purely as objects of pleasure and enjoyment. They tortured them in various ways let alone respect their opinions. In what way was Duryodhan's wife Bhanumati lacking in learning, intelligence, beauty and other qualities? Her generosity and nobility were incomparable. Had Duryodhan listened to queen Bhanumati in every matter, then sin, adharma, hatred etc. would never have touched him. It was because of Bhanumati's chastity, devotion to her husband, practice of dharma, that despite all the immorality the Kauravs were still alive. Bhanumati was dear to *sakha* Krishna. Because of her husband's neglect and lust, the poor thing stayed depressed day and night. On account of lack of mental peace and anxiety she was mostly unwell. If she died an untimely death, then the Kauravs would surely be destroyed.

We had all expressed our views. Kunti, who ever detested war and bloodshed, had expressed her opinion in favour of the *rajasuya*.

Still Yudhishthir was unwilling. He had left it all to the decision of Krishna Dvaipayan and Krishna Vasudev. When Krishna Vasudev was there, what was the need of anyone else's advice?

Krishna Vasudev said, "Maharaj Yudhishthir! You are fit to perform the *rajasuya yajna*. If a righteous monarch performs the *rajasuya yajna*, it brings about the establishment of dharma. Adharma is wiped out."

In a worried voice Yudhishthir said, "Will it be desirable to invite war and bloodshed by announcing the *rajasuya* just for the sake of satisfying my desire to be called emperor?"

Calmly Krishna Vasudev said, "The intention behind the *rajasuya* is not simply the expansion of the kingdom or despotism. Its significance is to acknowledge the superiority of dharma. In Yudhishthir's kingdom adharma has no place. This fact can be proved only by holding the *rajasuya yajna*. The *rajasuya* never opposes non-violence, peace or friendship. Rather, the *rajasuya* actually gives recognition to the king who protects dharma, gives him fame, unfurls the pennant of dharma on this earth. Therefore, king Yudhishthir! Without any delay make arrangements for the *rajasuya*. But before this, Jarasandh, the king of Magadh, will have to be slain. As long as so unrighteous a king as he, exists on the face of the earth, the establishment of dharma on earth is not possible. The king of Chedi, Shishupal, is the commander-in-chief of Jarasandh. He is no mean warrior. Therefore, first a campaign against Magadh will have to be launched. Thereafter, let arrangements for the *rajasuya* be made."

With the help of Krishna, Bhim and Arjun slew the sinful Jarasandh, king of Magadh. Then no obstacle remained to holding the *rajasuya*. All arrangements were completed in Indraprasth. Various responsibilities were entrusted to everyone. Arjun, Bhim, Nakul, Sahadev — all four returned after conquests in the four quarters. In all Aryavart everyone acknowledged defeat before the valour of these four brothers and the righteousness of Yudhishthir. Where the noblest hero of Aryavart, Krishna Vasudev, was the guide, where was the question of defeat?

Responding to Yudhishthir's humble requests, Bhishma, Drona, Dhritarashtra, Duryodhan etc. had arrived in time at Indraprasth from Hastinapur. All the kings of the country had been sent invitations. Everyone was overwhelmed by emperor Yudhishthir's politeness and heartfelt hospitality. The prosperity and wealth of Indraprasth left everyone astounded. In such a short time so undeveloped an area as Khandavprasth had been transformed into Indra's palace. Everyone was discussing this. From time to time on the pretext of jesting, Bhim kept adding fuel to their envy.

Yudhishthir divided the work among the brothers. Ashvatthama would take care of the hospitality of the sages and brahmins. Sanjay would welcome the kings and look after their needs. Kripacharya was vested with the responsibility of the security of the treasury. Duhshasan remained in charge of keeping everything in place. Duryodhan would take care of the valuable gifts brought from various places. Bhishma and Drona would provide directions regarding the arrangements and lay down the rules to guide everything.

Laughing, Krishna said, "O King-Emperor! Give me some orders too!"

Humbly Yudhishthir responded, "It is you who are getting this entire work done. Then what orders can I give you? Krishna! Truly speaking, it is you who are worthy to be emperor! Who am I? Everything is becoming possible because of you."

Krishna replied, "Am I that fortunate! I have one regret left in life, Yudhishthir! Not everyone is fated to be called an emperor."

Full of hesitation and doubt, Yudhishthir said, "In the world such great souls are also born who, despite being worthy of the highest honours, delight in conferring them on others."

Duhshasan could not tolerate this any longer, "Here you will keep flattering one another and we will sit around neglecting matters of state!"

Bhim laughed aloud, "There are people in this world who are not fit to be praised by anyone and who do not even have the good fortune of purifying their ears by listening to the just praises showered on others."

Krishna changed the subject, "I understand. So I am useless! Therefore, Yudhishthir will not give me any responsibility."

The great sage Krishna Dvaipayan laughed and said, "This has been obvious from your very childhood. Now only after the sacrifice is over will your effectiveness be proved. Is there any lack of work in the world? You can do precisely what you wish — who can stop you?"

The preliminary rituals for the sacrifice were complete. Grandfather Bhishma called Yudhishthir and told him, "It is the duty of the host to extend formal greetings to the honoured guests. Preceptors, priests, relations, scholars, kings and the beloved of all — these six types of persons have the right to be honoured with formal offerings. It is the custom to honour each by offering them an *arghya* each. However, he who is the most worthy among these six types, it is to him that the *arghya* must be offered first, according to the rules of the sacrifice. To such a person two *arghyas* should be offered."

Among the assembled guests who was the most worthy and fit to receive this honour? Muted discussions began among those present at the gathering. To receive the *arghya* was a matter of very great honour. Therefore, everyone began hoping that their favourite person would receive it. At this time Krishna was sought for. His advice too was required. But where was he? He was not near the assembly-hall. Jesting, Bhim said, "He has no responsibility after all. So he must be having fun somewhere."

Taking this harmless jest as bitter sarcasm, Duhshasan said, "Born in the Yadav clan, how can he find any interest in the *rajasuya* altar?"

Maya and I both became anxious. Seeking him, we found Krishna standing beside the gate made for the entrance of brahmins. I was stunned to see what was happening there. To salute the brahmins coming from afar, Vasudev was bowing down. Then with great care he was washing their dusty feet and wiping them with his yellow upper-cloth. His curved lips were a bright smile. Because of the exertion, drops of perspiration were dotting his forehead and cheeks, as though flakes of snow were falling on blue mountains.

I was startled, "Maya! What is this peculiar work *sakha* is doing! The work that servants and attendants should be doing — who has given this responsibility to Vasudev? By this not only is *sakha* himself being insulted but the honour of all the people of Indraprasth and of king Yudhishthir is being affected. Moreover, all of us will be regarded as grave offenders."

Maya, knowing everything, smiled gently and said, "*Sakhi!* Gently! Be patient! Vasudev's doings are not going to end with this only. Watch all he does."

"Why is he doing all this?" I asked in confusion.

Smiling, Maya said, "Because he is full of hurt! When Yudhishthir would not give him any responsibility, he began searching. He found no one willing to do this work and took it up himself. It is a good thing because on such a glorious occasion, who would like to do such a petty job?"

Worried, I was wondering what to do. Just then I noticed the brahmins had got up after taking some refreshment and *sakha* moved towards that place. I understood his intention. Swiftly I went forward taking Maya's hand, "Maya! With us here shall we let *sakha* do this?"

It seemed to me that Maya was hesitant. Letting go of her hand I went ahead. Before I could reach, Krishna had begun picking up the used leaves. Forgetting all my pride and status, good and ill, before everyone I caught hold of both his hands and pleaded, "*Sakha!* By reproaching Yudhishthir you are shaming me! Yudhishthir is the servant of the people of Indraprasth. Therefore, I am their maidservant. With the maidservant present, it does not look proper that you should do such petty things."

Laughing, Vasudev said, "No work is petty in this world. Even from the smallest work great results can be obtained. Look, today it is because I did that very task which you are looking down upon as petty, voluntarily, that such a great reward has been given me."

Holding on tightly to both hands of *sakha* with used leaves held in them, I kept looking at his face in amazement. What sort of reward has sakha received today? Looking down at my hands made lovely with begemmed bracelets Vasudev said, "It is because I was doing this work that the honourable lady Yajnaseni is, on her own, before everyone, standing for so long, holding both my hands. What can be a greater reward than this for any man in all Aryavart!"

Oh! I felt so shy. I let go of *sakha's* hands. Immediately *sakha* took up the used leaves. I wanted to catch hold of his feet and prevent him. But at that very time grandfather Bhishma, Krishna Dvaipayan appeared, coming towards us. Embarrassed, I drew away. I was thinking, "How noble is Krishna Vasudev! He does not differentiate between man and man. In his eyes master, servant, king, subject — all are equal. In life everyone remains lost in useless pride. Today he has opened our eyes."

Bhishma and Krishna Dvaipayan called Vasudev to the sacrificial altar. Before everyone Bhishma announced that Krishna Vasudev was the noblest man in all Aryavart. He was an altruist, wise, brave and fearless. Why only energy, strength, prowess and wisdom? He had indeed all the qualities and was the best of all and dear to all. He had dedicated his life to establishing dharma on earth. Whatever he had done since childhood till now had benefited the world. The supreme vow of his life was the destruction of the wicked and the protection of the virtuous. Hence, it was he who was worthy to be honoured first of all. The first *arghya* ought to be offered to him.

Shishupal was Krishna's cousin, but he hated Krishna. For, at the wedding of Rukmini, Shishupal had been insulted, as before him Krishna had abducted Rukmini and married her. Of course, Rukmini had wanted this. Shishupal opposed Krishna being offered the highest honour. And the Kauravs, burning with jealousy for quite some time, began supporting Shishupal, they being full of hatred against the guide of the Pandavs, Krishna. In grossly offensive language Shishupal began to abuse Krishna and the Pandavs. Hearing this, Sahadev got excited and said, "Those to whom the honouring of Krishna, dear to all, is intolerable, on the heads of those mean creatures I place my foot."

The events after this were terrible. Shishupal and his blind supporters became violent. In the meantime, disregarding their objections, on Yudhishthir's command, Sahadev presented Krishna with the first *arghya*. How could sinful Shishupal bear this enchanting scene? Wicked persons of the same mind plotted to ruin the proceedings and along with that kill Krishna.

The invited kings, sages, scholars, all were worried. If discipline was not maintained in the *rajasuya* sacrifice of such a virtuous and righteous king as Yudhishthir, then what was the point of being called an emperor?

Exactly at that moment, removing the doubts and turbulence in the minds of everyone, the Sudarshan discus sped through the air. In an instant it cut off Shishupal's head and returned to Shri Krishna's hand.

All were stunned! The next moment everyone surrendered to Krishna.

It was as though the death of Shishupal was the auspicious beginning of the oblation of the wicked in the *rajasuya* sacrifice. It seemed to everyone that there was no place for the wicked in Yudhishthir's kingdom of dharma. For the mission of his life was the destruction of the wicked. And Krishna himself was the guide of Yudhishthir and his brother Pandavs.

Everyone bowed his head before the King-emperor Yudhishthir. Everyone vowed that in the task of establishing dharma they would, according to the ability of each, provide assistance.

26

There was a specific interval between the day of the full moon and that of the new moon. But no one knew when sorrow would come after joy.

I, too, on that day was standing on the final step of happiness, prosperity, wealth and good fortune and thinking that in Aryavart there was no woman like me. What other happiness was beyond my grasp on this earth after this was beyond me.

It seemed that if there was any other happiness in this world even that could not be difficult for my husbands to get. Should I so desire, they would even bring the sun, the moon and stars to lay at my feet. She whose husband was the emperor, what was impossible for her to get?

Fate was laughing at my pride. The future is not visible and that is why there is so much pride in man.

Krishna Dvaipayan came to take leave of us. Yudhishthir, having touched his feet, was still recumbent. Emperor Yudhishthir promised with humility, "I will not pain anyone by uttering bitter words. I will not look upon my own children as different from those of others. I will not desire war and bloodshed. I will dedicate my life to making everyone happy by following the path of truth and dharma."

Blessing Yudhishthir, Krishna Dvaipayan said, "Many inauspicious events might occur in the coming thirteen years. No one can withstand the current of time. Innumerable kshatriyas might be destroyed. But without getting disturbed, keep on the path of dharma. For, it is in this that the welfare of the world lies."

Hearing the prophecy of Krishna Dvaipayan, Yudhishthir's face fell. His soul trembled. He said, "Is there no peace in this life? What is the inauspicious event whose turn it is now?"

Now Krishna Vasudev would leave. He had arrived from

226

Dvaraka many days before. Now he ought to get back. But thinking about *sakha's* departure I felt miserable. Why was the heart of the empress so weak? What was it that she lacked? I myself could not understand why I had grown so weak. It seemed as though the moment *sakha* left, the sky would fall on my head. Krishna Dvaipayan's prophecy set my anxiety and worry smouldering.

*Pranam*ing Yudhishthir, Krishna asked permission to leave. Yudhishthir, too, was disturbed. He said, "Govind! It is you who are worthy to be emperor. This achievement is not mine, I know. Therefore when my praise is sung in the world, instead of being delighted I am pained; I feel ashamed. Burdening my heart with sorrow and shame you are taking leave of as. The moment I think of this I feel extremely helpless."

Affectionately Govind caught hold of both his hands, "Brother Yudhishthir! It is good to be humble, but it is not right to consider oneself petty. It is you who have acted. I have but assisted. It is only dharma that can protect this earth. Therefore, it is in your hands that the responsibility of protecting dharma has been given through the *rajasuya yajna*. Man protects dharma and it is dharma that protects man. Do not forget this."

Govind took leave of everyone by turn. My sons surrounded Krishna, "Uncle, do not go!" Abhimanyu insisted, "I will go to Uncle's home." Krishna was caressing everyone, making much of them. He was advising them to concentrate on their studies.

Abhimanyu was the eldest. After him my sons were born at intervals of a year. Abhimanyu was absolutely like Arjun. It was difficult to say which son of mine was like whom. In each of them there was some semblance or other of the five Pandavs. The most surprising thing was that all of them seemed to have the eyes, lips and feet of Krishna. How did this happen? Perhaps it was because of my being engrossed in Krishna. My attention was ever on the lotus feet of Krishna. His eyes used to show me the path. His lips provided me the strength and inspiration to taste the nectar of life. Sometimes Krishna would jest, "*Sakhi*, your sons resemble me more than their fathers. Doesn't Bhim tease you about this?" I would blush with embarrassment. With lowered eyes I would reply, "This is only natural. Krishna has merged into my husbands in such fashion that they have become oblivious of their own entities. Therefore, if the children have become like Krishna it is only natural. Particularly, notice Arjun's son Shrutakirti. He is an absolute copy of *sakha*. How can I help this?"

Caressing Shrutakirti *sakha* said, "Where is the difference between my sons and Arjun's? We two *sakhas* are one soul. If you separate me from him, he becomes empty. If he is removed, I remain incomplete. Therefore, only you can say whose son Shrutakirti is."

Arjun laughed at *sakha*'s mischief and seeing him laugh, laughter overwhelmed me too. If he wanted to enjoy such jests, why should I get teased?

The children were consoled and sent away. *Pranam*-ing Krishna, I got up. By then my eyes had filled with tears. *Sakha*'s feet stopped. With a sad face he said, "*Sakhi*! Shall I be able to go to Dvaraka having seen your tears? Why do you give pain again? I vow that whenever you remember me I shall be present. But after your husband has become emperor, what help can this cowherd friend of yours provide that you will remember him?"

Again *sakha* hurt my pride! He knew that without him the emperor-husband was helpless like a leaf tossed on the river current. But knowing the state of my mind he was teasing me in jest. I folded my palms, "*Sakha*, I am offering you everything. Therefore, my pride too is yours. If you are not returning it, then why hurt me? Hurt me if you will, but come back, come back soon...."

"I will return. I shall come at the right time", with this assurance *sakha* left.

27

The pages of a book have to be turned, but the leaves of fate turn by themselves.

I had married five mendicant brahmin brothers. They turned out to be princes of Hastinapur! Then they got back the lost kingdom and for staying far from jealousy and unrest among cousins over the kingdom they had to establish their capital in barren, forested Varunavant. With what sacrifice, endeavour, pain and difficulty had they developed Varunavant into Indraprasth! The history of all the *sadhana* and labour was inscribed on my heart. The entire burden of the five had to be borne by me alone.

My husband was emperor. Indraprasth was the most prosperous city of Aryavart. From the viewpoint of wealth, prosperity, natural beauty, possessions, art, music, dance, literature and weapon-craft Indraprasth was the ideal of every kingdom.

I was the mother of five sons, but Subhadra's son was my first. My domestic life was replete with happiness, peace and possessions. I did not want anything more. The Pandavs stood by their own right. Krishna was their helper. Now to walk on the path of dharma and become one with the subjects in their joys and sorrows was my wish. Subhadra would look after the household. I would keep track of the world outside. The welfare of the suffering subjects had to be seen to. Food, clothing, housing, education — all these are the birthrights of man. If every citizen of Indraprasth did not have access to the minimum needs then Yudhishthir's being called emperor was meaningless, my name Yajnaseni was of no value.

I was thinking of immersing myself in the pursuit of public welfare as a mission when suddenly the dream was shattered.

Vidur, the discriminating, intelligent, most respected uncle-in-law, arrived from Hastinapur. In his hand was an invitation. The king of Hastina, Duryodhan, had sent an invitation to the king of Indraprasth, Yudhishthir. There would be dice-games with bets between my husband, Yudhishthir, and king Duryodhan.

My heart shuddered with some foreboding of evil. I urged my husband to refuse. Pleading with him I said, "Do not accept this invitation. For kshatriyas, playing dice is not desirable. It seems to me that behind the invitation for a dice-game there is some other plot of Duryodhan's."

Yudhishthir too was worried. In a grave voice he said, "Yajnaseni! Hunting, drinking, dicing and womanising, these four habits are the enemies of a king. I know this. Yet, if Duryodhan has sent this invitation with the permission of grandfather and the elders, then I will not be able to refuse."

"But you are not good at dicing — this too everyone knows. Defeat is certain, this too I can see clearly."

"Despite knowing for sure that he will be defeated, the kshatriya does not turn back."

"War and dicing are not the same."

"But I am not good at dicing and therefore, Duryodhan has challenged me. Despite knowing this, I cannot reject the invitation for fear of defeat."

"At least ask uncle Vidur once what is the intention behind this invitation," I pleaded.

Hesitantly and sorrowfully uncle Vidur revealed the truth. Duryodhan could not tolerate the glory and wealth of Indraprasth. The wealth and prosperity of the Pandavs had whetted his greed. He knew that even in seven lives he would not be able to equal the Pandavs. Therefore, on the advice of their wicked uncle, Shakuni, Dhritarashtra was persuaded to agree and the invitation to the dice-game had been sent. If not by force then at least by stratagem, to the extent of adopting the path of adharma, to loot the entire wealth and possessions of the Pandavs was the intention behind this dice-game. Shakuni will throw the dice for Duryodhan. There is none in the three worlds who can better Shakuni in the cunning throw of the dice so as to win.

Having listened to everything patiently, Yudhishthir gave directions to prepare for going to Hastina. I paled with sorrow and annoyance. I asked, "Even after knowing the intention of uncle Shakuni and Duryodhan, you want to accept the invitation?"

"Despite the deception of Gandhar king Shakuni being clear, the invitation has to be accepted. Every step in life is determined by fate alone. Therefore, instead of thinking otherwise, it is proper to take part in the game."

I was silent hearing the firm decision of Yudhishthir. What was the value of my refusal or consent or my apprehensions?

Without knowing how to swim, should one say "I must jump into the river; the call of fate cannot be rejected"? Then what would one call it other than suicide? Was Yudhishthir, unwilling to fight, accepting this invitation in order to avoid battle? Perhaps he was apprehensive that at any time the Kauravs might declare war out of greed for wealth. There was no sorrow in losing wealth and possessions on placing a bet so long as life was saved and remained peaceful. It was this that was the aim of Yudhishthir. Or perhaps arrogance had made him trust in fate blindly. Despite fate being powerful, man does enjoy the fruits of his efforts. How was it that wise Yudhishthir could not comprehend this truth?

If he had listened to my plea that day! The greatest disaster of my life could have been averted!

28

A menstruating woman was impure. So I was staying in a private mansion in Hastina. Accepting the invitation to the dice-game, *ma* Kunti and I had come with the five Pandavs. Of welcome, hospitality, affection, respect there was no lack in Hastina, no flaw. It was quite some time since the brothers had left, noting auspicious omens. I did not meet them. During menstrual periods, seeing the husband's face was prohibited. To see even the shadow of another man was sinful. Absolutely alone, I was seated in a corner of the room. Physically as well as mentally I was not alert. Though I was virtually a prisoner, my mind had flown to the assembly-hall, wondering what was the ultimate result. Silently I waited for news of the dice-game. Good or bad?

It was these thick, curly, long tresses of mine that were a major attraction of my beauty. While combing my hair Maya would say, "*Sakhi!* If the princes had seen your flowing tresses in the *svayamvar* hall then they would have considered themselves fortunate to commit suicide hanging themselves with your long hair. It is well that your hair was coiled up and covered with flowers that day and with a veil on top."

Now my hair was left loose. In my present condition, dressing the hair or decking up was prohibited. Except for a single cloth, even wearing undergarments was prohibited. In the separate apartments for female guests in Hastina's royal palace, with my wet hair drying on my back, I was idly passing the afternoon. Maya was seated next to me. As ever, she was praising my hair. Laughing, she said, "Those unfortunate men who are deprived of the chance of seeing the beauty of your hair, for them my mind fills with infinite pity!"

Irritated I retorted, "*Chheeh*, Maya! What nonsense you talk! For the lustful glance of another man to touch even the tip of a

232

married woman's hair is an insult. That is why the need of a veil and tying up the hair. Displaying one's beauty is the dharma of a courtesan, not of a wife. How do such peculiar ideas come into your head?"

Smiling Maya responded, "The attraction a man feels for a woman is natural, spontaneous. The attraction in a man's heart for a beautiful, talented, learned woman cannot be expressed in words. Therefore, all the princes of Aryavart going mad for you there, would have been no fault of theirs, rather..." Stopping midway, Maya smiled meaningfully, wickedly.

Annoyed I said, "Rather, the fault is mine. This is what you want to say?"

"The fault is his who has filled woman with beauty and men's eyes with the thirst for beauty," answered Maya.

In a dry voice I said, "Then go to him. Argue with him regarding the faults and good points. Why indulge in such talk here? And what is happening in the assembly-hall? Regarding that, there is not the slightest anxiety in your mind?"

Indifferently, Maya said, "What is the use of worrying? Can we do anything? What will be, will be. It is His wish. We have to dance accordingly!"...

Worried, I asked, "Maya, why don't you go and take a look at what is happening? What are the bets? Who is winning and losing? In front of so many learned, valiant noblemen of Aryavart, it does not seem proper for two kings to be engrossed in dicing — but no one would listen to a word of mine."

Maya laughed and said, "*Sakhi!* It is the princes who went for the *svayamvar* who are present as spectators in the dicing hall. They would be wishing that somehow Yudhishthir should lose..."

I burst out, "You know their secret desires so well. Tell me, what else do they desire?"

"They had seen virgin Krishnaa only once and were left with a life-long regret. The desire to console the heart by seeing the royal queen Krishnaa once is bound to be there." Maya spoke these words most naturally. But I was left stunned. Was Maya getting mentally unbalanced? *Chheeh, chheeh!* What sort of thoughts did she think! To remove the regret of people of the whole world I would display myself before them? Improper, unjust hopes and desires are the roots of regret. What did this matter to me?

I did not wish to argue any more with Maya. I did not like listening to such things. My anxiety was increasing. My body and mind — both were restless, disturbed.

There was a sound in the doorway. Was Yudhishthir returning victorious? I moved out of sight. How could I look upon my husband's face while menstruating?

Maya asked, "What is the news, Pratikami?"

Coldly the messenger said, "King Duryodhan's command is: queen Yajnaseni should appear in the assembly-hall."

Teasingly Maya said, "I was right — they are bound to want to see you."

My face flamed. Sharply I retorted, "Who is king Duryodhan to issue commands? I am not his subject. Has he forgotten so quickly that my husband Yudhishthir is emperor..."

Before I could finish, Pratikami said in a grim voice which crashed like a thunderbolt on my head, "King Yudhishthir, staked his entire immovable and movable property, male and female slaves, brothers and himself, and lost all. He ultimately staked his wife, queen Krishnaa, too, and lost. Therefore, queen Krishnaa is now the slave of the Kauravs. King Duryodhan's command..."

I was inside because I would not look upon Pratikami's face. Still, I was angrily wishing that I could glance at him once and burn him to ashes. How did he dare...? But, then, what was his fault? He was only an obedient servant.

In a steady voice I said, "Go, Pratikami! Go and ask my husband whether first he staked himself and lost or me? Till I get a reply to this I will not move from here." Nervous, Pratikarni went back. I kept standing stunned, inert. I was thinking, "What is this behaviour of Yudhishthir? Does even the most immoral uncivilized gambler ever stake his wife? Has anyone ever done such a detestable act in the history of the world?"

Doubling my anguish, Maya said, "Alas! What will brave Karna and the other princes be thinking? Of what sort is Yudhishthir's husbandly love? How grossly has he demeaned the daughter of Panchal before enemies!" I would have wept but my whole body was trembling with anger and excitement, which dried up all tears.

Just then Pratikami returned. In a polite tone he said, "King Duryodhan's command is that you shall have to come to the assembly-hall and question your husband in public. Along with the Kauravs, the other kings are waiting to hear your question and his answer."

I hardened my heart. In a steady but firm voice I said, "Go, Pratikami, ask my father-in-law and the elders what there opinion is. I shall accept their command. Listen, Duryodhan is not my lord. I cannot appear in the assembly-hall at his command. Have my husbands granted permission for this?"

With bowed head Pratikami went back sorrowfully. I was unable to think. Only the scene of the *svayamvar* hall was before my eyes. Those princes before whom with great pride I had rejected Karna, had garlanded the noblest warrior Arjun, today, before those very persons I, the empress of emperor Yudhishthir, the darling Draupadi of the five Pandavs, the queen of Indraprasth, the sister of Dhrishtadyumna — dearer to him than life itself — the bride of the Bharat dynasty and the *sakhi* of the perfect man, Krishna Vasudev, clad in a single garment, menstruating, like a helpless, unfortunate woman would appear in public in the assembly-hall? Will my husbands, specially Arjun and Bhim, stand this? And above all, having borne this insult, would I be able to go on living?

Full of anguish and anger I was thinking: was woman merely man's movable or immovable property? Was I part of Yudhishthir's movable or immovable property, male and female slaves, horses and elephants? Being a woman did I not have right even over myself, my own soul? If they had rights over this body of mine, did it mean they could do as they wished with me?

I saw nothing but gloom all around. That was when Nitambini

235

entered and silently stood before me. With bowed head and voice heavy with sorrow she began saying, "*Sakhi!* From your husband, king Yudhishthir, directions have come. Even in your single garment you should appear before your elder in-laws. Knowing that you are menstruating, they will surely take care to protect your honour."

Flaming in anger and horror I shrieked, "Get out, Nitambini! Do not show your face to me! How dare you carry such instructions to me?"

Like a tongue of flame my eyes and every pore of my body were burning. My anger against Yudhishthir I poured out on my companion. I began to make myself firm.

Right then with a loud, coarse laugh Duhshasan appeared before me. Full of shame I slipped out of sight. But shamelessly he came forward, "Come, lovely one, now you have become our property. Your self-respect, chastity, modesty, hesitation-keep them to yourself. Forget the five husbands. Accept Duryodhan and his ninety-nine brothers as your lords. You will see that such a catastrophe will never recur."

Out of shame, grief, fear, hatred, I shut my eyes. Duhshasan laughed demoniacally. It seemed to me that his lustful arms were advancing towards me. I moved backwards towards the women's apartments. I ran in that direction. Perhaps on reaching the feet of mother-in-law Gandhari my modesty might be saved or shelter would be available from sisterly Bhanumati or the other queens. But everyone's doors were shut.

Before I could cry out at the doors, Duhshasan put out his powerful hairy hand and catching hold of my long thick curly hair pulled hard. Helpless, I lost my balance. As the wild buffalo drags some broken creeper along, similarly Duhshasan dragged me to the assembly-hall. With great difficulty I tried to cover my breasts with my single garment. The end of it had slipped off my head. Face, neck, arms were all bare. The hair was already in disarray. Out of kindness they had covered my bare back from the sight of spectators. Like a creeper trembling in a storm, I was shivering with fear and shame. My diamond nose stud was sparkling like a star.

Even after dragging me into the assembly-hall, Duhshasan was pulling at my hair, as though I were a lifeless statue devoid of reaction, sorrow, emotion, excitement.

Laying aside shame and modesty I folded my palms, "Let me remain alone in private. I am single-garmented, menstruating..."

Laughing aloud Duhshasan said, "Whatever state you might be in, whatever you might or might not be wearing, what do we care about that? To us you are a mere slave."

To hide my anguish and shame my long blue-black hair was once again kindly covering my face. Duhshasan's barbaric behaviour was disarranging my single cloth. I was at a loss what to do. With difficulty I folded my hands over my breast. I began silently to pray to *sakha* Krishna. Who would come to my help in this extremity but Krishna?

In front of me were seated my heroes, my five kshatriya husbands, silent like offenders. Before their very eyes their wife was being insulted and they were sitting helpless, silent! At the other end were seated my father-in-law (blind, but surely he was hearing my cries? He must be aware of my helplessness), grandfather Bhishma (wise, valorous, celibate since birth, he too was a silent spectator), guru Drona, Kripacharya — all had become dumb. Seeing my state, Karna was perhaps savouring great self-satisfaction in the cruel joy of revenge. He kept looking at me scornfully out of the corner of his eye. The kings and princes present, good people all, were dumb. It seemed that other than Krishna there was no one in the world to help me.

Laughing loudly in glee, Duhshasan tugged at my hair, "Slave! Slave!"

Karna, Shakuni, Duryodhan and others were all encouraging Duhshasan.

More than danger, it is the apprehension of danger that frightens man. Once the danger is in front of you, I do not know from where the strength comes to face it, I do not know from where so much courage fills one.

With hands folded I looked towards the elders. My tears were flowing incessantly. Casting aside shame, modesty, I enquired loudly, "My elders are present in this assembly. They are all wise and brave men of Aryavart endowed with noble qualities. In my condition is it not shameful to drag me by the hair into this crowded hall? All are silent? Will no one answer my question?"

All were silent. A mild murmur arose and died down. Would any woman dare to demand an explanation of her elders with such firmness? No one could believe this.

Shakuni said to Karna, "The greatest offence a woman commits is to try to be learned. It is because she became wise and scholarly that her condition is thus! If she had grovelled at our feet and begged, perhaps she might have escaped such a gross insult. Just as knowledge and power enhance a man's attraction, similarly ignorance and helplessness increase the charm of a woman. However, Draupadi, strengthened by pride in her learning and wisdom, is like a burning tongue of flame. Can anyone have pity on her?"

Again I said, "I do not beg for anyone's pity. I demand justice. To protect the honour of women is the dharma of a king. Then does it befit the Kuru kings to insult the bride of their own clan? I wish to know: has my husband got the right to stake me after he has already staked and lost his own self?"

Even then everyone was silent. However, in a calm voice Bhishma said, "Immaculate one! One who is dependent does not have the right to stake someone else's wealth. But the wife is ever her husband's dependent. Therefore, whether, after having lost himself, Yudhishthir has the right to stake you or not, is genuinely a dilemma. I am unable to provide an answer. The way of dharma is extremely subtle. Explaining dharma is not an easy matter. Yudhishthir's very life is dharma. He is your husband. When he is silently bearing this insufferable insult against you and Bhim, Arjun, Nakul, Sahadev are ignoring it, remaining spectators in the hall, then what answer can I provide about dharma? Therefore, I do not feel like replying to your question."

Hearing these cruel, cold words of Grandfather whatever little hope I had left was ground to the dust.

Controlling my anger I said, "My husband, Yudhishthir, is not only the soul of dharma, he is also extremely simple and pure in nature. Taking advantage of his simplicity they have unjustly defeated him in the game. Only a king can play with another king. But deceiving Shakuni played for Duryodhan. In a dice-game one person cannot play for another. Even after knowing all this do the elders think that I have become a slave of the Kauravs?"

The question faded away in the air. Duhshasan again pulled my hair, "Stop this nonsense, lovely one! Legal arguments do not suit beautiful women. Now if you do as we wish, it will be well for you."

Helplessly I looked all around. All was blurred by my tears. I did not even feel like looking towards my five husbands. Seeing my helpless and pitiable condition, Bhim flared up in anger, "No-where in history will an instance be found of any man having staked his mistress, slave or even a prostitute to lose in a dice-game. When Yudhishthir staked us four brothers and lost, I remained silent. But I cannot forgive the crime of making our wife Draupadi the stake. For what offence will Draupadi suffer this insult? I wish to burn the hands that staked Draupadi and lost. Sahadev! Arrange for fire." It was not that Phalguni was not suffering for me. But in such a huge assembly how could he endorse the insult of his eldest brother? In a calm voice he said, "Bhim! Have you lost your senses? Yudhishthir is the eldest. He is like our father. In a game, victory and defeat do occur. What is the use of blaming anyone for that?"

The assembly was wondering at Arjun's nobility but it stabbed me to the heart. I thought, "Well! What respect for tradition and culture! So much respect! Elders must not be spoken ill of ... Arjun is advising Bhim while petty persons are insulting and outraging his wife. He is bearing it all. Is this the evidence of the great Bharatan civilization and tradition? Is this the heritage of the Aryans?"

A son of Dhritarashtra, Vikarna, taking my side said, "Devi Yajnaseni's question remains unanswered yet. In my opinion, Yajnaseni is not a dependent of the Kauravs. For Yajnaseni is not merely the wife of Yudhishthir. The other four brothers have equal rights over her. On the basis of what logic did he stake her? Further, did he retain the right to stake her after having lost himself? In my opinion, legally the Kauravs have not been able to win Draupadi."

All of a sudden Karna grew impatient. He told Vikarna, "Have you forgotten the past? Is it not because of this very Yajnaseni that one day all princes were insulted and defeated? Why so much of sympathy today? The extent to which Yudhishthir has rights over Draupadi, within that he did no wrong in staking her. Then if you feel that the insult of a woman is unjust and against dharma, has this woman not violated law and dharma? The condition of the *svayamvar* was piercing the target, that is manly prowess and ability. Why did questions of race, birth, history and family background arise there? Was that not unjust and devoid of dharma? If Phalguni was desired by her then what was the necessity of holding the mockery of the *svayamvar?* Why was the entire ruling class insulted? The final issue is that of a woman's chastity, modesty, shame, good character. Even the gods have prescribed one husband for a woman. But by accepting five husbands she has discarded her modesty, shame and womanhood. Moreover, she has profound intimacy with her husband's bosom *sakha*, Govind! I have heard that there is no earthly word by which that relationship can be described, that it is unearthly, heavenly. Therefore, the woman who, besides five husbands, is dear to yet another man, even to strip her naked in this assembly will not be committing any adharma, any injustice. For, we have won the entire kingdom, possessions, wealth of the Pandavs. They do not even have any rights over any clothes of theirs. First strip the five Pandavs, then arrange to honour Yajnaseni appropriately."

Stunned, I kept listening. Discriminating, knowledgeable, noble, handsome, the dearest son of Kunti was raging about the ancient insult he had suffered! Karna could utter such words! And for me? Whom he had desired at one time! Whom he worshipped in his heart? I placed my hands over my ears. Living was impossible.

Suddenly Duhshasan stripped my husbands of their garments. Wearing only a single cloth each, they sat without ornaments, with heads bowed. Who was present there to feel sad or ashamed for them? Before my own pain and suffering and shame, all the grief of others appeared insignificant.

Letting go of my hair Duhshasan began pulling at my garment. So this wicked person would actually translate into action the words of Karna!

Calling to the ten directions to witness, I said, "Since the beginning of time till today never has such a hellish, horrible thing happened, nor will it ever happen till the end of eternity. When Ravan was abducting chaste Sita, trees and plants, animals and birds — everyone shed tears. Even though born a bird, Jatayu opposed him and sacrificed his life. To rescue Sita, an army of bears and monkeys laid down their lives. But today, in the presence of elders, in the midst of the assembly, before everyone, the hellish scene of Draupadi's indescribable outrage went on being played, yet everyone remained silent, inert! Rather, everyone seemed to be waiting in anticipation for some thrilling scene of the drama. Alas! At one time comparing Dharmaraj Yudhishthir's personality to that of Ram I used to feel immensely glorified. For protecting the honour of chaste Sita how much sorrow and pain did Ram not undergo? He bore the profound anguish of raising the question of the test by fire to prove in public her chastity. While my husband having staked me and having handed me over to others is sitting there. A mute spectator, he is watching me being insulted. These wicked Kauravs are so much meaner and pettier than the demon Ravan. Ravan abducted Sita but did not rape her. Despite finding her alone he did not misbehave with her. Despite being moved by his perverted lust, he did not touch her body in the Ashok forest. He only kept begging her for love. That was natural. But here, wicked people, driven by

241

perverted lust, are insulting the bride of the Bharat dynasty and stripping her body naked in the assembly-hall! Such a gross outrage on womanhood will never be wiped out in history. The descendants of this country will blame the Kuru king for this. This lawless, gross injustice and tyranny of the Kuru clan will demean the entire male sex for all time. It will outrage all the chaste women of the Bharat dynasty and the entire female sex on earth. For this insult there is no forgiveness, for this sin there is no expiation."

After vomiting out this poison I was exhausted. I surrendered myself to Krishna. Pierced sharply by the arrows of my words, Duhshasan was roaring with excitement. He began pulling at the cloth round my waist. With both hands on my breast I was calling Krishna...

"O Krishna Vasudev! You know my heart. In whichever end of the world you might be, can you not understand how your *sakhi* is being tormented by the wicked Kauravs? In the long history of the world its blackest and most hellish chapter is being written. Are you unaware of that? O beloved of the *gopis*, Govind! This insufferable shame and anguish never occurred in the life of any woman. God willing, may it not be repeated in the life of any woman. O Creator! You know that the primitive man used to roam the forests naked. Even then the naked body of one woman would not have been stared at by hundreds of men all at once with such horrible lust. Even then a woman had her independent status and honour. But today this outrage on queen Krishnaa has surpassed all the crimes in the three worlds. From this insufferable shame and danger only you can rescue me. Govind! Save me!"

My lamentation was encouraging Duhshasan further. The more strongly he pulled at my cloth, with equal strength did I hold on to it with both hands. I kept trying with all my strength to cover my breast. Even after sinking up to one's nose, fools still keep depending on themselves so much! In his pride, how pitiable and oppressed does the condition of man become. I wanted to protect myself — but I was failing absolutely! Without total surrender of the self, God's compassion is not found. The moment this thought came to me, I forgot all shame, modesty, doubt. Leaving hold of that single cloth, I raised up both my hands. In anguish I cried, "Lord, I am not mine own. This body is not mine. Therefore, the whole responsibility of this body is yours. All is yours. Hurt, reproach, insult, shame, doubt, modesty, everything is yours. It is you who are the primal cause. I know nothing."

And truly, I became free of all shame, hesitation, sorrow, reproach, pain. On leaving everything to Krishna, if one got so much happiness, peace and courage then why did he suffer so much getting his own self entangled in every matter? Could even I comprehend this? At that moment, regarding Krishna Vasudev as God instead of as *sakha*, I was standing free from doubt and fearless in the midst of danger. Earlier, I had never been able to be so fearless and free from doubt.

Something was going on all around me. I was unable to know what was happening. I only saw the *sudarshan* discus spinning and through it Krishna's compassionate hand and from it layer after layer of cloth was covering me. Like holy water sanctified by *mantras*, grace was being showered on me. After that I did not know where all the sense of anguish and outrage within me disappeared.

Duhshasan was going on pulling my cloth. Till he grew tired and exhausted, he went on pulling with both hands. The more he pulled, the more my body would get clothed with costly garments. Seeing this amazing sight the entire hall was stunned. Shouts of "Sati! Sati!" resounded in the hall. Tired, defeated, exhausted Duhshasan tripped and fell on the heap of garments. Noticing this laughable condition of his, Duryodhan's companions, Kutila, Jatila, Kamana, Vasana, Karna's companion, Asmita, were commenting wickedly. Even now Duryodhan, uncovering his thigh and slapping it, was making obscene gestures towards me, inviting me to sit there.

Bhim's anger and excitement broke all barriers. He roared out, "Tearing apart wicked Duhshasan's chest I will drink his blood. Shattering that thigh of obscene Duryodhan I will appease the ancestors." I too vowed, "Till I wet my hair with the blood of Duhshasan's breast, I will leave it unbound thus."

Just then Vidur stated gravely, "This vow of Bhim will be the cause of severe danger to the Kuru clan. Bhim is exceptionally dedicated in fulfilling his vows. Moreover, chaste Draupadi's vow is even more terrible. What was to happen is over. Now free Draupadi. Yudhishthir's staking Draupadi after having lost himself does not appear to be proper."

Duryodhan laughed scornfully, "Then let the four Pandav brothers acknowledge that Yudhishthir is not their lord. I will free Draupadi." In a solemn voice Arjun said, "Before the dice game and during the dice game it is Yudhishthir who is our lord. But after having lost himself whose lord he can be, we do not know."

Now Dhritarashtra opened his mouth. With affection he said, "Krishnaa! You are the first among the daughters-in-law and the finest of all. Your chastity and devotion are honouring you today. You have revealed your greatness. I am extremely pleased with your dedication. What boon do you want? Speak!"

I looked at Yudhishthir for the first time and said, "Free king Yudhishthir. At least my eldest son Prativindhya will not be called the son of a slave."

"So be it", he said.

Yudhishthir sat with head bowed, full of grief and shame.

"Ask one more boon, Yajnaseni!"Dhritarashtra coaxed me.

"The fathers of my four other sons be also made free. Their weapons be also returned," I said calmly.

"So be it. But ask yet another boon."

"Forgive me, sire! The scriptures sanction up to two boons for a kshatriya woman. My brave husbands are now free. So long as they can bear arms, there will be no need to ask for any boon for their happiness and prosperity."

"But, auspicious one, you have not asked for your own freedom! I am asking you to take another boon. Then why hesitate?"

Full of reproach and hurt I said, "My husbands are courageous. My absence will not prove any obstacle to their happiness and prosperity. Had it been so then Yudhishthir would not have staked me in the dice game. He has several other wives. He did not stake them. Therefore, I am free. They will look after my husbands' needs."By the time I finished speaking, my tears had begun to flow.

Karna jested, "Well! What selfless devotion to husbands! Forgetting about herself, Yajnaseni, heroine of five husbands, is rescuing such valiant husbands as the Pandavs from the vast ocean! Perhaps she may not wish to return under the authorty of the Pandavs. So she has cleverly rejected the opportunity to ask for her own freedom."

"Excellent! Karna, you are extremely wise. Draupadi's anguish her husbands could not understand, but you have. The gathering is enchanted by the supreme chastity of Draupadi. If she is unwilling to return to the Pandavs then she can accept the Kauravs before this assembly, or our friend, the best of warriors, generous-hearted Karna is present here," mocked Duhshasan.

I flared up like a tongue of flame. Bhimsen was unable to tolerate this insult. He roared out, "Death is calling you, Duhshasan! A mighty war shall be fought. Because of this insult and humiliation of Yajnaseni the Kauravs will be destroyed. Lakhs of kshatriyas of Aryavart will be slain. The prophecy at Yajnaseni's birth will soon come true."

Yudhishthir stood up and restrained Bhim. With folded hands he pleaded with Dhritarashtra, "Permit us, sir! Your commands will be obeyed."

Generously Dhritarashtra said, "Go, my son! Live in peace with chaste Yajnaseni. Forgive this blind old man, Yajnaseni! I was forced to grant permission for such an unjust game of dice. If the son does not listen to the father then who will understand the father's helplessness more than me? But this outrage on you has also multiplied your glory. My sons will now understand the extent of their strength and prowess. The result of the dice game has shown how noble the Pandavs are. Yudhishthir's devotion to dharma, Arjun's patience, Bhim's prowess and daring, and Nakul-Sahadev's knowledge of rules and peacefulness have been revealed to the world. O Yudhishthir, now assuage chaste Draupadi's hurt and return to Indraprasth. Rule your subjects in peace. Establish amity with your foolish Kaurav brothers. Conflict does not resolve a quarrel. Rather, it destroys the whole kingdom."

Before leaving the assembly I *pranam*-ed everyone with folded hands. Humbly I said, "I beg forgiveness of all elders. While coming to the assembly-hall, on account of grief and excitement, I forgot the primary duty of *pranam*-ing the elders. I beg a thousand pardons. *Pranam ... pranam* to everyone and all."

After *pranam*-ing *ma* Gandhari preparations were afoot for returning to Indraprasth. Just then Duryodhan sent the invitation for playing at dice once again.

Sighing deeply Yudhishthir said, "It is this that is the trick of fate. I know that this time too I will lose. But it is not possible to reject the invitation." Yudhishthir left for the assembly-hall. I stood blocking his path. Seeing me furious, Yudhishthir gently said, "Step aside, Yajnaseni! Let me follow the path of dharma..."

Furiously I asked, "Husband! Despite the intolerable outrage and insult I suffered, you are not at peace? Is this your dharma? There is no dharma in answering the call of injustice. This is but your pride. You know yourself to be incompetent, yet you are not prepared to acknowledge it. Wife, son, brother, kingdom — crushing the peace, happiness, honour, security of all you wish to display your humility and devotion to dharma. Is this the dharma of a king?"

"If we reject today's challenge, will the Kauravs allow us to reign in peace even after our return to Indraprasth? Therefore, why hesitate in making a last effort and see what fate has in store?" said Yudhishthir and rejecting my advice went to the assembly-hall.

If I could have burnt myself to ashes, it would have given me peace. But I was born of fire, therefore the fire of anger and agitation did not turn me into ashes, it merely kept consuming me. Frantic with the burning pain I was moving here and there.

246

After such outrage I was waiting for what more the world had in store for me.

Maya consoled me, "Do not worry. The attention of wicked Duryodhan is concentrated on the wealth of Indraprasth. He will calm down on obtaining that. He knows that the Pandavs will not rest without taking revenge for your insult. Therefore, he does not wish that you return to Indraprasth. By any means he wants to exile you all.

"This is what will happen. Wherever the Pandavs go they will establish a capital like Indraprasth and live happily. Prosperity and happiness are like the dust of the road for the Pandavs. If you are with them then what is there that they cannot do? Do you not know that you are a portion of the goddess Lakshmi?"

Even in the midst of so much trouble and sorrow I could not but laugh, "Maya! Do you think that I am worried about the wealth of the kingdom slipping out of my hands? When I had placed the garland of choice round Phalguni's neck, he was for me a mere forest-dwelling mendicant brahmin. When I married the five Pandavs, they were princes without a kingdom. Then I was not sorrowful. The happiness and joy that were mine then I never got even after becoming queen of Indraprasth. I am not made of the ingredients that find delight in wealth and prosperity. But Yudhishthir's repeated humble surrender in the name of dharma at the invitation of injustice — this I cannot bear. Since I was staked at dice, my entire peace of mind has been destroyed. Instead of the agony of this insult and this anguish, to eke out an existence as the wife of a forest-dwelling humble gentleman will be preferred by any woman of character."

Perhaps it was fate that was on my lips. I had but finished speaking when news came that in the last dice-game Yudhishthir had lost his kingdom and, according to the conditions of the bet, the five brothers along with their wife would go into exile in the forest for twelve years. After that they would also have to live for a year in disguise.

For me the news was not grievous. I had lived in the forest with my husbands long before. But what would happen to the

subjects who had left Hastinapur to take shelter under Yudhishthir in Indraprasth? The men and women of Indraprasth would
have to undergo so much torment at the hands of Duryodhan
who was unjust and vindictive. As targets of the perverted lust of
the Kaurav brothers, the chaste, devoted women of Indraprasth
would have to suffer untold agonies. Was this indifference of
Yudhishthir towards the welfare of his subjects the dharma of a
king? While betting during the dice-game did he not think even
once of his subjects? If he was so indifferent to kingdom and
wealth, then why did he win the confidence of the people by
becoming emperor on the throne of Indraprasth?

Ramchandra invited grief by running after the golden deer.
But Yudhishthir ran blindly after dice — it was this that became
the root of all my sorrows.

In Yudhishthir's mind greed had no place. He was *sthitaprajna,*
his wisdom was not affected by joy and sorrow. The other brothers were silent followers. I, too, did not tell him anything. What
was the value of my words now?

The news of the forest exile of the Pandavs spread like wildfire
everywhere. Andhak, the Bhoj king, Krishnik, Dhrishtaketu the
king of Chedi, the mighty warrior Kekaya, my brother, Dhrishtadyumna, and father, Drupad, came to us. Yudhishthir took
leave of everyone. Father wanted to take me with him. I said,
"Father, do not deprive me of the opportunity of fulfilling my
dharma as a wife. How much suffering did chaste Sita not undergo with her husband? A similar opportunity has now arisen
in my life. I do not have the danger of a Ravan before me. For the
greatest outrage in my life has already occurred. Now all the
sorrow and want that will come will be minor ones. Do not
worry. He who protected me at the time of the supreme insult
will help me. After that, no sorrow or pain in life will be able to
overcome me."

Saying this I was *pranam*ing Krishna in my heart when I found
him in person before me. Eagerly I was going to touch his feet
when he caught hold of both my hands. I said, "Vasudev, in what
words shall I express my gratitude? Your deed shall be renowned

for aeons as a reassurance for the tormented. I will remain your handmaid for all time to come."

Krishna spoke in a sweet voice, "*Sakhi*, do not push me away with such words. I am your *sakha*. After all, what is it that I have done? When Yudhishthir was dicing, I was engaged in fighting king Shalva of Shaubha. Otherwise I would have stopped him from playing. Women, dice, hunting, liquor destroy the goodness of man. I was not in Dvaraka. Therefore, this disaster struck the Pandavs. The moment I got the news, anxiously I have rushed here."

Choked with emotion I said, "Lord, you can do as you will. Without you can anything occur anywhere? Who but you could tackle Draupadi's insult in the Kuru court? When Duhshasan dragged me by the hair into the hall, I was then menstruating, wearing a single piece of cloth. I, the wife of the Pandavs, Dhrishtadyumna's sister, your dear *sakhi* and the bride of the Bharat dynasty! Yet none prevented Duhshasan. My valiant husbands remained mute spectators. Duhshasan and Duryodhan's obscene words, gestures, Karna's sarcastic speech are even now piercing my being. In the royal hall the elders, warriors, scholars, all were seated. When Duhshasan began stripping me, none was there to help! It seemed to me I had no husband, no son, no brother, no friend, no father, no well-wisher! How terrifyingly helpless I felt! Who will understand that? I do not know where Bhim and Arjun's prowess and valour disappeared. Yudhishthir's humility and devotion to dharma-is this what it was? The destruction of the country where men do not rise to protect the honour of women is inevitable. The men of that country get a bad name and are abused. In such a situation it is on you that I depended, Krishna! When my faith in everyone was shattered, I surrendered myself to you. By your miraculous intervention not only was my honour saved but the honur of all womankind of this country. On the sacred soil of Bharata woman is not dishonoured — this you proved. Even though I was insulted, yet the glory of this soil was revealed before the world. It is this that remains a matter of consolation for me. O Krishna! I wish to spend my life as your handmaid. Only then, perhaps, may this debt grow somewhat lighter..."

Opening up my heart before my compassionate and understanding friend, Krishna, I sobbed into my *sari*. After the outrage in the Kuru court I had not uttered a word to my husbands. What was the point of displaying hurt and reproach before my husbands, who were the cause of my anguish and who, despite being powerful, did not come to my assistance? What further sulking can I do before such husbands any more? Finding so understanding a friend as Krishna, how could I control myself? After all I was a woman!

Folding his hands Krishna said, "Devi! My handmaid! You will turn me into an offender. I did not do anything at all out of the way for you. Whatever you had done, it was that debt that I repaid and am free now. In nursing me on the day of the ceremonial entrance to the new palace, you had torn the auspicious *sari* received from your husband to bandage my finger. In the shape of cloth it was that which I returned. By offering thread to get cloth in return — that is faith."

My eyes were tearful. Wiping his perspiration with a perfumed cloth, Krishna said, "Look! I have turned the gift of your affection into a kerchief and carry it about. *Sakhi,* Krishna is ever hungry for affection. Regarding me as your *sakha,* keep showering affection on me — that is all I want. I will count myself blessed. Treat me like that always."

I was amazed. Krishna was carrying around the strip of my *sari* as a kerchief! Every moment he was recalling that petty service!

It seemed to me that all the grief and regret of my life had been washed away. In a voice throbbing with love I said, "*Sakha,* you alone have the right to all the pure unsullied love of this heart. Since birth this heart has been offered to you alone. Do not shame me by repeating what you said."

Krishna laughed, "Krishnaa, you have been born of a portion of Lakshmi. Without your affection Krishna will be deprived of good fortune — remember this."

Finding Krishna's support, I was sensing strength within. In a firm voice I said, "*Sakha*, if those who were responsible for the horrifying outrage that Draupadi suffered in the Kuru court, for wicked misbehaviour, do not receive exemplary punishment, then the history of Bharata will be filled with shameful accounts of atrocities against women. Kings and princes will abduct beautiful women from their husbands' homes for quenching their perverted lust, will strip them in public. To enjoy the beauty of naked women with lust-crazed eyes will become the normal pastime of debauched men. *Sakha*, to me you are everything. What worry do I have? But if the Duhshasans and Duryodhans do not receive the fruits of their sins, then in future the fate of women is shrouded in the darkest gloom. I am surprised that even after attempting to strip the daughter-in-law of noble Pandu, the wife of the Pandavs, the dear *sakhi* of Krishna Vasudev, in the Kuru court, they did not die. When that wicked man was stripping me, helpless like chaste Sita I could have disappeared into the depths of the earth to hide my shame. If I had prayed, would not the earth have opened? But I did not do so. If I had done so my modesty would have been protected but the wicked would not have been punished. In the future this problem would remain unresolved for women. Tolerance is the ornament of women. But to bear injustice with bowed head is not the dharma of women. If the husband adopts the wrong path and the wife remains quiet, then everyone will suffer. The portion of sin in the world will increase. Innocent people will suffer the consequences of that sin. Therefore, even after the terrible outrage and the insufferable insult I am alive. Happiness, prosperity, enjoyment of the kingdom are not the aims of my life. Krishnaa has been reborn. The remaining days of my life I will fight against injustice, adharma, sin. I have sworn that I shall tie up my hair only after washing it in Duhshasan's blood. Otherwise, these tresses will ever remain loose. Though the world may call me an ogress because of this, the world must know that woman who creates, is auspicious, is also the destroyer of the sinful and the wicked. It is after washing my hair in Duhshasan's blood that I shall tie it up — Duhshasan who, regarding woman as weak, dragged me by the hair and insulted me. Then will the world know that while a woman's heart is delicate, it is not weak. O Krishna, if you do not help in fulfilling my vow, then this lovely creation of yours shall be crushed under the weight of sin."

Hearing my grim words Krishna was pleased. Reassuring me, he said, "Krishnaa, your anger and vow are just. Those who insulted you, those who looked upon you with lustful eyes in the assembly-hall, who encouraged sin — all of them will be laid low on the battlefield by the arrows of your husband, Phalguni. In the great war, Dhrishtadyumna will destroy Drona; Shikhandi will kill Bhishma; Bhim's mace will shatter Duryodhan's thigh; Dhananjay's arrow will slay Karna. Because of you, many kshatriyas will die. After your insult in the Kuru court, this earth cannot be saved from a great war. In age after age the breast of mother earth runs red with the blood of the wicked. The heavens may fall, the Himalayas may sink into *Patala*, the sun and the moon may collapse, the earth may split into a hundred pieces, but your vow shall be fulfiled. I shall leave no stone unturned in helping the Pandavs. Sakhi, do not grieve. What I say always comes true."

29

The hour of departure came. *Ma* Kunti broke down in grief. For the fatherless innocent children, what untold suffering had princess Kunti, wife of Pandu, not undergone! When her husband was king, even then, because of the jealousy and envy of Dhritarashtra, Kunti was deprived of royal comfort and had to bear the difficulties of forest-life. It was during that stay in the forest that her husband died. After the education of her sons, she had to take to the forest once again to save their lives. After the arrival of Yajnaseni as daughter-in-law, fate seemed to smile. *Ma* Kunti thought that now she would be able to pass the remaining days in peace watching over the prosperity of her sons. But sorrow was, as though, her shadow. Now the sons and daughter-in-law would suffer thirteen years of exile in the forest. If they were recognised in the year of their disguise then a second forest exile for another twelve years. Who knew whether, like king Dasharath, she might also have to give up her life without seeing her sons' faces! *Ma* Kunti was anguished over her sons and I was worried about my five sons.

The youngest son was still a breast-fed baby. How would I live without them for thirteen years? There was no way at all of taking them along. They would have to be left with Subhadra. They would certainly live comfortably with her, for did Subhadra love them any less? As Abhimanyu was dear to me, my sons were similarly dear to Subhadra. Kunti and Madri were the mothers of the five Pandavs, but the five were one soul. They were equal in Kunti's eyes. Subhadra would go to Dvaraka with Krishna, taking the children with her. The children too were very happy to hear of going to their maternal uncle's . And there were no words to express *sakha's* joy at the prospect of the children living in Dvaraka. But how did my heart understand all these things? Who except me would understand how much the pain of the forest exile would be increased by the absence of the children? If anyone could understand, it was *ma* Kunti.

Sorrowfully, *ma* Kunti said, "Daughter Krishnaa! You are chaste, faithful, learned. By the nobility of your nature you have brought renown to both families. What can I say to console you? Because of your grief and hurt do not neglect my sons. Keep note of Bhim's belly. Take special care of Nakul-Sahadev for they are younger and naturally hungry for affection. One more request: forgive Karna. The manner in which he has behaved with you is most regrettable. He has done so because of keeping bad company. Your terrible vow has shaken my heart. The vow is just. But Karna is blameless. he behaved like this because of the insults he has suffered since his childhood. Otherwise, he is extremely polite, humble — a gentleman. Do not entertain enmity for him. After all, he is my dharma-son."

Mother's eyes brimmed over. I was trying to appreciate Mother's pain. As a consequence of Mother's generous feelings, a trace of generosity reverberated in me too. I remained silent.

Mother remained in Vidur's home. Krishna and Subhadra left with the children. While leaving, Krishna said in a soft voice, "I am feeling jealous of the Pandavs. With a gem of a woman like you, what is there to worry about? It is a matter of great good fortune to be able to enjoy life in the forests, relieved of all responsibilities. My tender sister, Subhadra, will now bear the pangs of separation for thirteen years. Therefore, *sakhi*, you are fortunate. For taking part in your good fortune I shall definitely drop in at your forest cottage sometimes. *Sakhi*, without tasting food cooked by you, I shall not be able to pass these thirteen years. It is out of that greed that I repeatedly become the guest of the Pandavs."

I was delighted: "*Sakha*, is my delight any less in serving you food cooked by myself? After all, it is you who say that on receiving the touch of my hand food becomes amrita. Truly, is this a matter of little pride for any woman! Woman is the nourisher. The power to provide amrita from her breasts is woman's alone.

254

That is not in man. She is blessed because of this power of gifting amrita. The creator, too, is blessed. That is why a woman feels spontaneous joy in being able to feed a guest with food of his choice. O Krishna! I shall wait for you. If you are our guest from time to time, then by feeding you to your heart's content I shall also feel the joy of feeding my children to their fill. Children, guests, God, all are equally dear to me."

Krishna laughed, "Look, do not put me in the place of your children, guests or God. I am your *sakha*. You are my *sakhi*. This relationship is far more refined than any between two human beings. To give it a name is beyond the power and knowledge of man. It is in this that I take delight."

Sakha left. He promised to meet us.

We were walking along the royal road of Hastinapur towards exile. The citizens cried out at this sight. Hundreds prepared to follow us and came out on the road, leaving their homes. Yudhishthir restrained them, explaining, "Return and take care of *ma* Kunti, Dhritarashtra, Gandhari and grandfather Bhishma." Many brahmins did not agree to turn back. Where dharma was lacking, the lives and the dharma of brahmins would be endangered at every step. Therefore, Yudhishthir could not send them back. But, how would so many brahmins be looked after in the forest? Worried, Yudhishthir prayed to god Surya. Satisfied, Surya placed an inexhaustible copper vessel in his hands and said, "The most sublime gift is to give the hungry to eat, for that saves life. There is food for twelve years in this inexhaustible vessel. If anything is cooked in this vessel, till Draupadi has eaten, it will remain full. But once Draupadi has taken her share out of it, thereafter, for that day, the food will have finished."

*Pranam*ing Surya, taking the inexhaustible vessel, accompanied by the brahmins, with a steady heart we advanced towards Kamyak forest. For feeding the hungry the inexhaustible vessel was with me. Then the attractions of kingdom, wealth, property, prosperity — all appeared insignificant to me. Now in the whole forest none — neither people, nor birds and animals, nor even insects and worms, would remain unfed. My sad heart filled with bliss and contentment.

Dressed as forest-dwellers, all the five Pandavs were walking on the royal road. I was in the middle. The people of Hastina were tearfully showering flowers on us. None was able to control himself. The women were ululating. The elders were chanting *mantras*. Some were offering their invaluable treasures. Then Yudhishthir said, "Let your affection and good wishes form our sustenance. We cannot take any gifts. Renouncing everything we are entering the forest. The rights to these are king Duryodhan's. It is enough for us that you are eager to give us gifts."

After going some distance I saw that on the way Duhshasan and Karna were waiting with some attendants. I thought that perhaps at the time of leave-laking Duhshasan had come to beg forgiveness. Departure washes away all hatred.

Duhshasan barred our way. Placing a hand on his shoulder, Yudhishthir said, "Brother, forget the past. In a household, anger, reproach, sulking keep occurring between brothers. Then time smooths out everything. Distance and absence bring the separated close. By the time we return after thirteen years, having forgotten everything, we shall have grown closer. Krishnaa too will have forgotten those matters. Take care of your aged parents, grandfather Bhishma and *ma* Kunti."

Duhshasan laughed loudly and mocked, "You are a great hero in words. What sweet speeches! You imagine that hearing sweet things I will become forgetful? It is to see what money and wealth you are taking along that I am waiting here. Except for one cloth and weapons you cannot take even a straw with you. This is the command of Duryodhan."

Laughing Yudhishthir said, "Why did you take so much trouble? We are complying with the orders fully. You can see that besides what we are wearing and our weapons, we are taking nothing. Earrings, necklaces, bracelets, rings and even footwear we have surrendered to the treasury and come away."

Duhshasan laughed, "You are a hermit! But Bhim? He must be taking along a bundle of food."

In a rude voice I said, "Lord Surya has gifted us the capability of feeding thousands of people to their hearts' content. Then why should Bhim bring along a bundle of food from Hastinapur?"

"It is not that easy to give up a habit," said Duhshasan. Having inspected our weapons thoroughly, he let us proceed.

We had gone on only a little when Duhshasan's voice cracked like a whip, "Stop, Yajnaseni! You can throw dust in my eyes but you cannot deceive Karna. *Chheeh, chheeh!* Despite being a princess you are so greedy for a few ornaments? Anyway, that is typical of a woman's nature! The husbands are unable to provide even one ornament. Therefore it is only natural to be greedy."

I stood frozen. He kept staring again and again at the necklace on my breast, the bracelets on my hands, earrings, wedding rings etc. In a muted voice Karna said, "Take off all the ornaments. The borders of the kingdom will have to be crossed wearing only a single cloth. This is the command of Maharaj. Do not misunderstand us. We are only following orders."

Calmly I said, "*Ma* Kunti has made me promise not to bear hatred towards you. You are Mother's dharma-son, to be respected by us and dear to us. I am a married woman. Maya had stopped me from taking off the ornaments because of this. That is why I have them on. *Ma* Gandhari has granted permission for this."

"Gandhari is the queen-mother. We work under the king's commands," said Karna grimly. Duhshasan said in a coarse voice, "Before force is used, give up the ornaments yourself, lovely one! After taking off the ornaments, your beauty will not be diminished!"

Nitambini and Maya had come along to see us off. Maya took off all the ornaments from my body, even the nose-stud. Nitambini decked my arms, neck, hair etc. with flowers. In a sweet voice she said, "*Sakhi*, you are appearing pure and incomparable like a hermit-girl. Maya is very mysterious. Had you not listened to her, you would not have fallen into this predicament."

'I was unable to know how I was looking in ornaments of flowers. But my husbands were looking at me enchanted. I was getting lost imagining my incomparable beauty. Arjun quietly whispered, "How lovely do you look thus! After having seen this, why thirteen, I wish to live in the forest for three hundred years! Ornaments must be painful for your delicate limbs. It is only flower ornaments that suit you."

In shyness and delight I forgot the sorrow and pain of separation from the loved ones.

Suddenly I noticed Karna gazing at me fixedly as though enchanted. Not an eye was blinking. Flames of perverted lust were not burning in those eyes. A sweet, compassionate, muted light of affection was visible, lit secretly in a hesitant eagerness. My heart leaped. Then I cursed myself. He who was the cause of such gross insults to me — his infatuated stare was thrilling me! *Chheeh!* Not a jot of self-respect remained within me.

Glancing at him indifferently, I stepped ahead. Duhshasan and Karna again kept following us.

A little ahead among other people we came across Harita, guru Drona's wife, and Karna's wife, Rituvati. Trays of offerings in hand they were waiting on the extreme border of Hastinapur. The women of the city were waiting there to bid farewell.

Harita embraced me and said, "Krishnaa, forgive my husband. Despite being a preceptor and a brahmin, he did not act as he should have. He kept watching silently when they insulted you. As a result of this all his merit is destroyed. Know that by your curse their dynasty will be annihilated. He is dependent on the Kauravs, therefore, he keeps tolerating injustice. I acknowledge all his offences. Please do not curse my only son, Ashvatthama. May God ensure your welfare. You are the intimate *sakhi* of my lonely life. Only you can understand how much I am pained by your exile."

Laying my head on Harita's breast I, too, shed a few tears. I said, "Dear to my life, Harita! As Ashvatthama is your son, so is he like a son to me. I pray for your welfare. But, *sakhi*, who am I to forgive guru Drona? I am just a woman. In the eyes of scholars and wise men a woman has no status of her own. Honour and insult, character, nobility etc. — nothing is hers. This has been proved by my insult in the Kuru court. He whom I forgive-will God forgive him?"

In the midst of this Rituvati caught my hand — "Queen Krishnaa! I understand the burning anguish of your heart, for I too am a woman. The behaviour of my husband towards you — for that he himself is no less remorseful. The whole night he kept cursing himself; kept saying repeatedly 'In the great war it is death that will be the penance for my sin'. You will laugh if I speak of my husband's nobility. But, believe me, his character is appearing in this light because he has fallen into the company of the Kauravs. The anguish of the insult that day in the *svayamvar* hall was sharpened on account of being with the Kauravs. He grew inhuman. I know that he has committed a crime. As his wife, I beg forgiveness on his behalf. Rituvati's eyes were tearful.

Calmly I said, "*Ma* Kunti has made me promise that I shall not entertain any hatred towards her dharma-son. I have promised her. It is on her single word that I accepted five husbands. Therefore, despite his having insulted me in the Kuru court, I will say nothing to Karna. Remain happy, Rituvati! May your husband and sons prosper!"

I noticed that from a distance Karna was straining to hear our exchange. His eyes appeared moist.

Taking me by the hand, Rituvati stopped me. Taking valuable ornaments from the tray her attendants began to put them on me. As though bitten by a snake I shrank back, "What is this? Why ornaments? What will a forest-dweller do with ornaments?"

Humbly Rituvati said, "It is my husband's command that I should deck you in all my ornaments. You are his brothers' wife. On your going from here in such a mean dress he will have to suffer gross insult. King Duryodhan has no rights over these ornaments. All these are Karna's property. Knowing that Duhshasan would take your ornaments away, Karna sent me word to wait here with all my ornaments." Karna's favourite companion Asmita arrogantly said, "Do not be amazed at this small matter, *maharani!* Best of givers, maharaj Karna does not hesitate to give away his all, even his very life, as a gift."

259

Sarcastically I said, "He gestured Duhshasan to take away my ornaments and asked you to wait here with ornaments! An excellent instance of giving gifts indeed! But, Rituvati, even these ornaments are not earned by Karna himself. For, Karna did not become king of Ang on the strength of his own prowess. The royal crown on his head is the kind gift of sinful Duryodhan. Therefore, how can I accept Duryodhan's property? However, I shall remember. Karna's reputation as a giver shall also be tested. You took such pains for me, I am grateful."

Karna's face fell on hearing my words. Duhshasan flared up, "Alas! What gross injustice has king Drupad committed by handing over such a rare gem as Yajnaseni to such eunuchs! Now if he sees Yajnaseni proceeding to the forest in such a miserable state with her beggar-husbands he might wish to do penance for his sin by handing over his daughter to the valiant king of Ang, Karna. Princess! Now discarding these beggars accept wealthy and valiant Karna, or any other person. For, you have retained your chastity despite having five husbands. If you accept one more husband, then this indestructible chastity will not be affected a bit. So splendid a woman as you is to be enjoyed only by kings, not by beggars."

Duhshasan's vulgar comments infuriated Bhim, "Fool! Your bragging is but momentary. Just as you are piercing queen Draupadi's delicate heart with such insulting words, similarly shall I cut open your heart and offer it as *arghya* before her. Those who are supporting your comments, them too shall I send to hell..."

Noticing Bhim's fury, Yudhishthir took hold of him and calmed him down. I kept thinking that in future if anyone protected my self-respect and honour it would be this outspoken, transparent, quick-to-anger Bhimsen. He who, failing to protect the honour of his wife, to avoid war, instead of saving the honour of the kingdom, adopted renunciation and non-violence, might be a great soul of dharma. But actually he was a coward. One might feel devotion for such a person, but love was impossible.

30

Where generous nature spreads herself out spontaneously for the world, there how insignificant does man become because of his narrowness and selfishness! This I experienced immediately on setting foot in Kamyak forest.

After walking for three days along the banks of the Ganga, we entered the forest. The wonderful beauty of that place swept away all our grief, tiredness and depression.

Tall bamboo groves. Over them a verdant curtain of touch-me-nots. Behind them a teenaged girl was playing hide and seek. Sometimes she could be seen, sometimes she hid in the greenery of the forest. There was an indomitable urge in her to befriend us, yet she was full of shyness. Tinkling laughter, rhythmic steps, and suddenly her voice merged into the silence of the forest. I kept gazing, but she would not come in front. Yudhishthir, noticing that I was tired said, "Look, from time immemorial, Tandravati, the daughter of the mountains has been flowing incessantly on this difficult forest path, so far away from its birth-place. She has not grown tired! Her goal is the sea. While flowing to the sea she keeps turning the barren earth green. This is what life is. While progressing towards one's goal on the path of life, if a man is unable to bring about the welfare of his friends and relations, country and society, then what sort of life is that? Of what value is this body? The sea does not quench our thirst — the sweet water of the river does. Of what use is that property that does not remove the poverty of others? Today Duryodhan is the ruler of Hastinapur and Indraprasth. But if he is not interested in the welfare of his subjects, what is the use of that throne? Yajnaseni, the lessons that we shall learn during these twelve years of exile will be far greater than all the education we have had so far. It will provide happiness. It is for our welfare that God has sent us into the forest."

On the other side of the thick bamboo grove a waterfall could be seen. The sky hung over the greenery of the forest like a blue pandal. Could the sky be so blue! Deeper than the blue of the sky were those mountains. Small bits of white clouds had been sprinkled over them. There layers of clouds looked like the marks of ashes on the body of a yogi in meditation.

To break the meditation of the yoga-immersed mountains, the leaves and flowers of the trees had turned into nymphs in the rain. But the concentration of the mountains was not broken. The clouds were gradually falling off like ashes from the body of the meditating sage, turning into coverings for the foothills, blessing the earth with rain. Clouds here were free like wild birds. They were floating about as they wished, seeking the meaning of life.

Various types of creepers, trees, plants were intertwined; many kinds of flowers and fruit, big and small — nature in all her expanse was spread out, hinting at co-existence and amity. The trees standing on the earth were engrossed in striving for light. To drink in the sun each was striving to go higher and higher. Here each was mighty in its own place. All were tall, lovely, strong. But man! He wants to rise by making others small. Even if it was unjust, adharma, he would oppress others. The proof was the behaviour of the Kauravs towards their Pandav brothers.

The magic of solitude had entranced everyone. Yudhishthir grew philosophic. Arjun seemed lost in poetry. Bhim was thinking that we were the lords of this place. Nakul was admiring himself in the waters of the spring. Sahadev was seeking out a path in the forest and determining our future task.

In an enchanted voice I asked, "So, twelve years of exile will be in this Kamyak forest! Building our hut on the banks of the Tandravati, we will live in peace."

Yudhishthir asked Sahadev's opinion. He said, "Kamyak forest would be desirable from every point of view if the Kirats did not live here." Surprised, Yudhishthir asked, "What is the problem if the Kirats have their habitation here? We will make friends with them. It will lessen our sorrow of leaving friends behind. We will get integrated with them."

"But they will not become our friends. Out of fear of the Kirats even sages do not come to perform ascesis here. Brahmins and kshatriyas do not even enter Kamyak forest for fear of the atrocities of the Kirats."

I asked, "But what is the reason for enmity between them and brahmins-kshatriyas?"

Sahadev explained calmly, "One of the Kirats, Jara Ekalavya had prayed to guru Drona for education. If a child of Kirats is educated with princes, the princes might take it otherwise. Out of fear of the Kauravs, Drona refused the prayer of Kirat Jara. Jara did not give up. He made a clay idol of Drona and concentrated on practising archery before it. He mastered this art. Later, hearing of this and noticing Ekalavya's remarkable ability, Drona was worried that he would surely defeat and kill the Kauravs. To protect the Kauravs, Drona, on the pretext of asking for a guru's fees, cruelly asked for the right thumb of his simple, devoted, single-minded disciple, Ekalavya. How will the Kirats forgive that insult of the Kauravs and that fee demanded by Drona? That is why they are bent upon destroying the Aryans root and branch."

Bhim said, "But Yudhishthir and Arjun had pleaded in favour of accepting tribal Ekalavya as a disciple. Every man is equal. Therefore, Jara was not inferior in any way to a brahmin or a kshatriya. The Pandavs had interceded with Drona. Still, for the sake of the security of his employment learned Drona did such a deed. What is the fault of the Pandavs in this? Will the Kirats not understand this?"

Smiling sadly Arjun said, "People forget a hundred favours done to them. But a single harm and insult they remember all their lives. The Kirats may not be our foes, but they are enemies of kshatriyas. After coming away from enemies in Hastinapur, will we find happiness here in facing enemies again? Let us go to some other forest. Let the Kirats live in peace..."

"Impossible! We shall give up this place out of fear of the

Kirats? With Bhim present, will the Kirats display their might?" said Bhim angrily.

Yudhishthir said, "Violence and anger breed sorrow and are harmful for both sides. The victory won through violence may bring wealth, possessions, kingdom and power, but it does not give peace, friendship and happiness. It is not right always to adopt the path of violence. There is yet another magic for winning over the enemy. That *mantra* is known to Yajnaseni. Therefore, it will be good if she makes the arrangements for our living peaceably in Kamyak."

I understood Yudhishthir's hint. Eagerly I said, "In Kamyak there will be no distinction of class, caste, race. The injustice inflicted on Ekalavya will have to be made up here. There is enough cause for the Kirats to hate the Aryans. But by binding them in chains of friendship we will have to bring about the great union of Aryans and non-Aryans. In my hands is the inexhaustible vessel. Every day in Kamyak forest Kirats and Pandavs shall sit together to eat. I shall personally serve the food."

"I will remove the used leaves of all," Arjun happily said.

"After all, being *sakha's* disciple..." I murmured and smiled gently.

Suddenly a roar was heard. It seemed a thunderbolt had crashed. Sahadev informed us, "It is not a thunderbolt. The Kirat Kirmir has thrown a challenge to fight. He is the leader of the Kirats here. He is young, fearless and very strong. He is thirsty for the blood of brahmins and kshatriyas. Today is his chance. We are all in danger. Kirmir can pluck out a hill and throw it into the sea. Now may God help us!"

At once whirling his mace about Bhim ran towards the sound. We remained stunned. Sounds of fighting began. Depressed, Yudhishthir said, "On the very first day of forest life the earth will be red with blood. What can me more unfortunate than this?"

"But what is the alternative?"

"I know that Bhim will kill him. But by killing the enemy, enmity is not destroyed. Today after Kirmir dies, tomorrow some other Kirat will have to be faced. It might be that all the Kirats in the forest will band together and attack us. Even if Bhim and Arjun destroy the Kirat clan here, the Kirats will remain for ever enemies of brahmins and kshatriyas. Throughout the world this enmity will be established between the two races. As a result, not only we, but all humanity will be endangered. By saving Kirmir we might be able to build a bridge of amity between Kirats and Pandavs. But only Draupadi can save Kirmir from Bhim," said Yudhishthir.

Taking courage I advanced. I saw that having thrown him down, Bhim was showering blows with the mace on him. Kirmir was begging for pardon with folded hands, but Bhim was not listening. As Bhim was about to strike the mortal blow, I rushed forward and shouted, "Save Kirmir, my lord!" Abruptly, Bhim's hand froze in mid-air. Stunned by his furious appearance, I lost consciousness.

Later I got to know that the Kirat was alive. He could not understand which goddess had suddenly appeared and saved his life. The unconscious body of the goddess was lying on the ground. Kirmir ran and brought water in his cupped palms from the spring. He sprinkled this on my face and began rubbing my feet. I opened my eyes. Bhim was seated by my head; Kirmir was at my feet. The other Pandavs surrounded me. Finding me conscious, they were all relieved. Wiping his tears, Kirmir said, "Ma! Devi! Who are you? Parvati or Lakshmi? To save this ignoble person you put yourself in danger! Mother, how shall I repay this debt? Any command?"

Kirmir's simple, transparent words made me forget all my sorrow. "Kirmir, after calling me mother what else do you wish to know? Irrespective of age, a woman is mother embodied. Can the wife of the five Pandavs, Draupadi, not be the mother of Kirat Kirmir?" Kirmir sobbed.

"Mother, forgive me! Queen Draupadi is living in the forest-this I knew. But when did you reach Kamyak? Stay here as long as you wish. There will be no opposition, no danger, no difficulty here."

At once I said, "If even now the Kirats consider my husbands enemies, we shall leave this forest. But see, the Pandavs have never considered the Shabars inferior. Every man is equal — this view they hold firmly. That is why Draupadi accepted them in marriage."

"Ma, from today the Shabar clan is friend to the Pandavs. There will be no hatred for them in our hearts. It is because of the insult offered by the Kauravs that we were furious with the Aryans. To destroy the Kauravs is the supreme goal of our lives."

Yudhishthir said, "that is our supreme vow too. This has been our vow since they insulted Draupadi in the Kuru court. Therefore, our goals are the same. Now we have become friends of each other."

In a calm voice Yudhishthir continued, "When the earth was made, there was no difference between man and man. Man is the child of nature. Everyone has the same right to live on this earth. Sun, moon, rain, wind, the seasons, touch each man equally. It is man who has himself produced differences with other men. For the security of society, the development of civilization, responsibilities are divided among different members according to the abilities of a family. For the sake of society different castes have evolved. In a family no one is untouchable even though the woman cleans the used leaves of everyone, wipes the floor, washes the soiled linen. Then for doing the same work in society how can others become untouchable? Ram, the best of all men, had eaten fruit tasted by a Shabar woman. His status was not demeaned. Despite being the master, he made friends with tribesman Guha. He who distinguishes between men opposes the Creator. Dear Kirmir! Do not make us guilty. Gratify us by gifting friendship. You will see, sages will come to this forest. By their blessing, the inhabitants will benefit immensely. Civilization will develop by exchange of views."

How glorious it was that the emperor should beg for friendship with such humility!

Thrilled, Kirmir spoke in a choked voice, "Our fate is changing, that is why you have set foot here. I shall explain everything

266

to my friends and relations. My two brothers Kirat and Virat are dedicated to kill kshatriyas. It is up to Ma Panchali to bring them under control. The others I will manage. I am the leader of the Shabar tribe here. My word will be obeyed. After befriending Sugriv, Ram conquered Lanka and killed Ravan. Similarly, befriending the tribal chief, Kirmir, king Yudhishthir will conquer Hastinapur and slay the Kauravs. If you command, tomorrow morning itself the Shabar army will march on Hastinapur."

Folding his hands, humbly Yudhishthir said, "No, my friend, no! Do not misunderstand us. Conquering Hastinapur or killing the Kauravs is not the aim of our lives. After thirteen years of forest life if we get back what is ours justly, that will be enough. Even a day before thirteen years are complete we will not accept the kingdom of Indraprasth. To do so will be to violate the promise. We do not seek friendship out of any motive. We beg it for friendship's sake. However, it is true that it is in sorrow rather than in happiness, that a true friend is of help."

Kirmir was overwhelmed by Yudhishthir's nobility. Like lightning the news of friendship spread through Kamyak forest. Kirmir, Kirat, Virat and other forest-dwellers all came to meet us. Even wild animals came to make friends.

To celebrate the friendship I arranged for food. Cooking in the inexhaustible vessel myself, I had the Pandavs and the Shabars sit in the same row and fed them. That day the forest was *amrita*-full.

I announced, "As long as the Pandavs live in Kamyak, none will go hungry. Everyday the Pandavs and the Shabars will eat together. The Pandavs shall eat what the Shabars serve. I shall serve the Shabars. This is the rule that will be followed throughout the seasons."

Shouts of celebration hailing the Pandavs, dances, songs, resounded in the forest. Supremely content, I thought how noble man can be! By not recognising himself, how petty does he become!

31

The inexhaustible vessel was in my hands, but the whole day I had to keep hungry. For after I had eaten, food in that vessel would be finished for that day. Therefore, until everyone had eaten in the morning, at noon and at night I had to remain fasting faithfully, waiting for unexpected guests till midnight. I was not sorry at all for that. If by one person remaining hungry, hundreds get fed then it is better for that person to fast. Thinking thus, every day I used to feed the people in the forest, as also the birds and animals, insects and worms. Yes, in Kamyak forest even insects and worms did not go hungry. After everyone had eaten, I would forget my hunger and thirst.

Woman is mother, full of *amrita*. The moment a child is born, the man becomes a father and the woman, a mother. But the one who makes a stream of *amrita* flow into the child's mouth is the woman. In man there is no such ability. Therefore, a woman is *amrita*-full, nourisher, *Annapoorna*. It is the natural urge of a woman to fill the empty bellies of others and to rejoice in that. As a woman, I was born as a portion of the goddess *Annapoorna*, and quenching the hunger and thirst of others was a matter of delight for me. That was why Lord Surya had given me the inexhaustible vessel. I was ever grateful to him.

At times I recalled my own offspring, and Subhadra-Abhimanyu. All the men, women, children, young and old, of Kamyak forest would line up to eat. While serving food, a slight pain would rise in my heart — had my sons eaten? Would Subhadra be feeding them according to what they liked? Even today for my youngest son, Sahadev's son Shrutakarma, milk flowed from my breasts. Till the sad moments of my leaving for the forest, the milk of my breasts was his very life. There was no dearth of food in *sakha* Krishna's kingdom! But without mother's milk my darling would be weeping. He would be growing thin. And people would be recalling my cooking. Even Abhimanyu used to be delighted to eat what I made. Subhadra would take on the responsibility of all the children, but it was I who would feed them. By lavishing maternal care on the Shabar children I sought to forget the sorrow of separation from my sons.

Our cottage was at some distance from the Shabar habitation in Kamyak forest. Everyday I would go to the Shabars. Intimacy with them was increasing. The day I did not go, all of them came up to our cottage and ask, "What offence have we committed? Today we did not see you!" I had got chained to the innocent love of their simple hearts.

Kirmir's followers, Kirat and Virat, had both forgotten their vow of destroying kshatriyas. Now they were friends of the Pandavs, their followers. In Kamyak forest, there was no longer any hatred or violence. Sages and hermits could perform worship without any difficulty. Even the Shabars had begun taking interest in their rituals. Kamyak forest was becoming the place where the Aryans and non-Aryans united. The Pandavs dressed like the Shabars, putting on bark-garments. In dress and behaviour, too, they were growing to be like the tribal people. Bhim was virtually their leader. I dressed like Shabar women. We had become one in identity. We participated in their festivals, rituals, worship. We forgot that we were the descendants of some royal Aryan family. We even forgot that we had come from Indraprasth and that we would have to return one day.

It was only the thought of the children that caused pain from time to time. Noticing children at play in the Shabar habitations, I recalled my own. Milk flowed from my breasts. I grew feverish with anguish. I thought, if separation from children was to be my fate then why did my breasts not dry up? When I saw any Shabar woman suckling her child, my breasts would grow heavy and tears would spring to my eyes. I would ask my husband, "How long will I suffer thus?"

Yudhishthir understood my pain. Like a detached yogi he said, "Yajnaseni! Make your heart generous, vast. Consider all the children of this world yours. You will then find that the absence of five sons will no longer cause you pain. You are a mother, you have given birth, you are *amrita*-full. A mother's heart is as vast as the ocean. Let flow a flood of maternal love for the innumerable people of the world who are miserable, suffering, fallen. Gift love to all. You will see, thereafter none in the world will be as happy as you are."

Yudhishthir's words were like scripture. Every idea of his was eminently worthy. But how to accept them? To strengthen my mind, keeping Yudhishthir's words in my heart, I let flow a stream of maternal love into every corner of the Shabar villages.

The twin sons of Virat were Kambu and Jambu. Both were like dry skeletons. I was filled with compassion for them. Why were those two so thin in this lovely forest, full of fruit? Lying on the floor, they kept staring at me, sucking their dry fingers. How would that quench their hunger? They would cry now and again. I asked Kirat's wife Shriya, "Has their mother gone into the forest? Why are they so thin? Does the mother not look after them?" Shriya replied full of pity, "Yes, she has. But she will not return. Many days ago, a tiger took her away. The two were then two months old. Now I am their mother. Despite all my heart's love, my breasts do not fill with milk. For till now, I have not become a mother. So how do I give them mother's milk? That is why they are growing thinner. I cannot see any solution." With tears in her eyes Shriya was looking at them.

I did not think twice. Sitting down on the floor I took them into my lap. Milk flowed from my breasts. "Sister, do not take offence. I shall save them."

Shriya was delighted, "What is there in this to mind? This is a matter of great good fortune! But..."

"But...?" I asked anxiously.

Humbly Shriya said, "You are an Aryan lady. By giving your milk to a non-Aryan child your dharma will not be affected, I trust! You do know of the Ekalavya incident!" Holding her hand, I told Shriya, "Sister, forget the past. Aryan and non-Aryan are

270

distinctions made by men. The blood of all is the same. Mother's milk is the same for all. Give me the chance to earn merit."

In a steady voice Shriya said, "You will have to eat here. The food of the mother who feeds her milk to the child is different. Other food is harmful for the child. So, will you eat with us? Being an Aryan woman, how will you accept food in a non-Aryan's home?"

Compassionately I replied, "Shriya! Lord Ram had taken what a Shabari had tasted. His glory was not lessened by that. My husband, Bhim, has married the *rakshasi*, Hidimba. Arjun has married the Naga princess, Ulupi of *Patala*. We have friendship with people of the three worlds. Therefore, I accept your food as *amrita* and wish to let flow a stream of *amrita* into the mouths of both children."

Quickly Shriya gave me food. Without considering anything I ate. Then I suckled both children. With great contentment and peace I returned, realising the truth of what Yudhishthir had said. After that day when everyone had eaten, I used to go to the Shabar village. There I would eat with Shriya, then pour out all my maternal love. The two children gradually became strong and big. They would call me "Ma! Ma!". I was called the world-mother, *Annapoorna*! To the mother all children were equal. There was no distinction of race, religion, ruler and ruled. I was now happy. To the mother the only identity of man was the child, the child of immortality!

271

32

Today was *sakha*'s birthday, the eighth day of the dark fortnight of the month *Bhadra*. There would be celebrations in Dvaraka. *Ma* Kunti also observed Krishna's birthday with considerable fanfare. Preparing many types of sweets in the inexhaustible vessel, I distributed them among the inhabitants of Kamyak forest. In case any guest arrived, I kept waiting till the evening. Taking Kambu and Jambu in my lap, I fed them sweets. They were healthy now and had grown big. They had begun taking other food too. After they had finished, I suddenly thought of *sakha*. He would be looking so beautiful, ornamented with sandalwood paste and wearing garlands of wild flowers! Devaki and Vasudev would be distributing sweets enthusiastically. In the midst of these festivities would *sakha* think of me? The mighty ruler of Dvaraka, the best of all men, Shri Krishna on the one hand and, on the other, deprived of kingdom, the forest-dwelling Pandavs and their wife, Draupadi!

At the time of the exile he had promised to come from time to time to ascertain our welfare. But when? Till now he had not come into sight even once. I thought: "*Sakha*, on your birthday why are memories of you making me so restless? That enchanting form repeatedly swims into the mirror of my heart. Much as you relish eating what I prepare, do I enjoy any less preparing food for you? Since we arrived in Kamyak forest, so many unbidden guests have come. By the grace of the inexhaustible vessel it has been possible to offer them proper food. Today, too, many came and left after being served. But my mind is not content; the heart is not satisfied. Somehow within me a voice is saying, 'The guest will come; he is coming; surely he will come...'"

It was late in the evening. I had not eaten. Phalguni said, "Krishnaa, how much longer will you wait? What guest will

272

come so late at night? You have laboured all day. Now eat. You have fed everyone in this forest equally, sages and ascetics, tribal children, the aged, women, insects, worms. Now for whom are you still waiting?"

Firmly I said, "My heart says, *sakha* will be coming!"

"At this unearthly hour?"

"For *sakha* every hour is auspicious, do you not know that?" I said.

Affectionately, Phalguni took my hand, "Do you love *sakha* even more than me?"

"Shall I ask you the same question?"

"The answer will be, 'Yes. *Sakha* is the dearest of all.'"

"I, too, will say the same. But for the love of *sakha* I have no name, no limits, no earthly comparison."

With great affection Phalguni said, "Krishnaa! I am not jealous of *sakha* because of your love for him. I am jealous of you. I am afraid that in the supreme test of love you might surpass even me. And to *sakha* you might become dearer than me."

Laughing, I said, "Husband! I am within you and you in me. Whichever of us is dearer to *sakha*, what does it matter to us? Rather, if one of us is specially loved, that will benefit the other."

Now leaving aside jest he pleaded, "Do eat." Still I was hesitant. If *sakha* should arrive, then? What shall I offer him?

Phalguni reassured me. He said, "Even if he arrives, will he have remained hungry till now? Will the ruler of Dvaraka lack in victuals that so late at night he will come here in the forest to ask for food? If Krishna is wanting to be fed then serve the food once more. What I take I first offer to *sakha*. My life-breath is offered to him. Before accepting you I had offered you to *sakha*. What I eat, first *sakha* gets its taste. What I feel, first he experiences that. If you try to seek *sakha* within me then you will get him. Come, serve! I do not know whether I will feel hungry yet again or not."

Truly, there was no sense in waiting for *sakha* till so late. I also knew that despite Krishna and Arjun being in different forms they were identical and united in heart and soul. With great care, with total respect, with the delicate touch of maternal affection and mingling the sweetness of pure love, I put the remaining food before Phalguni. After offering it to Krishna, he accepted it. Eating what he left, I achieved supreme peace. Cleaning up the inexhaustible vessel I kept it away. I lay down thinking of Krishna.

I do not know whether I was sleeping or awake. Somewhere in the heart I heard the enchanting flute, and sandalwood-paste-smeared, yellow-clad Krishna was before me. With both hands outstretched he was saying, "*Sakhi*, I am limitlessly thirsty. This thirst will not be quenched with sweet water. That is why, not caring for storm and rain, I have rushed so far to you. I have heard you have become *amrita*-showering mother in Kamyak forest. At your *amrita*-spring no one remains unfed, not even insects and worms. Your heart contains the rejuvenating essence, *sanjivani*. Auspicious one, today on my birthday my throat is parched for a draught of *amrita*. Quench my thirst and glorify me."

I was thrilled, it brought me out in goose pimples. I was delighted. Within me I could feel the presence of mother Yashoda. Who was I, Krishnaa or Yashoda? I found that the solution to all my problems was standing before me: the child Gopal. On his face the incomparable radiance of the purity of the whole universe was shining. The butter and curd thief Gopal was now pleading for *amrita!* The *amrita* of my breasts was dripping. Cupping his palms, Krishna was drinking the *amrita*. In the form of my child Krishna had set foot here! He had removed the pain of a mother's heart by making me *amrita*-full. Immersed in maternal love I sighed, "Krishna, Kanhaiyya, Kanha..."

Touching me, Phalguni woke me up, "Why are you deliriously muttering Krishna, Krishna in your sleep?"

Helplessly I cried out, "Krishna! No, I was calling my own child. All my five sons had come in the form of Krishna. They were demanding *amrita*. With eyes heavy with sleep I was seeing my own sons in Krishna. In sleep pouring out the *amrita* of my breasts into my children's mouths my heart was satisfied." Truly, my dress was wet with milk.

Hearing my dream Arjun said, "The generous compassionate mother within you is distributing through Krishna *amrita* to all the children of this world. Even while asleep you have been thinking of the hungry children of the world. Your nobility is without comparison."

We were talking thus when *sakha* appeared. Outside the dense darkness of the dark fortnight, the incessant rain of Bhadra, yet in the cottage of the forst-dwelling kingdom-less Pandavs like a blue flame sat the perfect man, *sakha* Krishna!

Amazed, thrilled, Arjun said, "*Sakha*, on this dreadful night leaving Dvaraka how are you here in the forest?"

Smiling gently, Krishna said, "He who came into this world leaving the sanctuary of his mother's womb on such a terrible night, for him is there a 'proper time?' For him is any place impassable, unreachable?"

"But the reason for the sudden arrival? Is all well in Dvaraka? Subhadra and the children are happy?" asked Arjun.

Calmly Krishna said, "All is well. But the reason for my coming is different. Suddenly I remembered the taste of food cooked by Krishnaa. I thought: it is my birthday; she will have prepared lovely sweets of various types. I felt very greedy. So I came away. The whole day I was engrossed in thoughts of food cooked by Krishnaa. That is why I remained hungry. It seemed to me as though someone was waiting. So, without bothering about the problem of storm and rain — I came. See, I am completely wet."

The yellow cloth was sticking to *sakha's* body. From the curly locks drops of water were dripping constantly. Worried, Arjun quickly put his own dry clothes on *sakha*, wiped his feet, hair and body. But I? I sat doing nothing! Midnight! Now what would I offer *sakha*? After my eating the inexhaustible vessel was empty. I felt like ripping out my heart. I was thinking: 'But *sakha*, how will I give you food?' Why did I allow myself to be persuaded by Arjun to eat? I was used to fasting the whole day. What would have gone wrong if I had just fallen asleep for some time? He had come from so far to eat food cooked by me. Now with what would I satisfy him?

Wearing Arjun's clothes, *sakha* was looking just like him. Sitting up, pretending not to know anything, he said, "*Sakhi!* I cannot wait. I am dying of hunger." My eyes misted over. I could not speak. I was angry with Arjun and with *sakha* too. Should any guest come so late at night and waking up one from sleep ask for food? Did that not cross the bounds of normal decency? Moreover, *sakha* knew that once the inexhaustible vessel was empty, Yajnaseni no longer remained *Annapoorna*. Deliberately he wanted to put me in trouble. Well, it was his wish...

Phalguni was able to understand the state of my mind. Worriedly he asked, "*Sakha!* You felt like harassing Krishnaa on a rainy night like this? You are not content with all that has happened to her so far? Without your knowledge does anything take place in this world?"

Sakha did not pay attention to Arjun's words. Looking at me he said, "You did not keep even a little food? I had thought on my birthday you wil surely keep something aside. Having eaten up everything you went to sleep? I cannot believe this."

Full of reproach I said, "Yes, guests, if unfed, utter curses. Curse me. I will gladly accept it. She whose life itself is cursed-what has she to fear from curses?"

Scattering laughter *sakha* said, "Who says that your life is cursed. Come, *sakhi*, show me your palm. Where is your future in these lines?"

Before I could say anything he had taken my hand. Full of hurt and reproach I was thinking that I would draw it back. That is when Arjun whispered into my ears, "Show *sakha* your palm! His forecasts are very accurate. Moreover, in poring over your hand he will forget his hunger and thirst. You will also be saved from a guest's curse."

My hand was in *sakha*'s hand. He was looking closely at each finger. I saw that a particle of food was left on the tip of one of my fingers. Tired out, I had washed up in haste and somehow the food particle had got stuck to the finger and dried. Ashamed of having a soiled hand in *sakha*'s hand I was about to draw it away when *sakha* took up that very food particle and ate it like *prasad*.

276

I was amazed. What was this that he was doing — the left-overs of my food! He would make me sink in sin. But before I could even say anything, *sakha* was patting his stomach with great contentment.

Laughing, he said, "Oh *Sakhi!* If a single particle of food cooked by you is such a heavy meal, then I would surely suffer from indigestion if I ate much. It is as well that I arrived after you had finished eating."

I was cursing myself for my carelessness. And here *sakha* had belched, satisfied, and was praising my cooking! Stunned I was wondering about his miraculous powers. Faced with this, all my ideas of virtue and sin, dharma and adharma were becoming hazy. Telling us to rest, he himself lay down and left before dawn.

The secret of this dramatic entry and exit of *sakha*'s became clear the next day. The divine sage Narad had arrived. He was praising *sakha*'s love for his friends repeatedly. To save his friend from the curse of Durvasa *sakha* had rushed, on that dark rainy night, into the dense forest and had eaten that food particle.

Pleased with the service of Duryodhan, Durvasa, at his request, had arrived after midnight in Kamyak forest with his thousand disciples. Duryodhan was aware that before dawn the inexhaustible vessel was empty and I did not remain *Annapoorna*. He would accept the hospitality of the Pandavs and ask for immediate arrangement for food for his disciples. The helpless Pandavs would become the victims of Durvasa's fury and be destroyed.

But he whose friend was the saviour Krishna, why should he burn in Durvasa's curse? Having taken the particle of food stuck in my fingers, the universal soul of Krishna was content. And once the universal soul was content, Durvasa and his disciples, too, were content. Hardly had they entered the forest than their hunger was assuaged, their stomachs were full up to the throat! All this was the magic of Krishna. They understood and full of shame, Durvasa went back quietly with his disciples.

Hearing this from Narad I was delighted. Taking my left-overs, Krishna might have made me a sinner, but my husbands were saved from being cursed. My heart, mind and soul automatically bowed at Krishna's feet.

33

The vow of Karna of the golden armour and earrings was to slay Arjun. Born with this armour and earrings, he was invincible. Therefore, after the plot to destroy the Pandavs by means of Durvasa's curse failed, Duryodhan reminded Karna of his vow. In a grim, grave voice Karna said, "The first step towards the destruction of the Pandavs is the killing of Arjun. No power on earth can save him from the maw of death. It is for the killing of Arjun that my birth has taken place. God Himself will not be able to save him from me. If God alone was to do everything, then why did he give man so many limbs, brain etc.?"

Valiant Karna's vow spread throughout Aryavart like a thunderclap. Ma Kunti was sorely grieved. Her anguished lamentation reached Krishna's ears. Once sorrow had reached up to Krishna, no further worry remained. I had left every matter to him. The forest-dwelling five Pandavs were downcast with Karna's vow.

Suddenly *Devarshi* Narad brought news that Karna no longer had his armour and earrings. Therefore, it was not Arjun's but Karna's life that was in danger. Arjun's father Indra, hearing of Karna's vow, approached him in the guise of a brahmin and took away the armour and earrings as a donation. It was the armour and the earrings that were the secret of Karna's strength. Despite knowing everything, in his arrogance as a donor, Karna sacrificed his power and his beauty to Arjun's father without any regret.

Knowing that Arjun's life was now without any danger, I was reassured. But somewhere in a secret crevice of my heart from time to time a sad tune would play. Oh! If only Karna was not an orphan, if only his father's identity was known! His father would surely have made some efforts to protect his son. But he was helpless, orphaned. Deliberately he thrust himself into the jaws of

279

death. What joy would *ma* Kunti have in this? Karna was her dharma-son!

Narad announced: "Karna has obtained the infallible enemy-destroying missile from Indra. Therefore, there is no need to be sorry for Karna."

Again I became anxious for Arjun and the Pandavs. How strange was a person's mind! Hearing of Karna's vow regarding Arjun's death I became anxious about my husband. Then, the incident of the gifting of the armour and earrings filled me with sympathy and pain for Karna. The next moment I grew anxious once again regarding the Pandavs on hearing the news of Karna's having obtained the enemy-destroying missile.

I was all churned up with worry. In the midst of this *sakha* turned up. Seeing me, he said, "For whom are you worried — for Karna or Arjun? Both are equally skilled warriors and heroes. One is the son of Kunti the other is Kunti's dharma-son. I know that in *ma* Kunti's eyes her dharma-son Karna and her own son Arjun are equal. Do you too look upon them equally?"

I had never even imagined he would suddenly indulge in such jesting over Karna. At first, I was acutely embarrassed. I could feel my face had become crimson. That too could not remain hidden from *sakha*. The next moment I took hold of myself, "*Sakha*, the mind of man is not made of wood or stone after all. A woman's heart is naturally soft and delicate. He for whom there is so much love and sympathy in Mother, however great an enemy he might be, his death will not give me pleasure. Death may not be the appropriate punishment for an enemy. Birth and death are not in the hands of man. Why should man shoulder that responsibility? Death can be the solution to division, hatred, dislike. Therefore, it is natural for sympathy to arise in my mind for Karna. Further, on his having obtained the foe-destroying missile, it is even more natural for me to worry about Arjun."

Laughing, *sakha* said, "Once Karna saved you from drowning in the river. Sympathy for him is but natural. Ingratitude turns a man into a beast. However, do not worry about Arjun. Karna can use that missile only once. Thereafter it will return to Indra. What if Karna misses his aim that one time?"

Noticing the wicked smile on Krishna's curved lips, I was somewhat reassured. I thought, with Krishna here what was there for Arjun to fear? The next moment I said, "If I ever get the chance to save brave Karna's life then this heavy, oppressive burden of debt will be lifted from my mind. By saving my life, he has put me in his debt. Will such a chance ever come or not? If necessary, I wish to save Karna's life at the cost of my own and pay off this debt. I am in debt to one whose enemies are my husbands — whenever I think of this I am weighed down by depression."

Looking at me significantly Krishna said, "You are mistaken, *sakhi!* Your husbands are not Karna's enemies. Karna is your husbands' enemy. If he wishes, Karna can become the greatest friend of the Pandavs. It is only out of jealousy of Arjun that he has joined hands with the Kauravs. Regarding arrogance as manliness, he has invited his own death. If his life and death were ever to be placed in your hands, then it is death that he will choose. He will not turn aside from rejecting your kindness and sympathy. It is pride that is Karna's greatest foe."

The burden of debt is painful. To be indebted to an arrogant man is even more agonising than death. I thought it would have been better if I had died that day. If the current of my life had merged with the Yamuna's current, I would have been saved so much misery, so many dilemmas, so much anxiety.

34

Among the Pandavs there would be always discussions regarding winning back the throne of Hastinapur. But Yudhishthir would not participate in these. I would be angry at his silence. I would think, "He, because of whose short-sightedness the valiant Arjun, Bhim, Nakul, Sahadev and I, the daughter of Drupad, are living in the forest exiled from the kingdom, does not even think about any remedy for that injustice! A forgiving heart is the dwelling of God. But showing forgiveness to the enemy and the sinful is not the dharma of kshatriyas. One who displays only timidity or anger is not a proper man. Man ought to be gentle where necessary, and angry where required." Hearing such words from me, Yudhishthir would calmly reply, "The time of the destruction of the Bharat clan has arrived. Duryodhan is now king and he cannot forgive. If the king himself does not provide shelter to forgiveness, then he himself gets immersed in unforgivable crimes and sinful conduct. As a result, both kingdom and clan are doomed to extinction. Therefore, I have taken recourse to forgiveness. I have taken shelter in non-violence and truth. Let us see if the Bharat clan can be saved. It is then that my ascesis will be successful. Lust, anger, greed — these three are the doors to hell. Guided by anger and greed,no desire is fulfilled fully. Therefore, we should wait with patient hearts for the auspicious hour when fortune will change. Why think of conquering Hastinapur when we have only just begun our forest exile?"

Feeling let down, I would say, "Without action neither temporary happiness nor permanent delight is obtainable. Fate too is shaped by action. Without acting, how can fate be altered? Without thinking now of how to win back our lost honour at the end of the exile, how will the safety of the Pandavs be assured then?"

Even more calmly Yudhishthir would say, *"Dharma rakshati*

rakshitam. That is, if you take refuge in dharma, dharma will protect you. Therefore, under no circumstances can I renounce dharma. Yo are learned. Who will comprehend the nobility of protecting dharma more than you?"

Sulking, reproachfully with tearful eyes I would say, "Sakha is witness, this lord of dharma will abandon all four brothers and his wife too, if need be, but will not abandon dharma! But how dharma protects, the blazing instance of that is my insult, our forest-exile, Karna's obtaining the foe-destroying missile for slaying Arjun! How the Pandavs will remain alive does not ever seem to worry the lord of dharma."

Such words were being exchanged before Krishna when guru Krishna Dvaipayan arrived. Urging me to be patient he said, "Daughter Krishnaa! Just as being in a dilemma and grieving over matters relating to the victory and defeat, the life and death of your five husbands is natural to you as their wife, similarly, for Yudhishthir to remain unmoved after hearing everything, is equally natural. Still, I have come here to remove the anxiety of all of you. It is natural to be worried about the Pandavs not having adequate weapons to face a hero like Karna. Therefore, today I will teach Yudhishthir the *shrutismriti* skill. This he will teach Arjun. By means of this skill Arjun will be able to please Indra, Mahadev, Yama, Varun and Kuber for obtaining divine weapons. After obtaining the knowledge of the fire-weapon, Arjun need not fear Karna's foe-destroying missile. Are you satisfied with this, daughter?"

Silently I nodded my head in agreement. Vedvyas, after teaching Yudhishthir that knowledge, left along with Shri Krishna and Devarshi Narad.

35

Phalguni was leaving. Taking along the Gandiv and the inexhaustible quivers, he was proceeding to the Himalayas for obtaining divine weapons after stern ascesis. All the brothers were pleasantly bidding him farewell. Then these thoughts crossed my mind: "With so many brothers available, why is it Arjun on whom the responsibility for this stern duty has been placed? Could not the responsibility of obtaining the divine weapons from the five gods Indra, Mahadev, Yama, Varun, Kuber be divided among the five brothers? Phalguni is valiant, dedicated and powerful. Shall he not enjoy any happiness? Half of his life has passed in the forest, in stern penance. I had thought some years would be passed together in the forest. Among the brothers, Phalguni is the most poetic, most emotional. After he leaves for the Himalayas, the true agony of forest life will begin for me. What does nature gain by repeatedly taking my dearest man far away from me? How cruel does destiny become in giving me pain, in producing obstacles to my love for my husband! Even if Arjun is out of sight, he does not vanish from the eyes of the heart. Perhaps fate is unaware of this fact. Had it known this, would it have behaved so heartlessly? The heart trembles even to think of that."

Phalguni would have to be bidden farewell with a steady heart and a pleasant face. It was not out of any sense of hurt and reproach that he was proceeding to the Himalayas, but out of some desire. I asked, "When will you return?" The last time I knew that I would have to wait for twelve years. But this time there was no limit to the waiting.

Calmly Phalguni said, "Surely before the one-year-in-disguise. Can anything be forecasted regarding ascesis and its fulfilment?"

"Then?"

"Five gods are concerned. There is no chance of returning

before five years. It is difficult to say anything more. Why are you worrying? Even if I am not here, there are four other husbands after all. At this time, as forest-dwellers, they are free from all garbage. With them, like a forest stream, your days will speed by in unhampered joy, Krishnaa. Therefore, I am not worried about you. If I alone had married you, how much trouble you would have had to face! In the Pandav family, it is I who have to undertake such difficult tasks which occupy such long periods. Therefore, you would have had to spend the greater period of your life suffering separation. However, now that danger is not there. If you remain happy, then my sadhana too will become more concentrated."

I would remain happy, would forget the grief of separation from Arjun in the company of the other four husbands, would pass the time happily like an unhampered forest spring — how peculiar were these thoughts of Arjun! It was because of this that I felt even more sad. How would I explain to the lord of my heart that the speciality that his husbandhood had for me was quite different from the other four?

In this world who understood anyone else's mind and heart? There was no option but to regret that Arjun did not understand my heart's anguish. He whom I wanted every instant with me, was taken far away by fate repeatedly. What was the alternative but to accept with bowed head the directives Vyas had given in the presence of Krishna? After marriage I had to fight at every step. My time had been passed in worrying about the security of my husbands.

Again now sleepless nights would have to be spent for Arjun. I had thought that with my husband the pain of forest exile would be reduced, but in being separated from Arjun I would experience that pain a hundred times more.

With moist eyes Phalguni said, "Krishnaa, I leave for an auspicious task. After I return with the divine weapons, you shall be the chief queen of Hastinapur. Karna's arrogance will be broken. Killing Karna, I will take revenge for your insult. In all the acts of the Kauravs it is Shakuni who does the plotting, but the chief advisor is Karna. Be assured, Karna will not remain alive."

285

I knew that the death of Karna was assured. I also knew that where Krishna was, there was victory. The plans that had been made for the death of Karna would succeed and dharma would be victorious. Still the talk of Karna's death raised a tumult in my heart. Perhaps the profound maternal love in *ma* Kunti's heart for Karna had influenced me. I left everything to fate. With a smiling face I bade my husband farewell. Expressing womanly apprehension at the time of departure, I said, "I have heard that for obtaining the blessings of the gods one has to reach *svarg*. Rambha, Urvashi, Menaka and other eternally youthful and beautiful - *apsaras* live there. Take care that you do not maintain celibacy like last time! The last forest-exile was different. This time you are going with a momentous goal. Desire gives man temporary delight, but it does not get him to his goal."

Arjun joked, "Why? Are you jealous of the lovely *apsaras*?"

"Is it not natural to be jealous? Am I not a woman? Not human?"

"Who knows what will happen? The penance of even mighty sages has broken at the sight of these apsaras. I am a mere householder. Moreover, with the wife far away, how far can a man's arrogance be maintained?"

I felt angry with Arjun's jest. Throwing a fiery glance at him I said, "I think I shall commit suicide if I get news of your sporting with *apsaras*. You have seen what happened last time. I know that Krishnaa's fate does not tolerate the joys of husband, domestic life — anything. But it is you who will face problems. Last time you put forward the pretext of manliness in marrying the person you fell in love with. But if you fall in the snare of the *apsaras'* love, then there is no question of marriage, only of losing your reputation."

Catching hold of both my hands Phalguni said, "Krishnaa! You have still not been able to understand Krishna's *sakha* Phalguni! You have not been able to know his mind. When the time comes, yo will understand everything."

In Phalguni's touch was etched the purity of his heart. My jealous womanly heart was uplifted by that touch.

36

Do flowers bloom in the garden or in the mind's courtyard? Does fragrance reside in the petals of the flower or in the mind's petals? Is the musical note in the cuckoo's call or in the strings of the mind? Is spring actually there or is it imagined by the mind?

I did not know how nature's beauty, the sound of its music and the dreams of the mind, all vanished from a forest-life without Arjun. My heart was aching for visiting the holy *teerthas*. I wondered if during the pilgrimage it would be possible to see the saintly form of Savyasachi the yogi engrossed in ascesis. Lost in that scene, some time would pass for me. After I requested Yudhishthir a number of times for permission to proceed on a pilgrimage, he finally agreed. At times during the pilgrimage news regarding Arjun would be available from the itinerant sages. Arjun was practising *sadhana* in the Himalayas. On hearing of his welfare, my eagerness would become all the more intense. First he performed ascesis in the deep forests in the Himalayan foothills. Then, displaying his valour Phalguni obtained the *Pashupat* weapon from Shiv. Hearing of this, all of us were thrilled. Thereafter news came of his obtaining in a remarkably short while from Yama the rod, from Varun the noose, from Kuber various weapons of invisibility and brilliant energy. It seemed that Arjun would return very soon. It would not take long to get divine weapons from his father, Indra. Every day, every instant I would wait to welcome him. My nights were sleepless. It seemed he would be coming at any moment. In the glory of the rising sun, in the delicate loveliness of sunset, in the radiance of moonlight, in the music of the rains ... I would see dreams and shriek, "Phalguni, I will not let you go. I want no kingdom, no wealth! Only you should remain with me. How much of life has been wasted in separation. How little is left of our limited lives? At least in this final phase remain with me."

Bhim would grow irritated with my eccentricity. Catching hold of me he would say, "However learned she might be, a woman is but a woman after all. If you keep Phalguni tied to the end of your *anchal* then how will revenge be taken for your insult? How will injustice and adharma be destroyed? *Chheeh*, Panchali! You are so weak, so greedy for comfort..."

My wounds would bleed from Bhim's rebuke. The untied hair would feel too heavy. The mention of destruction of enemies would recall the terrible insult. I would regain self-control and say, "True, thrice true. No longer shall I raise obstacles in the path of Arjun's ascesis by moaning for him."

Nakul would mock my agony of separation. Sahadev would say, "Enough, Nakul! Yajnaseni does the right thing at the right time. Every day she keeps stoking the fire of revenge in Elder Brother's heart, pouring *ghee* into it. Otherwise would an embodiment of forgiveness and non-violence like our brother ever even mention revenge? And now you are mocking Yajnaseni's agony of separation! If you see her true nature, you will be at a loss. She is as tough as she is delicate. She is as forgiving as she is dedicated to taking revenge. She acts according to the needs of the occasion. At this time there is nothing to do except create poetry describing the season of separation. She is creating poetry. She will be able to present Phalguni something at least on his return." Truly, during this time I had completed a poem entitled, "The Season of Separation", of which the brothers had come to know. What would they be thinking of me!

The moment he heard the name of poetry, Bhim began to tease me, "Panchali, I too am going to Hidimba. Till you write a poem on me I shall not return. What will you write? Or will you breathe a sigh of relief on being free of me?"

Nakul laughed, "Then this poem will be, 'Draupadi's Lament'. That is, how she laments in your absence will be written in it."

Delighted, Bhim would say, "That is well! Draupadi's lament in my absence. Piercing through the firmament that voice will reach me. And hearing that lament, full of jealousy, Hidimba will kick up such a row that even Duryodhan in Hastina will be terrified. He will imagine that his fate is lamenting."

Nakul would laugh gleefully at Bhim's words. But Sahadev would say gravely, "Bhim considers a woman's lamenting as the proof of love. But it is Bhim who, among us all, loves Draupadi with the most open heart. Even if we wish, we cannot compel Draupadi to give us love. Whereas, whenever Bhim wishes, he can raise confusion in Draupadi. Despite our one-year condition of conjugal life, Bhim does not trouble Draupadi any less. In spite of being annoyed with this, it is on Bhim that she depends the most and has the greatest faith. Well, am I lying?"

All the brothers would look at me together. Laughing, they would try to jest away my pain of separation. Like a stone image Yudhishthir would see and hear everything calmly, unperturbed. Time passed, but Arjun did not return. There was no news of him either. Hermits returning from the Himalayas reported that he had left the mountain. As long as he was there, we were at peace. Now no one was able to say where he was and in what condition. The period of waiting was getting longer and longer. Eagerness was turning into anxiety. Not only I, but along with Yudhishthir all were anxiously waiting for news of Arjun. I had virtually given up eating and drinking. Who would bring me news of Arjun?

As though sent by God, that afternoon the hermit Lomash arrived at the door of our cottage. Arjun's whereabouts were known to him. Seeing my condition he said, "Devi Draupadi! Lay aside worry. Your heroic husband, having finished the task in the Himalayas, is now living very happily in *svarg*. He is trying to gather many weapons for defeating the Kauravs. His task is almost over."

"Then why is Arjun staying on in *svarg*?" I enquired anxiously. Calmly the sage Lomash answered, "After so many days Indra has got his son to himself! All his life his son has spent in forests and poverty. Now he is in the kingdom of *svarg*. Therefore, the king of the gods has requested him to stay for some time and refresh himself. He has acceded to his father's request. On seeing Indra's court in Amaravati, Arjun was amazed. He is entranced with the music of the Gandharvs and the dancing and singing of the eternally youthful *apsaras* Rambha, Menaka, Svarnprabha, Urvashi, Chitrasena, Kumbhayoni, Varuthini, Mitrakeshi, Chitralekha, Padmayoni etc. and is virtually helpless. On the advice of his father, Indra, he is taking lessons in dance, song and music from the king of the Gandharvs, Chitrasen. On the training being complete, he will return. While returning he will bring along from there other weapons like thunder and lightning. Therefore, do not worry about anything."

I was relieved on hearing that Arjun was all right. But he was in *svarg!* He was relaxing in the company of Rambha, Menaka, Urvashi, Chitralekha! I started feeling the agony of being in hell. They would immerse him in lust on the pretext of singing and dancing. I started cursing them. Why should their whole race not be extinct! I thought to myself, his task was gathering weapons and he was taking lessons in music and dance? Leaving behind the pleasures of *svarg* would anyone ever return? Would he at all remember the insult to which I was subjected in the Kuru court? Would he still remember that his brothers and wife were living in the forest without a dwelling? I was sitting engrossed in my thoughts, burning in my own grief. Watching my husband in *svarg* with the eyes of imagination, I thought living in hell was better.

Noticing my gloomy face, Sahadev spoke out, "Do not worry for brother! He is Phalguni, son of Kunti. He will never forget the anguish of the insult. Without extinguishing adharma, he cannot find peace even in *svarg*."

To encourage me, Sahadev said, "It will not be fair to lose faith in Arjun. You know whose *sakha* he is? To lose faith in Arjun means to lose faith in Krishna. Whatever Arjun has done till now has been for the welfare of Aryavart. When the time comes, some similar welfare may be achieved through this training in song and dance. Whatever the subject, education can be applied to a noble task. Now even if Arjun returns, still Elder Brother will not return to Hastina till it is time-however powerful we might become. Thirteen years of exile will have to be undergone. Therefore, what is the point of becoming worried over the matter of Arjun's return? Let him relax for some time in *svarg*. At least one of us is resting in comfort for some time!"

I was silent. How could I explain to Sahadev that pressing Arjun's feet was all that I desired! Without his company everything appeared hollow. Still, Sahadev's words provided encouragement. Arjun would surely return. After all, not only I but Subhadra too was waiting. And Subhadra was the darling sister of *priya sakha* Krishna. If not for me, for Subhadra he would surely return. It was this thought that helped give confidence to my sinking heart.

But obstinate is the mind of man! It is unwilling to accept anything! The days woud pass in roaming the *teerthas* with sage Lomash. But throughout the night heartache would not allow sleep to come near. When out of tiredness sleep overcame me, it would be full of nightmares. Sometimes it was the scene of insult and outrage in the Kuru court that would come up. Sometimes it would be the scene of being seen off honourably from Hastinapur by Karna. Sometimes I would see that my sons were remembering me and catching hold of my *anchal* were insisting that they would not let me go. And then again sometimes I would see Arjun surrounded by *apsaras*. He had become an expert in music, song and dance and was surpassing even the Gandharvs. In the midst of the apsaras Arjun appeared exactly like Krishna among the *gopis*.

My sleep would break. Recalling each dream would be a fresh stab of pain. But I could not share the pain of my heart with anyone. Even Maya and Nitambini were not near me. So only poetry was my dear companion. Letting the pain of my heart flow in poetry I would get some consolation. Year after year kept passing.

Arjun did not come back.

37

Sahadev understood me. For diverting my mind he advised a change of place by going on a pilgrimage with sage Lomash to the *teerthas*. After living for a few days in the Naimisha forest, visiting Prayag, Gaya, Gangasagar, proceeding along the western coastline we reached Prabhas. There Krishna, Balaram and the Yadavs greeted us. In Prabhas all the sorrow vanished in the midst of *sakha*'s hospitality. In talking with an open mind to *sakha*, my faith in Arjun was restored. With fresh enthusiasm and hope we went on.

Crossing the Vipasha river towards the Himalayas, we reached the kingdom of Subahu. By then I had become exhausted and weak. My diet was irregular because of worry and grief. I had insomnia. And then there were the difficulties of living in the forest. My health failed. I did not have the strength to take another step.

The forest was impassable in the direction of the Gandha-madan mountain. The Pandavs were advancing in that direction. I was unble to protest. How could I say, "I cannot proceed further"? It was Arjun who had sent the suggestion of going round the *teerthas* to sage Lomash. Yudhishthir had assumed that responsibility. I was fulfilling that duty with all the strength at my command.

With difficulty I had managed to go on when a violent storm arose. No shelter was visible to save our lives. Bhim was near me. He was holding on to my arm under a tree. But when misfortune struck, it came as an avalanche. Even the tree could not shelter us. It crashed, uprooted. Bhim sprang to safety, but I fell unconscious from a blow. I did not know till when I was unconscious. When I opened my eyes I found the sky clear, the storm had abated.

My husbands were seated by my head. A handsome boy sat

near me, massaging my feet with great devotion. On seeing him, I was reminded of my sons. Who were the fortunate parents of this young boy? And at whose behest was he engaged in serving me thus?

I was awash with maternal love. Gently I asked, "Son, who are you? Who asked you to massage the feet of an unknown woman? Whoever you might be, I am your mother. I cannot think of anything other than my sons. Tell me who your are, my child!"

Shyly the boy said, "By calling me your son you have said who I am. You are my mother, that alone is my introduction!"

Patiently I asked, "Still, who are your parents — the fortunate father and the mother who gave you birth? What is the objection to meeting them? By giving birth to such a virtuous son as you, your mother shall be glorified. I wish to congratulate her."

The handsome boy looked at Bhim. Bhim was smiling gently. It was the first time I had seen such a gentle, soothing smile on Bhim's face. Whenever he was amused, his laughter roared out. But today a new aspect of his personality was revealed to me. In an affectionate tone he said, "Hidimba's son, valiant Ghatotkach! Touch the feet of *ma* Yajnaseni! You may introduce your father to *ma* Yajnaseni. But do not introduce the ogress Hidimba to the royal bride of Hastinapur, daughter of Drupad, Panchali. For, the moment she sees Hidimba, the princess, the royal bride, the Aryan woman, Krishnaa, will forget all her education, training and culture and become an ogress. Then if two ogresses face each other, our plans of pilgrimage will be at an end."

Everyone broke into laughter at Bhim's joke. Ghatotkach *pranam*-ed me. Immediately I embraced him. By the very touch I experienced the delight of feeling my five sons and was filled with maternal love. Warmly embracing him I said, "Son Ghatotkach, my *pranam* to your noble mother. Despite living in the forest you are such a polite, gentle and well-behaved boy! That is the proof of the training she has imparted. Whenever he was angry with me, Bhim would go away to your mother, Hidimba. How much he must be harassing her that I can well imagine! Convey my repeated *pranams* and endless gratitude to Hidimba.

After we return to Hastinapur and the conflict with the Kauravs is resolved, come with Hidimba to your father's kingdom. There is no need for being invited for this. This is your right. Do not take Bhim's words as the truth. Do not think that out of hatred of my co-wife I shall begin quarreling like an ogress. Subhadra is my co-wife and stays with me in Indraprasth like my younger sister. Your mother is older than me in age and in experience. She is my elder sister, to be revered. Listening to your mother's praises from Bhim's lips I have certainly felt envious at times. But after seeing you today, my mind is full of only affection and respect for her. Tell your mother of my feelings."

Ghatotkach listened silently. Placing me on his shoulders he began to walk. Noticing my exhaustion, Bhim had summoned him. Carrying me tenderly like a flower, Ghatotkach sped like the wind through the mountainous terrain. Very soon we arrived at the Badarika *ashram*.

Ghatotkach folded his palms to take leave. I blessed him with long life and reminded him to come to Hastinapur. Seeing Ghatotkach, for some moments I even forgot the pain of absence from my five sons and Abhimanyu.

38

My tormented heart found some solace in the natural beauty of Badarika. It was from here that Arjun left on his journey to *svarg*. Therefore this was the ultimate pilgrimage spot. The sages and ascetics here told us that Arjun would return from *svarg* after five years. God knew what task he would complete there in five years. I thought I would wait here for five years. Everyone agreed to this. They began to pray for Arjun's return. I began to observe with great dedication fasts for his safe return.

In Badarika during my observance of vows the extent of Bhim's love was revealed to me. Whatever I desired he would fulfil immediately. On account of fasting and eating only fruits my body grew thin but the beauty and complexion grew radiant, pure and delicate like a flame. Bhim forgot his barbed comments, as though his very language underwent a change. Because of the elder brother's addiction to gambling and lack of foresight I was undergoing such pain — in this manner he would openly criticise Yudhishthir. And on the other hand Arjun was spending his time in *svarg* in enjoyment and luxury and torturing me on the pretext of learning music and dance — in this way he would criticise him as well. Nakul and Sahadev did not enquire about my health at all. They were busy with their own work. Therefore, Bhim would rebuke them too. In Bhim's mountainlike body flowed a veritable Mandakini of love for me. At times Bhim would make me forget the pain of Arjun's absence.

Five years were about to be over. Bhim and I were roaming in the forest. Suddenly the wind blew towards us from the northeast corner and a fragrant thousand-petalled golden lotus fell on me. I was enchanted with its wondrous fragrance and incomparable beauty. Spontaneously these words came out of my mouth, "If someone would bring me a hundred such flowers, I would string them into a garland and preserve it for welcoming Arjun. I have faith that sprinkling it with the drops of dedication and purity I will be able to preserve it for some days at least."

I had hardly finished speaking when like the wind Bhim sped away in the north-eastern direction towards Mount Kailash. It was late. Bhim had not returned. I was disturbed and narrated everything to Yudhishthir. Worried, Yudhishthir turned to Sahadev who informed him: On Mount Kailash, in Kuber's lake, golden lotuses that were extremely rare, bloomed. Without asking anyone, Bhim plucked a hundred. Because of not having obtained Kuber's permission, the guards of the lake obstructed him. Bhim flared up and killed many guards. Even now he was fighting them.

Hearing this, Yudhishthir was worried. Taking me along he went to Kuber and stopped Bhim from fighting. He was annoyed with Bhim. It was not proper to do such a thing without taking permission. Then Bhim said, "This work is actually yours. The husband's duty is to fulfil the desires of the wife. Draupadi's heart was set on the golden lotuses. It was your duty to bring her these. I have done it on your behalf."

In a steady voice Yudhishthir said, "It was also not proper for forest-dwelling, vow-observing Draupadi to be greedy for golden lotuses. Why were you plucking flowers without the permission of the owner? It is natural for women to be greedy for wealth, jewels and gold. At such times they forget to discriminate between what is proper and improper. But a man ought not to forget the distinction between good and bad under the influence of greed."

In order to prove the appropriateness of his actions, Bhim said, "Forest-dwelling Sita too had once desired a golden deer. For the sake of his wife, lord Ram ignored the question of good and bad. He ran after the golden deer. I am only an ordinary person. To fulfil his wife's desire, Ram promised to obtain the golden deer. Yajnaseni is the wife of five husbands. All are renowned for valour, prowess, heroism. How could I ignore her desire for golden lotuses? What has princess Krishnaa not sacrificed for our

296

sake? What suffering and insults has she not borne? Even while leaving the kingdom she had to bear the insult of having to take off her ornaments. And fulfilling this slight wish was my mistake!" Bhim was fuming with anger and excitement.

In a cold, calm, steady voice Yudhishthir said, "Lord Ram ran after the golden deer. What was its ultimate consequence? You also know what sort of grief and danger mother Janaki's desire for gold threw her into. In the lives of Ram and Sita it is from here that sorrow begins. Therefore, this is a warning for the people of the world. Had I not arrived here, your life too would have been in danger. It is not right to display valour without considering the pros and cons. Learned, scholarly, well-versed in scriptures, Yajnaseni forgot what is good and what is bad in the greed for gold! This feminine fascination for gold in Yajnaseni can become the cause of our destruction some day. I had thought Yajnaseni was superior to other princesses, but..." Yudhishthir could not continue. On the other hand, I was pale with shame, guilt, hurt and remorse. With difficulty I controlled my tears. Yudhishthir begged pardon for Bhim's improper behaviour.

Noticing my condition, Kuber sorrowfully said, "If Bhim had only intimated beforehand that devi Draupadi wanted golden lotuses, I would myself have sent hundreds of thousands of them. Bhim did not tell anyone anything. He did not even bother to take my permission. He simply began plucking the lotuses. That is why this situation occurred. Anyhow, what was to happen has happened. Now Bhimsen can present his beloved wife as many golden lotuses as he wished. Besides this, from my side I am presenting devi Krishnaa ten lakh golden lotuses. By the touch of the dust of her feet the lotuses of my lake have become even more beautiful. These fragrant lotuses are a hundred times more precious than gold. I can give them without hesitation as presents only to devi Draupadi."

I protested. Humbly I said, "I cannot accept your present. At this moment I am standing on the banks of the lake of dharma. I vow here that I shall never wear gold or silver ornaments and jewelry; that I shall never use them for enjoyment. You know that

297

I am inflexible regarding my vows. Therefore, forgive me, as these lotuses are golden and very precious, I cannot take them. Actually, a person's true ornament is not jewellery but his acts, personality and qualities. Despite being aware of this, because of greed I forgot myself. By warning me at the right time Yudhishthir has earned my gratitude."

Persuasively Kuber said, "Devi! If you do not accept my present I shall be deeply hurt. As it is, your name is virtually that of Krishna. Today after this uproar if you should return from the banks of my lake empty-handed, what will people say about me? Whether you use them or not, but save me from calumny by accepting my present. I am not in favour of wasting wealth, but I also do not hesitate to spend wealth on suitable work. You can put the golden lotuses to use in some noble purpose."

I sensed Kuber's sincerity. Light shone in the darkness. The dream that I had resolved to turn into reality after reaching Kamyak forest would become possible so soon! Humbly I said, "Sir, on account of the absence of harmony and good relations between the city-dwelling Aryans and the forest-dwelling non-Aryans the discrepancy that exists between the way of life and thinking of these two races bodes ill for the future. The forest-dwellers, far from education and civilization, consider themselves inferior to the Aryans. On the other hand, the Aryans regard themselves as superior to the non-Aryans. It is because of this misconception that enmity between the two societies is growing. If anything is done to create fellow-feeling in them then they will display friendship to the utmost. The proof of this is the harmonious life and friendship of the Pandavs with the Shabar tribe of Kirmir in Kamyak forest. But without any means of communication, there will be many obstacles to building a sound relationship. If the advantage of a road through the deep forest could be made available then it would be easy to maintain relations with them. They too would be able to visit cities and holy places. Consequently, it would be possible to establish integration between the Aryans and the non-Aryans, sages and hermits. Exchange of ideas, participating in festivals, marriages and celebrations of one another would be possible. In this manner, among them bonds of friendship and even of marriage could be forged. The endangered Aryavart can immensely benefit from this. Therefore, it is my request that in return for the price of ten lakh golden lotuses if roads could be built linking the forest of Kamyak, Dvaita, Naimisha and different places of the Himalayas, the ashrams of sages and Hastinapur, then my dream would be fulfilled. The Shabars, Rakshasas etc. have always been creating obstacles to the ascesis of sages. The sole reason for this is the absence of integration and communication. What do you feel about this?"

Yudhishthir was listening spell-bound. As for Kuber, he was astounded. Sage Lomash was approving and endorsing my words loudly. Nakul laughed and said, "Yajnaseni has suffered much crossing this difficult terrain. Therefore she is proposing the building of roads, temples, rest-houses in the forests. Yes, while returning, these will certainly reduce our difficulties, and everyone will also benefit."

With a gentle smile Sahadev said, "As a result of this many conflicts of Aryavart will be resolved. Today with sage Lomash presiding, let the foundation stone of Yajnaseni Integration Hall be laid."

Laughing, Kuber said, "Let Bhim now inaugurate the celebrations of today, for having married Hidimba, the sister of Hidimb, it is he who has laid the foundations of Aryan-non Aryan relations. Equal behaviour with everyone is Bhim's ideal. It is he who ought to lay the foundation of Yajnaseni Integration Hall."

Everyone applauded Kuber's announcement. With sage Lomash presiding, the auspicious beginning of the task of integration took place. On the earth dharma, truth, justice were endangered on account of the Kauravs. At such a time there was a particular need for such work. This was confirmed by the gods of *svarg* too who blessed us by showering flowers. This was not a matter of little encouragement and consolation for us. Completing this work we returned to Badarikashram. There we continued to wait for Arjun.

39

The grave detachment of the Gandhamadan mountain was up-lifting. I wished that I could remain for ever thus, lost in the beauty of nature, silent, indifferent. For some time past we had been waiting near the Gandhamadan. Arjun's five years in *svarg* were over. He would arrive at the Gandhamadan from *svarg*.

The sky was overcast that day. In the blue clouds I was painting Phalguni's dark beauty. Suddenly a supernal light gleamed in the sky. A bejewelled chariot gradually alighted on the Gandhamadan. Indra's charioteer Matali was coming with Arjun. The Pandavs were delighted. Without blinking I kept star-ing at Arjun's inimitable beauty resplendent in the supernal glow. He having stayed for five years in *svarg*, his beauty glowed with heavenly splendour. An other-worldly halo radiated from him. In delight, Bhim picked Arjun up and began dancing. Arjun was smiling gently. Everything about him seemed inimitable.

He touched the feet of the elder brothers, embraced the younger brothers. He had brought many expensive presents from *svarg*. For Yudhishthir, he had brought the map of that kingdom, its political lay-out, many papers concerning its administration. In future, Yudhishthir's goal would be the establishment of a kingdom like *svarg* on earth. He was very glad with these pre-sents. For Bhim, there were the rare nectarous sweets, fruits and tubers of *svarg*. Bhim immediately waded into them without waiting to sit down! For Nakul, begemmed bridles, saddles and a hunting dress from Indra's palace. For Sahadev, a remark-able instrument for ascertaining the movement of the stars and planets. Everything was visible in it, even the future could be calculated. Everyone was extremely happy with the presents.

I was standing silently, staring fixedly, lost in some heavenly dream. Bhim asked, "Anything for Draupadi?"

Laughing, Arjun came near me, "For you? What is there? Speak!"

My eyes were flowing with tears of joy. I said, "It is enough that you have come away from the enchanting *apsaras* of *svarg*. I do not want anything else."

Arjun took off a bejewelled necklace he was wearing round the neck and a precious crown from his head. Many precious golden ornaments he took out from the chariot. Keeping all of these before me he said, "Krishnaa! That day arrogant Karna had stripped you of ornaments at Duryodhan's command. I had vowed that day that I would adorn you from head to foot. For these five years how many presents of ornaments have I not received from gods! I have kept all of them carefully for you. Wearing these you will return to Hastinapur after the exile."

Silently I accepted them. The bundle of ornaments I extended towards sage Lomash saying, "Husband! I cannot break my vow. Now I shall never wear precious ornaments. All these ornaments of *svarg* will be utilised in the sacred task of establishing amity on earth."

Astounded, Arjun kept staring. He was unable to understand anything. Lomash narrated the entire history of the task of integrating the aryans and non-aryans. Arjun was overwhelmed with joy. Yudhishthir said, "I thought that princess Draupadi's burning character was filled with anger, pride, revenge only. But now I have understood how much of humanity and superhuman quality permeates it. A veritable Mandakini of kindness, forgiveness, compassion and love flow within her, a hidden stream like the Phalgu. How very late it is that I have got to know this! Inspired by Yajnaseni, the very nature of forest life is changing now, the differences between man and man are getting removed."

Taking both my hands Arjun said, "Krishnaa! It is your dedication and single-minded love that enabled me to remain indifferent in the face of the violence of *apsara* Urvashi's enamoured attacks. But as the price of that I had to sacrifice my manhood for a year. You will be sad to hear this. Still, because of Father's compassion I have been able to get out of Urvashi's clutches with just a year's eunuchhood instead of being condemned to be a eunuch for the rest of my life. Will you not tolerate my year-long eunuchhood with a patient heart?"

I was deeply grieved hearing this. Phalguni had rather remained in *svarg* than suffered the curse of losing manhood for a year. The man to whom I surrendered myself regarding him as best of all men, how shall I be able to bear a year of his troubled existence without manhood? Understanding my grief, Sahadev said, "Do not grieve, Draupadi! All happens on his direction. This curse on our brother can prove a boon during the year of incognito exile."

In a calm voice Arjun said, "I ignored Urvashi's offer of love. She cursed me to become a eunuch. But on father's request she altered it to a year of eunuchhood. Consoling me, father said, 'during the year of incognito exile Urvashi's curse will act as a boon.' Now Sahadev's words tally with what father said. The depression in my mind has been removed. Whatever God does is invariably for the welfare of the creature."

Hearing Sahadev's words, calling *sakha* I surrendered everything to him. I thought to myself, "If Krishna's *sakha* Arjun should have to bear the curse of a years's eunuch-hood then for this it is not Krishnaa but Krishna who will bear the shame."

40

The monsoons are a season of life. While living in Dvaita forest I realised this. While returning to Kamyak forest with Arjun on the way the Kirat chief, Subahu, welcomed everyone and requested that we enjoy his hospitality for a few days. By this time within the forest the advantage of a road had already appeared. Temples and rest houses had also been built. The forest-dwelling Shabars had begun visiting *teerthas* and the ashrams of sages in the Himalayas. Word of the love of the Pandavs for the Shabars and of my hopes for an integration of Aryans and Shabars had spread. In Kamyak forest changes were coming about in the lives of the Shabars. Therefore, we had the good fortune of enjoying the friendship of all forest-dwelling tribes. The Aryan–non-Aryan ill feeling that had existed on account of the hatred in the minds of the Kauravs had been removed by the principle of equality followed by the Pandavs. Gladly accepting the friendship of the Kirat chief, Subahu, we stayed there for some days.

I was keen to spend a quarter of a year in Dvaita forest. Here the rains appeared magical. Green showers spread their incomparable beauty everywhere. The Pandavs got ensnared in the magic of nature. Bhim and Nakul went hunting on the Yamun hill. That was where one day Bhim fell into the clutches of the serpent Nahush. Yudhishthir rushed to his rescue. It was found that the father of Yayati, ancestor of the Kuru dynasty, was Nahush who was cursed to become a snake by Agastya and was roaming for long years in the forest. To free their ancestor from this curse the Pandavs engaged in prayer. Yudhishthir provided the correct reply to Nahush's questions. Then Bhim was freed from the serpent's coils and Nahush himself, being liberated from the curse, disappeared after blessing the Pandavs.

Yudhishthir thought that for this virtuous act it was Subahu's kingdom which had been the chosen site. Liberating ancestors from a curse was a highly meritorious act for descendants. If they had not been living in Subahu's kingdom the Pandavs would not have this unique opportunity to earn the blessings of their ancestor. He expressed his gratitude to Subahu who with folded hands said, "Who am I? All is His wish. If that were not so, why would you have arrived in my kingdom?"

Bhim said, "Brother, we have many divine weapons with us. The entire Shabar clan is with us. We have the support of the Yadav clan and of Shri Krishna and Balaram. Now the blessings of our ancestor are also with us. Now why delay further? When will Panchali's hair be bound up? Duryodhan is bursting with pride, depending on Karna. After returning from his conquests, Karna is preparing for a great sacrifice. For this we too had been sent invitations. But they knew that without completing thirteen years we shall not set foot in Hastinapur. This invitation was like sprinkling salt on open wounds. After the completion of the great sacrifice, Duryodhan mightily praised Karna. Losing self-control, Karna declared in public that till he had slain Arjun he would avoid meat, wine, coition and would never refuse anyone anything. Therefore, the time has come to crush his pride. There is now no fear in returning to Hastinapur."

Unmoved, Yudhishthir said, "I have heard of Karna's vow. I know its gravity, too. Just now we will not be able to do anything. We have not held back out of fear. The time has not yet come. How can we return to Hastina? When thirteen years are over, including the year of incognito life, we shall return. First, we shall try to arrive at an understanding through peace, non-violence and co-operation."

I was depressed hearing of Karna's vow. Why did Karna ever remain jealous of Arjun? Was it because Arjun was dear to me? Because he had won me in the *svayamvar*?

Bhim understood my thoughts. He said, "Karna's anger against Arjun is solely on account of Draupadi. Although in youth, also he was envious after the winning of Draupadi that envy changed into hatred. Where there is a woman there is hell.

304

After the winning of Draupadi, everyone turned into our enemies."

I flared up at Bhim's blaming it on me frivolously. I was a woman. What was my fault in this? I was beautiful. How could I be blamed for that? Arjun won me. In this what was my crime? Karna did not win me — in this was I blameless? I did not know the answer to that question. All the blame accumulated and fell on me at this last question. Yet, was it not unjust on Karna's part to torment me throughout life?

Noticing my miserable condition, Arjun said gravely, "Do not worry about me, Krishnaa! I will not let Karna fulfil his promise. Father Indra made arrangements for the death of Karna long back. In the arrogance of being a donor he cut off his body armour and earrings as gifts. Since then the blood oozing from his body has not stopped. And still see his arrogance! Now there are so many divine weapons. What is the difficulty in killing Karna? Only on account of the foe-destroying missile it is natural for you to have doubts. If he is so full of anger regarding Draupadi, then calling on this pure forest land as witness I vow before everyone that till I have killed Karna I shall abstain from wine, meat and Draupadi herself. It is only after teaching Karna a fitting lesson that I shall be able to give Draupadi the honour due to a wife."

Stunned, I kept listening. I was thinking: "a woman is a giver of strength, inspiration and is auspicious. But whether it be Karna or Arjun, why do they take vows to remain far from women until they achieve their desired goal? Does the company of a woman suck out the strength of a man? Is this his lack of confidence in the strength of his character or is it due to the fear of a woman's charismatic attraction? By keeping woman far from his path of fulfilment does man give proof of his firmness or weakness? Aryavart's finest man, Krishna, never kept women far from his path of fulfilment! And yet in Aryavart he had accomplished many impossible feats. Krishna, the lord of many female hearts and the best of lovers. Before taking such a major vow Arjun did not even consult me once. I enquired of him in private.

In sharp sarcastic tones Arjun said, "Had you consulted me

before taking such a critical vow? Don't you know that till today my heart does not accept the year-long condition of conjugal life? That is why at any pretext I have kept myself far from you. After living for five years in *svarg* in the midst of *apsaras* the flesh and blood body of a woman is not something I desire. Therefore, even if today's vow keeps me far from you, it will not keep me far from your heart. I am aware that you too have borne many difficulties for my sake. The moment I look at you I understand that in my absence abjuring comfort and luxury like an ascetic you have disciplined the body. With four husbands present, why so much of difficulty? Is it not injustice towards these four? Krishnaa, from today, you must take greater care of them. This will help in achieving peace and steadiness. Now Aryavart is endangered by the injustice of the Kauravs. A great war is waiting for us. For being victorious in the dharma-war that will take place on earth three years later mental stability is essential. Therefore, I have made this vow only after careful thought. In our lives besides action, duty and protecting dharma is there any other duty? Do not misunderstand me."

I could not misunderstand my own husband. I knew that other than Krishna there was no second person as self-respecting and noble as Arjun. Otherwise, could he reproach me so sharply after such a long time?

41

Kamyak forest was waiting for us. Jambu, Kambu, Kirmir, Kirat and Virat and other Shabar friends were eagerly waiting. After we had reached, *sakha* Krishna along with his second queen, Satyabhama, came to enquire about our welfare. Krishna was delighted that Arjun had returned from *svarg* with divine weapons. He asked Arjun about *svarg*. Narrating amusing stories of *svarg*, Arjun entertained *sakha*.

On Krishna's arrival, I reproached him, "How did *sakha*'s feet turn this way after such a long time? While Arjun was in *svarg* you made no enquiries whether we were alive or dead. The moment he returned you remembered us?"

Krishna appeared stunned with amazement — as though falling from the sky. "Look *sakha*, how ungrateful and cruel a woman's mind is. As long as you were away I, leaving behind all the comfort of Dvaraka, kept following my friend's wife as her bodyguard on the difficult forest paths. For five years I could not even see my wives' faces in Dvaraka. For that let alone gratitude, she is showering blame on me!"

What can be a greater instance of *sakha*'s lies than this? Even at my silence Arjun smiled. *Sakha* tenderly said, "*Sakhi!* Say truly, every night on shutting your eyes did you or did you not have dreams of Arjun? Even while waking at times you saw Arjun's image in lakes, in the shadow of trees in the forest, in the snow flakes on the mountain — didn't you? Even in the mirror of your nails you saw Arjun! During the rains, lessening your torment of separation by getting wet on the forest paths were you overwhelmed by seeing Arjun's shadow walking beside you or not? Although by the time you called Bhim to show that shadow, it had vanished. Then regarding all this as your imagination, you used to remain quiet. Say, is all this false?"

I was amazed and asked, "*Sakha*, who told you? Till today besides myself no one knows all this. Every moment I would feel Arjun with me and the next instant it would seem a hallucination. I used to think that because I thought of him all the time it seemed thus. Out of shyness I used to remain silent. How did you come to know of all this?"

A little sadly Krishna said, "What the body has suffered who else will relate? *Sakha* was engrossed in the dance of the *apsaras* of *svarg*. Except for me who else would keep roaming by your side in the form of Arjun? At that time besides thinking of Arjun you did not even once think of me. This possibility did not even cross your mind that in the form of Arjun I might be roaming from forest to forest. Why should I myself reveal the mystery? Have I no expectations or self-respect? Did you not know that *sakha* Arjun and I are the same?

Hearing this I was stunned. I asked, "Is this the truth? At every instant, what I considered my mind's creation was *sakha* Krishna? One day I even thought that Phalguni had returned and was following me, keeping himself hidden in the jungle. When I told Bhim and the others, they laughed and teased me that even when I was wide awake I dreamt of Arjun. And except for me no one could see this shadow of Arjun."

Noticing my consternation Satyabhama said, "Krishnaa! You are talking like an ignorant person. Leaving us behind, your *sakha* remained the last five years in Badarikashram to look after the welfare of his friend's wife. By going to assuage the pangs of your separation from Arjun he has not pained us little in the pangs of separation from Krishna for full five years."

Pained, I said, "*Sakha* was in Badarika and none of us came to know of it! *Sakha* did not even tell us! If we had known then the anguish of Arjun's absence would truly have been reduced so much."

Sadly Krishna said, "I tried several times to tell you. Every time you mistook me for Arjun. Finally, writing a letter and keeping it in a golden lotus plucked from Kuber's lake I sent that to you. But immediately on seeing the flower you got lost in the

308

thought of stringing a garland for Arjun and expressed your desire to have a hundred flowers. My letter written with so much care was left unread."

Satyabhama said, "So, you wrote a love-letter to Krishnaa! Does it enhance your glory to despatch *sakha* to *svarg* kingdom and write love-letters to his wife?"

Krishna was taken aback, "Satya! Do not misunderstand! It was merely a letter of good wishes."

Sulking in reproach and hurt Satyabhama said, "Yes, I know what your letter of good wishes is like. Who does not know that the first love-letter in the world was exchanged between you and Rukmini? Your name will be the first in the list of writers of love-letters. If it was an ordinary letter then why was it placed in the midst of lotus petals?" During this conversation my shame doubled. How like a child Satyabhama expressed suspicion and sulked! Had she yet been able to understand her husband? Even if she was suspicious, was it proper to expose her husband in front of so many people?

Dramatically Krishna folded his palms and said, "Lady, please forgive me for past crimes. Whatever might have been in the letter, Krishnaa put it aside without reading it. Then why so much of discussion regarding it? That I am not at all fit to be loved has been proved by Krishnaa."

Arjun was listening to this exchange of pleasantries between husband and wife silently. He said, "There is nothing to worry about. The letter despatched by you has duly reached its destination. Even now Krishnaa has carefully preserved that lotus among her precious objects. When I returned from the kingdom of *svarg*, she showed it to me. Taking in its perfume she began saying, 'In these petals I can clearly sense the fragrance of Krishna. That is why I have kept it carefully.' If the letter you wrote is still in the petals then let us read it and see what it is like." Coming near Arjun, Krishna whispered into his ears, "One request: let Bhim not read the letter. He will be unable to comprehend the profound significance of the letter, this I know. On the

309

other hand, misunderstanding it, he will crush me with a single blow."

At that time Bhim had stepped aside and was engrossed in the sweets brought by Satyabhama. Sahadev and Nakul were occupied in talking to the Yadav bearers of the luggage. Yudhishthir was studying scriptures with hermits. Arjun laughed, "Only I know about this. To whom can I say that in my absence my dearest *sakha* was writing letters to my beloved wife? The shame will be only mine in this."

Laughing, Krishna looked at me, "It is lucky that *sakhi* has kept the lotus so carefully and recognised in it the fragrance of my touch. This is not a matter of little joy for me. The regret is that even Rukmini has not preserved my first love-letter."

Interrupting this exchange, Satyabhama immediately said, "So, the meaning of this is that you admit you wrote Krishnaa a love-letter!"

Laughing, Arjun said, "It is your love-letter that has enabled the stream of love to flow in the forest's flowers and leaves, rivers, fountains, animals and birds, human beings — in everyone. If *sakha* had not written love-letters then so much of uproar would not have taken place over the golden lotuses. Therefore, this offence of *sakha* relating to love is pardonable. For the greater good sacrificing the lesser self-interest is the ideal of *sakha*'s life."

The delight of Arjun's pure heart and his pure laughter thrilled me. I could find no comparison to the understanding and love between the two *sakhas*. Otherwise, whether in earnest or in jest, who could accept with such an open heart the matter of a friend sending a love-letter to his wife?

After the afternoon meal when everyone was resting I, with a heart throbbing with expectation and delight, opened the petals of the fragrant lotus. Truly, in the layers of the lotus was *sakha*'s indelible writing. With profound emotion I went on reading petal after petal —

"Priya *sakhi*!

For you I am OM that touches the soul, uplifts it, mingles it with infinity; that spreads out pervading creation, preservation

310

and destruction in the cosmos. In the midst of creation, destruction and life, the bond between you and me is inviolable, unbreakable. Look at this lotus. The sun is in the sky, but in the water the lotus waits. It finds the sun in the water. When the sun is reflected in the water, then it is on that reflection that it sheds its petals. The fulfilment of its life lies just in this. I am; I am being reflected in your heart. He who does not regard my reflection as me cannot find me. He who finds me has me reflected within him.

Sakhi! That which is the *mantra* of your dawn is also the music of your evening worship. I am near you. Why do you fear?

Your lifelong *sadhana's sakha.*"

As I read the letter, I became the lotus. I shed my petals on the reflection of the sun. I surrendered myself to the vastness of Krishna's love. I wrote my reply on the petals of a *ketaki:*—

"*Sakha,* lord of my heart!

For you I am a garden where flowers bloom. They do not know why they bloom. Sometimes the flowers wither away. Why they wither, this too they do not know. A flower knows this much that it withers even for the same person for whom it bloomed. So the fulfilment of a blooming flower and the pain of a withered one are offered to the same person. That person is you. He whom I seek in you is also no other than you. You are my Krishna, you are my Arjun, you pervade the world, are far above hope and desire. You are my *sakha.* Whether you are mine or not, I am yours, yours..."

Blown by the wind, the Ketaki letter was wafted from my hands to fall at his feet. Picking it up, he read it and smiled. I blushed. Looking down at his feet I was surprised to find later that Arjun was reading the letter while I had written it to Krishna. Behind Krishna was visible the smiling face of *sakha. Sakha* had understood everything even before Arjun finished reading the letter and said, "*Sakha,* it is wrong to read someone else's letter. This letter has been written to me by Krishnaa."

"But the letter fell on my feet", said Arjun.

Laughing, Krishna said, "Then the letter is yours but its

sentiments, words are for me. Before even reading it I had absorbed it all."

"How?" asked Arjun.

"It is this that is the difference between you and me. What you take in material form I absorb subtly. Draupadi is yours but her supra-physical entity is mine. This understanding has been arrived at between us long back. How are you arguing about it now?"

Arjun folded his palms, "Despite knowing everything, man behaves ignorantly. This is the illusion of the world. We know that the Pandavs are Krishna's, this world is Krishna's, Krishnaa too is Krishna's. Still, falling into illusion at times because of Krishnaa, one feels jealous of Krishna."

Laughing, Krishna said, "It is in the mis-step of the rhythm of life that its sweetness lies. Like the reproach and sulking of conjugal life, jealousy too creates a honeycomb. Therefore, apart from creating honeycomb in your domestic life I have no other intention, believe me, *sakha*. Between Krishnaa and you I am but a honeycomb."

Arjun and Krishna appeared identical to my eyes. Overwhelmed, I kept staring.

42

Loaded with fruit and flower, Kamyak forest had its own magic. A whole week passed with Satyabhama staying in its peaceful surroundings. Still she was not satisfied. Like two *sakhis* the two of us would frankly exchange our joys and sorrows, laughs and jokes. For many days I had not had a chance to unburden myself to Harita, Subhadra, Maya and Nitambini. Therefore, finding Satya near me, I talked a lot. Because of my affectionate response, she too grew garrulous. For a whole week she watched the sweet harmony of my domestic life with five husbands and was overwhelmed. Not only this, the attraction her husband Krishna — much desired by so many women — felt for me and his love surprised her. Perhaps she was also slightly jealous. I was able to be loved by five husbands and, by remaining happy myself, was able to make them happy too — this amazed her. Not only this. My mixing with Krishna and our boundless respect and love for each other being looked upon with such generous hearts by my husbands — these she was unable to understand at all. How I was able to manage such a terrible man as Bhim amazed her. During these seven days she quarrelled and argued with *sakha* Krishna. Every time Krishna called me to mediate. But as for my relationship with my five husbands, not even a trace of sulking or reproach reached Satyabhama, let alone argument, though I used to participate in all matters concerning the family. I put forward my own opinions and where necessary demolished those of my husbands. I even protested against Yudhishthir's statements and explained Bhim's arguments to him. Still she did not see any anger between us or quarrelling or ill feeling. On the other hand, in every matter my husbands would insist on my views and would not take any important decision without me. Seeing all this, Satya was absolutely wonderstruck.

313

Sticking to me like a shadow, she kept watching my work. What was the secret of my successful conjugal life? She was seeking the clue to the proper status of the wife in domestic life, but could not understand what it was. That afternoon the husbands had taken *sakha* to the Shabar habitations in Kamyak for some festival. Satyabhama eagerly asked, "Sister Krishnaa! How do you manage to satisfy all five husbands at a time? They appear ready to fulfil any wish of yours. Not a trace of unrest or dissatisfaction is visible anywhere in your joint lives. In Dvaraka, the eight chief queens and innumerable other wives, are unable to keep Krishna bound in the bonds of love. We never get to know when he goes where, what he does. Leaving behind the bonds of our love, when he gets entangled in the affection of someone else, we do not even get to know. For five years he lived in the forest taking care of you. *Sakhi*, have you any incantations, magical rites, or herbs and recipes for keeping the five husbands under control? Do tell me!"

Biting my tongue I said, "*Chheeh, chheeh*, Satya! Do not utter such words. Foolish and undiscriminating women take recourse to magical chants, herbs and roots for mastering their husbands. By this the husband's faith and confidence is broken. Often this makes the husbands fall into various types of terrible illness. Such women lose their husbands. *Sakhi*, you are Krishna's beloved wife. As your sister I advise you not to think of such foolishness Otherwise your husband will regard you as a mortal serpent and detest seeing you in his bed."

"Then by what means have you kept them bound to you?" she asked in eager curiosity.

I told simple Satya the mystery of my relationship with my husbands. "Satya, if you can, then follow this in your life. Removing pride from within me, I pour out my femininity like an offering of flowers before my husbands, made fragrant by the water of desireless action. I try not to be envious under any circumstance. My endeavour is to remain natural. I never eat or lie down before my husbands eat and lie down. I am up before they get up. I am never lazy in their work. If they return from a

314

long journey, I keep seat, water, food, resting place ready for them. Despite servants being available, I keep watch on household chores. I cook their favourite food myself and serve it with my own hands. I do not burden them with my own worries and anxieties. Rather, participating in their concerns, I offer my views. I do not spend too much time on toilet, bath and dressing. If my husbands are far away, I refrain from decorating myself. I do not take interest in matters which they dislike. Without their having to tell me, I am able to sense their likes and dislikes. I am never interested in arguing fruitlessly or rolling about in meaningless mirth. I maintain proportion in conduct, thought, action, eating, resting. The most important thing is that I never doubt them, nor do I ever shower them with unnecessary complaints. Similarly, I never keep anything secret from them. There is another special thing: before them, I do not utter a single word about their family or *ma* Kunti. I look on all of them equally, never discuss anyone's faults or qualities before the others. I anticipate their wishes, even their commands to servants. I never describe the wealth, prosperity, luxury of my father's house before my husbands. In the same manner, I never curse my fortune by comparing it with any other man's wealth and prosperity. So much so that in front of my husbands I do not mention any other woman as more fortunate than myself. I do not feel it necessary to display my innumerable desires before my husbands. I do not spend time in private with another man. I avoid women who are of a cunning nature. In front of my husbands I try to appear fresh, beautiful, ever youthful. It is because of the husbands that we are mothers, are fortunate, are mistresses of the household and are happy. Husbands are never hesitant in granting wives company, security, social status and motherhood. Therefore, is it not my duty to let them feel that I truly love them? Like Subhadra I, too, could have stayed back in my father's home. Why am I undergoing the sufferings of a forest life with my husbands? It is not only their happiness that is ours to share, but their sorrows too are ours. To lend courage and strength to husbands in misfortune and danger is the dharma of women. It is on this that I concentrate."

Satya was bewildered hearing this, "Stop, Krishnaa, enough! Let alone doing all these things, even listening to them makes me dizzy. I will not be able to do all this. It seems that even becoming a proper wife is the fruit of a regular *sadhana*."

I laughed, "It is here that you are mistaken. Instead of thinking that Krishna should be yours, why don't you become Krishna's? Just by that he will be enchained. Chandravali is one of the gopis and a great lover of Krishna. What is the difference in the attitudes of Chandravali and Radha? Chandravali's attitude towards Krisna is — you are mine. While Radha says — I am yours. Only because of this difference Radha becomes superior to Chandravali. My attitude towards Krishna is also the same. I say, 'O Krishna, Krishnaa is yours.' Since my very birth I have been in an attitude of surrender to Krishna. Those who mistake my attitude of surrender also fail to understand Krishna. The love of Krishna is not erotic in the human sense. My husbands understand this. Therefore, they even regard the love of Krishna as their good fortune."

With tearful eyes Satyabhama grasped both my hands and said, "Sister! You have not only won your husbands, you have even won Krishna. None of us have been able to understand my husband the way you have understood him. 'Krishna is mine' — saying this the eight of us are engaged in a tug-of-war. And Krishna is unable to be anyone's! Leaving us in Dvaraka, he has become Krishnaa's! From today you are my guru. I shall follow your advice. Only then will Krishna become mine alone — "

I laughed, "Sister, again you are on the wrong path. Not 'Krishna will become mine'. Say 'I shall be able to become Krishna's.'"

I do not know since when both friends were listening to our talk. Arjun broke in with a jest, "Enough, enough, Krishnaa! If you become Krishna's then who will be Arjun's? Speak, who is Arjun's? Answer! Otherwise to resolve the dilemma I shall summon Bhim here and the less I say of the results the better."

Without the least hesitation I said, "I am Krishna's; Krishna is Arjun's. So Krishnaa too is yours, what doubt is there in this?"

316

With eyes shut Satya was repeating, "Yes, I am Krishna's, I am Krishna's, I am Krishna's." She had forgotten herself. Tears were flowing from her eyes.

Asking for leave, Krishna said, "It seems, like Satya, I will now have to despatch all the eight queens to you. Only then will I be spared from that tug-of-war."

When Satyabhama had arrived I had enquired of the welfare of the five sons and Abhimanyu. During her departure I began to enquire once more. I was consoling my heart. They must have begun studying by now; how big they must have grown; while sleeping, eating, playing did they ever remember their forest-dwelling mother? — asking about all this, I broke into sobs.

To cheer me up, Satyabhama said, "Subhadra is there, all of us are there, then why should they miss you? They get whatever they want. Do not worry, sister. So many years have passed. It is only a matter of three years. They are extremely healthy and well-built. Abhimanyu now looks like Arjun's younger brother."

I wiped my tears and said, "They do not miss me at all?" My tears flowed faster. Seeing this, Krishna broke into laughter, "So remember, Satya! When we go back, the nephews must be given pain. Keep them hungry, send them to cut wood from the forest. Beat them too. Then they will remember *ma* Krishnaa very much. Then Krishna too will be very happy in this forest."

Wiping my tears and holding Satya's hand, I said plaintively, "Satya, do not listen to these terrible words of *sakha*. Being a man, how will he understand the state of a mother's heart? You can understand how painful it is to leave one's sons during their infancy and childhood. How will he realise that? Do not remind them about me. If they remember me, they will miss me and weep. Give my love to Subhadra. Tell her that I have brought back her husband from the kingdom of *svarg*. Also tell her that after Arjun's return from there Draupadi has not had a share in her conjugal bliss. For till Karna is slain, Draupadi is untouchable for Arjun. Despite being near him, Draupadi is now deprived of being of service to Arjun." While saying this, my face fell. To hide my tears, I got up and went inside the cottage.

317

43

The great sage Trinbindu's *ashram* appeared even more enchanting than Indra'a Nandan garden. I asked Arjun if it was really so. Entranced by the beauty of the *ashram*, Arjun too thought that Nandan garden would appear ordinary before this. My husbands had gone deep into Kamyak forest that day for hunting. I had expressed the desire to wait in this *ashram*. Leaving the priest Dhaumya with me, the five Pandavs left. Like a restless child I began roaming in the *ashram* garden. Being without pen and paper when I could not paint that poetic scene, it flowed out as sweet song. Like a butterfly I went from flower to flower, humming.

On the other side of the garden was the forest path. Some procession was coming with great paraphernalia, music and shouts. It must be some prince dressed as a bridegroom. They would have been attracted by my singing and turned towards the garden. Struck by my wondrous beauty, the bridegroom alighted from the chariot. Out of shyness, I hastily turned back into the *ashram* thinking, "*Chheeh*! My husbands are far away. Should I have been roaming in the garden like a young girl singing aloud?"

After a little while king Surath's son, Kotik, arrived at the *ashram* entrance. Holding on to a newly blossoming branch of a kadamba tree I was gazing at the blue afternoon sky and stringing together rhythmic lines of poetry.

Kotik was enchanted by me and said, "Incomparable one, who are you? Are you the daughter of nagas, yakshas, an *apsara* of *svarg* or a goddess? In the midst of the greenery of the forest you are blazing like a forest-fire. Flashing like lightning in the blue clouds you are enhancing the beauty of the forest. We have never seen such a beauty. You shame even the curvaceous waves of the ocean. The glory of your face is like a blue lotus in a lake. Your voice is the strumming of goddess Sarasvati's veena's strings. Whoever you might be, king Jayadrath of Sindhu desires to meet you. Husband of Duhshala, the only sister of maharaj Duryodhan, the mighty ruler of prosperous Hastinapur, king Jayadrath while on the way to marry the princess of Shalva kingdom has been stunned on the way on seeing your flawless beauty. He does not think it proper to proceed on his way without meeting you."

Hearing the name of the husband of my beloved sister-in-law I was delighted. It was only the Kauravs who were our enemies. Duhshala was a dear sister to the Pandavs too. I called her "Sushila". I had not met any relatives for many days. Therefore, eagerly giving my identity, I asked Jayadrath to accept my hospitality. No matter how many women a king might marry, a marriage enhanced his image. Therefore, Jayadrath's wedding journey was a matter of joy and glory. On such an auspicious occasion, if I did not convey my blessings and good wishes to my sister-in-law's husband, what would people say? What would my husbands' sister Sushila, think? And, on their return, what would the Pandavs too say to me? Yudhishthir would say I was envious. Bhim would describe me as narrow-minded. Therefore, I waited eagerly.

I greeted Jayadrath who was in his bridegroom's get-up. With warmth I said, "You did not recognise your elder brothers-in-law's wife? What is the meaning of behaving like a stranger and remaining at a distance asking for permission to meet? Even though I have seen you only once or twice, I have not forgotten your appearance. When you are the king of Sindhu, mighty Duryodhan's brother-in-law, then how will you recognise the exiled, forest-dwelling Pandavs' wife, Draupadi? How is Sushila? Does she ever remember me? Brothers might well become enemies, but their sister is common to them all. What would have been the harm if you had sent advance notice that you would be passing this way to Shalva? If they had known, the Pandavs would surely have waited for you. They have gone far for hunt-

319

ing and it is difficult for them to return before sunset. On their behalf, please accept my good wishes and blessings. While returning with the bride, if you should pass this way then please spend a night in the *ashram* of the Pandavs. The invitation stands from now itself. The Pandavs too will be glad."

Jayadrath gave no reply. He kept staring at me as though spellbound. Then he said, "Now I will not proceed to marry the Shalva princess. Lovely one! You might be my sister-in-law or anybody else, but it is you whom I wish to make my queen. To enjoy beautiful women is the glory of man. The man who obtains a beauty like you will be famous. The Pandavs do not deserve such a jewel. See in what a poor state they have kept you!"

I became a flaming fire in anger, "Enough, enough! Do not say a word more. Otherwise your death is inevitable at the hands of my husbands. Heinous sinner! Can anyone remain alive after insulting a married woman thus? You will have to do penance for this sin some day!"

How could my words be heard by lust-crazed Jayadrath? Dragging me by the hand he lifted me on to the chariot, saying, "Before me, the Pandavs are mere beggars. What harm can they do me? Lovely one, from today remain as the queen of Sindhu. That Duryodhan, who insulted you in the royal court — his own sister will be your slave. Surely you too will agree, that no greater revenge than this can be taken even by the Pandavs."

The chariot sped away. Kicking that sinner, I was about to leap down when he grasped me in both hands tightly. Helplessly I cried out, "Krishna, Krishna" and fell unconscious. When I regained consciousness I found myself lying on a bed. My husbands were seated anxiously all around. I was relieved. At least I had been freed from those sinful hands. Priest Dhaumya had pleaded with him not to force me. Kicking him away, Jayadrath had taken me on the chariot. Seeing this, Dhaumya ran to contact my husbands in the forest. Hearing the news, they ran and rescued me. But did they punish him properly or not?

Bhim reassured me, "Do not worry, Panchali. You are safe now."

In an angry tone I said, "I do not even wish to see the corpse of that sinner. Let his filthy body be thrown to the jackals in the jungle." Like rain following lightning, tears poured from my eyes.

Hearing my words, Yudhishthir said, "Yajnaseni! I had not expected such cruelty from you. Jayadrath has sinned. If the punishment of every sin were death then no one would remain alive on this earth. Men in general are attracted to lovely women. The discriminating man controls his desire. Jayadrath is bereft of conscience, so he insulted you. Do not forget that he is the husband of our only sister."

I flared up in fury and leaving the bed, stood up. Raging, I said, "You are perhaps even more forgiving than the best of all men of honour, Ram. For the crime of abducting Sita, Ram killed a wise man like Ravan. But because he is your brother-in-law, you will not punish him? Your wife being insulted does not pain you or excite you! The scriptures say that if the abductor of a woman or usurper of a kingdom should seek sanctuary, it will be unjust to let him live. He is the chief enemy of society."

Bhim supported my contention. Arjun, Nakul, Sahadev were silent. Yudhishthir began to explain the nobility of forgiving. Gradually I calmed down. Truly, man has filled this earth with so many sinful desires that at every step dharma, justice, truth are in danger. It is true that if the punishment of every sin is death then there will be no man left. The working of our society is such that throughout life a woman has to suffer because of sin. If Jayadrath were given the sentence of death for his sinful act, then for the rest of her life Sushila would suffer the agony of widowhood. Thus, the punishment would have to be suffered not by Jayadrath but by Sushila. A man does not incur sin by enjoying many women, it only enhances the glory of his manhood. In some circumstances, even if we consider it sinful, no one will describe it as an unpardonable crime. That is why there is such arrogance in man. There are many instances of abduction of beautiful women. Therefore, Jayadrath had not done anything overstepping the limits of society. He was a man and moreover a king. It is a kingly right! I felt angry with society. First I felt full of reproach against my husbands, and then against God. Whoever's fate is full of grief is created as a beautiful woman by God. However, Sushila too was a woman like me. She was faithful to her husband, full of love, pure in conduct. Without any fault why should she have to undergo the ultimate suffering?

In a voice heavy with tears I said, "Then free Jayadrath. What is Sushila's fault? If the rules of society are not altered on Jayadrath's death, then why burden Sushila's life with grief? If the desire for another's wife were an unpardonable crime and shameful for man, then there would not be so much of sin and perversion in this world. Chaste Sita's life too would not have been so sorrowful. After the killing of Ravan and the destruction of Lanka, rape and beastly tyranny over women would have vanished from earth. For men, women have also become something to be won like kingdom, wealth and prosperity. He whose might is greater, wins the wives of others. That Jayadrath failed was my good fortune. If Jayadrath had won then by rights I would have become his mistress." I pardoned Jayadrath but began cursing womanhood for the inequality in the rules and laws of society for the sexes.

Shaving Jayadrath's head, Bhim forced him to acknowledge servitude of the Pandavs; made him *pranam* me hold my feet and beg forgiveness. Out of fear of his life, Jayadrath did all this. The king of Sindhu dressed in bridal finery was standing with shaven head in a single cloth! In disgust, I averted my face and spat, "Let alone the touch of a conscienceless lust-crazed man, even seeing his shadow is improper for a chaste woman. *Chheeh*! You are not even fit to touch the dust of my feet."

Shaven-headed, half-naked Jayadrath was lying full-length on the ground doing *pranam*. Bhim and Nakul laughed uproariously. I came away from there.

Ashamed, defeated, frustrated, Jayadrath did not return to his kingdom. He sat down to perform penance in Hardwar to please Shiva. Shiva appeared before him. He asked the boon, "Give me the weapon to defeat the Pandavs in battle. Even if it be for a

322

single day, I wish to defeat the Pandavs." Shiva replied, "I understand your intention in asking for this boon. By defeating them, you are eager to obtain the desirable woman, Draupadi, in accordance with the rules of kshatriya conduct. However, I have already given my most powerful weapon to Arjun. Yes, for one day you will be able to defeat the four Pandavs other than Arjun."

Having obtained Shiva's boon Jayadrath went about boasting, "So, my desire shall be fulfilled. Karna will defeat Arjun and I the other four. Between the two of us we shall enjoy Draupadi. Draupadi is used to being enjoyed at once by several men, so there will be no difficulty."

Hearing this news Bhim angrily told Yudhishthir, "You see the consequence of forgiveness? Of course, the obsession of winning Draupadi can make anyone go mad. What is the fault of Jayadrath?"

But I said, "So the fault is mine? That it is sanctioned by the scriptures for the woman to be enjoyed by the enemy after her husband has been defeated in battle, is the true fault. But who will understand that? Who will oppose the scriptures?"

44

For diverting the mind we went to Dvaita forest for some days. My mind was restless. My beauty and youth seemed curses to me. Arjun had taken the vow not to touch me. The period of exile was about to end. Yudhishthir was busy with plans for the future. Bhim would keep roaming in the jungle. Therefore he would sometimes stay with Hidimba. By this time roads had been made in the deep forests. So Bhim would not tease me unmercifully as in the past and harass me. Nakul kept himself occupied in dance and music and celebrating festivals in the Shabar villages. Sahadev was engrossed in thought regarding the incognito period of the exile. As a matter of fact I was leading an absolutely lonely life. Gradually I had passed beyond desire and lust, as though this was the first step of an ascetic life of renunciation. Towards man's lust and my own lovely body and youth, disgust was accumulating in my mind. At the root of all our suffering, insult, the exile of the Pandavs, loss of kingdom, was the frustration of not winning a beautiful woman. That woman was myself — Krishnaa! Who knew what evil was waiting for us after returning to the kingdom following the exile? Duryodhan, Duhshasan, Karna, Jayadrath, the eyes of all were fixed on me. But what was my fault except being beautiful? Sometimes I would pray, "O Lord, instead of this beautiful body give me peace, give my husbands peace, return peace to Aryavart. Taking all my beauty make the earth beautiful, make the human heart beautiful!" But who would listen to my prayer? I saw that on account of prayer and celibacy my complexion was improving. My body was gleaming with an other-worldly radiance. I was becoming even more beautiful. It was as though fate was deliberately pouring out all beauty over me alone, to torment me.

45

That day seeing my face in the waters of the rivulet I was entranced. Some sort of foreboding arose in the mind. It seemed as if some virile man might rape me. After all, it was by rape and injustice that this world was now proceeding.

Suddenly a shabar youth came running, "*Ma*, a handsome man has been found lying in the jungle, bleeding from his body and his ears. He has a crown on his head. Even while bleeding, he was engaged in hunting, and disregarding the loss of blood he hunted down a tiger with great skill. Suddenly bitten by a poisonous snake he has fainted. All our herbs and roots, incantations have proved fruitless. The poison is flowing through his veins. The sage Viprapad has declared that you have the power to control birds and animals. If you command, the poisonous snake will suck out the poison from the man's wound. His life will be saved. By killing the man-eater in Dvaita forest this man has done us a great favour. If his life is lost in this fashion then out of fear no one will enter Dvaita forest."

Without wasting any time I sped to the unconscious body of the youth. *Arre!* Mighty gift-giver Karna! The wounds from gifting the body-armour and ear-rings have not yet healed. Looking at him I felt that he was a cruel donor. If he were not extremely cruel and stern then would he have earned the glory of being a donor by flaying himself? Sympathy for the cursed man awoke in my heart. The very next instant the memory of his vow to slay Arjun flashed in my mind. Now, after a few moments, there would not remain any reason to be afraid or anxious. The poison would remove the thorn from Arjun's life automatically. The very source of Duryodhan's strength and arrogance would dry up. He would come himself to beg sanctuary. Why just Indraprasth, even the royal throne of Hastinapur would be ours. By killing Karna, Arjun would not have to be guilty of causing *ma* Kunti's heart grievous pain.

I did not know why, my resolve weakened. The tender woman within me grew anguished visualising the grief, pain and death of a man. The compassion of Kunti within me also awoke. Unknowingly, the mother in me took over. Before me lay a man in the jaws of death. I could save his life. And he was no ordinary person. He was the supremely handsome and valiant hero, Karna! Moreover, he had also saved my life!

I forgot that this man was my husbands' enemy. The cause of my insult was left far behind. The form of Karna sprinkling thorns on the path of my future vanished. Only a valiant hero, the dharma-son of sinless Kunti and my saviour, was lying unconscious, inert before me.

I hummed the chant for summoning the serpent. It was as though it were waiting for my summons. At my command it sucked at the wound and slowly began removing the poison. Then in a trice it disappeared somewhere into the deep jungle. Some signs of movement appeared in Karna's body. At my gesture, Shabar youths applied herbal medicines to his body. The bleeding stopped. His wonderful strength came back. Regaining consciousness, he sat up. Before he could open his eyes and look around, I left the spot. The gratitude of an egotist like Karna will also not be free of egotism. Bearing that burden was beyond my power. He saved my life — I discharged my debt, that was enough. There was no need for gratitude.

I heard Karna's attractive baritone. He was saying, "Who is the lady? Lady, whoever you might be, I *pranam* you. You have saved my life, you are like a mother. I have never seen my mother. Whatever I have sensed of my saviour has filled my life with blessings. Forgive this cursed offspring all mistakes and omissions, all offences. For you are a mother and you are forgiving. If not against you, I have been committing offences against another woman. My desire to torment her goes on increasing, for I am a man and my manhood cannot forget the insult it has suffered. Perhaps till death that will not be forgotten. Today I had brought

Duryodhan along to torment her by displaying our prosperity. But I am returning a brazier burning with poison. Devi, embodiment of power, I salute you! I have always been a worshipper of strength and beauty. But without tormenting that woman I am not able to go back. Devi, forgive me..."

Hurriedly I returned by the forest path. Spontaneously, like clouds heavy with rain, my tears flowed. The frank confession of the anguish of Karna's heart had touched the mother in me, had touched every string of my heart. Silently to myself I forgave all the crimes and injustice Karna had committed against me. Why? Only a mother could forgive all the offences of her child...

Reaching the *ashram*, I conveyed the news of the arrival of Duryodhan and Karna and related the incident of gifting Karna his life. Hearing my account, Yudhishthir and Arjun exclaimed, "Excellent, excellent!" Yudhishthir said, "Wonderful! Yajnaseni has done yet another virtuous deed." Arjun said, "Because of Yajnaseni the opportunity of killing Karna remains. If Karna had passed into the jaws of death today, I would have been deprived of the joy of killing him. The world would have remained ignorant of my valour. Today Yajnaseni has acted as an extremely discriminating and wise woman."

Bhim was irritated, "Draupadi is greedy for praise. Gifting our inveterate enemy life, under the pretext of nursing him, she is gathering applause. Although it is because of Draupadi that Karna is our inveterate enemy." Hearing Bhim's words throbbing with anger, I was certainly somewhat pained, but I remained silent. He was, after all, always like this.

After some time news arrived that the gandharv king, Chitrasen, had imprisoned Duryodhan. The gandharv king was sporting with *apsaras* in the lake in Dvaita forest. Duryodhan kept staring at them improperly. Noticing his lust-filled gaze, the guards requested him to leave. He did not listen. A fight with the gandharvs broke out. Karna was absent from this fight. Duryodhan was defeated and imprisoned. Hearing this, the five Pandavs immediately rushed to Chitrasen. Seeing his friend, Arjun, Chitrasen was delighted. Requesting the release of

Duryodhan, Arjun said, "We beg forgiveness for the improper conduct of Duryodhan. It is the wish of our elder brother, Yudhishthir, that you donate him his liberty. After all, the Kauravs are our brothers. In our presence if he remains a prisoner, that will adversely affect the reputation of our family. In the name of our mutual friendship, please release him."

Chitrasen was surprised, "*Arre!* It is for insulting you that he had arrived with his soldiers to display his wealth. When your father, Indra, heard of this, he sent me to teach him a lesson. And you are requesting me for his liberty!"

"This is the fitting punishment for him. Having set out to display his wealth to us, to have his freedom restored to him by our kindness and help — will that be any less an insult to any man?" asked Arjun, smiling.

Chitrasen let him go. "Touch the dust of the Pandav's kindness". The Pandavs asked Duryodhan to touch Chitrasen's feet. Having touched their feet, sunk in shame and insult, he returned to Hastina.

Reaching the *ashram*, Bhim said, "Look at Karna's slyness! Leaving his friend in danger, he slipped away. Does this befit a man?"

Gravely Sahadev said, "Karna is definitely an egotist, but he is not by nature a lustful or debauched person. A man of his unimpeachable character is rare in Aryavart. As he did not like Duryodhan's vulgar behaviour, he came away. Because he hates Draupadi, at times he has behaved unbecomingly with her, but he is far above lust."

Karna was my inveterate enemy, but my head bowed with respect for him.

46

Anxiety about the year in disguise was disturbing everyone. Only Yudhishthir was unperturbed. We were all apprehensive that if the Kauravs were to pierce through our disguise, then we would have to suffer another twelve years of exile. It seemed that Yudhishthir desired this very thing. Immediately on returning to Hastina war was inevitable. He was aware of this eventuality. He was assuring us, "What has to be will be. Why worry about it from now?"

That day we had got tired roaming in Dvaita forest. Yudhishthir felt thirsty. Sahadev went to bring water from the nearby lake. When Sahadev did not return, he asked Nakul. After Nakul when even Arjun did not come back then Bhim went. Yudhishthir and I kept waiting till noon for the four. My mind was filling with foreboding. Yudhishthir was next to me, still I felt that the world was empty. Finally, both of us left for the lake to find out what had happened.

Reaching there we saw all four lying sound asleep. I thought how utterly irresponsible they were! The elder brother was waiting thirsty and here they were asleep even at noon! I sat beside the feet of the third Pandav, Phalguni. He appeared very tired and worn out. My mind was apprehensive, disturbed. The poor man spent his whole life in forests, celibacy, ascesis and worry. Now he had further vowed not to touch me. As though I was the greatest sinner on earth. I was thinking all sorts of things when Yudhishthir said, "Yajnaseni, you are learned. There is no alternative but to acknowledge defeat before the truth. Everyone dies at some time. But I am only grieved that all of them left us before their time."

I could not comprehend anything. Who had left? Who was he referring to?

For the first time Yudhishthir was shedding tears. Recalling the qualities of his brothers, he was cursing his thirst. Now I understood that my four husbands were dead. I broke into tears with my head on Arjun's feet. I forgot Arjun's vow and clutched his feet to my bosom. Then I fainted.

To bring water for sprinkling on my face Yudhishthir stepped towards the lake. He had but put forward his cupped palms to scoop up water when a bird perched on a tree spoke, "Yudhishthir! First answer my questions correctly. Otherwise you, too, will die like your four brothers. I am a Yaksha, the guardian of this lake. All four tried to drink without answering my queries. The consequences are before you."

Yudhishthir stopped. Patiently and with the greatest care and seriousness he gave the correct answers to the Yaksha's questions. I had regained consciousness. Hearing Yudhishthir's profound answers, even in the midst of so much sorrow, I was filled with respect for him. Before his unfathomable wisdom, my own intelligence and knowledge appeared insignificant.

Satisfied with his replies the Yaksha said, "I am pleased with your answers. I will revive whichever brother you choose. Tell me: Which of the four?"

I was seated holding Arjun's feet. I was thinking selfishly that the gift of Arjun's life would make me happy, but all four were my husbands. If only one was to be brought back to life, then I wanted that it should be Arjun.

But just then Yudhishthir said, "Save Nakul."

Although this gladdened me, yet I broke down at the thought of Arjun not living. Whose would be such a life of predicaments as mine?

Surprised, the Yaksha too enquired, "Bhim and Arjun are your two arms. They are Kunti's sons. But leaving them aside, why have you asked for the life of Madri's son, Nakul?" I too was asking myself this.

Giving the supreme example of fairness, Yudhishthir said, "*Ma* Kunti's eldest son, I, am alive. I want that in the same manner Madri's eldest son, Nakul, shoud remain alive."

330

The Yaksha was extremely pleased with his impartiality. At once he restored all four to consciousness. As though from sleep they all awoke. I was still clutching Arjun's feet, wetting the shores of the lake with my tears.

Arjun quickly removed his feet, "As a wife, all are your husbands. You ought to behave in the same manner with all. I had won you, therefore to show love and anguish for me alone is unjust. If we countenance injustice then the defeat of the Pandavs is inevitable. Krishnaa, remove this mountainous burden of unjust love from me. That is all."

I thought that my grief would provide Arjun with some encouragement. But lecturing me regarding justice, law, rules he again turned me into an untouchable. My tears kept flowing, washing away the guilt and sin of loving my husband.

47

Peculiar scenes thronged this predicament-filled act of my life-drama. In the city of Virat, capital of Matysa kingdom, we had taken shelter in the palace in disguise. If a year passed without problems, then the curtain would be rung down on the sorrowful play. Before the final curtain, the climax of the play was being enacted. Thinking in this fashion, I tried to remain patient.

Somehow four months of the incognito life went by. Yudhish-thir was in the Virat royal court by the name of Kank. He had assumed the role of an expert in the dice-game. To play at dice night and day for entertaining the king was his task. From where the grief of our exile began, it was there indeed that our grief would end. Coming to know that the brahmin Kank was Yudhishthir's friend, King Virat honoured him greatly.

My supremely powerful gastronomic husband, Bhimsen, had chosen a task to his liking. He was the cook of the royal palace: Vallabh. After coming to know that for some time he was cook in Yudhishthir's palace under the direct supervision of Draupadi and was also an expert wrestler, Virat had appointed him chief cook.

Of the role of my husband, Arjun, handsome as the god of love himself, it would be best if I did not mention anything. Whatever pained me seemed to be inscribed in his fate! Now he was the teacher of dance and music, the eunuch Brihannala. He was now putting to use the music and dance lessons learnt from the gand-harvs and Urvashi's curse. Hearing that at some time he had been companion of princess Draupadi, his status was considerably enhanced with Queen Sudeshna and princess Uttara. Devoid of virility, Phalguni now wore saris and hid the mark of bowstrings on his body and shoulders. Making a long plait of his hair he adorned it with flowers. He wore many ornaments in his ears, nose, and on his hands, arms, waist, feet. Coloured his lips, put vermilion marks on his forehead, collyrium in his eyes and dressed himself like a woman. Besides teaching princess Uttara dance, during feasts in the palace he entertained the queen and the city women by presenting performances of dance and music. I tolerated the disguise of everyone, but seeing handsome Arjun dressed as Brihannala I was overwhelmed with anguish. Wonder-struck at his dancing skill, everyone would applaud. I would go away from there and break down in grief. I was aware that this state of unmanliness, ridiculous gestures, womanly voice and facial expressions, swaying rhythmic gait — all were only for some days. Could any woman even in dreams bear such a condition of her husband? In the female apartments when women are engrossed in fun with Brihannala, I would strive to keep my patience intact despite my depression. Brihannala's feminine gestures and expressions would vastly amuse the women. I wished I could shriek out, "Who is Brihannala, do you know...?"

But the next moment I would harden my heart like stone. Tears had to be restrained. I would go away from there. Instead of Arjun, if Nakul had assumed this role, it would have been a different thing. For he was fond of ornaments and dress, conscious of his looks. Such a transformation of Nakul would have pleased me too. But the husband whose sole pride, glory and confidence were his virility and valour — seeing him in this role I grew sad.

Nakul had taken the name Granthik. Nakul having been Yudhishthir's stable-keeper in the past, Virat easily agreed to appoint him as guardian of the horses. Sahadev devoted himself to serving the cows with the name Tantripal. Virat handed over to him the well-being and security of his cattle. In their chosen roles, Nakul and Sahadev were probably the most content.

These were the roles of the five Pandavs, sons of king Pandu, in their incognito exile! Now what about the predicament of the daughter of Drupad! Draupadi was Sairandhri, queen Sudeshna's maid for dressing her hair.

Queen Sudeshna had been enchanted with my beauty. However, she was apprehensive that if she kept such a beautiful woman in the inner apartments even her aged husband might get infatuated. I had pleaded, "Maharani, I am married. My five gandharv husbands are in exile on account of their ill fortune. Therefore, for keeping body and soul together I have come to you. When they return, they will honourably take me back home. Therefore, do not be anxious regarding my beauty. I do not wish to attract anyone. And if anyone does get attracted, it will go ill for him. My gandharv husbands will not hesitate to punish him sternly. There is only one request: I shall not obey the commands of any male and shall not touch leftover food." Since then I had been queen Sudeshna's trusted companion. Covering my untied hair with the *anchal*, I used to devote myself to dressing the hair of queen Sudeshna and princess Uttara.

Yudhishthir was enjoying himself thoroughly. Day and night he was engaged in playing dice with Virat. He even had his meals with the king.

Arjun spent the time entertaining princess Uttara and queen Sudeshna. He lived in a separate room in the female apartments. There the maidservants would joke and jest about Arjun. I would redden with anger and bid them go about their own work. Mocking me they would say, "Why are you so disturbed? Not content with five husbands you have left home and come here. Now divert your mind for some days with Brihannala. In the royal female apartments Brihannala is the only means of entertainment. The entry of men is prohibited here. Yes, there is a brave man, the queen's brother Keechak. He is attracted to you. Hastinapur's royal bride, Draupadi, despite being married to five people is termed chaste. By fulfilling Keechak's desires, your chastity will not be affected. Keechak does not even glance at us. Otherwise why would we jest with this eunuch?'"

In anger and disgust I would flare up. Apprehending that in the flames of my anger the entire secret would be consumed, Arjun would take my hand and draw me aside in private. He would say, "Come, *sakhi*, let us talk in private. Ignore their words.

I belong to everyone. If the king wishes, his; if the queen wants, hers; if you desire, yours..."

The maidservants dissolved in obscene laughter. I felt like weeping. I could not say anything.

Softly Arjun would say, "Krishnaa, considering play-acting as the truth you are suffering. It is a matter of just a few days. This night of sorrow is about to end."

Suppressing my anger I would say, "He whose valour and virility were my teenage dreams, how can I bear this role of his? I can tolerate nothing in this play-acting — your dress, gestures, expressions — nothing." Looking at him, my grief would increase. Wiping my eyes, I would walk away.

Bhim would labour hard day and night. After his arrival, the other cooks began handing over their work to him and relaxing. Bhim did not care about this. Preparing tasty food he would serve everyone. After everyone had eaten, he would sit down with the vessels and finish off all that was left. Before coming to Virat, he was the one who was the first to eat after food was made ready. The slightest delay in cooking and he would raise a storm. Where food was concerned, all his patience and knowledge vanished. And here with what great difficulty he remained hungry till the last man had eaten. He fed others. Keeping his mouth closed, controlling his greed, he served food to others. I would break into tears, thinking, the moment food was ready with what love I used to feed Bhim and here I was but a servant! What rights did I have here!

When Bhim would sit down to eat then maidservants, cooks and others all would gather round to watch the performance and laugh. They would say, "The poor chap has never seen such royal food. Thanks to his good fortune he has got employed here. Now he is in seventh heaven".

I wished I could slap the faces of these maidservants, but I had to control my anger. I would say, "I have heard that prince Bhim of Hastinapur also used to eat like this. For him the ability to consume great quantities of food is something to be proud of, as he is a prince. But Vallabh is a cook. Therefore, this ability looks like the greed of poverty. Who knows, tomorrow even Vallabh might become a king. His strength is like a king's."

The maidservants would collapse in giggles, "When Vallabh becomes king you may be a queen. This must be the fantasy you are indulging in. If with five husbands you are fated to become a servant, then what is the harm in depending on Vallabh? Whether he becomes a king or not, his appearance is certainly that of a king." Then with an obscene gesture they would laugh shrilly. And I, furious and disgusted, would rise and leave.

Life was going on in the midst of this anguish burning within me. Only Uttara was the sole oasis in this desert. Looking at Uttara I used to forget the sorrow of separation from my children. Her flawless delicate beauty, pure youth would cool my agitated heart and make it honeyed and soft. Embracing her, I would sometimes say, "If my son were a prince I would make you my daughter-in-law. And if by some miracle my son should win royal throne then it is you who will become his bride." With the curiosity of youth Uttara would ask, "When you are so beautiful, how handsome must your sons be! If your gandharv husbands are so powerful, so valorous then will not their sons be valiant too?"

I would describe Abhimanyu's beauty, valour and super-human genius to Uttara. She too would listen entranced and say, "I believe that only he who is brave and handsome deserves to be king. If the king's son is unfit then why should he have any right to the kingdom?"

I, too, would silently support this statement of Uttara's. I would think that if this would be so then the ruler of Hastinapur would not be Duryodhan but Karna. But it was the jest of fate that Karna was not a prince, that was why all his valour was being mocked.

When Uttara and I sat together talking to each other, my sorrow would hide somewhere. I would become fresh, beautiful, normal. That was when Keechak would come and tease Uttara. Keeping Uttara in-between he would gesture to me in various ways indicating his lust. The attraction which I felt within me for a man's valour, courage and learning, to the same extent I detested his lust and blind desire. Therefore, I was disgusted with Keechak. He sent several gifts to me through the maidservant, Malati. I returned them. Ultimately, he sent me a letter setting down his naked lust. I threw it into the fire. In reply I told the maid, "Tell lust-crazed Keechak — why is he inviting sure death? For him, I am a poison-woman."

But Keechak was shameless. A debauch was like a beast and what shame did a beast have? What insult could it feel?

On finding an opportunity, I told Yudhishthir about Keechak's conduct. For, at this time, Arjun had no strength, manhood and he was unarmed. If I told Bhim he would react so violently that our disguises would be revealed. Our lord was Yudhishthir. I had thought that by telling him my grief would end. But he remained indifferent. Before justice, dharma, tolerance, forgiveness and generosity his wife's honour, helplessness, grief, pain and insult were nothing to him. Seeing my bewilderment, helplessness, anger and disgust, he would recite ethical axioms to me, "Yajnaseni! You are intelligent and learned. If a person does not protect himself, no one can save him. Carefully avoid falling victim to Keechak's lust. Do not do anything whereby our secret will be in danger. For, then we will be helpless. The time to reveal our identity has not yet come. With so many beautiful women in Virat's palace, why did Keechak's eyes fasten on you? You ought to have been careful from the beginning..."

There was no chance to give vent to my anger. I could not even relieve myself by shrieking aloud. Yudhishthir was not the type of husband to whom you could convey anything by shedding tears. I had wept before him and would not weep again. This had been my vow since long. He who did not give any importance to hurt and reproach, sulking before him was ridiculous. For, his own hurt in my sulking increased the flow of my tears. If tears could be freely shed before anyone that was before the open-minded, blunt-of-speech, Bhim. If he perceived the truth behind my tears, he would even cross the ocean for me. But I was afraid of him. If he heard that Keechak's wicked eyes were on me, he was sure to kill him. And the result would be that the secret of our identities would be out.

With great care I tried my best to protect myself. Then I surrendered myself to God. The husband was the wife's God. If he was unable to protect his wife then how could he be God? Only the man who could protect could be God. Therefore, placing *sakha* Krishna on God's pedestal, I used to worship him. It was he who was my friend in danger, my saviour. Therefore, he was my God, the lord of my heart, to be remembered every dawn — my most intimate friend. Even if he was afar, by establishing his presence in the heart I used to avert danger.

48

That day arrangements for some celebration had been made in Virat's inner apartments. It was Sudeshna herself who was presiding over the celebrations. Yudhishthir was playing dice with Virat after a meal. Bhim was busy in the kitchen. Arjun was occupied in dancing. Nakul was lookijng after the horses of the guests. Sahadev was preoccupied in the stables, as usual.

Uttara and I were seated near queen Sudeshna. Everyone was enchanted with Brihannala's dancing. Only I was suffocating. That Phalguni, who in the *svayamvar* hall had defeated all the warriors and won Krishnaa, was dancing among women to entertain them in the private apartments! What irony of fate!

All were laughing. I was biting my lips and striving to hold back the tears. That is when queen Sudeshna gravely said, "Sairandhri! Take a vessel and bring scented wine from Keechak's rooms."

In a hurt tone I said, "Maharani! I had told you beforehand that I would not perform any low task. At this time Keechak is drunk. In this condition it is insulting and dangerous for any woman to enter the rooms of a lust-crazed man. Therefore, excuse me."

Queen Sudeshna had never treated me as a servant. She had kept me as though I were her dear. But today in a stern voice she said, "You know the consequences of disobeying my command, wife-of-five-husbands, Sairandhri?"

I stood up. Was Sudeshna hatching some sort of a plot to gratify her brother's lust? We needed shelter for a few months more. Otherwise all our efforts would go to waste. Calling on Krishna, carrying the vessel for wine, I stumbled towards Keechak's apartments.

I knew that I was entering a blazing fire, advancing towards

unfathomable depths of an ocean, answering the call of a raven-
ing beast to quench his lust. Before Keechak's strength I was
insignificant. Despite my five husbands being present, it was
I who would have to protect myself. My womanhood was in
danger, still my feet must press forward. Even the criminal condemned to the stake walked up to it, not by his own wish, but his
feet moved on that path by royal command. My condition was
precisely the same. There was no difference between jumping
into a hungry tiger's cage and setting foot in Keechak's rooms.

At Keechak's door I broke down in helplessness. Calling on
Krishna, I said in my mind, "*Sakha*, it is you who are my God! My
beloved! The honour and insult of your dear *sakhi* Krishnaa is all
yours. Save my honour."

Keechak was lying in wait. The moment he saw me he stepped
forward with both arms outstretched. Seeing this sudden assault,
I gave him a hard push. Losing balance, he fell down. Like a
frightened deer I fled and reached the place where Virat and
Yudhishthir were playing dice. Keechak in his drunken state
rushed behind me. In front of everyone catching hold of my hair
he threw me down and kicking me showered obscene abuse on
me. Amazing! Yudhishthir went on casting dice unperturbed. He
did not even raise his head to look at me! Bhim suddenly arrived
there. Forgetting everything in his fury, he was but looking at a
large sapling when Yudhishthir anticipated him and said, "Mr
cook, what is the matter? What do you have to do here? If you
want wood, go to the jungle. Do not disturb the game here." At
Yudhishthir's command, controlling his fury, Bhim went away
from there.

Shaking with rage and insult I addressed king Virat, so that
Yudhishthir could hear, "The paths to justice are barred from all
sides to women. Debauched men outrage me and insult me in
public, but regarding it as inconsequential without interfering in
it you keep playing dice. If the king does not protect a woman
then he ought to grant her permission to commit suicide."

King Virat remained silent. His kingship was dependent on
Keechak's strength of arms. What could he answer? On his

340

behalf, Yudhishthir replied, "Sairandhri, we do not know the full facts of the case. So how can justice be done? You should retire to the inner apartments. Matters relating to women cannot be discussed in the royal court. Those who are in charge of the private apartments will look into this matter. At this time they are all engaged in the celebrations. Therefore, let this night pass. It might be that one of your gandharv husbands might arrive to take revenge for this insult. Go, inform Vallabh to arrange for the night's food early. Tonight everyone will rest for all will be tired. See that our game is not disturbed."

Yudhishthir cast the dice again. Wiping my tears, I returned after saying, "Perhaps only after my chastity has been violated will my gandharv husbands take notice. Then it is only my corpse that they will find. By giving them my all as my husbands, perhaps I committed a sin. What I am suffering is the punishment for that. My eldest husband cannot tolerate any disturbance in his dice-game. It is because of this game that my very life has been choked out of me. Despite being aware of this, he does not bother. If my respect for him lessens should he blame me for that?"

Yudhishthir bowed his head and remained silent. I came away. I understood his hint and told Bhim everything. According to Bhim's advice I begged Keechak's pardon and invited him to meet me at midnight. Seizing this chance, Bhim finished him off. Regarding Bhim as God I *pranam*-ed him, letting my tears fall on his feet. The whole night on the dirt floor of the kitchen, I kept shedding tears of gratitude on Bhim's broad chest. He kept petting me, consoling me, encouraging me to live on.

In the morning it appeared that my gandharv husband had fought with Keechak and killed him. My status in the inner apartments increased. It seemed to me that the night of sorrow was about to end.

The news of Keechak's death spread like lightning throughout Aryavart. The greed of the Kauravs was whetted. They attacked to loot the wealth of Virat. On account of Keechak's absence, Virat was weak. Defeat was inevitable. The king made preparations to surrender. But cleverly the Pandavs defeated the Kauravs and Karna. Virat's independence remained intact. Worsted in battle, the Kauravs returned to Hastinapur. Later, getting to know the true identity of the Pandavs, Virat was delighted. The hoped for day of liberation arrived. The exile of the Pandavs came to an end with a battle. Who knew what the future had in store?

49

After thirteen years of suffering the first fulfilment of a wish occurred in the auspicious wedding of Uttara and Abhimanyu. Virat proposed that Uttara be married to valiant Phalguni. But pure of conduct, virtuous Phalguni explained, "I am Uttara's dance-teacher, like her father. Therefore, it will be desirable for her to marry my son, Abhimanyu." For the first time the secret desires of my heart were being given voice by Phalguni.

With great pomp the wedding of Abhimanyu with Uttara was celebrated. Subhadra, Balaram, all the eight queens of Krishna, my five sons, my father, brother and many other kings came to participate in the marriage. Only mother Kunti could not manage to come. She lay unwell in Vidur's home.

Enchanted with the young bride's flawless radiant beauty, Subhadra said, "Elder sister-in-law, although in beauty your daughter-in-law will not be able to surpass you, still it is difficult to find anyone as lovely as her. Now I leave the responsibility of finding other daughters-in-law to you. I have five more sons. Choose carefully for them beautiful princesses. They must be such that even you will be outshone by them."

Everyone was laughing aloud at Subhadra's words. With a deep sigh I said, "Let them first become worthy men. Since their very birth they have been scattered here and there. Who knows what fate has in store for them..."

For so many days I roamed in the forests, leaving my sons elsewhere. Today I lacked the courage to call them my own. Still, hearing Subhadra's words how many matters typical of a mother's heart awoke in me! In fantasy, I began to see my five sons wearing crowns, flanked by flawlessly lovely princesses. My eyes filled with tears. What other joy did I want? This was enough. If this dream came true, I would then retire to the forest.

After the wedding, taking Abhimanyu and Uttara with us, Subhadra and I left for Vidur's home. Mother Kunti's blessings had to be taken.

Tormented by the sufferings of her sons, perhaps it was mother Kunti who was the most delighted by this marriage. In advanced age, lying in bed, for diverting the mind from the sorrows and pains of life, the young bride Uttara was an enchanting toy. In Uttara's happy domestic life perhaps Kunti could forget her traumatic conjugal life and sorrowful motherhood.

Om shantih, shantih, shantih! Efforts to establish peace on the one hand; on the other the challenge to battle. In the midst of this, all my dreams about the rest of my life were ground into the dust.

The Pandavs completed the year of disguise after the twelve years of exile in the forest. By all canons of justice their half of the kingdom, Indraprasth, ought to be handed back to them. But all the efforts went to waste on account of the selfishness and sinful plots of the arrogant, jealous, wicked Kauravs. After this, what other alternative except war was possible?

If peaceful understanding is possible then what is the need for war? Man is inclined towards peace. It is the beast that incessantly engages in quarrels, bloodshed and fighting. But invariably the final result of war has only been death, lamentation, bloodshed, destruction. One party wins, but both sides suffer heavy losses. The loss that society faces because of war makes victory and defeat ultimately equal for the victor. Therefore, till the very last, war ought to be put off and Yudhishthir was engaged in seeking out a peaceful solution to the problem.

Father Drupad had gone to Hastinapur with his priest for evolving a peaceful solution. He returned in despair. The Kauravs were not prepared to part with anything. Therefore war remained the only alternative. Hearing of the warlike preparations of the Pandavs, Dhritarashtra despatched Sanjay as messenger to the Pandav camp with the advice to abjure conflict. However, this meant that they ought to become mendicants. He said, "O king! Without battle the Kauravs will not give you even five villages. Therefore, you are preparing for battle. Getting a kingdom by war will you get peace? The kingdom that you will get through the death of friends, brothers, well-wishers — what peace will it get you? What is the value of joy got through bloodshed in this evanescent life? This is but another name for sorrow. If you want to win your kingdom through bloodshed, then what was the point of suffering exile for thirteen years? All your nobility, virtue, merit and fame will be destroyed by war. Therefore, O King! however heroic you might be, do not engage in so heinous an activity as war to win wealth and kingdom. Rather than this, living by begging is superior. It will be appropriate to build a hut in the forest and live as a *sannyasi*, renouncing this world."

Yudhishthir was lost in thought. He had ever opposed war. But in this situation would it be proper for a kshatriya warrior to return to the forest without fighting?

Noticing Yudhishthir's worried face, Bhim said, "Begging might be a brahmin's dharma, but it will be adharma for a kshatriya. Brother! Have you forgotten the injustices of the Kauravs — the insulting of Draupadi, the lacquer-house conspiracy, sending us to barren Khandavprasth? This adharma of the Kauravs is nothing new. Because of the jealousy of blind Dhritarashtra our virtuous and peace-loving father, Pandu, despite being the king of Hastinapur, was forced to spend most of his life in the forest along with his wives. It was in the forest that he died. Our mother, Kunti, is a royal queen, queen-mother, but has taken shelter with uncle in poverty and sorrow. Leave aside our own lives. Whatever we have borne from birth till now has been the result of the injustice, adharma, lies, unfairness of the Kauravs. It is unjust to seize other's property or wife through battle. But to fight for winning back what is justly ours is the glory of manhood. Till now we have suffered everything. More cannot be borne. If we let this suitable opportunity for takng revenge for the insult to Draupadi slip by, life will not be worth living."

In a calm voice Arjun said, "Do not be excited, brother! We have here our *sakha* Krishna, the wisest and most just man of Aryavart. It is he who will decide the course of our future action."

Sakha Krishna was seated quietly, listening to everything unmoved. In a grave, resonant voice he spoke, "I desire the welfare of both the Kauravs and the Pandavs. I want their conflict to be resolved. Even now the peace-making efforts are continuing. Today dharma and peace are in danger in Aryavart. Our aim is that they are re-established. If the Kauravs are not agreeable to peace then it is war that shall have to be the last alternative. Now the issue is not restricted to the individual disputes between the Pandavs and the Kauravs. It is no longer a family quarrel. It is now a conflict between dharma and adharma, ideals and meanness, truth and falsehood, virtue and sin. Therefore, for the sake of dharma, ideals, peace and the welfare of mankind, to suffer, if necessary, bloodshed, loss of life and property is the dharma of kshatriyas. Now the unity and integrity of all Aryavart is in danger. If Aryavart falls to pieces, seizing the opportunity, gods or demons will gobble it up. Aryavart will lose its identity and then will come the darkness of subjection. In that, not only the Kauravs and the Pandavs but all the innocent inhabitants of Aryavart will lose their peace, joy and good fortune. Therefore, now the question is of the integrity of the country, of protecting dharma. Whether it is the Kauravs or the Pandavs who are deserving, if they who deserve it do not get their rights, then in the interest of the general welfare it will be necessary to go to war. If the Pandavs discarding attachment to the kingdom become forest-dwellers, it will not harm them. The harm will be suffered by the innumerable inhabitants of Aryavart. It is proper for the reins of the kingdom to be placed in the hands of the righteous, the just, the good ruler. Cattle, brahmins, children, women, dharma, tradition — all are in danger today. The goal of this great war will be their protection. If the proposal for truce is not acceptable to them, then it will be war."

All were in agreement with Krishna's view. I had been thinking of war from the very beginning. Otherwise how would the sinners receive their proper punishment? If the Kauravs were not punished, why would the coming generations fear sin? Every day, in broad daylight, they would go about stripping women and looting their chastity.

Preparations for going to war were complete. Still, honouring Yudhishthir's request, *sakha* himself went to Hastinapur. He asked for merely five villages for the five Pandavs. Just with that they would engage in establishing peace in Aryavart on the strength of dharma. But wicked Duryodhan, despite being aware of the heroism of the Pandavs, rejected the offer of peace, depending on Karna's prowess. He did not even scruple to insult Krishna.

Karna's advice was, "Once five villages are given over to them, by the means of cunning *sakha* Krishna's plots and stratagems it will not be long before the throne of Hastinapur also passes into the hands of the Pandavs. Therefore, do not give them even a needle's point of land in Hastinapur."

Sakha Krishna returned. News of the great war spread everywhere. Aryavart was stunned. The victory of dharma was assured, but who was not aware of the terrifying consequences of war?

Because of the selfishness and greed of the Kauravs entire Aryavart was in danger of being dragged into the horrors of war. Krishna repeatedly sought to convince Dhritarashtra and blamed him for this war. As the blind king was blind to the good and ill of others, similarly, he was blind in his love for his son. This was the cause of the grief of the Pandavs. It raised obstacles to their just inheritance. If Dhritarashtra desired, the war could be averted. The son's obstinacy and wicked nature were only pretexts for Dhritarashtra. Despite Krishna saying all this, his truce proposal was rejected. Declaring war, he returned from the Hastinapur court.

Karna came some distance to bid him farewell. Bhishma, Drona, Kripacharya and other great warriors were reluctantly supporting the Kaurav cause, out of compulsion. But it was actually Karna who was their mental strength and the source of their power. Making a last attempt Krishna tried to persuade Karna. Should he agree, Duryodhan might listen to him.

Ma Kunti was in Vidur's home. After the exile she was in considerable mental anxiety over the uncertain future of her sons. I, too, hearing of her illness, went there. That war was inevitable, before giving this news to the Pandavs in Upaplavya town, it would be appropriate to inform Kunti of this. Krishna requested Karna to accompany him up to Vidur's home.

Knowing war to be inevitable, both Krishna and Karna were grave. Krishna advised him to reconsider the peace proposal, but in a single word Karna refused. In a voice throbbing with arrogance he said, "In the hero's horoscope turning back is never written. After having rejected it once, Duryodhan will never consider the proposal of truce. How can I give him this advice?" Then, in a mocking tone he said, "Arjun has gathered weapons after roaming this earth, the heavens and the nether regions. During the exile, the entire Shabar tribe has joined the Pandav camp through Krishnaa's efforts. The support of all non-aryan clans will be available to the Pandavs. The support of the miracle-working personality of this era, Krishna, is also on their side. Then why such fear of war? Why are they faint-hearted?"

Seeing his efforts to restrain Karna going to waste, Krishna said, "Karna, you are Kunti's adopted son. Behind this is the silent lamentation of her helpless maternity. You have never bothered to listen to that. Is there any woman in Aryavart who has suffered as much as she? Vasusen! During Kunti's unmarried state you were born of her womb. The source of infinite light, the tremendous deity Surya is your father. You are Kunti's first child. Out of fear of public scandal and society, she placed you in an earthen casket and let it float down the river. But in every throb of her heart your memory is present. After finding you in Radha's home and hearing how she had come by you, Kunti recognised you. By adopting you she sought to assuage the mute agony of her heart. Legally, you are the eldest son of Pandu, the eldest brother of the Pandavs. It is my duty to reveal this to you before the war begins. For, I am your maternal cousin, your well-wisher. Till now you have been fostering enmity against your own brother. You have repeatedly insulted and outraged the wife

348

of your younger brothers. Even now you are firm in fighting against your own brothers! Mother Kunti is suffering mortal agony from this prospect. Now consider: taking whose side is your duty?"

Karna sat down in astonishment — "I am Kunti's son! The god Surya himself is my father! And all my life I was deprived of my just rights on account of being considered of low birth. At every step I found only insult and shame. Kunti gave birth to three sons from different gods. In the same manner Karna came into Kunti's womb from Surya's seed. Truly, the first offering in worship of the sinless virgin maiden is Karna! By the time she gave birth to Yudhishthir, Bhim, Arjun, she had been enjoyed by Pandu and other gods. From this point of view, Karna is a sinless godly infant. It is from the blessing of a sage that he has been born. Yet, because of the false pride of parents, the attachment to social status and prestige, he has been walking with bowed head on the paths of society as an insulted man. Today in the final moments, all that sorrow and anger is rising. It cannot be controlled. Brother Krishna has unravelled the mystery so late that Karna's path cannot be changed any more."

Krishna was watching Karna struggling with the dilemma and said, "Brave Karna! There is still time. Come, join the Pandavs. Accept the blessings of mother Kunti. Your union with the Pandavs will bring the whole world to your feet. Forge all the sorrow of the past and fight for the Pandavs. Besides enjoying the whole world, obtain Draupadi, too, and establish the supremacy of your prowess."

Right within his grasp the most beautiful woman in the world, the one desired by innumerable men, Krishnaa; and on the other side the arrogance of manhood, of his own vow, of the pricking of his conscience. Heavenly bliss on one side; death on the other. But the bliss would be the gift of Krishna. Would it be better to lay down his life fighting at the call of manhood, or for the sake of his life, to take advantage of Krishna's offer and in this penultimate moment to betray his foster parents and bosom friend, Duryodhan, breaking his vow to change sides? Karna was not afraid of death, for at the very next instant after birth he was thrown into its clutches. What Karna feared were cowardice, infamy, fear itself. Therefore, it was death that Karna desired.

In a grim voice Karna said, "I know that victory is where Krishna is. The meaning of taking the side of the Kauravs in war is death. Yet, I have enough confidence in my own prowess. I am still confident of defeating the five Pandavs, for the foundation of my heroism is my own valour. Instead of the blassings of Kunti who, for the sake of her honour, comfort and welfare, threw me into the jaws of death at birth, it is the blessings of my foster mother, Radha, that I crave. Friend Duryodhan, who at every step bolstered up my crushed manhood, helped me in misfortune — even knowing his defeat to be certain I cannot desert him. Karna cannot betray out of fear of death. Nor will he deny his foster mother out of greed for a kingdom. Therefore, O Krishna! Kindly do not make a public declaration of the mystery of my birth. Otherwise, a righteous and generous-hearted person such as Yudhishthir will surrender everything at my feet. You know that I get deeply disturbed over gifts, pity, kindness, compassion. Therefore, may Yudhishthir be victorious — this is my wish as his elder brother."

The arrogant man's eyes were moist. His voice throbbed with affection for Yudhishthir. Yet he remained firm in his decision. A man who was so arrogant as to consider Krishna's blessings and good wishes as pity and compassion, his dearest friend could only be death.

Instead of being delighted on seeing Karna after such a long time, mother Kunti broke down. Embracing him, she agitatedly asked, "My son, how cruelly have you ripped off the divine blessing of the body-armour and earrings for donating as gifts! Do you know how many inauspicious dreams I have dreamt about you since that day?"

Calmly Karna said, "*Ma*, for the protection of your dear son, Arjun, those have been taken away from me under the pretext of a donation. Why do you worry over this?"

"How will you understand my heart..." Controlling her tears, she was petting Karna. I was anxiously waiting nearby to hear the results of the truce proposal. Oh, what a unique scene was being enacted before my eyes!

For passing on the news, Krishna said, "Then, Karna, you are not agreeable to my proposal to support the Pandav camp. Now be prepared for war. Seven days from now is the new moon under the Margashirsha asterism. That day on the banks of the five lakes in the dried-up bed of the holy Sarasvati river in 'Kurukshetra' the Pandav-Kaurav war shall begin. The significance of 'Kurukshetra' is that it is the field of work. Righteous deeds alone are true work. Unrighteous acts are evil. Therefore the true meaning of 'Kurukshetra' is 'the field of righteous work'. To fight for establishing justice is true work. To fight for fulfilling unjust hopes is to do evil work. Therefore, in Kurukshetra it is righteous work and truth that will be victorious. Inform the Kauravs of the day for beginning the war."

Hearing the certainty of the war, Kunti fainted. She had repeatedly encouraged Yudhishthir to fight, but knowing of its certainty her heart failed her. The moment *ma* Kunti regained consciousness she began to weep. So wise, patient, all-tolerating like earth itself, *ma* Kunti — what sufferings had she not borne? The word war did not terrify a kshatriya woman. Moreover, the victory of the Pandavs was assured. Yet *ma* Kunti was weeping! But surely she was not so faint-hearted? Why was she losing control? Why was she so distraught?

Taking the dust of Mother's feet, Karna returned, sad. Indistinctly, Mother said, "May you live long, son! Good fortune attend you!" Then tears burst forth.

Sakha accompanied Karna up to the chariot to bid him farewell. Placing a hand on Karna's shoulder he said, "You saw Mother's condition! She is worried about Arjun, but far more than that about you. You are the son of her virgin life, therefore out of shame and embarrassment she is unable to speak out anything. But she is deeply worried for you."

With a painful heart Karna said, "This sorrow of *Ma* is the result of her own action. I am only sorry that not knowing that

351

devi Draupadi was the wife of my younger brothers, I insulted her in many ways. As the wife of my younger brothers, she is like my daughter-in-law. And yet I led the onslaught on her modesty and honour! For that I beg forgiveness from you." With a choking voice and moist eyes, Karna grasped Krishna's hands.

Krishna said, "Yes. Krishnaa is waiting for the opportunity to avenge her insult. But even she will forgive you on getting to know of your true identity. Her heart is so tender and generous. When the time comes, she will get to know everything and accord you due respect. Karna, I wanted to hand over the whole earth to you. Krishnaa too would have become yours. As the eldest brother of the Pandavs, in terms of the words of Kunti, justly Krishnaa ought to be your wife too. Even she could not tempt you to support the Pandav cause. Now what can I wish for you? You have no faith in divine power. Good wishes and blessings for welfare you reject as pity. Therefore, the final words that I shall speak are these, 'Manhood and pride are not the same thing. May your manhood be victorious. May your pride be destroyed.' This is my only wish."

Embracing Krishna, Karna bade him farewell and left, saying sadly, "When I desired your friendship, I threw it away by harbouring enmity for the Pandavs. When friendship is being offered, I am not in a position to accept it. For, I have pledged myself to the Kauravs. Therefore, O Krishna! Should I be alive at the end of the great war, then will your friendship be mine. Otherwise, I shall wait for you on the other shore."

Krishna kept looking compassionately at Karna. I was astonished with Kunti's son Karna's devotion to friendship and kept contemplating admiringly the pride in his word and his manhood. But my eyes were moist. Why? With what feelings did the eyes of Krishna, beloved of the Pandavs, brim over with tears for Karna?

Even I myself could not understand this.

50

Only a mother could understand a mother's heart. I could feel every bit of Kunti's sorrow. Noticing her condition I did not go with *sakha* to Upaplavya town. Before the war started I would have to go to the Pandavs. It was I who would have to apply the vermilion victory mark on their foreheads. Arranging the tray of *arghya*, it was I who must perform the *arati* and with a smile send them to the battlefield. But now for the next few days it was necessary to stay with mother. *Ma* had grown extremely restless. Whatever might happen in the war, knowing that sorrowing for sons was written into her future, she had broken down.

It might be that along with the Kauravs, Karna might die, or the Pandavs might be killed. In both situations *Ma* would have to weep for her sons. Which stone-hearted mother's heart would not break into pieces!

Kunti had ever suffered on account of the poverty and sorrows of the Pandavs. If the Pandavs were her expressed pain, Karna was her secret agony. It was like having a particle of dust in the eye that gave great pain. But that pain could not be expressed to anyone. The torment of a thorn lodged in the corner of the nail in a healthy body — how could that be explained to someone else! Karna was such an unbearable pain for *Ma*. People see the healthy body but it is the wound in the corner of the nail that wracks the whole body with pain. But I was able to feel *Ma*'s condition. I wished I could ask her to give me some of her pain so that I could suffer some for her sake and reduce her burden to some extent. But *Ma* was even now embarrassed to speak the truth before me. Her love affair as a young virgin is the supreme shame and embarrassment of a woman's life, even though it is absolutely natural. If one has a mind then it possesses the capacity to feel. And if enthusiasm is added to that capacity to feel,

353

then waves of love flow there. These waves, out of fear of society, dashing their heads on the shores turn back into the foaming current of conscience, but sometimes wet the feet of an unknown traveller. The traveller's feet become clean when the water dries, but the waves sweep away into themselves all the garbage, thorns, stones, keeping them all gathered in the depths of the sea of the heart. On the surface, all seems pure, blue, crystal-clear. Can anyone bare her inner condition to another? *Ma*'s condition was also exactly like this.

I was like *Ma*'s shadow, ever accompanying her. I wish I could say, "*Ma*, I know everything. I too am a woman, wife of five husbands. I would mingle my grief with your sorrows. Who will know the pain of secret sorrow so well as I? I have accepted five husbands with a clear mind and heart. Regarding myself as a flower offered in adoration, I bloom afresh at every dawn and spontaneously shed myself at the feet of the deity. Yet, do I have no secrets or frustration? How can that be? Is it possible for me to speak out openly all that is there?"

Laying my head on *Ma*'s feet I washed them with my tears, saying, "*Ma*, what is your sorrow? Can I not share it? What shall I do for you? Say something! It is on your word that I wrote such a chapter in the history of this world as had never been written before by marrying five brothers. Now what impossible task can there still be that I will not be able to perform? Why are you wasting away? In the war, victory will be of the Pandavs, this my heart is convinced of. Have faith in my words. Where Krishna himself has consented to be Arjun's charioteer, how can any question of defeat remain there?"

Ma's tears would flow, "War is inevitable. Heroes will be slain. The destruction of kshatriyas has become certain. This is my sorrow. I am afraid for valiant Karna. If he had fought in the Pandav camp, I would have had no grief."

I became silent. To hope for that which is not possible is bound to invite grief. He who rejected the gift offered by Krishna, who could persuade him?

Suddenly that day Mother went off to the banks of the Ganga.

Her body was weak, wasting away in worry. She had pain and fever. What work did she have on the banks of the Ganga at this unearthly hour? Surely she was not going to give up her life in the Ganga in case she had to grieve for her sons?

I followed her in another chariot. Later, I was annoyed with myself. But how could I leave her alone in that condition?

Keeping my chariot behind a tree, I hid myself, waiting for mother. I could see her. I could hear her words too. I despatched the maids here and there to gather flowers. Gradually she advanced towards a solitary spot on the bank. There brilliantly handsome Karna was chanting the vedas, having completed the evening ablutions. his superbly formed body appeared remarkably attractive in the rays of the setting sun, as though pure radiance was scattering from his entire presence. I was enchanted seeing that pure appearance. Not for a single moment did I remember that he was our inveterate enemy, that I was a married woman!

After *pranam*-ing the sun Karna looked back. Seeing Kunti, he poured water on her feet, *pranam*-ed her and said, "*Ma*! How are you here at this unearthly-hour? What service can the son of charioteer Adhirath and Radha do for you?"

Ma looked at Karna fearlessly and declared in a frank, open voice, "My son, the person who takes the shelter of truth does not suffer. I have come to remove grief by revealing the truth. Son, you took birth in my womb from the seed of the god Surya. You are not the son of Radha and Adhirath. Do not pain me by taking their names. I want that you should remain with the Pandavs. They are your uterine brothers. If you fight with them, brothers will kill each other! I will not be able to bear that. The world will be blessed if Karna and Arjun unite. My life will be blessed! I will be blessed, my son Karna! It is the duty of the son to satisfy his parents. To keep my word, Draupadi accepted five husbands. I have come with the confidence that in the same manner you too will keep my word."

Above, the god Surya revealing himself said, "Yes, Karna! It is Kunti who is your mother. I am your father! It is your dharma to

355

keep Kunti's word. As my son, you ought to be devoted to dharma."

Karna looked straight at Mother. His voice was clear, firm, "Parents are the son's dharma, his gods. But keeping even your word will destroy my dharma. My parents are Radha and Adhirath. To give birth to a child is not within one's power, but bringing it up is surely within one's reach. When you yourself did not fulfil the duty of a mother then how can you expect a son's duty from me? That sungod who makes all things in the world visible, why did he hesitate till now to reveal the identity of my father? When my manhood, pride, honour were being ground into the dust before everyone, where were you then? How much of insult and humiliation have I suffered since childhood! Who is responsible for that? In Draupadi's *svayamvar*, when Dhrishtadyumna demanded my introduction, then was the sungod not present in the heavens? I looked up at the sky seeking the invisible secret of my birth, but he went on observing silently. Then what duty of a father did he fulfil? Because of being the sons of Kunti, Bhim and Arjun got all the opportunities and facilities. Did I get anything at all? You kept tolerating all the insults and humiliations heaped on me. You remained silent life-long. Of what value is this revelation of my birth today at this ultimate moment? I cannot break my promise. This I have told Krishna too. I have rejected the temptation of winning the whole world along with Draupadi. Leaving Yashoda weeping, Krishna left for Mathura, but I cannot do so. I am indebted to the Kauravs in many ways. Whether it be dharma or adharma, it is the duty of a man to pay off his debts. Without cause I kept assisting in insulting and outraging your chaste daughter-in-law, Draupadi. It is this guilt that is bowing me down. Today I understand that full of reproach against that selfish mother of mine I avenged myself on Draupadi. *Ma*, now I cannot keep your word. Forgive me. I also beg forgiveness of Draupadi. May she remain ever fortunate and may widowhood never touch her. May victory be with the Pandavs."

Ma sobbed out, "My son, your hurt and sulking are natural. but if you fight against the Pandavs, the question of Draupadi

356

remaining fortunate does not arise at all. Since leaving her father's home she has been bearing only sorrows."

Forcefully Karna said, "Mother, now the reason for your arrival here is clear to me. All right, I promise that besides Arjun I shall not lift weapons against the other four sons. For, if I take up arms against them, they will die. Arjun is my equal as a warrior. Since childhood I have been his rival. Because of him, my manhood has been insulted at every step. I shall only fight with him. His father took away my body-armour and earrings. Therefore, perhaps I may die at his hands. Let Arjun live and enjoy the kingdom. Otherwise, it is he who will face death. And I too shall have to go the world of the dead. I shall die fighting. Or if Arjun dies, then I shall also die with him. There is joy in challenging a brother and obtaining victory. But after killing, there is no liberation from the grief of fratricide. He from whose brotherly love I was kept deprived all my life, why should I be deprived of bearing the sorrow of grieving for him? Therefore, unwanted from both sides, discarded at birth by mother and father, it is death that is preferable — that is true, for Karna. Karna is not afraid of death. He fears pity, compassion, betrayal. Give me leave. This is the final meeting in this birth. At the final moment you accepted me as your own; for this Radha's lowly son is grateful. The time for living in the glory of being Kunti's son is past. That is the regret left in life."

Karna took the dust of *Ma*'s feet. Embracing him, *Ma* said, "My son! Your unfortunate mother blesses you ... may you earn fame."

Karna laughed, "I know you will not bless me with 'Be victorious' or 'Live long'. For that will block the path of welfare of the five sons. Between one son and five sons, it is the five whose lives will be of greater concern. However, drawing sustenance from your blessings, I shall endeavour to earn fame. It is death on the battlefield befitting a hero that makes a man famous. Your blessings will come true."

At the final moment, hurting mother with the accumulated reproach of his whole life, egotistic Karna left. Helpless, Kunti remained standing, wiping her tears. Gathering in both hands

Karna's footprints left on the wet sand, she wept, "Karna, Karna! My son Karna! ... May my death come before yours!" She collapsed in the dust there.

I ran to her and lifted her up. Supporting her body burning with fever I said, "*Ma*, evening has set in. You are the queen-mother of Hastina, bride of the Puru dynasty. What will people say if you are seen lamenting here at such an hour?"

Mother became like a small girl. Pouring out all her grief, she said, "At least someone now knows my inner agony. The five Pandavs, despite being my sons, could not understand my pain. For they are men. How will they appreciate a mother's pain? Krishnaa, one request. Do not reveal to Yudhishthir or the other brothers Karna's identity."

"Why? Otherwise during the battle they will be extra careful not to take his life?", I said without thinking.

Calmly *Ma* said, "You do not know Karna. That anyone should out of kindness save him from death, even this he will not tolerate. Moreover, today's battle is not between Karna and Arjun. This has been transformed into a world war. On one side is justice, on the other injustice. On one side faith in the divine power, on the other perversion of selfishness and arrogance. Here it is not a question of individual gain and loss. Even if Karna is in danger, dharma should not be endangered. If Karna gets victory, the kingdom will belong to Duryodhan and then justice and dharma will vanish from the earth. Leaping into this great war, the people of the world wish to establish dharma and justice. Individual interests ought not to be given predominance if they block the path of general welfare. Therefore, for the sake of the welfare of the world, I shall have to suffer. There is no other alternative."

From a helpless girl *Ma* Kunti was transformed into the majestic world-mother. *Pranam*-ing her in my mind, I counted myself blessed.

51

That day right from the morning arrangements for worship were on. A variety of dishes and sweets were being prepared. *Ma* had returned after offering *prasad* in Shiva's temple. The priest was making arrangements for performing worship to celebrate a birthday. Whose birthday was it? Despite all efforts I was unable to recall. It was not any of my husbands or children. Then for whom was this worshipping? Surely *Ma* Kunti was not labouring under some delusion? Without any occasion she was celebrating a birthday!

Noticing the doubt in my mind *Ma* said mildly, "Today is the day my eldest son, Karna, was born. Every year I worship only in the Shiva temple. Nothing is done at home, in case anyone gets to know about it. Today there is no fear of that. You know all this. Let me celebrate my son's birthday once at least. But see that Vidur does not get to know of this...", *Ma's* voice was tremulous with apprehension.

For pleasing *Ma*, I too threw myself into the work with great enthusiasm. The *prasad* was distributed. The priest was praying for long life of the eldest son of Kunti. *Ma* could not control her tears. The priest had been told that *Ma* was making arrangements for performing rituals for the welfare of her sons. When the priest asked, "In whose name is the prayer to be made?", *Ma* replied, "There is no need for any name. Make the prayer for the sake of Kunti's eldest son. The eldest son is the head of the family. There-fore, that will signify the welfare of all in the household." Repeat-edly the priest worshipped, praying for Kunti's eldest son, and *Ma* kept shedding tears silently.

At the end of the worship Kunti told Vidur, "Today my heart wants to seat my dharma-son, Karna, next to me and feed him *prasad*, for the five sons and grandsons are far away." Vidur said,

"Why worry about this? Send an invitation to Karna. He will not have any objection to coming to my residence."

Receiving the invitation, Karna began to consult the Kauravs. Duhshasan said, "Careful, friend! Never trust women who have been enjoyed by many men. Moreover, both Kunti and Draupadi are in Vidur's residence. You are our mainstay in the war. Only three days are left. I scent some stratagem in the invitation. It is you who are the danger to Arjun. So it might be a plot to get you out of the way. What can't a woman do to save her son's life?"

Everyone supported Duhshasan and advised that Kunti's invitation should be ignored. But Karna said, "Kunti has recognised me as her dharma-son. Therefore, she can never do any such heinous act. By apprehending this, you are insulting Kunti's motherhood. I may be the enemy of her sons, but I am her son after all! She can never violate dharma."

Duhshasan again urged, "Kunti might be your mother, but Draupadi is no mother. Draupadi is specially fond of Arjun. Therefore she is your enemy. She may mix poison in your food."

In a grave tone Karna said, "Krishnaa is the noblest woman of Aryavart. In her mind flows a stream of limitless affection even for birds, animals, insects and worms. You do not know that in Dvaita forest my death was sure from snakebite. It is Krishnaa who saved me by her miraculous powers. Without waiting for my gratitude, she left the place. Still, from the loosened hair, swelling and free like blue ocean waves, and the incomparable physical beauty I recognised her. She who is lifegiver is also, in a sense, mother. Will she, who saved my life once, be able to take my life?"

The invitation was accepted. Karna came to Vidur's residence. *Ma* Kunti eagerly served Karna food. First she put a sandalwood paste mark on his forehead. Placing the *prasad* in his mouth, in a voice drenched with tears she said, "Today is your birthday."

Surprised, Karna asked, "Birthday? I have never observed it in my life. What is the point in observing any day other than the day my parents found me in the waters? Yes, they have been celebrating the memory of the day they found me."

With tearful eyes *Ma* said, "But every year on your birthday I offer prayers in the Shiva temple, light a lamp, donate gifts and feed guests. I had no way of informing you."

While eating Karna said, "Then I give permission to observe this first and last birthday in my life. Who knows whether after the war I shall remain, or..."

Ma fell silent, shedding tears. Wholeheartedly, with all the pending emotion of a mother's heart, she fed her neglected, ignored, cursed son to her heart's content. Karna too, eating silently, tried to please *Ma*.

After he had eaten, seating him near her, *Ma* said, "My son! The bitter comments of the Kauravs on my invitation and its reply I have heard from Vidur. Once you had rescued Krishnaa from the river. Krishnaa too saved your life in Dvaita forest. Hearing all this, I think that between you two there was never any ill feeling or enmity. Whatever unpleasant incidents occurred, in those, others were the players. By befriending the Kauravs, you became the victim of the misapprehensions of others. Before the war such misapprehensions ought to be removed between Krishnaa and you. She wishes to tell you something."

Hesitantly Karna said, "I have already begged Krishnaa's forgiveness. Why all this in the last moments? What's done can't be undone..."

Kunti did not listen to Karna. Coming to me she said in a pleading tone, "Daughter! Hearing that for lessening my grief you are prepared to do anything, I was hopeful. Karna did not keep my word. I have faith that he will keep your word. Quite naturally, Karna has been attracted to you since long before. For my sake, will you be able to request him for the last time?"

I was taken aback. After knowing that Karna is Kunti's eldest son, my heart had filled with sympathy and respect for him. But demeaning myself, would I be able make any silly request?

Noticing my dilemma and the lines of anxiety etched on my forehead, *Ma* said gently, "You are my daughter-in-law. Your honour is even more important than mine. I shall never ask you to do anything which might harm the honour of the daughter-in-law of the Puru dynasty. Simply request Karna this much that — though he may not join the Pandav camp, let him under some pretext not fight for the Kauravs either and remain far from the battlefield. If you ask Govind, he will tell you the pretext. By doing just this much my unfortunate son's life will be saved."

I could well understand *Ma*'s helplessness. I agreed to make the request.

Karna was waiting for me. Hearing that I wanted to tell him something, his heart was beating fast. I entered the room with Maya and *pranam*-ed him. The moment he saw me, Karna forgot all his regrets and remorse. Perhaps he was reminded of the defeat in the svayamvar hall. In a mocking tone he blurted out, "By making what sort of request to charioteer's son Karna now does the future empress of all Aryavart desire to make him an offender?"

Humbly, using Maya as the medium, I expressed my request.

Karna laughed aloud, "Despite knowing my death to be certain in war, Krishnaa is persuading me towards suicide? The special moment for suicide arrived in my life on the day of Krishnaa's *svayamvar*. But considering that suicide is the coward's way out, I desisted from it despite all the self-disgust born of the insult and Krishnaa's injustice. And today at the final moments of my life Krishna wishes to see me deprived of the auspicious opportunity to leave my body in a manner befitting a hero! Why?"

In a hurt voice I spoke through Maya, "Maya! What an emotional outburst! The meaning of refraining from war is to live long. This is the desire of *Ma*. Knowing that Karna's life is endangered in this war, *Ma* is anxious. Therefore, grieving in *Ma*'s grief, I am making this request. War does not last forever. After the end of the war, dharma and peace shall be re-established on earth. Then there will be no obstacle to the Pandavs and Karna unitedly ruling the kingdom. If good people govern in unison, it will benefit all mankind. And this Karna regards as suicide?"

In a grave voice Karna said, "I have heard Krishnaa is a learned woman of Aryavart, well versed in the scriptures. But I am surprised to hear that for her life means the number of years one lives. It is cowards or the timid who stay away from the battlefield under some pretext out of greedy attachment to their lives. Such living is even worse than death. He who deliberately tries to remain far from the battlefield actually slays his own self. Karna is, at least, not such a coward. Karna is capable of destroying the entire Puru dynasty and becoming king of Hastinapur. But he is not attached to the royal throne. Rather, Karna considers a heroic death preferable. Therefore, by making such a request, *Ma* has insulted my manhood. I shall not be able to honour this request of *Ma*."

I was unable to tolerate Karna's arrogance. It was out of concern for *Ma* that I had come with this request. How could he boast of being able to destroy the whole Puru dynasty? Did he not know the valour of Arjun? I was irritated. Keeping Maya in-between us I said, "Maya! Valour and heroism are the glory of a man, but to offer proper respect to parents and elders is also an integral part of a complete personalty. Arjun honoured his mother's words and made his four brothers take part in marrying the bride he had won. Is Arjun not a brave warrior?"

Mocking, Karna said, "Lady! I acknowledge that your husband is brave. But I fail to understand what sort of man he is. If I were in Arjun's place, and *Ma* had ordered that the woman I had won in the *svayamvar* was to be shared by other brothers, I would have violated that command. Taking my beloved with me, I would have left that kingdom. Now, as a son of Kunti, should *Ma* order me to accept Krishnaa as my wife, I would immediately reject it. Yet I am ready to lay down my life for *Ma*. I do not consider blindly obeying improper directives as the sign of manhood. This is the only difference between Arjun and myself."

Standing inert, I kept burning in the leaping flames of arrogance and manliness.

Pranam-ing him again, I was returning when in a soft and humble tone Karna said, "Lady, you are now the wife of my younger brother, like my daughter-in-law! May you be fortunate! Moreover, you have saved my life and assumed the status of my

363

mother. The cursed son of Radha *pranams* you. Forgive all the crimes of this birth. In the next birth, I shall wait for the opportunity to do penance for them."

With both palms folded, Karna saluted me and begged leave with moist eyes. How strange is the mind of a woman! A moment earlier I was disgusted with Karna's egotism. Now his moist eyes and pained voice were destroying my mind's fortress of pride. My heart was wishing it could take him under my *anchal* and rescue this rare man from the jaws of death!

In a tearful voice I said, "For the mistake committed by my brother in the *svayamvar* hall because of which you have suffered insult and humiliation, as your daughter-in-law I crave forgiveness."

"In this birth this is the final meeting. The daughter-in-law is ever to be forgiven." Saying this, Karna left the room. He did not even look back, and sat in the chariot.

52

The fourteenth night of the dark fortnight. A huge circular field of five *yojans* was the battlefield of Kurukshetra. Here on either bank of Hiranyavati river were the Kaurav and Pandav camps. The ominous silence preceding a storm prevailed all around.

After the night the rays of the dawn would shine on Kurukshetra. The great war would begin. My dear brother, Dhrishtadyumna, was the commander-in-chief of the Pandavs. Grandfather Bhishma was the chief commander of the Kauravs.

My presence in the Pandav camp was absolutely necessary. For I was their wife, their inspiration. With victory marks placed on their foreheads by me, after looking upon my auspicious face, they would embark on battle every day. However, after this I would depart for the secure tents made for the stay of women. Therefore, without me the Pandavs would become powerless. In my subconscious mind pride was lurking. It was natural for any woman to have such pride. My husbands had more than one beautiful wife. My dearest husband, Arjun, had among his many wives the sister of *sakha* Krishna, Subhadra, too. But here no necessity had arisen for their presence. So I was the best among all these wives, incomparable in my chastity despite having married five husbands. My mind's pride was being reflected on my face.

Laughing, *sakha* said, "*Sakhi*, I have been watching you since evening. You are looking most thrilled. Not a trace of fear or apprehension. Are you not terrified of war?"

Proudly I said, "I am a kshatriya woman! Moreover, I have husbands. Is it improper to hold the belief that all will be well with my husbands? After all, it is faith that is the key to success..."

Sakha's teeth gleamed in laughter. "So, is war inevitable tomorrow? Although I had given my word to drive Arjun's chariot in the Pandav camp, at the last moment I have backed out. They will not face any problem. What can they fear? Many heroes are on their side. Beside them is so inspiring, chaste and faithful a wife as Krishnaa!" No sooner had Krishna's words ended than terror and despair overcast the Pandav camp.

The Pandavs were seated around Krishna. Downcast, Arjun said with folded hands, "*Sakha!* What is the fault of this unfortunate? Why such words of despair at the final moment? Even if you do not fight, still we have taken refuge with you. If you are not on our side, then where is there any question of war? Ultimately, we will be ridiculed. What is my fault?"

In a deeply hurt tone *sakha* said, "You have no fault in this. The fault lies in my principles. I have ever remained on the side of dharma and truth. To destroy falsehood is my dharma. The pure heart is my station. But it seems to me that we who are preparing here for war have kept some secrets in our hearts. For the sake of truth I am ever cruel. Therefore, I shall be compelled to be cruel and return to Dvaraka tomorrow morning."

With folded hands Yudhishthir said, "Vasudev! What pretence is this? What sort of friendship is it to desert the boat in midstream? What is it that you really want?"

He was glancing at me sideways and laughing. Maya was giving him company in laughing too. When Maya laughs in this fashion I understand that fate itself is laughing. Maya's laughter is a veritable treasure-house of deception.

In a grave voice Krishna said, "This is a dharma-battle. Therefore, before the war the mind shall have to be made open, clean, pure. Only then shall I be able to become Arjun's charioteer. Otherwise, give me leave."

Bhim was irritated, "Enough! On such a petty matter you raised a veritable storm! Now we shall each of us frankly declare our secret weaknesses before everyone. I shall begin..."

Krishna stopped him, "No, no. Not thus. Let it start from the eldest brother."

Yudhishthir with downcast face said, "Even now I wish that this war did not take place. If a solution to the problem can be found without war even now, it will be acceptable to me. It is to avoid war that I staked my wife at dice and was prepared to lose. If we had not gone into exile then, the Kauravs would have tried to take Indraprasth by force. Despite having been born in the kshatriya clan, to detest war is the weakness of my character."

Bhim straightforwardly announced, "As mine is the larger share in food, in enjoying Krishnaa too my portion should have been more. Because of this not happening, I get annoyed with Krishnaa and Krishna. Further, I tend to eat too much, therefore I am always thrust into the jaws of danger. Therefore, I feel reproachful towards my mother and brothers."

With bowed head Arjun said, "For honouring Ma's words I combined with my brothers to marry Krishnaa jointly I feel agitated about this. I wish Krishnaa was mine alone! To think thus is the weakness of my character."

Shyly, Nakul said, "Krishnaa is more beautiful than me, is flawless, therefore I feel envious of her. It would have been nice if she had been less attractive than me."

Sahadev's voice was full of sadness, "My weakness is my *ma*. We feel proud of introducing ourselves as Kunti's sons. Kunti's maternal love is incomparable. But the name of the person who gave us birth, the wife of Pandu, Madri, will gradually be forgotten and someday it will vanish from the pages of history. Sometimes it is this that pains me. It is the duty of the son to keep the memory of his parents alive. Therefore, is this weakness of mine not natural?"

Krishna's pure laughter was heard, "All of you have unhesitatingly spoken out the truth. Your faces are shining like mirrors. I am glad."

"Then you have no objection to becoming the charioteer of Arjun, Vasudev?" asked Bhim. Smiling, Krishna looked at me and said, "How can I say as yet? Your beloved Draupadi is still silent."

On my behalf Maya said, "Why are you dragging queen Krishnaa into this? She is a lady, do you not know that? Is there any account of what comes into a woman's mind and when? Can every thought be uttered in public? Moreover, will any wife be able to say anything before her husband?"

Sakha laughed, "Maya, you interfere in every matter. Why do you become a barrier between Krishnaa and Krishna? Is Krishnaa an ordinary woman like my sister, Subhadra, or the other wives of the Pandavs? She is as chaste and faithful as she is beautiful and learned. The mind of the chaste woman is pure like the sunlight. On the mirror of the chaste wife's mind not even the shadow of any man other than her husband is reflected. Why should Krishnaa feel any hesitation in opening up her mind? Rather, that will enhance her glory and I too will be able to agree once again to remain in the Pandav camp."

Caught in a dilemma I kept thinking in silence. How dangerous could Krishna prove to be when the time came! The great war would break out in the morning. My husbands were anxious and restless. At such a time should I frankly expose my mind? It would raise an unnecessary storm in their agitated minds. How would I send them to fight with agitated minds? I had no hesitation in declaring the weaknes of my mind. But Krishna's statement had to be answered cunningly. On the one hand Krishna's presence was essential; on the other, it was my duty to keep the minds of my husbands steady and calm. What a terrible quandary my dear *sakha* had placed me in!

Laughing, Krishna said, "*Sakhi*, why are you keeping quiet? Is the weakness of your mind so very grave?"

Affectionately I glanced at the pure faces of my husbands and said, "I have heard from *Ma* Kunti that Krishna is all-knowing. The hearts and minds of all are open to him. I have heard that he destroys pride. He does not permit anyone's pride to remain. So he has created this drama for destroying Krishnaa's pride. Krishnaa's mind is not hidden from Krishna. Even then if he wishes to hear it from my lips, I shall not hesitate."

All were watching curiously. Maya was smiling. Krishna remained pretending ignorance like a simpleton.

I said, "I have many weaknesses. For I am no goddess but a human being. If I begin to describe them one by one then the very hour of t is great battle will pass by. Therefore, I am declaring only the chief weaknesses. The first weakness of my heart is my dear friend, Madhusudan! From the moment I was named, I used to feel that there was some subtle, unearthlly, unseen but unbreakable bond between Krishnaa and some miraculous person named Krishna. The name of that relationship is not known to me. If it is known, then Krishna will know it. The second weakness of my heart is the same as *Ma* Kunti's weakness."

"What is that?" Krishna asked like an innocent child.

Calmly I said, "It is Kunti's sons that are my second weakness. It is my failing that the sympathy of my heart cannot cross the sons of Kunti. *Ma* Kunti'e sorrow and weakness are her sons. It is because of her sons that she has suffered all her life. With *Ma*'s grief I mingle my own sorrow. I am attracted to all of them — from the eldest son of Kunti to the youngest. What woman will not, after all, feel a weakness for a moment towards tremendous manhood! But in that weakness there is no touch of fickleness, hope or desire — this is well known to Krishna."

"My third weakness is the third Pandav, Arjun! He is valiant and gentle, therefore the entire responsibility of the Pandav family falls on his shoulders. The other four share his glory. Because of this at times I get annoyed. When the burden of getting divine weapons fell on Arjun, I wondered, like any ordinary woman, why that responsibility was not divided by the five Pandavs among themselves. What sort of justice was it that the efforts of one would be enjoyed by four? However, this was my meanness. I have made an offering of my life to keep the five Pandavs bound together, yet blinded by love for Arjun I thought of sowing dissension among them. Although the next moment, full of remorse, cleansing myself of the meanness, I would curse myself."

Exposing my weaknesses before my husbands my eyes filled with tears. I saw that my dearest Arjun's eyes were also moist. I felt blessed having exposed my weaknesses. Silently, in my heart of hearts, I was expressing gratitude to Krishna.

With an affectionate glance Krishna said, "Glory to you,

Krishnaa! In using words you have surpassed even Krishna! By saying that you are attracted to all Kunti's sons, from the eldest to the youngest, you have opened up your pure heart. Some day after the war I shall explain this statement further."

Krishna was smiling gently. The Pandavs too were content with my frank admission.

Suddenly I said, "Is most respected Krishna devoted only to seeking out the weaknesses of everyone? Has he no weakness of his own? He should also purify his heart today in this sacred hour today before the battle."

Clapping his hands, Bhim laughed out aloud, "It is only Krishnaa who has the ability to compel Krishna. Speak, child Krishna, what is your weakness?"

Krishna was embarrassed. In that state he said, "My weakness is spread throughout earth, the heavens and the nether regions, everywhere. Playing with the infinite universe is my weakness. Whoever loves me most, I harass him the most. He whom I love, I throw into danger. He who imagines, 'Krishna is mine' — I become an illusion to him. He who imagines, 'I am Krishna's', I become bound to him. That which I build, I also destroy. It is in this that I find delight."

Folding both palms together, Bhim said, "Enough, enough, child Krishna! Listening to your list of weaknesses our minds have been crushed! For, we love you. It is you who constitute our world. Then, if you destroy that..."

Yudhishthir *pranam*-ed Krishna.

Round Krishna's head was an ineffable radiant halo! A supernal glow was radiating from him, seeing which all agitation and anxiety of mind and heart vanished.

This was necessary for the Pandavs before the war.

53

Time was invincible, infinite. Eighteen days were so insignificant in it, so ordinary. Like the blinking of an eye, how swiftly was the horror of the eighteen-day war swept away in the current of time!

That eighteen-day current of the time-ocean obliterated everything. Everything was destroyed. In the ocean of great Time, a small wave, the Battle of Kurukshetra, rose and disappeared. The war was over. Pitiful defeat on one side; terrifying victory on the other!

Could victory be so terrible, awful, full of despair! An earth devoid of people. Friend and foe, wise and foolish, brave and cowardly, old and young, father, brother, teacher, friend, husband, son — all were licked up by the slavering tongue of war.

Now with whom would the victory celebrations be held? Those who were loved most had been snatched away from me by the great Time. My father Drupad, brothers Shikhandi, Dhrishtadyumna and their sons, Virat and his sons, my dearest son, Abhimanyu, Kunti's supreme weakness, valiant Karna — hidden in the corner of my heart as a gentle emotion like a mole on the chest — innumerable subjects and soldiers, our sons Ghatotkach, Iravan and ultimately my own five dear-as-life-itself sons were all slain in the war. Sinless, delicate children even before blooming lay down to sleep in the battlefield to satisfy the blood-lust of battle-hungry blind men. Eleven armies of the Kauravs and seven of the Pandavs went to eternal sleep in the bloody river of the battlefield. Among the heroes, Kritavarma, Kripacharya, slayer of my sons, Ashvatthama, on the Kaurav side, and on the Pandav side the five Pandavs, Krishna and Satyaki remained alive at the end of the war.

Joy and sorrow, hope and despair came and went at the blinking of an eye. On every day of the war excitement was at the

371

peak. One moment news to rejoice in would arrive, the next would bring sorrowful tidings. I knew that dharma was wherever Krishna was. Where Krishna was that was where victory was. Victory was playing hide-and-seek with me. Still I knew that victory would be mine. Happiness, prosperity, honour, all would be mine. For, I was the wife of the virtuous Pandavs, the sister of Dhrishtadyumna, the mother of Abhimanyu and the *sakhi* of Krishna. Yet victory left one thus — stripped of everything!

I had encouraged the Pandavs for war, but kingdom, wealth, prosperity were not my goals. To avenge the insult and punish the offenders were my only aims. I avenged the insult and the offender was also punished. But what did I get? That in a dharma-war the offender was punished, but the innocent did not suffer — where was this written?

What was the fault of my darling Abhimanyu? He had taken birth with the beauty, qualities and heroism of Arjun. Therefore, I loved him too much. He knew that after entering the discus formation of the army there was no return. Still Yudhishthir despatched such an innocent boy to fight seven chariot-heroes? Before sending him, he did not even ask whether he knew the trick of coming out of the discus formation after breaking into it! Must always Arjun or his son move into the jaws of death? What was the substance of which Yudhishthir was made? As if he had nothing called a heart! Were virtuous people heartless?

While living far from my sons in Virat's city, I had showered love on Uttar and Uttara as though on my son and daughter. I brought Uttara as my daughter-in-law with so many dreams of joy applied to her eyes like collyrium! Uttar and his brother were slain in battle. Teenaged Uttara was pregnant and in that condition she lost Abhimanyu. How could I bear any more? Subhadra had always been a believer in fate. She was simple. After the death of her only son she was struck dumb. Uttara became virtually insane. Arjun was overwhelmed with sorrow. Yudhishthir was silent, unperturbed!

The hellish killing of Abhimanyu was paining me even more. As many as seven chariot-heroes jointly slew him! And the leader in this slaughter was Abhimanyu's eldest uncle, the son of Kunti, Karna!

I broke down in the sorrow of Abhimanyu's death. I had then thought that perhaps this sorrow would be assuaged by the death of Karna. News of Karna's death arrived. The chariot-wheel of Karna had got stuck in the mud. He had alighted to lift it when at the direction of Krishna my husband, Arjun, slew the unarmed Karna! Why did Arjun do this? The killing of *Ma* Kunti's eldest unarmed son took place on the field of dharma! Karna's death could not lessen the agony of losing my son, Abhimanyu. Rather, the killing of Karna in that helpless condition doubled my sorrow.

Making my heart stone, I had to bear the grief of Karna's death. I had thought that it would be Duhshasan's death that would lighten my sorrow. Duhshasan died. At one time I used to be frantic in eagerness to bathe in Duhshasan's blood. Bhim kept his promise. With handfuls of wicked Duhshasan's hot blood he washed my unbound hair. My heart, burning with the insult, had been satisfied, but was not at peace.

Every fibre of my open tresses was touched by that red, fresh, hot blood. Human blood flowed down my face and shoulders. Every strand of my hair stood up with the smell of fresh blood. It seemed as though all the delicacy of my self would be wiped out in a horrific delight.

But instead of the heart's burning reducing, the leaping flames went on rising higher.

At one time I had imagined that Duhshasan's blood would bring peace to my heart. Now it seemed that drinking blood only satisfied the beast. Anyone who has the slightest feeling of humanity in him cannot ever achieve peace by sporting with human blood. However much I might be immersed in revenge, I was a woman. How could I find peace through human blood? Rather a helplessness, disgust, detachment from life, profound remorse and sorrow overwhelmed me. Seeing the huge body of Bhim and Duhshasan's blood I had shivered to see the beast hidden in man. Even as red as this would have been my Abhimanyu's blood, the blood of my father, friends, brothers! The earth can never be satisfied drinking blood. For she is the mother, life-giver, bringer forth of heroes!

Repeatedly the earth has been drenched with the blood of heroes because of man's narrow selfishness. Man's blood is shed on her breast. But does blind man ever appreciate her sorrow and pain? Bloodshed, horror, can never give peace to anyone, can never quench the agony of anyone. Now it was this that the bathing in Duhshasan's blood was telling me. Bhim brought another handful of blood to pour on my hair — I shrieked out, "Enough, enough! Let me live. Take me to some other earth! O my lord! I cannot bear this! In Duhshasan's blood I can smell the blood of Abhimanyu. It seems that the blood of all human beings in the world carries the same, identical smell. Do not make me an ogress..." I fainted.

When I regained consciousness, I was in the camp. Someone was seated by my head. I felt a tender touch on my forehead. Tears were falling drop by drop. The smell of blood was still overpowering me.

I heard the voice of *sakha*. He was saying, "*Sakhi*, compose yourself! The punishing of Duhshasan, the destruction of injustice, is the law of great Time. By the death of wicked persons like Duhshasan the earth will become sinless. Once again dharma will be established on earth. This is the goal of my life and yours. It is at my command that great Time is going on destroying the wicked. It does not befit so intelligent a woman as you to lose your composure in this fashion."

I broke down and was in tears. I said, "*Sakha*, where is my son, Abhimanyu? What sin had he committed? Why did great Time snatch him away? What sin will the world be free from by his death?"

Sighing deeply, Krishna said, "*Sakhi!* This is truly the terrible consequence of war. For the welfare of the world in the course of destroying the wicked, even saints and sages have to make sacrifices. For the sake of the world's welfare individual interest has to be renounced. The individual has to lay down his life. In the

374

cause of the world's welfare, Abhimanyu has sacrificed his life. By dying a valiant death he has gained heaven. In the history of the world the name of Abhimanyu will shine for ever."

Lamenting, I complained, "The mother's sorrow is not wiped out if the son lives on in the pages of history. No mother craves for her son's death even if he attains immortality by dying a hero's death. You are a man. How will you understand a mother's heart?"

Smiling sadly Krishna said, "Yajnaseni! I am Abhimanyu's maternal uncle. When you were in the forest, I was at his side. His upbringing, education, training in weapons, taking the entire responsibility of these I was making him *sakha's* fitting inheritor. I was not just his uncle, but his father, mother, teacher, friend, everything. I ought to be grieving the most at his death. But I am aware of the motions of time. Therefore, I do not grieve over death. Compose yourself. If you behave in this fashion, who will help Arjun to regain composure? If you see him overwhelmed with grief, you will understand what I mean."

Sharply I retorted, "*Sakha*, the third Pandav loves you more than his own life. Is that why you have pained him thus? Is this your principle?"

Sakha's voice was calm, "In the war when overcome by attachment brave Arjun sat down discarding weapons speaking of not taking up arms against friend, brother, teacher, grandfather, then for removing that delusion and inertness from his mind I had to explain the mystery of the soul's immortality, birth and death, virtue and sin, creator and created, and all the truths concerning the world on the battlefield itself. Therefore, Arjun will overcome this sorrow gradually. Do not worry about that."

I recalled what I had heard from Arjun's lips about that unprecedented event on the battlefield. To remove *sakha's* inertness, Krishna had revealed to him his universal form. In the battlefield itself Arjun saw Krishna's innumerable mouths, innumerable blazing eyes, innumerable limbs, innumerable sharp teeth. His body had expanded filling the whole sky. The radiant golden body was blazing with energy. In the mouth, fitted with tusks terrifying as the all-consuming flames, were visible innumerable suns, moons, stars, planets! In that very mouth Arjun saw everyone. Seeing that form, Arjun had become dizzy and had prayed, "O Vasudev, restrain this form of yours".

Then was Krishna great Time! It was he who was the creator and the destroyer, God Himself!

Ma Kunti had recognised him properly. That is why despite being his aunt she *pranamed* him!

If the soul was immortal, if after the death of the body the soul united with the creator, then why grieve over death?

For a moment I too, forgetting my grief, stood up and bowed before *sakha*.

Maya's voice was heard, "Uttara is fainting repeatedly. This is not the time for *pranam*-ing Krishna."

I was once again overcome with grief.

54

Duryodhan's thigh had been shattered. After being struck down he was counting the moments before his death. The war was over. After Father's death the people of Panchal were sorely distressed. That day I had gone to Panchal only to tell them that they were not fatherless. My brave brother, Drona-slayer Dhrishtadyumna, having conquered the enemy was still alive. The moment peace was re-established in Hastinapur, he would return to look after the subjects. I was satisfied after informing my sister-in-law of Dhrishtadyumna's welfare. She was in deep distress, waiting for him.

The whole night we sisters-in-law, forgetting all sorrow, kept spinning dreams of future happiness. Abhimanyu, Ghatotkach, Belalsen and all the other sons of my co-wives were dead, still by God's grace my five sons were well. Looking at them it might be possible to forget the sorrow of losing the other sons. Right from childhood they had been deprived of their mother's love. A few days after their birth I had gone away into the forest. Now I could give them a mother's love to my heart's content. Besides this, what desire for enjoying any other happiness was left in me!

Having seen war, bloodshed, death, lamentation, all for kingdom, my mind's attachment to throne, wealth, possessions had been broken. No delight was left in becoming queen. Once the sons had grown up, handing over the kingdom to them I would be a queen-mother. As the wife of five husbands I had spent the whole life in trouble. Now, at least, as the mother of five sons I would be able to draw my breath in peace for some days! I would try to seek out the meaning of life in their laughter and joy, seek out my darling Abhimanyu.

The whole night I kept dreaming: the faces of my laughing, playing children, scenes of their marriage, their enthronement, and scenes of playing with their children, petting them. *Apsaras* were descending from heaven to garland them. Perhaps my daughters-in-law were looking like *apsaras*. The dream broke. My heart was beating fast. What was all this I saw? What can be the significance of this?

Who could I ask for the meaning of this dream? There was still time till dawn. But just then the news arrived — Drona's son Ashvatthama had attacked at night and killed Dhrishtadyumna and all my five sons as they lay asleep! My sister-in-law and I fell unconscious. Who would console us?

Such a defeat at the moment of victory! The cruel jest of fate! How would I bear this grief? I was already distressed with the sorrow of losing Abhimanyu, Ghatotkach and the rest. This terrible news virtually took my life away. There is perhaps no sorrow greater than that of losing one's son. No words are adequate for that. Death is the only antidote for this grief.

They were asleep, beheaded, in a sea of blood like sinless flowers — my five delicate children: Prativindhya, Shrutasom, Shrutakirti, Shatanik and Shrutakarma. The smile had not faded from their lips — some sweet dream of the night had not yet been wiped off their eyes.

Taking my sons' corpses in my lap again and again I was wailing, lamenting. Clutching someone's decapitated head and another's torso to my breast I fell unconscious. How could a mother losing as many as five sons at a time retain her composure?

My five husbands were overcome with grief. Today the creator had made everyone sonless. They were all looking away from one another. Tears were mingling with the sons' blood. Only Govind was consoling everyone.

After some time I forgot myself. Like a demoness I shrieked out horribly, "Without destroying that sinner Ashvatthama and taking revenge on that slayer of children, I will not even be able to die in peace."

Bhim understood. Noticing my firm resolve not to touch food and drink, he stood up. Just then news arrived that after hearing of the death of the five sons, Duryodhan had given up his life. Bhim became alert at this news and set out to capture Ashvatthama. Seeing that terrible appearance once more I shrank back. Was earth on the verge of a cataclysm? Was there no end to death at all?

Yudhishthir, Arjun and Krishna had also set out in search of Ashvatthama. Suddenly a mild tremor awoke in my heart. Drona's wife Harita was still alive. In her life, Ashvatthama was the only means of existence. Drona was dead. After the death of Ashvatthama, Harita too would be a victim to grief for her son. Yes, Ashvatthama was a sinful soul. But Harita was like my mother. She who did not know what it was to grieve for a son would slay someone else's son to take revenge. How could I do so? A moment ago I was weeping, "Oh God! Do not let even enemies suffer the loss of sons!" And how could I now kill Ashvatthama and drown Harita in grief for her son? By killing Ashvatthama, my five sons would not come back. Then let sinful Ashvatthama live. Let him live long, suffering all pains. In Hastina, let at least one mother, Harita, be saved from grieving over her son. I called Krishna. In a gentle voice I said, "Pardon that sinful soul. Tell Bhim, there is now no need to capture Ashvatthama and bring him here. That sinner shall himself suffer the consequences of his sins. Fate will see to that. Who am I to punish?"

Smiling, Krishna said, "Panchali! A thousand *pranams* to the incomparable embodiment of compassion and forgiveness."

Bhim's voice was heard, "Panchali! Here is the wicked Ashvatthama. Tear open his heart and drink your fill of his blood. Quench the agony of losing your sons."

I did not even lift up my eyes to see his imprisoned state. Turning my face away I said, "I do not even wish to set eyes on this sinner. My soul will be sullied by his touch. Husband! Be kind. Take him away from my sight. Drive him out of the boundaries of the kingdom. He has no place in this kingdom." My tongue was dripping fire but the eyes were raining tears. I could not bear any more and fell unconscious.

379

Sinful Ashvatthama was not even fit to be forgiven. Having been forgiven by me, afraid, he ran into the forest. Ultimately, to destroy the progeny of the only dynast of the Pandavs, Abhimanyu, waiting in Uttara's womb for deliverance, he released the Brahma missile. It was the friend-in-need Krishna who saved the child in Uttara's womb by despatching the discus. Like a green blade of grass in a cremation ground turning into a flower through the rain of Krishna's compassion, the last hope of the Pandavs kept growing in Uttara's womb.

55

Death is more generous than life. Death is more composed. Those who were enemies yesterday, today their death drenches the heart with tender compassion. Those who were wicked, lustful, sinful till yesterday were made composed, steady and unperturbed by death today.

Those who were slain as enemies in the battlefield, considering them as brothers, after cremating them, the rites for the dead will have to be performed to ensure the welfare of their souls.

That heart-rending scene of the meeting of both separated families on the battlefield! How could that ocean of grief be described? A hundred sons, their many sons, brothers, cousins — losing them all, Dhritarashtra, Gandhari, the Kaurav wives were seeking out their dear ones among the piled-up corpses. With them was *ma* Kunti.

I, the five Pandavs, and Krishna too were searching for our relatives.

Ma Gandhari and Kunti were weeping in each other's arms.

All the Kaurav women, overwhelmed by grief, were lamenting for sons, husbands, friends, brothers. All the women of Hastinapur had lost their beauty, overcome by sorrow. All were pale with the shock of widowhood and destruction of the family.

From this point of view my grief was somewhat less than theirs. My five husbands were alive. They were victorious, although this victory was being observed in the cremation ground next to the flaming funeral pyres.

On seeing *ma* Kunti I sobbed out. With my head on her breast I said, "*Ma*, my darlings, my sons! My Abhimanyu! Where are they? Why won't they be seen any more? What shall I do with this kingdom? If one has no children, what will one do with a kingdom, with wealth and possessions?"

Ma patted my head and said, "Daughter! The grief that is yours is also mine. I am seeking the body of my ever-neglected, reproachful, proud son, Karna. Till death he remained insulted because of my sin. In death he found his befitting, heroic departure. Repeatedly during the war Bhishma, Shalya, Jayadrath insulted him as charioteer's son. Even so wise a man as Bhishma mocked him as half a chariot-warrior, *ardharathi*. My unarmed darling met death at the hands of Arjun."

Hearing those words of *Ma* it seemed as though only Karna was her sole son and Arjun someone belonging to the opposite camp! Though a hundred sons remain alive, it is for the dead son that compassion wells up in a mother's heart.

Stunned, overwhelmed with grief, all were gazing at the battlefield of Kurukshetra. How horrible, heart-rending was that scene!

Lakhs of corpses, split into parts, limb by limb. Bloodied hair and skulls. Bodies without heads, heads without bodies, chests split apart, lumps of flesh, bones, intestines — what a horrible scene was spread out on the battleground. Horses, elephants, men, the blood of all was mingled as in a sea. Wherever one looked one heard only the howling and raucous cries of jackals, vultures and crows. Tearing of flesh, drinking of blood, dragging of bodies were going on. Hastinapur had turned into hell.

Widowed women, shorn of prosperity, were looking for the bodies of their husbands, fathers, sons, brothers in that hell and, finding their corpses, were shrieking, clasping them to their breasts.

In the midst of the battlefield, ignoring the horror of death, lay the resplendent hero, Karna, like a second sun. Because he was the sun's son, death had only touched him. His body had not mortified or become noisome.

Kunti was standing near the feet of the corpse. I was behind her. *Ma*'s tears were falling on the corpse's feet. All the hesitation, shame, scruples, fear of public calumny that affected the female heart, had been swept away by death. Unnerved by grief at her son's death, the mother had forgotten that Karna was her pre-

382

marital son. Taking Karna's corpse in her lap, she wailed aloud before everyone. That lamentation pierced through the heavens. Surya grew compassionate, red, pale and began to set.

Stunned, Yudhishthir was watching. He noticed that *ma* Kunti's feet were absolutely identical to Karna's. In the assembly-hall, during the insulting of Draupadi, when he had got excited over Karna's barbed comments, Yudhishthir had calmed down in amazement the moment his eyes fell on Karna's feet. Today he saw that they were *ma* Kunti's feet. *Ma* Kunti was lamenting for dead Karna. What was the meaning of her weeping — as though for a son?

Spontaneously, Yudhishthir's eyes filled with tears. All were stunned, surprised. Controlling her grief, *ma* Kunti said to Yudhishthir, "My son, as Kunti's eldest son you have suffered much. As the chief of the Pandav family many responsibilities were cast on you which you discharged too. Actually, you are not Kunti's eldest son. He who was deprived of the glory of being Kunti's son all his life, was actually the eldest son. Today he lies before you on the ground. He is your eldest brother, son of Surya, mighty hero and donor, Karna! Despite being the fruit of a sage's blessings during my virginity, he has lived a cursed life on earth. Ultimately he lost his life at his brother's hands."

The sacred battlefield was today a crematorium, above friend and foe, rich and poor, high and low — everyone. Everyone had been placed on the same footing. Standing on this sacred earth Kunti exposed the supreme secret of her life before her sons. Then she broke out into lamentation.

Arjun, gazing with moist eyes at the composed body of Karna, lying like the setting sun, was cursing himself.

Forgetting all scruples and mingling my tears with Ma's, I too was weeping in honour of proud Karna's departed soul.

Innumerable pyres flamed up. Karna's mortal body caught fire. Pride, arrogance, the desire to be victorious ignoring divine power, all had vanished. Only the glory of his manliness kept ringing in my heart.

With surprise I saw, Karna's dear companion, Asmita, had

leapt into the pyre and was being burnt to ashes. Throughout life it was Asmita who kept Karna near her. Today death swallowed her up too.

Life cannot overcome pride, but death overcomes even the ego. Bereft of arrogance, Karna's face was resplendent as the morning sun in the flames of the pyre, appearing pure, delicate. It seemed as though I was looking at a god in the flames of the pyre. *Ma* Kunti and the Pandavs kept shedding tears.

Standing near me, Krishna was consoling *Ma* and encouraging the Pandavs, "Man is bound by both divine power and manhood. If either is lacking, then like Karna, despite having everything, one is frustrated in every act. There is a challenge thrown by manhood too. Karna had that. But without the combination of prayer with manliness, arrogance devoured him. So long as man is alive, the ego shall remain in him. The meaning of this is not that death is the only means of overcoming the ego. There is a means of doing away with the ego while being alive — it is by surrendering oneself, ending one's ego. Uniting effort and prayer, surrender yourself. Then you will truly live. Otherwise, you will be finished."

"An egoless life is impossible. But discarding the petty ego, nurture a noble pride. That is: O Lord, I am yours! That is when I can be proud. That petty pride of Karna was the pride of his own ego. Arjun too is not devoid of ego. But his pride is noble. I pride myself on your strength — this is Arjun's attitude. Karna would say, 'I am great on account of my own efforts'. Arjun says, 'Because of you I am great'. Just this is the difference between the two. Otherwise in valour, prowess, manliness they are equal. The bodies of both were different, but the power was the same."

"It is because of pride that Karna was destroyed. Destroying pride, Arjun remained alive and victorious. Therefore, do not grieve for Karna. No one destroys anyone. In the current of time, man himself brings about his own destruction."

Overcome by grief for her sons, *ma* Gandhari, hearing Krishna's philosophic lecture, said in fury, "O Krishna! You are expert in the scriptures. You are master of miraculous powers and the close friend of the Puru dynasty. What is impossible for you? If you wished, the Kauravs could have been saved from this destruction. There is no joy in acquiring a kingdom after destroying the enemy. It is in the presence of the defeated enemy that the glory of enjoying a kingdom lies. See, Yudhishthir has acquired a kingdom. But having lost all his relatives along with the Kauravs, how he is cursing himself! It is you who are responsible for the destruction of my sons..."

Krishna's voice was calm, "Devi! Greed for the wealth of others, seizing the kingdom of others, envying, insulting women — it is for these reasons that your sons were destroyed. How much suffering did a virtuous soul like Yudhishthir undergo on account of being addicted to playing dice? What had I to do in this? Till the end I was engaged in trying to establish peace. The consequence of war is always loss of life and property, destruction of civilization and distress to mankind. In this both the offenders and the innocent, the peaceable and the violent are harmed. On account of ignoring my peace proposals the Kauravs were destroyed."

Standing near the funeral pyres of her sons, Gandhari said in anger, "O Krishna! However much you may justify yourself, it is you who are the cause of everything. If I have the slightest power of meritorious acts, then I curse you — as today the Bharat dynasty has been destroyed, similarly some day in the same way your clan will be destroyed. Thirty-six years from now, your friends and relations, too, engaged in conflict with one another, will be destroyed. Like the Kaurav women, the Yadav women too will lament the loss of husbands, sons, relatives. Dvaraka will be lost in the sea."

I was stunned. Knowing the grief of the destruction of a family, despite being a woman, how could she curse someone else? Moreover, it was the glory of the Yadavs, the perfect man, Krishna, whom she had cursed. Was this the generosity of her maternal heart? A woman does not become a mother by giving birth to a hundred sons. The mother's heart is vast like the sky itsef. It is all-enduring like the earth. Like the sea it keeps hidden gems of compassion.

There was heard in *ma* Kunti's low voice a prayer, "O Vasudev! Without your allowing it, the destruction of the Yadavs cannot occur by anyone's curse. O Madhusudan! May not even the enemy suffer the grief of losing his family, his sons. Only this is my prayer."

Krishna smiled in that crematorium, "Devi Gandhari! You have the power of some merit and that happiness shall certainly be yours. For my relatives and family, addicted to liquor, will fight amongst themselves and die. For establishing dharma it is necessary to destroy adharma. Therefore, if my sons discard the path of truth, then tomorrow falling into the grasp of time they shall be destroyed root and branch. Exactly thirty-six years from now there shall be the change of an era in the stream of time and your curse will bear fruit."

Even God Himself accepted a heartless curse for proving the power of the merit earned by a woman.

The flames of the pyres shot up higher and higher with all the unguents and oil poured into them. In death-desiring, grief-over-whelmed hearts, there was a portion of waking life. As though the upward shooting flames of the pyres were warning, "Become vast. Lose yourself in the being of the creator. Then whatever be your sorrows and grief, you will be able to overcome them. The significance of life will be realised."

56

Thirty-six years of ruling the kingdom without sons and friends was, for Yudhishthir, the curse of the acts done by him. At every moment the sad, accusing eyes of the sonless widows of Hastinapur would condemn him, "This is that king Yudhishthir, the very soul of dharma! Obsessed with dicing, he lost his kingdom and wife and laid the foundations of war. Ultimately, having lost everything, he is enjoying the kingdom! The cause of the sorrows of innumerable subjects is none but Maharaj Yudhishthir."

I shared their sorrow. Fifteen years went by in serving blind Dhritarashtra, Gandhari and *ma* Kunti. Later, deciding that they would pass the rest of their lives in the forest, *ma* Gandhari, Kunti and Dhritarashtra left.

At the time of departure, *ma* Kunti said, holding Yudhishthir's hand, "Son! No one is as unfortunate as I am. Even after getting the kingdom, I never had the joy of being a queen-mother. For, I kept ignoring and being unjust to a son like Karna all his life, ultimately lost him. Every instant it is this sorrow that keeps stabbing me to the heart. Now at the end this is my request: Son! On the anniversary of his death, perform the *shraddh* of your eldest brother, Karna; pray for the peace and happiness of his soul. I never observed his birthday publicly. There is no hesitation in asking you to observe his death anniversary."

Tears were flowing when *Ma* left. There was no sorrow in her for leaving behind the five sons. Because of recalling the death anniversary of her ever-ignored son, sorrow for him was overwhelming her.

Now no other work was left. No elders were left to be served! Nor sons and daughters to be loved and petted. Life became a painful burden. Time passed with great difficulty.

Only one support was left, *sakha* Krishna! He came from time to time. We too visited him. Some time was passed in this manner. Sitting together, Arjun and I sometimes remembered *sakha* and spent the time discussing him. Arjun recounted the philosophy expounded by *sakha* on the battlefield. How many memories bloom like flowers in the garden of the mind! One has to go on living with the help of memories.

The ninth day came to mind, when grandfather Bhishma had vowed to destroy the Pandavs the next day. Consternation broke out in the Pandav camp. When life was at stake, who could sleep?

Sakha Krishna came to me, "The chariot is ready. Come, let us go to a place." I asked, "Where have I to go so late at night with you?"

Laughing, *sakha* said, "If it was a matter of taking you somewhere then I would have done that long ago. You cannot understand *sakha* even now? At least on this moonlit night it is hardly the hour for taking a turn with you in the chariot!"

I got into the chariot. It stopped near the Kaurav camp. At night, near the Kaurav camp! What did I have to do there? Was it that for saving the lives of the Pandavs *sakha* would present me as a gift to the Kauravs?

In the dark, *sakha* was walking on, leading me by the hand. He said, "Go carefully so that even your footsteps are not heard, no one's sleep is distrubed. We have to go straight to Grandfather's tent. If the Kauravs wake up, danger will arise." I took off my footwear and was about to put them down when *sakha* took them from my hand saying, "There might be some noise in keeping them down. What if someone wakes up? Noticing female footwear outside Bhishma's tent they will grow suspicious, and then all will be spoilt." I saw *sakha* standing with my slippers in his hand! I was overwhelmed with shame and embarrassment. Even in such a dangerous moment he jested, "Any valiant prince of Aryavàrt will count it his good fortune to take these slippers in his hands or even on his heart or head. Fate has placed this luck in my hand today. Do not delay, go ahead."

I immediately went on ahead and bowed down to the ground

at the feet of Grandfather. In the faint light Grandfather could not recognise me. Perhaps it was some woman with a complaint. Automatically the words, "May you be fortunate!" escaped his mouth.

Oh! Now I was able to comprehend *sakha's* words. Pushing back the *anchal* from my forehead I said, "Grandfather! May your words be true, this is my only prayer." Recognising me he was full of astonishment. "Daughter Krishnaa! Who suggested this plan to come to the Kaurav camp so late at night for hearing these very words? Who but Krishna can do this..."

I recalled that *sakha* was standing outside, slippers in hand! I was most embarrassed. What could I say to Grandfather?

Knowing that the purpose had been achieved, *sakha* also came inside and said, "Now please keep your word. You have given her the blessing to remain fortunate. Then how can you with any justice destroy the Pandavs?"

Grandfather laughed, "Krishna! I had heard of your games. But today I have seen it with my own eyes. You are roaming around in Hastina with Krishnaa's slippers? It is difficult for lifelong celibate Bhishma to appreciate what joy you get in doing footwear-service to women! However, when you have taken so much trouble, there is no alternative to telling the Pandavs tomorrow of the secret of my death. Now you may rest assured regarding the Pandavs."

Krishna laughed and said, "What trouble is there in this? It is because of your vow that I got the chance of picking up the slippers of Draupadi. There is so much joy in doing this work."

In the presence of Grandfather I was dissolving in embarrassment. What had *sakha* not done for us! He ate my left-overs, picked up my slippers, became my husband's charioteer, drove the chariot. Today I understood that there was nothing that Krishna could not do for his devotees.

The perfume evaporated from the dried petals of flowers offered to gods yet the fragrance of sandalwood and frankincense kept coming. There was no joy in the pain-and-sorrow-filled experiences of the past but the memory of Krishna, like the fragrance of sandalwood and frankincense, filled the mind with pure bliss. Everyday I would think: "Krishna! It is because of you that I live. It is you who are before my eyes in waking, sleepng, dreaming. When Phalguni and I sit, it is *sakha* who is between us." After the death of Karna, Phalguni had completed his vow. There was the opportunity to lead a conjugal life once more with me, but that inclination itself no longer remained. The loss of sons and the guilt of the killing of Karna had turned the mind away from worldly pleasures. Therefore, whenever we were together, sorrow would split us into two. That was when the thought of Krishna would unite our souls, revealing the new significance of life. Finding me overwhelmed with grief, Arjun would speak about Krishna and when Arjun would be depressed, I would take refuge in memories of Krishna. For keeping the five husbands happy, I would send word to Krishna from time to time to visit us. For driving away the post-war sorrow, what recourse was available to us other than Krishna?

57

Year after year passed by. To save the Yadav clan from destruction Krishna prohibited drinking of liquor in the kingdom. I thought that even if Dvaraka should be submerged still if Krishna was there, everything for us was there. Who could destroy him who was self-born?

Sakha had not come for many days. News reached us that Krishna had called Arjun to Dvaraka. After Arjun left for Dvaraka I felt a little hurt — so he felt like meeting *sakha*, but did not think of *sakhi!*

But the news with which Arjun returned — would I be able to describe that? The very sky seemed to have collapsed on me; the earth seemed to have slipped from under my feet. Fighting amongst themselves after getting drunk, the Yadav clan had destroyed itself. Balaram had accepted death. Krishna Vasudev had left this mortal frame being struck down by the arrow of the Shabar Jara. Having performed the obsequies of Krishna and Balaram, Arjun had returned with Krishna's grandson, Vajra.

The great passing of Krishna had taken place! The end of an era had come about. Arjun became powerless, and I, lifeless. I thought, Time is the most powerful force. No one has the power to escape Time. The terrible Kaliyuga was, as though, only waiting for Krishna's passing. After the beginning of the Kaliyuga it seemed to Yudhishthir, the incarnation of non-violence and dharma, that the time had arrived for the great departure, that now he had become unfit for the royal throne. No, in the Kaliyuga, Yudhishthir, devoted to justice, could not remain on the throne. It was this dilemma that faced me.

The throne remains, kings change. Men come and go but the mighty current of Time keeps flowing. Without Krishna, the

391

Pandavs were as justice without dharma! Everyone knew that the time for Yudhishthir to abdicate had arrived.

Parikshit, son of Abhimanyu and Arjun's grandson, was installed king of Hastina. Vajra, the grandson of Krishna, became king of Indraprasth. Handing over the burden of the kingdom to the last scions of both *sakhas*, Yudhishthir was at peace.

He assigned their responsibility to Subhadra. Obeying Yudhishthir's wish, I left for the Himalayas with the five husbands for climbing to *svarg*.

Reaching *svarg* in one's own body was no small temptation. If that temptation was rejected then it was not possible to climb to *svarg*. I had left behind kingdom, wealth, possessions, everything. But had greed left me? Was life without greed possible!

Looking back, I saw Maya running behind us. Maya did not leave me! Why? Like some bond, Maya was pulling me back. Why?

A creature is bound by the triple thread of the three *gunas: sattva, rajas, tamas*. Tamas gives birth to attachment. From rajas come addiction and desire. Sattva produces purity. Still, sattva was a bond. If tamas and rajas were shackles of iron then sattva was a chain of gold. Therefore, even though the desire to reach *svarg* through the Himalayas was *sattvik*, it seemed to me like chains of gold round my ankles. For, even this had been transformed into an attachment for me. If the desire for getting a kingdom was shackles of iron then wasn't the desire to attain *svarg* a chain of gold?

Who was free of attachment? I? My husbands? could a man who had attachment achieve *svarg*?

Attachment blinds a person. But to proceed onwards, some attachment, some desire for results does exist within a person. Therefore, like a blind man, without considering what is right and what is wrong, he keeps walking on the path, just like us.

While walking on I mused: "What did I get in this birth? What did I lose? Why did I come? What task was accomplished through me? What ought to have been done by me?

"Food, sleep, sex, the pleasure of a kingdom, etc. — I got

392

everything in life. Still it seems that my life has remained unful-filled. What is wanting? Why have I borne so much sorrow, grief, pain, in life? I feel that with Yudhishthir as husband any woman will have to suffer..."

And while thinking thus, my feet slipped on the golden dust of the Himalayas.

My five husbands, whom I had regarded even as my five senses all through life and who had been my companions in life after life, did not even look back. They kept on walking straight ahead on the path to *svarg*. I was alone at death's door!

Bhim's voice could be heard, "Brother! Draupadi has fallen down!" Yudhishthir said in a steady voice, "Draupadi is herself responsible for her fall. She was too fond of Arjun. It is this that is her sin. Bhim, keep down your mace here. It is the mace that is your arrogance. There is no place for arrogance in *svarg*. Do not turn to look back. Keep going."

Obeying his brother's command, Bhim put down his mace and went forward. As a sign of the journey of the Pandavs to *svarg* Bhim's mace lay on the breast of the Himalayas.

It was here that *ma* Kunti, Gandhari, Dhritarashtra, virtuous Vidur had also spent the last days of their lives. That is where I lie. Ahead the temple of Bharat is visible. It was on this path that Bharat, the devoted and obedient younger brother of Ram, had proceeded into the solitary reaches of the Himalayas for penance. At the time of our forest-exile Yudhishthir got this temple built here. Today after doing *pranam* in the Bharat temple all five left me behind and travelled on.

Pride is an obstacle on the path to *svarg*. Can anyone be free of pride in this world? I was the royal queen of Hastina. Sacrificing father, sons, brother, friends — everyone, I had won the status of queen. How can it be that there will be no pride in my mind? There was enough scope for pride in that life. But even that life did not seem fulfilled to me. Today I lie alone on the way to death. My arrogance has certainly been removed. But helpless-ness is waiting to swallow me up. Helplessness is filling me with a sense of want. Today I am realising that life is not just pride, and nor is it only full of helplessness. It is between these two that the stream of life keeps flowing. Both pride and helplessness have significant roles to play in life. Pride by itself blinds a person, while helplessness fills him with a sense of want. But if the pride and helplessness, instead of being petty, are noble then life becomes fulfilled. Then man thinks: "O Lord! I am but your creation and that is the source of my pride." Then when he thinks that all his strength, all his support is He alone, then his soul soars upwards and the doors of *svarg* open up to receive it.

Today I, too, offering my pride and helplessness to you, am becoming noble. Without you, both pride and helplessness of man are meaningless, fruitless.

58

Whose is this sweet flute? It is cleansing this bleeding interior, making a stream of feelings flow. Someone is humming in my ears, "Life is not for enjoyment, but for feeling." Who is showing me the path, drawing me away from a life of pleasure to a life of feeling? Calling me, "Come...come...I am waiting for you!" Who is this invisible companion? Is it Maya?

No. Maya slipped, fell down and died long back. The name of this door of the Ganga in the Himalayas is Mayapuri. On setting foot here, Maya disappears. I am now free of Maya. It was Maya that had kept me in bondage. I kept agonising in grief, sorrow, insult. And not recognising that enchanting Maya I would say, "O *sakha* Krishna! It is you who are paining me." Truly, how much did I have to suffer on account of failing to know you? What was my fault? Whenever I resolved to annihilate my ego and turn to you, Maya blocked my way. She turned my mind downward. Today death appears more pleasant than life. For, life was ruled by Maya, while death is freeing me from Maya.

Sakha! Annihilate me for my drawbacks, annihilate me! Throughout life I kept demanding — give, give me happiness, prosperity, worldly pleasure. You gave me everything. You also poured into my lap all the sorrows of the world. Today I am asking for something else — take me, take me, O Krishna! Finish me, exhaust me! Make me indivisible. He who is not separate from you is the true devotee. Am I not your devotee? O *sakha*, will you be able to deny this?

Sakha! Dearest of all! I shall not ask anything for myself. I am asking this for this beautiful earth, the last thing I beg in this life. You are God. There is nothing that you cannot give. Will you not give what I ask for?

The first thing I ask for — O Krishna Vasudev! Whatever has

happened in my life — let it not be repeated in the life of any other woman. Lay down a rule that no woman will ever have several husbands at a time. Keeping myself indivisible, the pain of being divided is known to me.

The second thing — Compassionate Krishna! Do not let even the enemy grieve for his sons. There is no grief in the world greater than this. Who knows this more than me?

The third thing — the pain that I suffered in the court. Let no other woman in the world ever have to go through this. Make women beautiful, but do not make men so lustful.

The fourth thing I ask is for this world, for the coming dynasties of this Kalyuga. O Krishna, supreme worker of welfare, I have suffered one war. Even now the mother's heart in me hears the lamentation of mother earth. Therefore I request that because of race, religion, language and colour let no country split into parts like Hastina and Indraprasth. Inequality is the variety of Your creation. Let not the integrity, unity and purity of any country be destroyed. because of this. I have suffered the consequences of the great war. Both sides fighting in a war suffer losses. Both the victor and the vanquished lose their friends and relations. Civilization, culture, wealth, life — all vanish.

From lord Vyas I have heard that five thousand years from now man will reach the pinnacle of achievement of civilization, culture and science. With the help of science he will establish contact with planets and stars. Then if, because of a wrong decision, power-hungry persons launch a great war, what a terrible situation will arise on account of the weapons created by that very science! O saviour in distress, Krishna, on the destruction of this world it is you who will labour for a new creation and civilization. O Creator! Therefore, as you went to Hastina in Dvapar for establishing peace, similarly, for giving warning in advance, why do you not whisper into the ears of the thoughtful people of Kaliyuga in the honeyed tone of your flute, *Shantih! Shantih! Shantih!*

If your music of peace proves fruitless, it is you who will be compelled to descend on earth. Two paths are yours — either peace or destruction. Man has understood very well the sorrow of taking birth on earth with this mortal frame. Then why does he not choose the path of peace? For the welfare of creation, national integrity and world unity are my fourth demand.

Sakha! the fifth thing I ask for — I, Panchali, the heroine of five heroes, the princess of Panchal, and the mother of five sons. With the fifth demand I shall complete the final chapter of my body made up of five elements. What will the final matter be? *Moksha? Svarg?* Liberation? It is this that is the demand of a creature's soul. But my demand is the opposite!

I do not want *moksha,* salvation. I do not want to reach *svarg* in this body — not even liberation. It is rebirth that I crave. You are surprised, *sakha!* I do not want *svarg.* That is the habitation of the gods. If anyone reaches *svarg* in his own body, it will be Yudhishthir. For, despite being virtuous, he is cruel towards human beings. He is more than a man, he is a god. To go far from earth in order to attain *svarg* has been his lifelong *sadhana.* My other husbands are normal people. Definitely they will one by one slip and fall. Instead of undergoing the suffering of reaching *svarg* in one's own body, the effort to turn one's own motherland into a heaven will be preferable.

Sakha! Many omissions have occurred in this birth. Even if it was for the sake of justice, I wanted war, sought the opportunity for revenge, encouraged my husbands for war. Today I think that if I had vowed from the beginning to establish peace then the innocent men and women of Aryavart could have lived on.

For the faults of this life give me rebirth and on this same sacred earth: the earth where you took birth in a mortal body. The soul of Bharata is permeated with Krishna, bliss, love. It is a heart full of love that is the foundation of such grace. You cannot love God if you detest man. Therefore, O greatest of lovers, let me be born as a lover. Let me be born again and again as the beloved of Krishna and a lover of the world.

I am realising the Krishna consciousness of great Bharata. Spirituality and the feeling for dharma will touch the consciousness of all mankind. Some day the entire world will be filled with the consciousness of Krishna. The meaning of Krishna is darkness. It is darkness that is the womb giving birth to light. Therefore, a world enveloped in the darkness of danger and difficulty and error can only be uplifted through spiritual consciousness. And then Bharata will be the pathfinder of the whole world in friendship and peace. O Creator Krishna! For the faults in my present birth, let me be born again and again in this land of Bharata.

I do not want an entire life. Even for a moment, with the hand of a worker, the eyes of a knower, the heart of a devotee let me be born for your sake, die for your sake. *Sakha!* it is you who are the world, the universe. Living and dying for you means living and dying for the world. On being born thus, perhaps I may be freed of the faults of the present birth. My life will become meaningful. Living on earth, dying on earth, my soul shall attain heaven. More than attaining heaven in this body, it is the soul's attaining heaven that I like.

Today I have no sorrow in dying. For I am dying with the wish to be born again on this sacred earth of Bharata. On the way to death instead of your name, it is the voice of your flute that is on my lips — *Om shantih, shantih, shantih!*

In the troubled human mind of Kaliyuga may this enchanting sound of the flute keep playing in the same way — *Om shantih, shantih, shantih!*

Finis.

Sakha, I began this letter to tell you of my grief. And I have come close to the pain and suffering of the world. I have set down before you that play of which you are the hero. It seems that my story remains incomplete. Having finished the letter, I am going through it. Having read it, I am wondering if I should begin the letter all over again. Begin from the end, end from the beginning... what is this that I am doing?

It is you who have said, life does not end in death: it begins there; it puts on a new dress. Then what is the harm in writing 'finis' at the beginning of the letter and beginning at the end?

My body is lying here, the soul is flying away like the petal of a flower where, pierced by the arrow of Shabar Jara, your bleeding feet have bloomed as lotuses with innumerable golden petals in the empty black Krishna-full sky. You had thrown towards me one day exactly such a golden lotus of a thousand petals in full bloom and aroused in my heart a lotus-love! Caught in the bonds of maya that day, I did not understand that it was not a lotus but your loving feet that you had extended towards me.

Innumerable torn petals are coming blown from somewhere, creating that very same lotus of innumerable petals. Again these lotus petals get blown away somewhere. They are torn away, to unite again. There is no diminution in the shape of the lotus or its petals. Neither do they increase.

I see the face of each and every one of those for whom I was mourning, having lost them, in each petal in your lotus-feet. My father, brothers, sons, *ma* Kunti, Gandhari, friends and relations and ultimately heroic Karna — all are getting united as petals! I am being blown away to be united in that very blooming lotus. Whatever I have lost, I am going to take. Now I have realised that attaing your lotus feet is the supreme fulfilment. Where there is supreme fulfilment there is no distinction between friend and foe, dharma and adharma, race and caste,. In those very lotus petals I see everything and realise this: What is emptiness is really fullness; creation is really destruction; the beginning is really the end.

Therefore, it is with *'finis'* that I am beginning my letter. For this is not a letter; this is my life. After all, it is the reiteration of life that is my wish.

Where did I end the letter — ? Yes — may the sound of the enchanting flute keep playing in the inner being of universal mankind — *Om shantih, shantih, shantih!*

'The Beginning'.

AFTERWORD

Draupadi is a challenge of womanhood, the embodied form of action, knowledge, devotion and power.

Such a woman — who has faced torment, insult, mental and emotional dilemma like Yajnaseni Draupadi — has not yet been born on this earth.

Beautiful women have been tormented and insulted throughout the ages by lust-blinded men. But that the bride of one's own family should be stripped before many wise, qualified and honourable men who all keep sitting silently to gaze at her naked beauty — a darker chapter than this will not be found anywhere in the written or unwritten history of the world. In fact, no account of such an outrageous incident can be found even in epics, poetry, novels and drama. Not only this. Because of the words which slipped inadvertently from the lips of the mother-in-law, princess Krishnaa was compelled to take five husbands. There are a few such instances in the Purans, but in the history of the civilized world it is a gooseflesh-raising event. On account of her outstanding chastity, Krishnaa remains one of the five *satis*. But on account of having accepted five husbands, Krishnaa was abused again and again by the Kauravs and Karna as a harlot, enjoyed by many men. In the life of Krishnaa, the unfailing companion of the Pandavs in their joys and sorrows, a series of griefs of various types came. But her self-confidence never gave way. Ultimately, her feet slipped for the first time on the golden dust of the Himalayas. Krishnaa was deprived from attaining heaven. Alone, in a helpless condition, she was forced to give up her life.

All of us know something of Krishnaa's sacrifice, dedication, strength of character. The name of the younger sister of a lady known to me is Krishnaa. Leaving her debauched drunkard of a husband she is living in her father's house. Everyone said

400

Krishnaa should remarry. But in our society today the remarriage of one discarded by her husband is not that simple and easy. For diverting her mind, Krishnaa went away to her brother in West Germany. Sometime later, she married a young man there. She has two children now, a son and a daughter. Her conjugal life is comfortable. But the peculiar thing is that those who were at one time sympathetic towards Krishnaa, said after the second marriage, "Well! When her very name is Krishnaa, she could be happy only after taking a second husband. *Arre!* The Krishnaa of the Mahabharat took five husbands, and still not being satisfied, was attracted to Karna and Krishna..."

I was deeply pained by this comment. Not because of any remark regarding the Krishnaa of the Kaliyuga, discarded by her husband. Today men shed crocodile tears for men — this is a matter of no consequence. The root of my sorrow was such thoughtless words for the unique, learned, devoted and powerful woman, Krishnaa of Dvaparyuga. This can be the individual view of someone. But how far do we know Krishnaa? How much knowledge do we have of the majesty of the *Mahabharat* and of its noble culture? How many have read thoroughly the original Sanskrit or its translation or Sarala Das' Oriya *Mahabharat?* The blind have gathered to look at the elephant — in that fashion, without having read the *Mahabharat,* on the basis of hearsay we sully our own culture.

Portraying Krishnaa in the form of Yajnaseni, I am placing her before the culture-loving readers of my country. The incident mentioned above kept pricking me, so I have put it down.

Chiefly I have depended upon the *Mahabharat* created by Vyasdev. I have also been influenced to some extent by the Oriya Mahabharat of Sarala Das. Some imaginary incidents and characters have been merged into the core narrative. At some places, the sequence of events of the original Mahabharat has not been followed. I have tried to present a psychological picture of Krishnaa as a woman living a predicament-ridden life, full of variety.

It is the supreme human being, Purushottam Krishna, who is the protagonist of the *Mahabharat.* Krishna and Krishnaa —

through the integral link between these two names I have depicted a relationship of spiritual love. Many writers have previously shown this *sakha-sakhi* relationship of spiritual love between Krishna and Draupadi. Faced with the superhuman personality of Krishna, which woman in any era could help loving him?

Only this is my wish: that in the soul of this world, sorely beset by war, that final prayer of Yajnaseni should reverberate: *Om shantih! shantih! shantih!*

PRATIBHA RAY